# INHERITANCE
## of STRANGERS

# *Bilingual Press/Editorial Bilingüe*

# NASH CANDELARIA

# INHERITANCE
of **STRANGERS**

**Bilingual Press/Editorial Bilingüe**
BINGHAMTON, NEW YORK

ISBN: 0-916950-58-1
Printed simultaneously in a softcover edition. ISBN: 0-916950-59-X

Library of Congress Catalog Card Number: 85-71527


PRINTED IN THE UNITED STATES OF AMERICA




*Cover design by Christopher J. Bidlack*

*Back cover photo by Victor Samoilovich*

# The Rafas of New Mexico

Francisco Rafa — b. 1641 Río Abajo / d. 1680 Río Abajo (Taos Rebellion)

m. 1667 Madalena Gutiérrez — b. 1653 Río Arriba / d. 1720 Los Rafas

José Antonio Rafa I — b. 1675 Río Abajo / d. 1770 Los Rafas

m. 1700 María Trujillo — b. 1680 Santa Fe / d. 1725 Los Rafas

Concepción (Navajo chief's daughter) — b. approx. 1710 / d. Unknown

Félix Blas Rafa (out of wedlock) — b. 1725 Los Rafas / d. 1765 Buffalo Country

m. 1750 Juana Armijo — b. 1732 Río Abajo / d. 1784 Los Rafas

José Antonio Rafa II — b. 1755 Los Rafas / d. 1850 Los Rafas

m. 1775 Rosalía Baca — b. 1759 Los Rafas / d. 1829 Los Rafas

Francisco Juan Rafa — b. 1781 Los Rafas / d. 1857 Los Rafas

m. 1807 Estela Lucero — b. 1791 Alameda / d. 1873 Los Rafas

**José Antonio Rafa III**
b. 1821 Los Rafas
d. 1906 Los Rafas
m. 1854 Gregoria Sánchez
b. 1831 Los Rafas
d. 1898 Los Rafas

- Carlos 1821-1847
- Josefa 1809-1883
- Clara 1811-1889
- Andrea 1829-1909

**Francisco Leonardo Rafa**
b. 1856 Los Rafas
d. 1916 Los Rafas
m. 1875 Florinda Chávez
b. 1859 Los Chávez
d. 1920 Los Rafas

- Carlos José 1858-1903
- Consuela 1863-1934
- José Blas 1865-1898
- Andrea 1869-1937

**Carlos Antonio Rafa**
b. 1881 Los Rafas
d. 1971 Los Rafas
m. 1896 Matilda Griego
b. 1879 Los Griegos
d. 1974 Los Rafas

- José Leonardo 1876-1890
- Rosa Florinda 1882-1948
- Gregoria 1883-1923
- Juanita 1885-1951

**José Hernando Rafa**
b. 1906 Los Rafas
d. 1971 Spain (on bus to Sevilla)
m. 1927 Theresa Maria Mathilda Trujillo
b. 1911 Albuquerque

- Tomás 1895-1950
- Eufemia 1896-1977
- Carlos 1899-1976
- Gregoria 1901-
- Juana 1908-
- Daniel 1911-1960

**Joseph Rafa, Jr.**
b. 1931 Los Angeles, CA
m. 1954 Margaret Winston
b. 1932 Chicago, Illinois

- Joseph III b. 1955 Anaheim, CA
- William b. 1959 Fullerton, CA
- Theresa b. 1961 Newport Beach, CA

"Our inheritance is turned to strangers, our houses to aliens."

Lamentations 5:2

1

Los Rafas, U.S. Territory
of New Mexico, 1890

"It isn't true that you used to be a priest, is it Grandfather?" Leonardito's solemn little face and furrowed brow had turned intently toward José Antonio, and the boy's voice had been a whisper. "Priests can't be grandfathers; it would be a mortal sin."

"Mortal sin? What would you know about mortal sin, changuito?" At which the boy's lower lip had trembled, and his eyelids had begun to blink. "Hey!" José Antonio Rafa had placed a wrinkled hand on José Leonardo's back and rubbed it. "My big boy isn't going to cry just because I called you a little monkey, are you?"

A solemn shake of head. Then, still blinking, the sly question again. "Were you, Grandfather? A priest? Tell me."

The old man had turned from the dark-eyed intensity of his brown-faced little grandson. His eyes had narrowed and he could not completely swallow the smile that twitched at the edges of his mouth. With so young a boy, there was so much you could not tell. So he would evade the difficult questions and instead tell Leonardito little things about his own youth. Amusing stories. Wondrous oddities. But not the hard things, the painful things. He had been saving them for later.

Now that the boy was old enough to understand, José Antonio felt too old to explain. Too old and too tired. The years had eroded his passions so that he accepted things he once would have fought. Or even worse, he had become indifferent to them.

The clatter of hooves and the squeak of buggy wheels jarred him from his reverie. As the rhythm slowed and the sounds stopped, he slid upright against the apple tree on which he leaned and strained his eyes. The Anglo was striding up the dirt path with forthright purpose. He was almost to the door of the little adobe house before José

Antonio recognized him. James Smith. A neighbor. The biggest land-owner in Los Rafas.

"¡Demonio!" he thought. "What now?"

The door opened cautiously and the round, dark face of his daughter-in-law, Florinda, peered out. The sound of their voices carried, the Spanish words a soft murmur that José Antonio could not understand. Then Florinda stepped down the crude wooden step to the ground and pointed back behind the house. The two heads nodded in accord and now Smith was pointing in the same direction.

"No!" José Antonio thought, struggling to his feet. But before the thought became a shout, Señor Smith had turned and headed back toward the main ditch that bordered the fields. The only answer was the slam of the front door as Florinda returned to her chores.

"He's not there," José Antonio said aloud to himself. "Francisco took the wagon and—" But it was no use. No one would hear. He blinked solemnly at the house from which he could hear the shrewish screaming of his daughter-in-law as, one by one, his younger grandchildren sulked their ways outdoors, punctuated by four volleys from the slamming door.

"He's not there," José Antonio said again, the words a reminder that propelled him after the visitor.

He walked through the small apple orchard, casting an indifferent glance at the tiny green fruit that would eventually grow into the somewhat larger sour fruit. Through the trees to his left was the big house, his own house. His wife, Gregoria, stood at the kitchen door with folded arms as the screaming grandchildren ran toward their Nana.

Better her than me, he thought. Why was it that as he grew older his ears became more sensitive? Not like so many of the old ones that he knew who could not hear anything less than a shout. And why was it that those who shouted the most had the least to say?—thinking once again of Florinda.

Then he was clear of the trees and the ditch, across which the short, slender figure of his oldest grandchild, Leonardito, waved at the approaching Señor Smith.

Not Leonardito, the old man thought. I should remember to call him Leonardo. He's almost a man now. José Antonio smiled, seeing the solemn face with traces of dark hairs softly framing the upper lip.

He measured the ditch with his eyes, then walked toward the dirt-covered planks that spanned it. By then he could see Leonardo and Señor Smith nodding as they turned and stared toward him.

"He's escaped again, Grandfather." Leonardo's face was pale, and his eyes shifted nervously. José Antonio and Señor Smith nodded greetings as Leonardo continued. "Don James says he's in with the goats again. I'll get the horse and follow behind the buggy."

It was a short ride, west along Rafas Road, then north toward Los Griegos. Past fields with tips of green thrusting their way up through the dark soil. José Antonio rode silently in the buggy alongside Don James, whose only comment was the wordless encouragement he clucked to his horse.

Don James. How strange that sounded. Don did not go with James. It went with Jaime. Or Francisco. Or José Antonio. But Don James — José Antonio could not bring himself to use the word with the Anglo name. Señor Smith. Or Mr. Smith. Yes, better Mr. Smith. Yet the men who worked the Smith place called him patrón. Boss. Which was all right since he really was their boss. But to a neighbor? Mr. Smith.

The horse trotted automatically up the path to the house. An American house. Large. White-painted wood with a sloping roof. Out of place among the flat-roofed adobes that dotted Los Rafas. But then that was another sign, like "Don" James, that things were changing.

There was even that house in Albuquerque — and José Antonio smiled as he thought of it — that a rich trader had built like a castle. How strange that these Yankees with their democracy and independence would build houses that aped the royalty of Europe. Castle indeed! Even the Spanish at their most pretentious did not build castles in this Territory of New Mexico. Adobe was good enough.

"Whoa!" Mr. Smith nodded toward the shed as Leonardo drew his horse alongside the buggy and dismounted. "He's back there," Smith said. "When I tried to get him out, he just sat on his haunches and howled."

Leonardo and José Antonio exchanged glances. Even now they could hear the unearthly howl above the frightened bleating of the goats. The old man dismounted from the buggy thoughtfully, then laid a hand on Leonardo's shoulder.

"Don't worry," he said, trying not to look into the embarrassed eyes of his grandson who was on the verge of tears. "He'll come with us."

"Do you want me to help?" Smith asked. José Antonio could tell from his voice that he really did not want to, and he shook his head, knowing that the man would be relieved.

"All right, Leonardo." José Antonio led the way past the shed to the goat pen.

Several of the goats ran toward them as they approached, bleating their anxious goat cries through the spaces between the fence railings. He was in the corner like Smith had said, on his haunches, stalking a nanny.

"Pedro!" José Antonio commanded. The large head turned, cocked over one shoulder, and the fierce eyes stared at them, unrecognizing. "Come here, Pedro!" Still no recognition, though the eyes burned less brightly now as if they were turned inward, sorting through memories. "Pedro. It's me. Don José Antonio Rafa."

Finally there was a flicker of recognition, a dawning, and the edges of the hard mouth turned upward in a smile. A low growl, almost a laugh, escaped from his lips, and Pedro tossed his head toward the billygoat who stood his ground threateningly in the opposite corner of the pen.

"Mira ese cabrón," Pedro said, still smiling. "I'm going to make a cuckold of him."

The nanny that he stalked into a corner let out a bleating cry and burst along one side of the fence to break free, but Pedro was too quick and she stopped, stiff-legged, and backed once more into the corner.

"Oh, Grandfather—" Leonardo cried.

"Leave her alone, Pedro!" Don José commanded sharply. Once again Pedro cocked his head toward them. His bewildered eyes blinked as if, finally, some new thought was coming through. José Antonio's voice was gentler now, soothing.

"Don Pedro," he said. "It is unbecoming for a man of your dignity. Your stature."

"Her name is Esmerelda," he answered in a hoarse, wistful voice. "In her land she is a princess."

"But this is your land, Don Pedro. And here it would never do. You have your hacienda to think about. Your family. Your peons."

Thoughtfully Pedro looked from José Antonio to Leonardo, staring at each until a ray of recognition flickered at them. His wild expression softened and he looked at the frightened goats as if he did not understand.

"Come along, Don Pedro. We have to go home." José Antonio extended a hand toward the center of the pen where Pedro had sat down, finally assuming a more human posture. Then, in a quiet aside to Leonardo, "I'll take him on the horse. Everything will be all right now. You go back and get his room ready."

"What will Don James think?" Leonardo's voice was shaking, tearful. "You're crazy!" he hissed at Pedro who did not hear as he struggled to his feet. "Our family is disgraced!" The boy turned and ran before José Antonio could admonish him.

Pedro took José Antonio's hand and climbed out of the pen. When they walked back around the shed, Mr. Smith was looking across the field at the receding figure of the running boy.

"He refused a ride in the buggy," Smith said.

José Antonio watched until he could no longer see Leonardo. Then he mounted the old horse and pulled Pedro up behind him.

"Thank you, Mr. Smith. My apologies for any trouble it caused you."

Pedro turned toward the shed from behind which they could still hear the bleating of the unsettled goats and he waved. Only José Antonio could hear his whisper, "Adiós, Esmerelda."

The horse clomped along the road. After the turn onto Rafas Road it increased its speed, knowing that home was near. But as they drew closer, Pedro began to squirm restlessly and groan his animal-like sounds.

"Don Pedro!" He became still and quiet. "We are nearing the hacienda, Don Pedro. You will have to set an example." The answer was a soft whimper, but then he sat quietly until they drew up beside the shed behind the big house.

The door was ajar and José Antonio looked about as if he might find the answer to how Pedro Baca had escaped. The boy must have forgotten and left it unlocked, he thought. Or perhaps Florinda had forgotten when she last fed him.

He dismounted and put out a hand to help Pedro. Then the bellowing started. Like a bawling calf. Florinda stuck her head out the door of her house and screamed at them. "Stop that howling, you loony!"

"Come on, Don Pedro," José Antonio coaxed. But the frightened eyes were watching Florinda, and Pedro began to whimper again. Finally he swung a leg over the back of the horse and slid down the side, but he stood just outside of the door still whimpering.

"I'm sorry, Don Pedro, but you have to go in." José Antonio took him firmly by the arm and tried to lead him into the shed, but Pedro resisted with strength increased by fear.

From behind, José Antonio heard the sound of running bare feet, then Leonardo was beside him, helping shove. "¡Andale!" the boy scolded. "If you don't go in, Mamá is going to come out and tie you to the bed."

His resistance dissolved and he walked docilely to the pallet in the corner and threw himself on it. "They're after me," Pedro said. "They come through the walls at night and try to kill me. They want my land. All of it." Then he began to shake uncontrollably and cry.

"Crazy man!" Leonardo hissed.

But José Antonio saw him slip the bottle into the filthy rags that served as blankets and he was looking at Leonardo when the boy turned his gaze back toward him. Caught, he blushed and looked away from his grandfather.

"You might as well be feeding him poison," José Antonio said, moving toward the pallet and the hidden bottle.

"Mamá said that at least it keeps him quiet."

José Antonio reached for the bottle but before he could lift it, Pedro's hand gripped his. "No," Pedro said. "Not my medicine!"

José Antonio hesitated. He looked at the pleading face of the unshaven old man. An old man much the same age as he. An old man once young and full of hope, reduced to pleading for a bottle of wine to help him blot out the misery of his condition. He let go of the bottle. Pedro clasped it to his breast and a smile lit his miserable old face.

As José Antonio turned to leave, he saw that the boy had left, and he shouted after his grandson. He locked the door and looked through the orchard past the ditch toward the field and shouted again. "Leonardo!"

The boy slowed from a run to a walk and at the third shout he turned and came slowly back. I ought to give him a good one, José Antonio thought angrily. Him and that heartless daughter-in-law of mine.

But when the boy's fearful eyes at last met his, José Antonio remembered the solemn face of a few years past looking up at him and whispering: "It isn't true that you used to be a priest, is it Grandfather?" But what Leonardo said now in his soft, nervous voice was, "Yes, Grandfather?"

"I want you to show respect to that old man," he said sternly. The boy stood still, eyes downcast. José Antonio's voice softened. "Remember when you used to ask me if I had once been a priest?" Leonardo nodded. "And I told you stories of the old days?"

"About the conquistadors," Leonardo said warily. "And the Moors. About the great Indian rebellion and Dead Man's March. About how to tell which plants in the desert were good to eat. About witches and saints. About how to break a horse."

"There is more," José Antonio said. "Things I could not tell you when you were small. Now that you are almost a man it is time that you learned about them. About him." He motioned his head toward the shed. "Because that old man, as much as anything, is the story of what happened to our people in the twilight of our days."

## 2

The story could not be told all at once. There was too much work to be done on the farm, and at fourteen years of age Leonardo had to shoulder a man's burden. As the oldest of his parents' children, it was his duty not only to help his father in the fields but also to teach his ten-year-old brother, Carlos Antonio, how to do some of the simpler tasks on the farm.

José Antonio thought a great deal before he began to tell the story to Leonardo, trying to understand what it was that had happened to them in the forty years since the Americans had conquered New Mexico. Back then when he had been a young priest and forsaken his vocation to help his family.

I do not want to deceive myself about ancient glories, he thought. I never believed in them. Glory was always in the future. In heaven. In God. But as I get nearer to that, I think more about the past and how it might have been. About our loss of vigor. About giving in instead of fighting. As I grow older, I sometimes have regrets. Sometimes wish that I had fought more and accepted less. But what will I tell Leonardo?

\* \* \*

"Long ago there was our land," he told Leonardo. "A beautiful land called New Mexico. Its borders started far east of us at the Mississippi River and extended west to the Pacific Ocean. That was when people thought California was an island. It also started north of us at the upper edge of what is now the state of Colorado and extended south to the borders between Mexico and the United States — along Texas, the New Mexico Territory, and the Arizona Territory. It even crossed those borders — it had its own boundaries in the old, old days — into northern Mexico.

"That was a long, long time ago when the white man first came here. It was they who named it New Mexico. They were our ancestors from Europe who gave us our language, our religion, and many of our customs. It was they who married our other ancestors, the Indian peoples who still live here."

"But Grandfather," Leonardo protested. "We are not Indian. We are Spanish!"

José Antonio did not respond to his grandson's protest as he continued. "New Mexico has been a land of change. Of movement. Of conquest. For hundreds of years before the European, the Indian tribes and nations fought among themselves. They captured slaves. They took lands and hunting grounds and places where there was abundant water. But before the European they did not have the horse, so these changes came slowly.

"The peoples lived in isolation, and since there were relatively few of them, they seldom intruded on each other's lands. Some of them — many of them — became peaceful farmers living in permanent homes where they tended their fields and worshiped their gods and raised their families much as we do. Their ancestors still live in the pueblos up and down the Río Grande Valley."

"But Grandfather, what does that have to do with old Pedro Pedo?" There was a smirk on Leonardo's face. Pedo meant fart.

"Don Pedro Baca!" José Antonio said sharply. "An old man deserving of respect."

"Don Pedro," Leonardo echoed cautiously.

"Now don't interrupt," José Antonio warned. He went on. "Then, of course, came the conquest. The Spaniards sailed in their ships from across the ocean. They came by land up from Mexico to this place. They had such hopes for it — such a burning desire to find treasure as they had found in Mexico — that they named it *New* Mexico.

"Among the illustrious names of those early explorers was Baca. Only the name was not Baca back then. It changed over the years. It used to be Cabeza de Vaca. Head of a cow."

Leonardo looked surprised. Cabeza de Vaca, José Antonio thought. The boy had no doubt heard the name, but as with most names he had never thought about the meaning.

"It was a name given to the family by a king of Spain back when the Moors ruled that country. When not everyone had a family name. There was a great battle between the Spanish and the Moorish armies. The Spanish were seeking the Moors to destroy them, pursuing them across the countryside, but they had lost them.

"The advancing army came upon a shepherd who pointed the way. He had marked the place the Moors turned with the skull of a cow. The Spanish overtook the Moorish army and won a great battle. As a reward the king named that nameless shepherd Cabeza de Vaca. From that family came warriors, explorers, Don Pedro.

"It was men like that who came to this New World, to this New Mexico. Now the struggles were no longer just with nature nor between Indian and Indian. Now the struggle was between Indian and Spaniard. One man taking another man's land. The history of the world.

"Then later the struggle was between Spaniard and Mexican. For those families who stayed had become Mexican. Had taken Indians for wives. Had become something different from their ancestors in Spain generations before. From that struggle was to come the Mexican nation. A great nation of which New Mexico was to be a part for only a short time. For from the east came the other New World European: the Anglo."

The boy was yawning and his eyes were heavy. I should say "tortilla!" José Antonio thought. Then his hungry belly would wake him up. Or I could say "play" and his feet would twitch and dance with life.

The boy yawned again and spoke as if he really did not know that he spoke. "That was when you were a priest, wasn't it, Grandfather?"

José Antonio nodded. "It was the last conquest. The Anglo took from the Mexican what the Mexican-Spaniard took from the Indian who in turn had taken it from other Indians. The strong take from the weak."

"But the weak shall inherit the earth, Grandfather," said the boy, looking very sleepy now. "That's what the priest says in church."

"No," the old man answered, shaking his head. "The weak may be blessed, but the earth still belongs to he who takes it."

Now Leonardo's eyes had almost closed but José Antonio had barely begun his story. He shook his head in reproach although he could not help but smile. Facts and dates were only the dry skeleton of history, destined to crumble into dust and blow away in the winds of the mind, while the heart and soul of history throbbed within the humans who were its inheritors. In Don Pedro, in his drunken sleep, locked in the shed. In Leonardo nodding in boredom at an old man's recitations.

# 3

"¡Desgraciado!" Leonardo ran from his mother's angry shout out of the kitchen and into the orchard. "You come back here with that tortilla or I'm going to smack you good!" How could she smack him if he ran away? he thought. "Wait till I tell your father, you good-for-nothing!"

But it was too late to worry about what his father would do. The stolen food was so temptingly warm that he could hardly wait to slip into his favorite hiding place just over the hump of the ditch near the big house.

He slowed to a walk and looked at his booty: two tortillas. In his haste he had not realized that he had been so lucky. His mouth watered at the prospect of this treat. Two all for himself. Not cold leftovers to be haggled over after the grown-ups had eaten their fill. Or to be ripped into pieces by the grabby little hands of his brother and sisters. The thought gave him such pleasure that he burst into laughter.

He was already chewing the first bite when he dropped to the ground and leaned against the shallow embankment, out of sight of both houses. He stared up into the still blue sky of a late afternoon but saw little. It was as if his eyes were covered by invisible shutters that deflected his attention inward to the taste and feel of the warm food.

The hard, tight knot of hunger softened and dissolved. A glow of satisfaction radiated from his stomach out to the very tips of his fingers and toes. Now at last he saw the sky, watching a crow glide through the air looking down on the corn and bean fields as if undecided about the choice of good eating.

This must be what heaven is like, Leonardo thought. A full belly. A quiet place to rest (he patted the ground). And no one after you about this or that (cautiously he turned toward both houses, but they were silent).

A long sigh escaped his lips, ending in a tingling shiver of contentment. Only one more wish, he thought. A little tobacco. A nice cigarrillo.

"Ay, Jesucristo," he whispered to the heavens. "How about a little cigarrillo for this miserable sinner?" He laughed at what he thought of as a private joke, mimicking the words he sometimes heard his grandfather mumble about being a poor, miserable sinner.

Then he leaned back, his hands behind his head, and closed his eyes. His mind was filled with visions of tobacco. All shapes and sizes. Rolled in corn shucks. Rolled in paper. Rolled in tobacco leaf. Fine turd-shaped cigars wafting their healthy masculine aroma into the air.

He could almost smell them burning, so strong was his desire and his imagination. Wait! Was that aroma his imagination? No. It couldn't be. That was the real thing. It had to be. He popped open his eyes and turned about, searching with his nose for the origin of that ecstatic burning. Watching hopefully for a friend who might share this pleasure with him. But there was no one and the aroma had disappeared.

He looked suspiciously at the shed behind the big house. Was the old loony enjoying the luxury of a cigarrillo in the dark of his adobe prison? Leonardo closed his eyes and sniffed the air in that direction. But no—Nothing. Or was there? Perhaps just the faintest trace, the memory of a cigarrillo.

Furtively he crept along on all fours to the shed. He looked about again before rising to the small open window that was visible only from one corner of the big house.

"Psst!"

No answer. He placed an ear against the opening and listened. Nothing. Until his ear felt warm, moist breath, and Leonardo turned to see the old man's crooked mouth smiling at him through the bars. The boy dared not scream, although he was shocked by this startling apparition.

"They're coming to take my land," Don Pedro whispered. "But I'm ready for them. I have my pistola right here." He nodded toward the filthy mattress against the wall. "And my vaqueros will be lying in ambush. There is no way that they can take the rancho from me. Would you like to help?"

Leonardo peered into the dim cell. There was no pistola in sight and no tobacco either.

The old man leered at Leonardo. "I'll make you my heir if you help. You'll be richer than the mind of man can comprehend. You'll own land that would take days to ride across on a fast horse. These little farms here in New Mexico—they're nothing. In California I lose more land than this when the wind blows across my rancho. It will be all yours when you're my heir. All you have to do is help me."

"Do you have any tobacco?"

"What?"

"Tobacco, you old loco. To make a cigarrillo."

"Tobacco? I don't grow tobacco on my rancho. I raise cattle. Horses."

"No, you old fool. Do you have any tobacco in this—this hacienda of yours?"

Don Pedro looked around his room uncomprehendingly. Then a thought seemed to lodge in the net of his mind. "You will be my heir," he whispered. "Don't tell the others. They'll be jealous. All you have to do is help me."

Leonardo peered into the dark recesses of the shed once more, searching for a pouch that might contain what he wanted. If there was anything at all, it had to be on the old man. But how could he smoke it? No one would trust him with a flint.

"Help me," came the plea.

"Help you what?"

"Let me out. I have to see Esmerelda. We have to be ready when they come to take my rancho from me."

"Do you have any tobacco?"

A sly, crafty look crossed Don Pedro's face. "Yes," he answered. "I'll give it to you when you let me out. Just unlock the door."

The old fool, Leonardo thought. Every wrinkle on his face says "lie." Tobacco, hah! I have as much faith in his tobacco as I have in his California rancho.

"Please," the old man pleaded. "You'll never regret it."

"Liar. Stop lying to me or I won't bring you your medicine anymore."

"No!" The outburst ended in an animal-like howl.

"Shut up, you dummy." Leonardo's heart pounded as he glanced fearfully toward the big house. Don Pedro howled again, a shriek that sent shivers through the boy. "Just wait," he warned. "Just wait." Then he ran quickly, silently toward the ditch. He slowed only after he had passed safely from view. He could hear his mother screaming as the old loony howled even louder.

That old crazy, he thought. As crazy as—he couldn't think of what old Pedro was as crazy as. The craziest thing that ever existed. Why would Grandfather take in old Pedro Pedo? What was Pedro to him? Then he remembered. It had something to do with his grandmother, his Nana. They were related. Old Pedro was her brother. Or her primo, her first cousin. Anyway, the one who went to California. Or was it his parents who had gone to California? Something like that.

Leonardo mused on this puzzle as he trod across a neighbor's field, having crawled through the barbed wire without really thinking about it. The dirt road that led north was just ahead. There, sitting on the edge of the field, was his older cousin, Ernesto Chávez, a tiny column of smoke rising from his cigarrillo.

"Cousin. How goes it?"

Ernesto took the cigarrillo from his lips with thumb and forefinger and spat into the dirt. "You got any money?" When Leonardo shook his head, Ernesto feinted a lunge at him and Leonardo turned his overall pockets inside out. "Damn!" Ernesto said. "I know of this sweet card game tonight with money just waiting to go home with me."

"Sorry, cousin."

"How come you're not out in the fields breaking your ass? What are you up to?"

"Nothing." Ernesto spat again and leered as if he didn't believe him.

"How about a puff?" Leonardo asked.

"I don't like anybody slobbering over my cigarrillo. Get your own."

"Do you have any extra tobacco?"

"Tobacco costs money."

"God, what I wouldn't give for a smoke."

"You'd really like a smoke, huh?" Leonardo nodded. Ernesto smiled as he thought something over. "No," he finally said. "You haven't got what it takes."

"What do you mean?" No response. "What do you mean, Ernesto? Tell me. Aren't we cousins? Next to you I'm the oldest cousin in both Rafa and Chávez families. Man, we're close!"

"You really .think you have what it takes?"

"How should I know if you don't tell me what it is?"

Ernesto uncurled himself and stood abruptly, like a jackknife snapping open. Lean and hard, he towered over the smaller Leonardo. "Come on," he said.

They crossed the road and cut through another field. When they reached a grove of cottonwoods, Ernesto put out his hand and nodded toward the white frame house.

"Don James's place," Leonardo muttered.

"In the back, in the storage area in the barn, there is enough tobacco to smoke for a hundred years. That rich gringo wouldn't miss the little we'd take. And there's more than tobacco there."

"I don't know—"

"Coward," Ernesto said irritably. "I knew you didn't have what it takes."

"Don James keeps a gun."

"And dogs," Ernesto mimicked. "So what? If you want tobacco, there's tobacco."

"I'll have to think about it."

Ernesto's derisive laugh lashed Leonardo and he could not look his cousin in the face. "I'll be here tomorrow night at sundown," Ernesto said. "If you have any guts at all, you'll meet me here. Until then, so long, cuz." With that he turned and ambled across the field.

"So long, cuz," Leonardo echoed.

# 4

Leonardo's howling stopped and José Antonio knew that it would not be long before Francisco would rap on the door and enter.

Gregoria placed a hand on her husband's shoulder. "It's over," she said. "That boy. What did he do this time?"

"A whipping does not help," José Antonio said. "If it did, we'd all be saints."

He felt her strong farmer hands begin to knead his aching shoulders. "Do you feel all right, Tercero? Should you be going to the meeting?"

"I'm all right," he grumbled.

Then the two staccato knocks and a red-faced Francisco entered, scowling. The two old people looked at each other before they spoke in unison, "Hijo."

"Mamá. Papá."

"What is it this time?" Gregoria asked. José Antonio remained silent. It was none of his business — or hers.

"That boy will never amount to anything," Francisco said. "The minute I turn my back he drops his hoe and disappears to God knows where. Then after supper off again until who knows what hour of the night. When I ask him what he's up to, he says: 'Nothing, Papá.' Nothing? What kind of an answer is that? You don't disappear for hours to do nothing."

"Maybe he has a girl."

"He better not!" Francisco turned to his father. "How are you, Papá? You don't have to go to Smith's if you don't feel up to it. I can go alone. I know how to handle it."

José Antonio stood. He plucked his sweat-stained Stetson from the door peg and motioned to Francisco. "Come on."

"Are you sure you're all right?"

"Yes," he snapped in irritation.

They boarded the old wagon silently. José Antonio looked at its dry, sun-bleached wood, a great improvement over the carretas of his youth. He recalled the intolerable squeal of ungreased wooden axle on crude wooden wheels and the occasional unexpected and violent cannonade of a snapped axle on those old Mexican carts. It seemed that they were forever replacing axles before they could continue their journey.

José Antonio sighed as the old horse plodded along. "Did a whipping do you any good when you were a boy?"

Francisco stiffened. "Sometimes young people are possessed of the devil and one must root it out."

José Antonio's eyes narrowed as he glanced at the sullen Francisco. The matter was closed, he sensed that. He did not like to interfere in his children's lives, even when it involved his grandchildren. Yet his son was wrong.

"Remember. Leonardo is only a boy."

Francisco snapped the reins viciously and the horse lurched forward, barely increasing its speed. They rode in silence until they turned off Rafas Road toward the Smith place.

"Who are they going to nominate this time?" Francisco finally asked.

"There's talk about Plácido Durán."

"Jesus! What happened to Martínez?"

"I don't know. The only talk I've heard is about Durán."

Francisco spat over the side of the wagon. "He's nothing but the hired peon for that Anglo crowd downtown. At least Martínez listens and tries to help. You don't see him running around after that bunch picking up their droppings and acting as if he discovered gold. What the hell! We might as well elect an Anglo and forget all this pretense."

"We'll see when we talk to Smith."

"Where's the money coming from to back Durán?" José Antonio shrugged. "From the railroad people," Francisco said. "And the real estate developers. If we did some of the things they do, we'd be in jail. Or hanging by a rope from some tree."

Francisco fell silent, still angry, having shifted his anger from Leonardo to the local políticos. José Antonio thought about the compromises one had to make in life, that whether one compromised or not, things turned out the way they were going to. Much of the time it didn't matter what you did except to yourself. To your pride. Your sense of honor.

They turned into the Smith place and Mrs. Smith ushered them into the living room, rich with its red woolen carpet and oak furniture shipped all the way from Chicago. There were no niches in the walls with votive candles burning before small wooden figures of saints. And the air was sterile—devoid of the aroma of humans or food.

They sat self-consciously on the stiff, cushioned chairs waiting for James Smith. "Is the man from New Town going to be here?" Francisco asked in a subdued voice. Somehow this house, for all its sterility, was like being in church.

"I don't know."

After a few moments footsteps approached. "I'm sorry to keep you waiting, gentlemen." Smith shook hands with them formally, stiffly. "Don José. Don Francisco." Smith sighed as he sat down. "There's a thief loose around here. I was just out in the barn. Jesse said it had been broken into." Jesse, whose real name was Jesús, was his hired foreman.

José Antonio and Francisco exchanged glances, thinking unspoken thoughts. One of us, is what José Antonio thought. One of our people has to be the thief.

"There are more strangers around than in the past," Francisco said. "Everywhere you look there's an unfamiliar face. The railroad brings them in every week."

Smith stood abruptly and went to the door. "Martha!" A moment later she came with coffee and set it on a small table. "There. Now we can get down to business."

"Where is Señor Gertz?" José Antonio asked.

"He won't be here."

That meant they were only going to talk about Old Town. Gertz was the merchant from New Town who represented the new interests. The Anglo interests. Merchants. Businessmen. Professional people.

"The word from party headquarters," Smith continued, "is that Plácido Durán is our man." He took a sip from his cup and waited, but there was only silence. "Now you gentlemen know the rural area. Los Rafas. Los Griegos. Los Chávez. How will Durán do here?"

When they hesitated, Smith spoke out again. "I want to know! We've got to win this election! Now tell me. What about Durán?"

"There are stronger candidates," José Antonio said. "Men that our people would back with enthusiasm."

"Like Enrique Martínez," Francisco added.

"Stronger candidates? Does that mean they won't vote for Durán? That they'll vote for the other party's man instead?"

"Who knows? Does a crow care which ear of corn it eats when they all look the same and it's hungry?"

"Don Francisco. What do you say?"

"Durán is not that well-liked. People won't say that to your face. They'll drink his beer and eat his barbecue at a rally. But underneath, where it counts—I don't know."

"What's the matter with him?"

José Antonio and Francisco looked at each other. Finally, José Antonio shrugged. How should he put it? "People don't trust him," he began. "Like . . . statehood. You know how he stands on statehood. Our people don't buy that.

"Look. We've been part of the United States since I was a young man. Over forty years. California became a state right after the war. And here we are, still only a territory.

"You know what people say? California was overrun by Anglos during the Gold Rush, so there were enough of them that it was safe to become a state. They couldn't be outvoted by Mexicans.

"Look at the Territory of New Mexico. First the Anglos in Arizona pulled out and formed their own territory from what used to be New Mexico. Then other pieces were carved out of our territory to give to Colorado and Nevada, which later became states. Here we are still not a state. We may be U.S. citizens, but we're second-class. Definitely second-class.

"Since we were conquered, fifteen states have been admitted to the Union and here we still are. What do you think our Spanish-speaking people think about that?"

Smith's face reddened. "Durán has never made any public pronouncement about statehood."

"He doesn't dare. But people know how he feels. He'd prefer that we stay a ward of the Federal government forever rather than take our rightful place in the Union."

"There are problems," Smith said. "Our small population. Our lack of wealth. As a territory we enjoy privileges and protection that—" But José Antonio shook his head and Smith let his words trail off and took a new tack. "What you're saying is that the Spanish-speaking people know how he feels and disagree?"

"Statehood is only one of many issues. Many feel that his position on unsettled land claims goes against the interests of our people." He didn't say what Durán was for: the railroads and the land developers.

"In other words, Durán is too much of an Anglo for their tastes."
José Antonio avoided Smith's eyes. What he said was true. Smith
was no fool.

"There are many who favor Enrique Martínez." José Antonio was
surprised at the restraint in Francisco's voice.

"Martínez is a troublemaker," Smith said. "Besides — and I mean no
disrespect — we are not here to choose our party's candidate but to elect
him. The matter is settled. It will be Durán. Even if the matter were
not settled, the men uptown would never agree to Martínez."

"It will be difficult."

"It may be that we can raise more money than usual for our campaign. We can take over every cantina in town the week before the
election. The key will be to make sure that everyone — and I mean
everyone, alive or dead — goes to the polls. We should have enough
money to grease a lot of palms."

"I don't think a dollar a vote is going to be enough," Francisco said.
"People will want more than they are used to getting."

"No!" José Antonio could barely restrain his rage. Startled, the others
turned alertly toward him. "You say, Mr. Smith, that we are not here
to select a candidate. Fine. I see that. But I'm not here to buy votes
either. I have been the party's man in Los Rafas for years. Ever since
the early days when I worked with the lawyers validating our land
grants and as a representative in the territorial legislature. I will talk
to people. Try to persuade them. I will help them. Do them favors.
They will listen at election time. But I will not buy votes. As God is
in heaven, I was once a priest. I am still a Catholic. There are some
things I will not do."

The air was charged with silence. Francisco picked up his cup and
gulped the contents in one swallow. Smith's face turned a deep red.

"Nobody's asking you to buy votes, Don José. That is not the policy
of our party, although it's hard to restrain some zealous party workers."

"A dollar a vote will not be enough," Francisco said. "No matter
who does it and how it's done. I mean no disrespect, Father. I'm just
trying to be a realist. If someone tries to buy votes, it will cost them
a lot of money. The best way to win an election is to have the best
candidate."

"Enough of this talk," Smith said. "That's not why we're here. I'm
not asking you to buy anything. I hope you'll forget that the matter
ever came up. We're here to discuss our liaison with Los Rafas and
surrounding areas. Let's look at it area by area, family by family, and
see how the vote lines up."

José Antonio began. Two hours later he and Francisco were in the wagon making their way home.

"I still think it's a mistake," Francisco said. "Even Smith must realize that by now. There are too many voters we are not sure of, even some who normally vote the party line. Why the hell didn't someone consult us? They make all the decisions over in New Town, then expect Old Town and the ranchitos to fall in line."

But José Antonio was not thinking about the election. Off in a field his still sharp old eyes saw two figures duck out of sight. His grandson, Leonardo, and — he strained his eyes to see. Ah. There. Ernesto Chávez, that troublemaker and potential jailbird.

Francisco urged the old horse on as José Antonio weighed this new consideration. He decided not to tell his son. He would talk to Leonardo himself.

# 5

Francisco had kept his own counsel after the meeting with Smith. If his father had not been there, he knew that Smith would have drawn up to him confidentially. "How much more than a dollar a vote?" he would have whispered, and Francisco would have told him. "I'll talk to the men uptown. There's not much in the election fund yet, but maybe we can do something." Then he would have slapped Francisco on the back and winked. "I like doing business with a man that understands."

Son-of-a-bitch! What did *Smith* understand? Mierda, Francisco thought. From the absurdity of making Durán their candidate to the belief that he, Francisco, was his man. Smiling that shining, pure, hypocrite's face at José Antonio. "Of course not, Don José. We wouldn't buy votes." How could his father be so naive?

He spat into the dirt street as he secured his horse to the hitching post. It was early yet and the streets of New Town were almost empty. Even the cantinas were quiet, although a few red-eyed stragglers made their way in for a morning pick-me-up.

Later on, near train time, the tempo would quicken. Parades of people — whole families from some outlying ranchito, or a Navajo squaw in full regalia with her brood trailing behind her, or white-haired viejitas who seldom left their little adobe hovels — would scurry to the station to marvel at the puffing iron monster that was importing progress from back east. Few realized that after a short stop, progress would get back on board and not get off again until it found a permanent home in California.

The hardware store was empty except for the clerk who ran a hand through his thinning sandy hair and nodded at him. The transaction took but a moment, and then he was out in the street again. Francisco would rather have patronized one of the traders in Old Town, but when you needed something a little out of the ordinary, you would be more likely to find it in one of the stores in New Town run by the German Jews. Couldn't even speak Spanish when they came out here from Europe with little more than their peddler's carts, but they learned it. Didn't speak English much better than some of the Hispanos, but they spoke it well enough to sell to the other Anglos. And they prospered.

Francisco mounted his horse and headed toward Old Town. He could see the signs of growth everywhere. New buildings. Stores. Hotels. Cantinas. Trading posts. Before, there had been nothing but desert.

A buggy passed on its way to the railroad station. A few early risers bustled along the board sidewalks. People who a few years ago did not even know that there was such a place as Albuquerque. Settlers drawn west by land, by the prospect of homesteading, the lure of gold, the railroad.

It all puzzled him. What did they want, these aggressive gringos? Why did they work so hard for so much when they did not take the time to enjoy it? When you looked at politics, at trade, at the railroad, at the cattle business down south, it was almost all Anglo. Run by intense, serious, purposeful men who worked like machines, denying themselves the pleasures of life: of home and family, of more than a business-like drink or two, of a lively dance, a woman. What the hell! he thought. A crazy way to live.

He marveled, watching the beehive come to life as his horse trotted through New Town. Although there was not that much distance in space between the old and the new, there were decades in time. There was no gradual transition between New Town and Old Town, just an abrupt change and suddenly you were fifty years behind the times. Sleepy adobe rather than wood frame. A few people moving as if there were no hurry, as if there were all the time in the world. And they were right, Francisco thought. Where were they going that they should be in a hurry? To say a prayer at San Felipe Church. To pick up a yard of calico at one of the stores. To go home to a meal of frijoles and chili. An hour sooner or later would not change anything. Since we all end up planted in the ground anyway, why hurry?

He crossed the acequia madre, the main irrigation ditch, passed the impressive castle that was a rich Anglo merchant's home, and was on the way toward Old Town plaza. As he turned toward the square, a shout greeted him.

His brother-in-law, Armando Chávez, waved and ambled across the plaza toward him. He hitched his horse and waited, glancing from the church toward the Armijo trading post to see who else was about this morning.

It took awhile for Armando to reach him. There was no hurry. Not like in New Town. One always had an hour to spend with a friend. Maybe two. One could take a day off from field work to run an errand. To have a drink. Catch up on the gossip in the shade of a cottonwood.

"¿Qué tal?" Armando was a short, dark man whose round face gave the impression of heaviness, although his body was stick thin. He was smiling. He always seemed to be smiling. A quip ready, as if life, no matter what, was a funny story waiting to be told. "I saw that swayback," he nodded at Francisco's horse, "and knew it was my favorite brother-in-law."

"Mierda."

Armando laughed. "I hear the big boys have decided who we're going to vote for in the coming election."

"What have you heard?"

"Come on. You're the big político. When someone breaks wind in city hall your nose starts to twitch. I hear you're going to run Durán."

"Who told you that?"

"Oh, a little bird. 'Durán,' this little bird said, 'savior of the people. A man on every side of every issue. Whose right hand has grown twice its normal size and turned green from being in the cash drawer so long.' Is it true, Francisco? Would those assholes uptown run Durán?"

"That's what I hear."

"Jee-sus. I think I'll move to Texas. At least there they don't let a Mexican vote. Or if they do and you vote for the wrong man, they take you out to the nearest tree and stretch your neck for you. Clean and simple. You know exactly where you stand. None of this phony voting for a handpicked candidate."

Francisco nodded. Anytime you wanted to tell the whole world and Los Rafas, you just started with Armando. His nonstop mouth was better than the newspaper. So Francisco kept his thoughts to himself.

"We ought to form our own party." Armando said. "Republicans. Democrats. Now challenged by Tortilla-Eaters. We could take over the territory. We outnumber them."

"Sure. Except with a Republican governor appointed by President Hayes, it would be hopeless."

"Come on. Smile, hombre. I'm only teasing." Francisco did not smile. "What you up to in Old Town today? Oh, I know. It wouldn't have anything to do with that sister of mine, would it? It's her birthday next week, and she nagged at you not to forget it. I can hear her now." He gave such a startling imitation of Florinda that Francisco finally grinned.

They walked along the south side of the plaza toward Armijo's. He would go in and look for some nice cloth so Florinda could sew herself a new dress. Something pretty. Some color other than black, which was all you saw around here because people were forever in mourning. Somebody was always dying. A husband, brother, cousin, nephew, in-law. Sometimes the plaza looked like a parade of crows.

"Look. Look." Armando jabbed him with a sharp elbow. "The friend of the people, Plácido Durán himself. He's probably going into church to empty the poor box. Look at those clothes. Wheee! Frock coat. Silk vest. String tie. Fancy boots from Chicago. Black gringo hat. He ought to be dealing cards at the Silver Dollar. Or soliciting customers for the girls at La Cucaracha." Armando shook his head and laughed.

Francisco cleared his throat and spit. In a moment Durán would turn and see them. His face would light up and the edges of his mouth rise in that automatic smile of his.

"I haven't got time for him," Francisco said as he hurried to the nearest store.

"Maybe he'll stand a voter to a drink," Armando said. He turned from Francisco and called across the plaza. "Don Plácido! What a pleasure —"

Bullshit! Francisco thought, rushing into the store. I'd rather vote for that clown Armando than for Durán. He hurried to the bolts of cloth, shaking his head and mumbling to himself about the inexplicable stupidities of politics.

# 6

The day started out hot. The desert sun rose in all its vigor, beaming with intense indifference on man and beast, old and young, weak and strong. Only a fool or an Anglo would work on such a day.

José Antonio sat in the cool of the big house. He could hear his wife in the kitchen. She would be finished with chores soon, relieving him of the pinprick of conscience he felt as he sat while she worked.

Outside, the heat imposed quiet the same way it reduced motion. With no one out, there was no one to make a sound. Oppressive heat brought with it a blessing. He would not hear his daughter-in-law screaming across the yard at her children or husband.

Still, José Antonio listened, his ear cocked for the sound of bare feet on hot, dusty ground. He had asked his grandson to come to him. Soon, he knew, the inside of Francisco's house would heat up as the outdoors already had. Heat up from the friction of personality on personality, until Leonardo would burst from the house as from a prison. Trying to diminish by distance the nagging staccato of Mamá's harangue or else propelled by a blow from his father's impatient hand. Then the boy would remember that Grandpa wanted to see him.

José Antonio listened until he dozed, not quite asleep yet not fully awake, an old man's sleep. Until he was suddenly aware of the quiet flicker of his wife's treasured Mexican fan beside him, moving the still air in the adobe coolness of the thick-walled house. Then a door slammed in the distance, followed by the slap of feet on earth.

"I'm going to tell him about the old man," José Antonio said.

"Why does he need to know that?"

"He is not a child anymore. I want him to know what can happen if he doesn't watch out."

Gregoria shook her head. "It won't happen here. Maybe in California. In Texas certainly. But not here."

"It's like the devil. If you watch out for him, he never comes. The minute you relax your vigilance, he steals up to you in the most innocent of disguises. The boy needs to know what has happened in the past so he can know what to look out for in the future."

"Craziness!"

"What do you know?"

Then the soft knock before Leonardo let himself in. "Whew. It's like an oven out there." He dropped onto the floor between his grandparents. "They're arguing about la política," he said. "Papá has to go to some meeting and Mamá doesn't want to let him."

"I saved you an empanada." Gregoria stood. "And I'd better see about Don Pedro. He may be thirsty." She furrowed her brow and shook her head at José Antonio in wordless displeasure at what he planned to tell their grandson. José Antonio ignored her.

Leonardo devoured the homemade turnover in three fast bites. One moment his grandmother had handed it to him, the next moment it was gone, and he was wiping his mouth with the back of his hand.

José Antonio did not speak until the back door slammed. "Remember what I told you about the Bacas?"

"Skull of a cow. On the hill to point the way the Moors had gone."

"Well. There's more to it than cow skulls. Our own desert has more than enough of those.

"Your grandmother's mother was a Baca. Don Pedro is your grandmother's first cousin. But he is more than that. As a young man his father went to California where Don Pedro was born. In turn, Don Pedro returned to New Mexico as a young man to trade horses. He met and married your grandmother's older sister, Rebecca. So you see, he is both cousin and brother-in-law. He is a special person."

\*   \*   \*

Don Pedro's father settled in a beautiful valley in California. It was north of the capital and presidio of Monterey and south of San Francisco, bounded by mountains.

The foothills on the west rose to the redwood-forested Santa Cruz Mountains, from whose peaks you could look further west to the Pacific Ocean. On late afternoons thick white fog or heavy clouds spilled over the green mountaintops like giant sea foam slowly breaking on a primitive shore. The Diablo Mountain Range to the east and south was dry brown and desolate, standing guard against forbidden entry. While toward San Francisco the southernmost finger of the Bay gently touched the shore of the valley. Surely Eden could not have been more blessed than this beautiful land.

Settlers were few, so nature's bounty was for the taking. Because of the Bacas' political connections and illustrious name, approval of their grant was a foregone conclusion. The certificate, signed by the comandante of the district and duly witnessed, was but a formality. The comandante was a dear friend.

"Take more if you wish," he said. "My God, there will never be many people in this place. The Indians are too lazy and too ignorant to make anything of it. It would be sinful to let it go to waste."

"But also a sin to take more than one can use. You are too kind. If fifteen thousand acres are not enough, I will come back."

"Now that the mission lands are being liberated from the blood-sucking priests, there are families who have been granted ten times as much. But—" With a sigh, the comandante returned the Bacas' petition, the priest's report that accompanied it, and the signed certificate. Los Palos was legally theirs.

Don Pedro passed an idyllic childhood on the rancho. The eldest of eight children, he was the leader and heir apparent. When their vaqueros broke horses, the pick of the herd was his. When the first apricots ripened in their orchard, the most golden of the fruit was set at his plate while the Indian maid watched eagerly, enjoying his pleasure almost as if she had savored the fruit herself. When a new book found its way on a ship from Acapulco to San Francisco Bay, he was the first to whom their governess would read the exciting story and the first to ponder the mysterious lines and curves that spelled out the secrets of the world on the pages.

But even then the seeds of change were being planted. For on the day of his fourteenth birthday Pedro met Samuel Barker, the first Anglo in this Mexican California who was more than a foreign curiosity to him.

He had awakened early, anticipating the day of festivities. There would be guests from neighboring ranchos. The priest from Mission San José would dedicate the day with mass. The large, dour padre would, as always, pat Pedro on the cheek too sharply for it to be really playful and remind him: "Christ died for our sins. So you, muchacho, must live for God." But what the padre really meant was that the mission no longer owned miles of land and hundreds of Indians and that the Bacas should remember to tithe generously as well as set a bountiful table for the corpulent padre.

Pedro had dozed off again when quiet singing and the giggling of his four younger brothers and three sisters woke him.

"Estas son las mañanitas
Que cantaba el Rey David"

Then his mother's smiling face peered through the open door. "Follow the string," someone said. "Hurry up."

Amid the giggling and the clatter of footsteps, he took the yarn tied to his bedpost between thumb and forefinger and followed its long and convoluted path through the rooms of the house and finally outside to the corral.

Pedro's heart pounded with excitement. He knew every stallion, every colt, every gelding, every mare, every filly, every mustang, every pony on the rancho. It had to be something new. The grooms grinned silently and nodded at his approach.

"Where is it?" he shouted. The grooms nodded again and jerked their heads toward a beautiful two-year-old in the back that Pedro had never seen before.

"He's a racehorse," Don Pedro senior said. "Bred and true. From a line of champions. It's in the blood. Like you, son. Just like you."

Right then Pedro named the colt Campeón, "Champion." Afterward, he barely heard the padre mumble his way through a rapid mass. He scarcely touched his breakfast. He had to try out his new colt. He mounted Campeón amid cheers and, accompanied by the senior groom, rode off toward the foothills.

"Go easy," the groom warned. "He is young. Do not ride him too hard too soon. He must be brought along slowly and properly."

But even on that first cautious ride, never had Pedro ridden such a magnificent animal. He knew there was not its equal in all of California. He ached to ride him full speed. Match him against all comers. Let him proclaim his name to the world: Campeón!

As they rode back to the rancho, two riders approached from the south. More guests. Pedro recognized the comandante of the presidio who had ridden all the way from Monterey.

"Ah," the groom smiled. "Now there will be some excitement. When the comandante and the padre meet, we may see the fight of the century. It was a mistake to invite those two within ten miles of each other."

But it was the second rider who attracted Pedro's curiosity. A man he had never seen before. An Anglo. Samuel Barker.

## 7

The celebration continued through the day, climaxing in a feast that went on until midnight. Pedro dropped into bed a tired but happy boy. Long after he retired, others found beds for the night. Not just the large number of permanent residents — the family, servants, ranchhands — but also their several guests, some of whom brought tents for their servants.

Although there was no clash between the comandante and the padre — they were both on their best behavior — Pedro was not disappointed. The guest who intrigued him most was Señor Barker. He studied him whenever he found himself near the Yankee.

"Samuel Barker!" the man had said when formally introduced. His hand shot out like a ramrod to grip firmly and pump twice, as if squeezing milk from a cow's teat.

"Maryland. That's where I'm from. Leastways before I became a sailor. But I've sailed my billion gallons of ocean now. Hoisted more tons of cargo than my tired muscles care to remember. It's time to settle down. Go back to my first love."

"What is that, Señor Barker?"

"Horses. Beautiful horses. This certainly is the country for them."

With that, Señor Barker winked at Pedro. Later, Pedro had seen him from a distance leaning on the corral admiring Campeón. When Barker had turned away there was a bright gleam in his eye and a smile tugged the corners of his mouth.

He knows good horseflesh when he sees it, Pedro thought. That made Señor Barker a friend automatically.

Barker left early, paying his respects to Pedro's father, the comandante, the padre, and the owners of ranchos in the area.

"You must send this young man to see my horses," Barker said, resting an arm on Pedro's shoulder. "Bring your magnificent birthday horse. I have a racehorse too. Brought it on board ship from New Orleans. Once it has its land legs again, we must have a race." His voice dropped to almost a whisper. "I challenge you!"

Pedro's chest swelled with pride at being treated as an equal. He envisioned Campeón easily outdistancing the seasick horse from New Orleans.

Pedro smiled as he snuggled into bed. The smile was still on his lips as his heavy eyes closed.

\*　\*　\*

One afternoon the very next week Don Pedro senior told Pedro to be ready to ride the next day. There was business in San José, and it was time for Pedro to learn more about running the rancho. Also, his father added, San José was not far from Señor Barker's place. It might be diverting to look at some horses.

Early the next morning, Pedro, his father, and his Uncle Ignacio mounted the horses that had been made ready for them. "But where is Campeón?" Pedro protested. He did not want to ride the wretched plowhorse that the groom had brought him.

"He is young and must begin his training. Besides," his father added slyly, "we need to see what the challenger is challenging us with. Racing is serious business."

Despite Pedro's protests, they rode in the cool of the morning. Soon the early mist burned off, and Pedro forgot his irritation. He was a man among men. A compañero who was addressed as an equal by his father and uncle. In these past few days he had crossed an invisible boundary that left his little brothers and sisters behind in their childhood world. He glanced secretly at the men he rode beside, and his heart soared with elation. Soy hombre, he thought. I am a man.

Their business in San José was brief. Pedro saw little that he recognized as business. He was introduced to some men as his father's oldest son; there was polite and unhurried conversation about horses and cowhides and crops. After the third such visit, where they were served lunch, Don Pedro said, "It's time to look over a few horses, Ignacio. What do you think?"

They rode quickly now, with a sense of purpose that had been lacking during the morning. Barker's rancho was small by Mexican standards. It lay south of San José on the flatlands bordering the trail to Monterey. The one-story adobe house sprawled casually back toward the corral. Beyond the corral was the smooth oval of a racetrack.

Samuel Barker greeted them with a shout, leaving the group of workmen surveying the track. "Don Pedro," he said with enthusiasm. "Don Ignacio and young Don Pedro. Welcome. I'm so pleased that you've come. It gives me an excuse to let my men do the work they are paid for without me having to tell them every little thing." He walked up to Pedro and looked askance at his mount. "But where is your Campeón? As you can see," he extended a hand toward the workmen, "we are making ready for your challenge. We prepared the track just for you."

Pedro knew he was being teased, but it pleased him nevertheless. "Campeón is in training," he said seriously. "He is a young horse and must be brought along slowly."

Barker nodded at the wisdom of this as he led them past the corral and barn to the track.

"It's exactly a mile around," Barker said. "I dare say it's the only such track in California. None of this local straightaway racing for me. Let the horses go around so everyone can see. It beats staring a mile down the countryside at clouds of dust, not knowing whose rear end is whose. No, sir. A round track. It's the only way."

They leaned against the fence to look at the horses. "We are just starting," Barker said. "There are only six choice racers now, but there will be more."

Pedro watched with a critical eye. There were several times as many horses as good or better on their own rancho. He was disappointed, hoping there would be something worthy of challenging Campeón, but from what he saw none of the horses was remotely in his class.

"Which one would you race against Campeón?" Pedro asked.

"It would have to be a young horse," Don Pedro said. "Our two-year-old must be matched against an equal."

Barker stared at his horses as if in deep thought. "That little gray filly is the only two-year-old in the lot."

She was a pretty little thing. Almost a toy. And would have made a charming mount for one of Pedro's sisters. Pedro tried to restrain a smile.

His father looked questioningly at Barker. "Is that the one you brought from New Orleans?" Barker nodded.

Like his father, Pedro narrowed his eyes and turned once again toward the gray two-year-old. He scrutinized her long, slender legs. Her delicate conformation. As the filly moved, she seemed to subtly favor her left hind leg. Barker is no fool, Pedro thought. Was he truly serious about a race or had he merely been indulging a young neighbor?

"May we have a closer look?" Don Pedro asked.

Barker ordered a groom to bring the filly. Once again they studied her with practiced eyes. All Pedro could see was the subtle hesitation of her hind leg. As if she were stepping carefully, looking for soft ground on which to place her hoof. But Barker and the groom seemed unconcerned.

"Has she a name?" Pedro asked.

"Palomita. Little Dove."

Don Pedro stepped up to Palomita and calmed her with swift, experienced hands, stroking her soft gray coat, inspecting her from flank to legs to teeth, paying attention to the questionable leg while not seeming to.

"We would love to race, wouldn't we Pedro?" Don Pedro said, patting the filly affectionately on the flank. "But neither of us has seen the other's young horse run. It would be a game of blind man."

"I have confidence in Palomita, Don Pedro. While your son's Campeón is a magnificent young colt, I am willing to make a match. With no handicap, even though the average colt is bigger, stronger, and faster than the average filly. But then Palomita is not average."

Don Pedro turned to his son, eyebrows raised. Pedro nodded eagerly. "What about the rules, Señor Barker? What conditions should we discuss?"

A thoughtful silence as Barker gazed across the corral toward the other horses. "Well—" He turned toward Don Pedro and Don Ignacio. "What did you gentlemen have in mind?"

"Distance," Don Pedro replied, looking at the others. "Shall we say one mile?"

Don Ignacio nodded. "That's about right for young horses."

"How about once around the track?" Barker asked. The others nodded in agreement.

"When?" Pedro asked.

"How about four weeks from today? That will give my Little Dove time to work off her sea legs."

Again they nodded, and Pedro glanced once more at that hind leg of Palomita's.

"What about riders?" Pedro asked excitedly.

"That should be up to the owner of the horse," Don Pedro said, as if it were of no consequence. But the boy knew that he should be riding Campeón. He was certain his father would agree.

"Fine," Barker said. "Likewise the saddle will be the choice of the owner."

"Agreed."

They stood quietly in a group, all smiling, all satisfied regarding the impending match. Pedro looked forward with anticipation to riding Campeón to a great victory. His father and uncle no doubt were thinking of a wager or two. While Señor Barker smiled for who knows what reason.

\* \* \*

Four weeks went by quickly. Don Pedro, the head groom, and Pedro devoted their energy to the training of Campeón. They marked off a mile-long stretch on the flattest, most remote area of the rancho and took Campeón out every morning. After much discussion and argument, they agreed that Pedro should not ride bareback, but that their most skilled leather craftsman should fashion a lighter than normal saddle to reduce weight yet allow a firm seat.

Campeón's workouts met all their high expectations. The young stallion was a magnificent runner, unquestionably the fastest two-year-old ever at Rancho Los Palos. He was spirited and strong, and though hard to handle at times, he loved to run. Even in workouts with older horses, Campeón showed his heels, blazing the mile-long stretch as if it were nothing at all.

Although Don Pedro watched with satisfaction, a certain uneasiness nibbled at him. "Ignacio," he said to his brother one morning. "A colt will almost always outrace a filly. It's like pitting a man against a woman. Then there was Palomita's leg. Yet that crazy Yankee is willing to race . . . without a handicap. I don't understand."

"He's a fool," Ignacio answered. "He has been a sailor too long and forgotten what he once knew about horses—if he knew anything."

"I don't like it."

"Well, hermano. I could always send someone over to spy on them." When Don Pedro did not answer, Don Ignacio nodded emphatically. "I'll do it!"

"I think," Don Pedro said, "I will only make a small wager on this race. It does not feel right."

Ignacio laughed. "Don't be a fool. It is a chance to make a killing. Time to bet everything. Once Campeón has won, Barker will never bet against him again."

*        *        *

Young Pedro grew more excited as the day of the race approached. He was not interested in gambling. Even if he had something to wager, it would not have obsessed him the way it did the grown-up men. To Pedro the contest was of prime concern. Winning was everything, bringing with it honors and acclaim. To be the victor was the object. And to be recognized for it.

So the boy concentrated on the training, both of Campeón and of himself. He practiced a fast breakaway at the start, holding a firm rein during the middle stretch of the race, then gradually building up speed toward the three-quarter mark, with an all out drive to the finish.

The day before the race Pedro felt that nothing could beat them. He and Campeón were almost one, like the mythical centaur that was both man and horse. He barely heard their spy's report; it did not really concern him. So what if the filly no longer favored her left hind leg, the last sea leg to become earthbound? And that she circled the track rapidly, but not so rapidly as Campeón. Wasn't that to be expected? The only question, in all fairness, was whether or not the filly should have a handicap. His father and uncle strongly disagreed.

They rode leisurely to Barker's rancho before midday, pulling Campeón along in a large wagon. A stall had been reserved for the horse, and Samuel Barker welcomed the men to his house. There they would rest and relax until the race the next afternoon.

At night as they lay on their pallets, Pedro could hear his father and uncle arguing. "How can I accept a man's hospitality and not bring up the question?" Don Pedro was saying. "The filly should be given a handicap. A horse-length or two. If she is no faster than our spy said, Campeón would still win."

"We made an agreement. Wagers have already been made. It would just confuse everything. He had his chance. It was Barker himself who said no handicap."

"Pedro, what do you think?"

The boy sat up, surprised that they had asked his opinion. "Uncle is right. Señor Barker said no handicap."

"See?" Ignacio said.

"I don't like it," Don Pedro said reluctantly.

Pedro lay back, too excited to fall asleep. What was it that bothered his father? Nothing could go wrong. During the last workout Campeón had blazed the mile straightaway like a meteor. What would be different tomorrow? He would blaze another fast mile around an oval instead of on the straight. It was that simple.

Early the next morning the crowd began to gather. Some had come from as far away as Monterey and San Francisco. Bets flew back and forth. Not just gold and currency, but land, saddles, horses, cattle — whatever of value that someone else would agree to. Uncle Ignacio had wagered six good horses and a piece of land in the hills west of San José. He was smiling, as if thinking how the gold he would win would help make improvements on an undeveloped part of the rancho. Pedro's father and Señor Barker had shaken hands over a small wager of two hundred pesos in gold.

After the horses were paraded around the corral for all to see, Don Pedro called Pedro. "It's time to take Campeón for a warm up on the track. Take it slow. Let him try the curves; they will be new to him. And remember our plan. Away fast. Hold him firm through the middle of the race. Then build up to a fast finish. Are there any questions, hijo?"

Across the corral Samuel Barker was having a quiet discussion with his mounted rider. While Pedro listened to his father, his eyes watched his opponents with dismay. It was the first he had seen of Barker's man. He was no human, but a wizened miniature. Sunburnt. Hard-faced. With large strong hands and a body the size of a child. He sat high on the horse on a flat saddle that was nothing more than a piece of leather cinched around Palomita. The stirrups were short and far forward on the horse, altogether very peculiar.

"Father?" He nodded toward Palomita.

Don Pedro cast a studious glance across the corral. "He must have trained a small ape to ride on a toy saddle. Don't worry. We Mexicans have always been the best horsemen in the world, and you have the best horse." He patted his son on the leg and Campeón on the flank. "Buena suerte."

As Pedro rode toward the track, he took a last look back. His father's face was expressionless, watching the monkey on Palomita urge the little filly forward. "All right, m'love," he heard the rider say in an accent he did not recognize.

The horses limbered up along the straightaway nearest the spectators. Pedro took Campeón into the first turn. He was strong, this young stallion. It took all of Pedro's strength to keep him from bearing out in a straight line instead of holding to the curve.

As they walked back toward the starting line, Palomita drew alongside. Again the accent and language he did not quite understand. "You'll have all the bloody fun you want when you hit that first turn full speed, mate."

Then the starter beckoned to them and they stopped beside him for instructions. Once around the track, Pedro thought. Start fast when the flag is dropped. Hold him steady down the back straightaway. Then build up speed to the finish.

He glanced nervously at the other rider who sat astride Palomita nearest the inside rail. The little monkey's smile annoyed him. "We'll see who's smiling at the finish," Pedro whispered to Campeón.

The handlers led the horses to the starting line and held them steady while the flag poised motionless in the air. The crowd noise faded so that all Pedro could hear was the breathing of his horse and the thumping of his own heart.

The starting flag dropped. There was a roar from the spectators. The horses broke as if launched from a catapult. Palomita rushed into the lead in spite of Campeón's fast start. Then they were into the turn and Pedro saw the little filly hug the rail, the shortest distance around the track, as if she were attached to it.

"Come on!" he said to Campeón. "Turn!" But the young stallion bore wide, and it took all of Pedro's effort to keep him from going wider.

As they came off the turn, Pedro could see the rear end of the other rider raised high as he leaned over the flying filly. Hold Campeón steady down the backstretch, his father had said. But that damned filly and her monkey rider were ahead.

No, Pedro thought. He could not let that little horse stay in front. "Come on, Campeón!" he shouted. But the filly hung on gamely, and they were into the second turn before Campeón's head bobbed even with Palomita's tail.

"All right, Campeón! We have to stay on the inside now. We can't lose any more ground!"

Palomita's rider looked back over his shoulder as Campeón was gaining. As they went into the turn, the filly bore wide, and Campeón swung even wider to avoid bumping her. Then the rider pulled Palomita quickly and agilely back toward the rail while Pedro fought hard to keep his mount from losing ground. He pulled Campeón hard to the inside and saw the quick backward smile of Palomita's rider.

"Bastard!" Pedro cursed. "You did that on purpose!"

They had rounded the curve and were now on the last stretch to the finish line. Build up speed! Pedro thought. Drive for the finish!

But he had lost ground on that last curve and Campeón was three lengths behind.

"Now, Campeón! ¡Andale!" The colt responded, flying like a demon, while up ahead Palomita's rider was flailing at her with a whip.

Pedro could see the judges at the finish now, could see the other rider whipping the filly as if that would propel her across the line, could see the gap closing while the finish line loomed closer and closer.

"¡Corre, Campeón!"

"Run, you bloody little filly!"

A roar from the crowd as they crossed the finish line. Did we get her? Pedro thought as he slowed Campeón before turning him back toward the judges. Alongside he heard Palomita's labored breathing and a shout from her rider. "The race is not always to the swift! Sometimes it's to the smart!" But Pedro did not comprehend, and it wasn't until the judges surrounded the filly that he realized he had lost.

The shouts and applause drove him away from the winner with a heavy gloom. As Campeón stepped from the track, Pedro looked down and saw the disappointment on his father's face.

Behind his father his uncle stood stunned, not yet understanding what had happened. Then Ignacio turned abruptly, not daring to look his nephew in the face, and slumped off, a beaten and depressed man.

Pedro burst into tears. It was his fault. They should have beaten that filly by a good six lengths. He had not held Campeón tightly enough around the curves. He had let Palomita's monkey of a rider block him wide on the last turn. He had been so confident of his horse that he had not ridden a smart race.

"That's all right hijo," he heard his father say. Then he felt the strong arms help him down from the saddle, and his father put an arm around his shoulder. "We will win next time. We'll train Campeón on an oval track."

"It's all my fault!"

"No, hijo. You rode a good race. She beat Campeón by less than a head's length. It was just that . . ." Don Pedro squeezed his son's shoulder. "He outsmarted us." The boy looked up and saw the puzzled expression in his father's eyes. "We were so pleased about no handicap that we ignored the oval track and the curves. Barker is a smart man."

"Uncle Ignacio is furious at me."

His father shook his head. "He's more angry at himself. At his greed. Ah," he said, raising his arms wide and letting them drop, "what can an honorable man do but pay his debts?"

Pedro wiped his eyes with the back of his dusty hand. They were through the crowd now, approaching the corral. Along the way he had heard expressions of condolence, seen the sad headshakes of friends who too had lost their wagers.

"Let's clean up and go home," Don Pedro said. "We've had enough for one day."

\* \* \*

Leonardo's head nodded. "Leonardo!" he heard his grandfather say.

The boy shook his head, bewildered, and looked up into his grandfather's solemn face. "Sí señor."

"What do you make of that race?"

"They lost."

"Is that all?"

"The fastest one doesn't always win."

"And . . . ?"

Leonardo's sleepy eyes were alert now. He stared at his grandfather, trying to fathom what answer the old man wanted. "They were outsmarted?" he said in a questioning voice. The solemn look on José Antonio's face relaxed a bit. But the boy could sense that there was more. "I don't understand," he finally said. "It's just a story about a race. It isn't even very important."

Grandfather's face clouded and he blinked his eyes in silence for a moment. "It was the first time the boy Pedro had ever had dealings with an Anglo. It wasn't to be the last.

"He learned that there are more ways of making war than with rifles and cannon. There are subtle wars that one must learn to recognize and prepare for. Wars do not have to kill. They need only have one side win. Whether it's a horse race or title to a piece of land or a woman. Whatever it is that two want and only one can have."

"I see, Grandfather." But the boy did not see.

"There is more to Don Pedro's story," José Antonio continued. "For his first encounter with an Anglo was the least painful. But more of that another time."

# 8

After she left José Antonio and her grandson, Gregoria took a clay pot and tin dipper from the kitchen and stopped at the pump before she unlocked the shed.

Don Pedro sat on the floor in a corner staring at the door. "I brought you some water," she said, placing her load on the small rough table. "How are you, Pedro?" He didn't answer.

She was angry at her husband and did not want to return to the house while he poisoned their grandson's mind. So she sat on the edge of the pallet, placed her hands in her lap, and gazed at her brother-in-law. Who was crazier? she thought. José Antonio or Pedro?

She thought of her beloved sister Rebecca, Pedro's wife, and tears filled her eyes. "You are the only one of your family left, Pedro," she said. There was a flicker of recognition on his face and he grunted at her. "Do you want some water?" He sat immobile, staring at her.

Gregoria wiped her tears with her apron. He had not gotten better. The craziness still lay submerged behind his wary eyes. Usually the spells only lasted a few days, but this one had gone on for over two weeks now.

"When you get better," she said, "you can go back to your room in the big house."

He blinked and a tear rolled down his cheek. "Rebecca?"

"No. Rebecca's gone." He shook his head as if he didn't understand.

How would Tercero feel if I were no longer with him after thirty-six years and five children? she thought. How would I feel if he were no longer with me, even though I am angry at him now?

Pedro stirred. She watched him, trying to see in this dirty, unshaven, crazy old man the bridegroom who had taken her older sister to California. Gregoria had been nine — no, ten years old. The bride had been eight years older. Beautiful in the wedding gown that had been their mother's. More beautiful than any bride Gregoria had ever seen, even her own daughters.

She had been a flower girl, and she remembered her own sweet dress that she had been so proud of. "I'm just like a bride," she had whispered to herself. "A beautiful young bride." She had swirled round and round, the skirt billowing and whirling until her mother had told her she would fall and ruin it before the ceremony if she did not stop.

My God! That had been fifty years ago. Her mother had still had three years to live. Papá had not yet started to drink so heavily. She had not met José Antonio, not even known that he existed for he had been a young seminarian in Durango.

"Agua." The croak startled her, but this sign that Pedro was surfacing to the real world was gratifying. He drank greedily, then with a sigh pushed the empty dipper toward her for more. He drank the second dipperful more slowly.

"You must be feeling better," she said.

"It's very hot."

"Do you want Leonardo to take you for a walk by the ditch?"

"The heat is good for the corn. You can almost see it grow. But the animals don't like the heat. They're not growing any more."

"I'll send Leonardo."

A crafty smile twisted his mouth. "They want to take my rancho and my horses, but I won't let them."

"No, we won't let them."

"I have the fastest horses in California."

He was back where he had not been for twenty years, back in California. Were those intervening twenty years a blank? It was hard to tell. Sometimes it was as if New Mexico did not exist for him, and he was reliving over and over the nightmare of his previous life.

His voice dropped to a whine as he held out an empty bottle. "Is there any more medicine?"

Gregoria stiffened. It angered her that Florinda gave Pedro cheap wine to quiet him when he was at his worst. It was sinful to abuse the man that way.

"We're out of medicine," she said, taking the bottle.

His face clouded with disappointment. "Will you get more?"

She did not answer. Pedro stood and helped himself to another sip of water. He smiled as if to say: See. There are other things to drink besides medicine.

"Are you hungry, Pedro?" He shook his head. "I'm going. I'll send Leonardo after awhile."

Gregoria latched the door behind her. If it were up to her, she would let Pedro roam free even at his worst. Her only concern was that he might injure himself. Other than that, what could he do? He was a harmless old loony. Every settlement — and most families — had at least one.

She slammed the kitchen door behind her. José Antonio should be through sermonizing by now and she would not have to listen to his nonsense. What ever possessed him to tell Leonardo about Pedro and California she did not know. But the old priest was stubborn once he set his mind on something. "Old priest" was what she called him when he stiffened into his moral, upright attitude. It infuriated her. As if being honest were the only virtue. There were some things people did not need to know and it was not really a lie if you did not tell them. But that old priest . . . Bah!

"Leonardo," she called.

"He's gone," José Antonio said.

She picked up her fan and sat next to her husband. "What nonsense did you tell him today?"

"Nothing."

"Humph!" As she folded her arms across her chest, she saw his lips tighten into a hard narrow line. Then she thought of Pedro and her sister Rebecca and looked hard at the stuffy old priest beside her. It was ridiculous how the two of them tensed like angry bulls. What was there to fight about? They had so much and they differed over so little.

She saw his stubborn look and almost laughed. For some reason it struck her as funny. She took his face in her hands and gave him a playful kiss. "Are you mad at me because I don't want to tell Leonardo about things he'd be better off not knowing?"

"Sometimes you make me damned angry," José Antonio said. "Usually when you tell me something I already know but don't want to hear. Sometimes you don't even have to say anything. All you have to do is look at me.

"I bored him," José Antonio said. "He is at an age when he cannot listen. Remember Francisco? Or José Carlos? Leonardo may never know why Pedro is the way he is if he doesn't listen. He'll never know what happened to him and his family in California. So how can he appreciate New Mexico if he does not know what terrible things happened to our people in other places? How can he learn what to watch out for so that those terrible things never happen again?

"He is the oldest son of our oldest son, the one who stayed. The others? Why would Carlos want to go to Mexico to prospect for silver? Or José Blas join the army? It was as if they couldn't wait to grow up and leave, while Francisco stayed."

Gregoria felt a sadness when he mentioned their other sons. Of course they were grown men who had a right to go wherever they wanted, but that did not lessen her sadness. At least their daughters had married local men who kept busy farming and kept them busy raising children.

"You want Leonardo to stay here and carry on the way the Francisco carries on," she said.

He nodded. "One madman and two wanderers in the family are enough."

## 9

It was after dark when Francisco saddled his horse and set off for the meeting. He could hear Florinda screaming at the children and the echoing bellow from Pedro in the shed. A malicious smile lit his angry face. Somehow it seemed right that a shrew should be answered by a crazy man.

"What meeting?" she had started in on him this morning. "If it isn't la política then it's the cantina with those drunken bums you call your friends. When are you ever home? You never think about me. I'm just your slave around here. Yours and those wild children of yours. Why don't you let your father go to the meeting instead? It's his job, not yours. I think you do it to spite me because you know I don't like it."

On and on and on. All day. The same words in the same noisy scream that was like a whip snapping at his ears. Until he had enough — more than enough — so that when the children were outside he smacked her one just to shut her up. Not a very hard one. He had slapped her harder other times. But all he had done this time was change the screaming to crying.

As he rode slowly past his parents' house, he looked at the light in the window. How was it that those two old people had lived together so long and so tolerantly? They did not always agree, yet he had never heard the infernal screaming and arguing that was such an accustomed part of his own married life. He cleared his throat and spat viciously into the dark.

The proprietor of the little cantina, a distant cousin, nodded in silence as Francisco entered. Then the proprietor walked through a side door into the little store that was the other part of the same small building. The room was empty except for a shadow at a corner table.

"He's putting out a guard," the man in the shadow said, "to tell them it's a private party tonight."

Francisco sat. "Where are the others, Martínez? The guest of honor is here but not those who invited him."

Enrique Martínez lit a cigarette and Francisco could see his face in the brief flare of flame. "There is no guest of honor. We're just friends getting together for a visit."

"I'll light the lamp. I feel like a damned owl in the dark."

Soon they were bathed in a soft, flickering glow. "I almost didn't make it," Francisco said. "That damned wife of mine." Florinda Chávez Rafa was known for her tongue and temper as were many of her Chávez kinsfolk. Too much inbreeding, some claimed. Too many first cousins marrying first cousins. Or even worse, some whispered. Offspring from unnatural couplings forbidden by God and decency.

The side door to the store opened and the proprietor ushered in two more men who glanced furtively around the cantina, then walked to the table.

"Griego. Lucero." Francisco said.

They exchanged quick nods. "So," Griego said. "Armijo's late again."

They sat quietly. Soon Ignacio Armijo rushed in, bustling with importance. The proprietor set five glasses and a bottle on the table.

"Well," Armijo said. "You're all here. Good." He rubbed his hands briskly as if he could not wait for the meeting to begin.

"Gentlemen," Martínez said as Francisco poured. "To what do I owe this honor?"

The others looked at each other as if uncertain who should speak. It was Griego's idea, Francisco thought. It was he who had approached them, suggesting that they talk to Enrique Martínez. But then, as José Antonio's son, he might be considered the spokesman for the senior político in the area. Only he had not told his father about this meeting and neither had the others. They knew to a man that Don José would not have joined them. Would have advised them to forget the matter and support the party's nominee.

Francisco saw the eager look on Armijo's face, the lips parted, ready to speak. "Pablo," Francisco said to Griego. "It was your idea." Armijo closed his mouth, the irritation on his face obvious.

Griego put his drink down and wiped his mouth with the back of his hand. "Well. You all know some of it. The party's nominee is going to be that bootlicker, Plácido Durán. Francisco, you were there with Don José when the gringo Smith told what they had decided in New Town. Told, mind you. Not asked or suggested. Now we're supposed to deliver the vote, whether we want Durán or not."

"Yes, yes," Armijo said impatiently. "We know all that."

Griego continued. "Sheriff is probably the most important of the elected offices. Whoever is sheriff has real power." He clenched a fist and shook it over the table top. "Laws written in books mean nothing unless a sheriff interprets them and enforces them. When it's not our man, like the incumbent, you know who gets screwed."

"You're damned right, Pablo!"

"So there we are," Griego said. "Plácido Durán. Shit! We might as well have an Anglo in office, if he's elected. Frankly, I don't think Durán can come close to beating the incumbent. I can't deliver the vote for him in my area. Even if we register goats, cows, and chickens. Anyway, goats and cows and chickens are too smart to vote for Durán."

"It's that way everywhere," Francisco said. "Don José and I told Smith, but he didn't want to talk about it."

"Doesn't he want to win?"

Francisco's lower lip protruded, his eyebrows raised, as he shrugged. "Of course. But he doesn't understand. Those Anglos in high places don't see it clearly. They think that just because they want something that automatically makes it so."

"The point is," Griego said, "it's still early enough to do something about it. That's why we're here." They all turned to Enrique Martínez. "That's why we asked you to meet with us."

"You can get elected," Francisco insisted. "You would represent the Spanish-speaking people fairly. They know that. That's why they'll vote for you."

The words faded to silence. All eyes were on Martínez, waiting. "Gentlemen," he finally said. "I'm deeply honored by your trust and support." He stared at his half-full glass as if looking for an answer in the reflection from the amber liquid. "It's . . . it's very difficult.

"First of all, the major parties have picked their candidates. They have the money, the organization, and the connections to elect whomever they want. It hardly matters what the voters think. They can run a jackass and still make a race of it.

"That means that anybody who is not a nominee of a major party is out in the cold. No chance. Even if a new party were started, it would take money and people. Hell! How are you going to raise money from voters who barely have enough to eat? It takes time to build an organization. We only have a few months.

"Finally, even if that miracle occurs, what are the chances of winning? The independent candidate would probably be a well-known man who deserts one of the major parties. So at best he would split that party's vote. The opposition would only have to hold on to its own vote and it would win in a landslide. Even if this independent candidate could cut into the opposition's vote, he would have to do it to an extent that is not really possible. The best that might happen is a run-off between the two top men, which means more campaigning, more organization, and more money.

"That's what I see, friends. We would need a series of miracles and I don't even have hope for one."

The other men stared at each other in silence. Having known them so long, Francisco felt almost certain of what was going through their minds. Quiet Lucero, who was nodding sagely, was agreeing with Martínez. "Yes," Lucero would say in his low lisp, "it would take more miracles than we are capable of. We'll just have to do the best we can for the party and wait for another time. Next election. It won't be long."

Armijo, who was leaning forward eagerly, staring at Martínez, was probably thinking: "The hell with all the reasons why we can't! We've got the best candidate. We'll have the backing of many of the Spanish-speaking. We have a good chance. If we don't do it now, we'll never do it."

And Griego, the shrewdest political mind in the group, would probably say: "Martínez is right. We've been over this ourselves. Too many miracles. Too little time. After Durán loses, we'll get our chance next time. If we do our job for the party, after having told Smith what we think, they'd be fools not to listen to us before the next election. Would you run then, Martínez?"

The first to speak was Pablo Griego. "What would Don José think, Francisco?"

The question stung. What did it matter what his father might think? He was not a partner in this. Never would be. He would be for the party, no matter what.

"What would happen," Francisco countered, "if Durán refused to be the candidate?"

Eyebrows raised. Chests inhaled deeply. "And if my hens laid golden eggs," Armijo said. "That man salivates in public for the job. He'd dishonor his wife, mother, and four daughters to be sheriff."

"The party would have to pick another candidate," Lucero said.

"Of course." Francisco looked shrewdly at those around him. "All we need is to persuade Durán that it's in the best interests of the party . . . and himself."

Silence again. They avoided each other's eyes. They all knew what it meant. Although Durán might be a jackass and a fool, he had not survived and progressed as far as he had by quitting. It would take drastic persuasion.

Enrique Martínez tossed off the rest of his drink and stood. "Well, caballeros, I think the real meeting is about to begin. You realize that I can't be a participant in such a meeting. By right I shouldn't even know that one is taking place." He winked at them and scratched his cheek. "In fact, I don't know." With which he turned and left the cantina.

"The meeting," Francisco said, "will come to order."

# 10

Sunday Mass was more than a religious occasion. It was a social occasion too. In fact, more social than religious for many. After Mass people would gather in the plaza outside San Felipe Church and pass the time with family and friends before riding or walking back to their little farms.

Sisters, in-laws, cousins would catch up on the family news and escape the monotony of their daily lives for just a while. Men would talk of weather or crops or horses or politics. Young men and women would flirt in excited, laughing voices or whisper confidences while aiming discreet glances at their current object of interest.

For boys of Leonardo's age, there was an opportunity to break away from adults and gather with cousins that one saw only occasionally. He was the oldest of the cousins on his father's side of the family and treated his younger cousins with disdain. The more interesting ones, the older ones, were his cousins who were children of his mother's sisters and brothers.

This Sunday he knew that Mass would be a respite from his mother's nagging. Yet he did not feel like going to church. Even the prospect of seeing his older cousins was not enticement enough. He worried that the oldest of the Chávez cousins, Ernesto, might be there. It was unlikely. Leonardo had not seen Ernesto in church since sometime last year, but the remote possibility still unnerved him.

"You'll go to hell, you ungrateful boy!" was his mother's loving comment as the wagon turned into Old Town plaza. As the wagon slowed, Leonardo leaped to the ground and waved toward a group loitering on the west side of the plaza. "I'd better see you inside!" his mother screamed after him.

"Hey, Leonardo," one called.

"Hey, cuz," another echoed.

"You know what happened to Pancho last Sunday?" All the cousins gathered around except Pancho whose sunburned face turned deep red.

"I'll get you!" Pancho spat angrily as he turned on his heel and crossed the plaza. He stood beneath a tree with his arms folded belligerently across his chest.

The storyteller continued, occasionally glancing at Pancho from a corner of his eye. "He was at the altar rail going to communion. I was right next to him. The old padre was coming down the line, mumbling away while he passed out the wafers. Just as he got to Pancho —" But it was too much, and he started to laugh.

"Aw, come on, man. Tell the story."

"Just as he got to Pancho . . . it got very quiet. The padre had not started his little prayer yet. Anyway, he was standing there with the chalice in his hand when Pancho broke wind. You could hear the high-pitched whine all through the church."

He started to laugh again and wipe at the tears in his eyes. "Then," he finally managed. "The old padre's eyes popped wide open and his Latin came out real loud. Almost like a shout. But it was too late to drown out the sound. Or maybe he was trying to bless the foul-smelling wind from the holy Pancho. Anyway, the old padre's nose started to quiver and I could hardly keep from laughing when my turn came. I almost choked on the wafer. Pancho turned red as a chili and this cloud of stink followed him all the way back to the pew. Everybody in church stared at him."

The sputter of giggles broke into loud laughter and they looked at Pancho. "Oooh, Pancho," someone teased. "How could you?" He responded with an obscene gesture.

As Leonardo laughed, an arm fell across his shoulder, gripping him painfully. "Well, cuz," Ernesto Chávez said in mock surprise. "I didn't expect to see you here. Where were you the other night?"

"I can't talk," Leonardo said. "Mass is about to begin and I have to go in."

"Of course." But Ernesto's grip did not loosen. "I have to talk to you, understand?"

"Hey. Let's go," one of the group said. "We'll be late."

"Understand?" Ernesto repeated.

"Yes. After Mass."

But Ernesto still gripped him tight. "I'll be waiting," he warned. "Right here. If I don't see you . . ." He pushed Leonardo roughly toward the others who were rushing into the church.

Just as the priest entered, Leonardo saw his mother search through the crowd. When she finally saw him, she nodded. "Good," her expression seemed to say. "This is where you belong."

He sat uncomfortably through the service, trying not to think about Ernesto waiting outside. He did not want to see his cousin. He was sorry that he ever got involved with him, but he did not know what to do about it. Ernesto had attached himself to Leonardo, not through kinship but through a stubborn sense of pride. Leonardo had promised to meet him again after their initial foray but had not shown up. Now Ernesto was more determined than ever that they get together.

Why did I ever do it? Leonardo thought. He had been tempted by the tobacco in Smith's storeroom. He had not thought of it as stealing. It was more like discovering a treasure.

They had met beyond the ditch on the west side of the Rafa fields, under the shadow of a cluster of cottonwoods.

"What about the dogs?" Leonardo had asked.

"Don't worry. I've been making friends with them and I brought them something to eat. I'll take care of the dogs while you get into the storeroom."

They made their way in shadows as Ernesto told him what he was supposed to do. He handed Leonardo a tool to force the lock. The tobacco was stored on the right. You could find it by the aroma and the feel. The cured tobacco that was ready for smoking would be in gunny sacks. Leonardo would grab what he could carry while Ernesto entertained the dogs. If there was any sign of trouble, run like hell.

The snap of the breaking hasp sounded like a cannon shot to Leonardo. He had cringed in the dark, certain of discovery. But the house remained still. The rest was just as Ernesto had said and they were soon on their way, each carrying a sack.

That should have been the end of it, but it was only the beginning. Leonardo had to be more careful than ever that his parents not catch him smoking; they would want to know where he got the tobacco. Finding a hiding place for the loot almost drove him to despair. There was no spot on the farm immune from his family's eyes. Finally he dug a hole in a remote corner of a field and buried it, not caring that it might rot in the ground. He smoked portions of the small quantity he carried on his person in stolen moments in hidden places. The pleasure was poisoned by guilt and fear of discovery. Worse, the more he avoided Ernesto, the more Ernesto sought him out.

Mass was over. The crowd moved out slowly, but Leonardo held back. For a moment he thought of going to one of the holy statues and kneeling in prayer. But he really did not want to pray and could not bring himself to lie in God's house. Finally only a few stragglers remained and he knew he could no longer avoid his cousin.

Ernesto waited across the plaza from the church, an arrogant smile on his lips as he watched Leonardo approach. "You must have prayed long and hard, cuz," he said. "You're the last one out."

"What do you want?" Leonardo said. "My parents won't be here long and they expect me to go back with them."

The older boy flipped a knife from his pocket and whittled ominously on a twig. "Where were you the other night?"

"I . . . My parents wouldn't let me out of the house."

"Come on."

"It's . . . it's true."

"You've been avoiding me."

"No I haven't. I've been busy."

Ernesto poked the knife toward him and scowled. "Mierda. You're afraid, that's why. Chicken. You think you're a man, but you're nothing but a snotnose." Leonardo stood silent, trembling. "What if I told your mamá on you?" Ernesto's voice was mocking and his eyes glinted cruelly.

"You wouldn't."

Ernesto smiled. "I need your help on another job."

Everything inside Leonardo screamed no, but his voice came out a whisper. "I can't."

"You'd better!" The knife jabbed at him like an accusing finger.

"Leonardo!" He never thought he'd be glad to hear his mother's call.

"Remember," Ernesto warned. "You're my partner. Meet me at the trees again. Tonight after dark."

"Leonardo!"

"I have to go."

"You'd better not forget if you know what's good for you."

## 11

José Antonio noticed that suddenly Leonardo helped on the farm with an energy and thoroughness that brought smiles to his father's normally solemn face. In the evenings the boy would come to the big house and ask him to continue the story of Don Pedro.

José Antonio was pleased at this interest and at his grandson's new-found zeal for work. One never knew when a young person finally saw things in their true light and took up his inevitable responsibilities. It was gratifying to see signs in one so young, even if they should prove to be only temporary. Soon enough life would force Leonardo to take up the permanent yoke.

"When did Don Pedro next have dealings with the Yankees, Grandfather?"

"Later. Much, much later. At the time of the war."

"Which war? There have been so many."

"The Mexican War. The one in which your great-uncle, my brother Carlos, died fighting to keep the Yankees from stealing this land from Mexico.

"Since then there have been the Indian wars, too numerous to mention, with the Yankees trying to pacify the tribes that we as Mexicans could never defeat.

"And the great war between the Yankee states over slavery. Which always made me wonder how a nation that loved freedom so much still had slaves over thirty years after Mexico had abolished slavery. In this war the Confederates from Texas captured Albuquerque."

"That's the one in which Mamá's Uncle Nasario fought?"

"Many of our Spanish-speaking New Mexicans were in the Union Army. And like many of our quarrels with Anglos, this one was again with Texans."

"But when you were talking about Don Pedro you meant the Mexican War."

"That's right, hijo."

*   *   *

When the Mexican War began, Don Pedro was already a young man. A few years before while on a horse-trading caravan to New Mexico, he had met and married Gregoria's sister. Now he was the father of four and, as the oldest son, helped his father manage the rancho.

In the years since Pedro's memorable fourteenth birthday, California had been in a constant state of turmoil. The winds of liberalism blew across the old political landscape. California became an autonomous part of Mexico with its own California-born governor—a Californio, as native-born, Spanish-speaking citizens were called. With these political changes came the ever-present rebellions—perhaps rebellion was too grandiose a word—but there were arguments, plots, pronunciamientos punctuated by occasional gunfire. Occasionally someone might even be wounded or killed.

The major event though was the final downfall of the missions. These twenty-one jewels of Catholicism and enterprise up and down the length of California were emasculated. The Indians were abandoned to shift for themselves, some all too inadequately. Mission lands and stock were leased or sold and millions of acres were thrown out for bid to those rancheros with connections or money or both. No longer did the padres have the economic and ecclesiastical power that had for so long ruled this land.

Don Pedro senior added to Rancho Los Palos with reluctance. He was not given to large ambitions. The Bacas had all the land they wanted. If one worked too hard, one never had time to play. But with others making bids for mission lands, he thought that he ought to take a share, if not for himself, for his children.

With this added land came the need for more workers and the Indians from the missions more than filled the need. Don Pedro senior was a man known for his kind heart and easy ways, so there were always many who wanted to work for him.

As for the Yankees, more and more came to this Eden. The United States consul openly urged the Californios to become part of the U.S. Many American seamen settled, married local women, and became Mexicanized gringos. For the most part, these seamen got on well with the Californios. But from across the plains came trappers and farmers, far different breeds. The settlers wanted land. With much of the choice land already granted to the great ranchos, conflict was inevitable.

One morning Don Pedro put aside the account books he kept for his father and stepped outdoors for a breath of fresh air to clear his confused head. It was abundantly clear that the wealth of Rancho Los Palos was to a certain extent illusory. True, they owned twice as much land as they had received in the original grant. Not only did they raise horses, but now they raised cattle for the hides and tallow that filled Yankee trading ships. Their farming operations made them self-sufficient. Yet with all the money coming in from their main source of income, cattle, there seemed to be just as much money going out. Not only for fiestas and bailes — what was work for if not to allow such pleasures when the day was done? — but there were other expenses. Don Pedro felt that his father paid their workers, peons and Indians alike, much too generously. The old gentleman was lavish with gifts to family and church. With all of these leeches sucking the wealth from the rancho, it would not take much for them to be in debt. A bad year or two would do it.

Don Pedro turned his back to the morning sun to loosen the muscles made tight by sitting at a desk reviewing accounts. He shook his head in confusion. How could a family own such wealth and have so little to show for it?

His eyes traveled full circle, surveying the rancho, staring at the mountains to the west where they still owned timberland. As he turned his gaze north, his keen eyes saw a tiny cloud of dust that signaled an approaching rider. He stood, lost in thought, watching the cloud grow larger. The horse was moving quickly. Urgently. As if on a mission of importance. But it was a great distance away yet, so he strolled past the main house toward the stable.

After a brief exchange with the chief groom, Pedro turned back toward the house. The horse and rider had almost arrived and he recognized one of the vaqueros who had been sent on an errand to the big rancho to the north.

"Don Pedro!" the excited shout came. The vaquero reined his horse viciously and leaped from its back, removing his sombrero and standing breathless with heaving chest. "Rebellion, Don Pedro!"

A look of shock crossed Pedro's face, and he placed a hand on the vaquero's shoulder as a sign that he should catch his breath.

After a moment the vaquero continued. "I was at the great rancho by the bay when the news came," he said. "That Yankee bastard Frémont and his men have kidnapped Don Mariano Vallejo and members of his family. They have declared an independent Yankee republic with a bear emblem as its flag."

"Texas all over again," Don Pedro said. He did not say what else he thought. That it served Vallejo right for befriending so many

Yankees over the years. It was well known that Don Mariano was the best friend the gringos had in Northern California.

"The prisoners were taken to Fort Sutter. No one knows what the crazy Bear Flaggers will do next."

"Gracias, Joaquín. I'd better tell the old Don."

The vaquero walked slowly toward the bunkhouse as Pedro turned toward the main casa. His father sat sleeping in a rocking chair in the parlor.

"Señor," Pedro said softly. The old Don shook his head as if warding off a fly. "Señor."

After a few chews of almost toothless gums, eyes opened to slits. "Yes, yes," he mumbled irritably.

"Excuse me, Father, but there is news important enough that I should interrupt your nap." The old Don sat up, his eyes now completely open, and nodded impatiently. Pedro told him.

The old Don shook his head sadly. "Rebellion? No, hijo. Not rebellion. Out and out banditry. Poor Mariano. This is the thanks he gets for all his kindnesses to the Yankees."

"What about the other Yankees here in the north?"

The old Don dismissed the idea with a wave of the hand. "There will be no stampede to join the Bear Flaggers. Can you see Don Samuel Barker following Frémont and his cutthroats? Never. An independent republic? Another Texas? No. Most Yankees would much rather that California become part of the United States directly. I do not see the Yankees rushing to join Frémont."

"Still, I think we should put out extra guards."

A slight nod from the old Don. "We should watch out for these bandits and protect our livestock and our fields. That's how we should treat them — as bandits."

"What do you think the military will do?"

If it were up to me," he said, "I would ignore them. It would not be a rebellion if Yankees refused to join them and Californios refused to fight them. It would be a mistake to dignify that rabble by engaging in war with them." Again he shook his head sadly. "Poor Mariano. When you invite a viper into your house, you are asking to be bitten."

"I'll call together the family and the workers to let them know," Pedro said.

"Only the family, son. Your Uncle Ignacio. Your brothers and cousins. The foremen. But not all the workers. It would only alarm them. Set out extra guards. Do not send anyone off the rancho unless it is absolutely necessary. We will stay here and take care of our own."

"Sí, señor."

A few weeks later, as the old Don had predicted, the rebellion failed to spread. True, horses and cattle were stolen here and there. A few fields were wasted. But on the whole the situation was in a state of quiet suspense and the men at Rancho Los Palos went about their work much as always.

One morning Perdro sought his Uncle Ignacio before having a talk with his father about their financial condition. Where did Don Ignacio think they might reduce expenses or increase income? Should they reduce the wages of the workers? Cut back the size of their staff? Should they sell their prize horses that contributed to their pleasure but not to their profit? Or sell a piece of land — perhaps the mountain property above San José — or the timberland further west? But Don Ignacio was nowhere to be found.

He asked a dozen people before one of the house servants looked at him in surprise. "Oh, Don Pedro," she said. "I forgot. Don Ignacio and his two sons went to the landing on the bay. Someone wanted to sell them a boat."

"That's off rancho property!" he protested. She shook her head in bewilderment; she did not know that. "¡Demonio! The old Don will be mad as hell when he finds out."

He decided to wait and speak to his uncle before he spoke to his father, so he went back to work. In midafternoon Pedro remembered and asked if his uncle had returned. No one had seen him.

He left the house and looked north toward the bay, but there was no sign of approaching riders. Pedro frowned. More than enough time had passed for them to ride to the landing and back a half dozen times. Certainly no boat he knew of could require such long negotiations. He began to worry. Everyone on the rancho had been emphatically forbidden to leave the property until this Bear Flag nonsense had been resolved.

He waited another hour before he rounded up a search party. "Señor," he said to his father. "We'll be back before dark. They have been gone too long."

Pedro led a dozen armed vaqueros on the short ride to the bay, just beyond the north edge of the rancho boundary. They reined in as they came within sight of the landing and peered toward the water's edge. Nothing. Just the quiet afternoon breeze blowing through the wild grass. Not a sign of the three men, their horses, or the boat.

"Careful," Pedro said as he led them slowly toward the landing. The quiet water had receded so that the wooden piles stuck out from the muddy bottom.

They scattered and searched the area. There were signs of horses, more than three. Fresh signs from today or yesterday at the earliest. They dismounted and carefully combed the area on foot.

"Don Pedro!" one of the vaqueros shouted.

Pedro saw him approach waving a sombrero. He turned over the wide-brimmed hat, its crown dusty from where it had lain. "It looks like Don Ignacio's," he said.

After more fruitless searching, Pedro directed the men to fan out and search the underbrush in an arc extending from the landing. As he led his horse along the edge of the mud flats, he saw a cloud of dust in the distance. Then, mounting to get a better view, he watched them approach. Some two dozen vaqueros escorted a cart across the valley. Two of the riders waved, then galloped toward them. As they came nearer, Pedro recognized Don Arturo Soto, whose rancho lay on the west side of the bay. Pedro spurred his horse toward them and drew alongside Don Arturo. There was a sorrowful, hesitant look on his neighbor's face.

"We have been looking for my uncle and cousins," Pedro said.

Don Arturo lowered his eyes, and his voice trembled although Pedro could not see his averted face. "I have terrible news, Don Pedro." Pedro looked at the vaqueros escorting the cart, and the significance, the premonition, sucked the breath from him. "There was a Bear Flag patrol —" Soto began. "One of my brothers had sold Don Ignacio a boat —" Then he shook his head and leaned across his mount to embrace Pedro. "Those goddamned Yankee murderers!"

For a moment Pedro's vision went blank: all he could see was a dark gray curtain over what had been the intense brown-green grass on open fields, the blue edge of the bay, and the clothes and horses of the approaching riders. He felt faint and he fought the drowning sensation. Fought the void.

"Are you all right, Don Pedro?" The voice was filled with concern and Pedro felt another arm on his other side steadying him.

After a bit the wave of gray passed and he shook his head weakly. "I'm all right," he finally said. "I must see them." He spurred his horse toward the cart, followed by the two Soto brothers.

"Halt!" Don Arturo shouted to his men.

Pedro dismounted, wiped the perspiration from his face, and slowly walked to the cart. The driver turned and drew back the serape cover. They were lined up lengthwise like neatly stacked logs of wood, Don Ignacio in the center flanked by his sons. The blood stains on their shirts had hardened to almost black-red around the bullet holes.

"They . . . they've stolen their clothes!" As if the theft of boots and jackets and trousers was the final outrage. "Oh, my God! Ignacio. Lalo. Juan." Pedro threw himself on his uncle's body and wept.

The others stood by at a respectful distance and watched quietly. Don Arturo silently motioned to a vaquero to ride out and gather the Baca party. By the time Pedro's tears had stopped and he had dismounted from the cart, his men were riding toward them.

"Those murdering bastards!" Pedro said. He heard the mumbling in the background as the vaqueros conversed in undertones. Then he turned to Don Arturo who stood beside his brother, both with sombreros in hand as at a funeral. "How did you find them?" Pedro asked.

Soto took him by the arm and they squatted on the ground in the shade of the cart. "A tragedy," Don Arturo looked at Pedro, his dark eyes blinking. "Don Ignacio had bought a boat that my brother wanted to sell. So my brother and three of the Indians from our rancho rowed across. They were to meet Don Ignacio at the landing on this side.

"I warned them to be careful. There have been armed guards at our rancho ever since those crazy Yankees started their so-called rebellion.

"As they crossed this narrow finger of the bay, they saw riders along the eastern shore. A Yankee patrol working its way south toward the landing.

"Then they saw Don Ignacio and his sons waiting for the boat. The Yankees were hidden by brush and at some distance. As the boat drew close to shore, they yelled and waved at Don Ignacio, but they could not make themselves understood. The men on shore must have thought they were shouting greetings because they waved and shouted back.

"All of a sudden the Yankee patrol sensed that someone was at the landing. They had seen the boat. They galloped and quickly surrounded your uncle and cousins. What happened next one of your cousins told us before he died.

"The Yankees accused them of being enemy soldiers and opened fire. No other explanation. No questioning. Not even to see that they were unarmed. Just a hail of bullets. One of your cousins fell first. His brother, the one who survived longest, fell on the wounded young man to shield him. One of the Yankees shouted: 'Kill the other son of a bitch!' And more shots rang out.

"By then it should have been obvious that the three were unarmed and not soldiers. How could they mistake your old uncle for an enemy soldier? Your uncle looked at them in shock. 'How could you animals kill my sons for no reason at all?' he said. 'You had better kill me too!' Another shot rang out and Don Ignacio was dead.

"Then the rebels stripped the bodies of boots and other clothes, took their horses, and rode off.

"Meanwhile, those in the boat had rowed out of gun range and waited for their departure. A few rebels stood on the landing and shot at them and cursed before they rode away.

"They waited until the Yankees were far off before they rowed ashore. Your cousin Lalo was still alive and told them what he could. He died as they rowed the bodies back across the bay to our rancho. We placed them on a cart and set out with a guard to Rancho Los Palos."

The vaqueros from Los Palos had gathered round by this time and listened. One of them, a grizzled, white-haired old mestizo, crossed himself and began to pray aloud. Others joined without thought, although most of the men, including Pedro, seldom attended church.

After prayers there was a brief silence as their thoughts focused on their dead countrymen. Pedro placed a hand on Don Arturo. "Thank you for all your help in this tragedy. I will never forget it. God grant that we suffer no more from these barbarian gringos." He rose and briefly instructed his vaqueros to return to Los Palos.

"It would be a privilege, a duty, to escort you the rest of the way," Don Arturo said. "We could do no less."

Together the three dozen horsemen rode in solemn procession, accompanying the death cart to the rancho.

# 12

The murder of the three Bacas plunged the rancho into gloom and bitterness. A priest was sent for and the bodies were buried in a corner of the rancho under a cluster of live oak trees. The plots were marked with three white crosses that reminded Pedro of the crucifixion. Neighbors from miles around traveled in armed parties to the funeral. To show that the Bear Flaggers did not represent the attitudes of all Yankees, the Baca's Yankee acquaintances were there, including Samuel Barker with a new man, a lawyer, who promised to take the murderers to justice.

The old Don took the tragedy harder than anyone. In the recent past he had dozed and rocked in his chair, leaving the business of the rancho to his oldest son Pedro. Now he could hardly sleep at all, prowling the quiet rooms of the house at all hours, trying to drink himself into insensibility. One morning they found him drunk and moaning, spread-eagled across his brother's grave.

In July, just one month after the so-called rebellion, Commodore Sloat sailed into Monterey Harbor and declared California under the protection of the United States. Even this takeover without casualties (unless one considered the woman who bruised her leg rushing from church when the landing was announced) was met with gloom at Los Palos. It did not matter that the Bear Flag Republic was no more. That would never bring back to life their beloved dead who had been so cruelly and needlessly murdered.

When news of Sloat's landing came, the old Don merely opened another bottle of brandy and continued drinking. If they had landed but two weeks earlier, his brother and nephews might be alive. Samuel Barker's lawyer friend, John Archer, sent a note that perhaps now it might be possible to pursue justice. But even this brought no joy to Don Pedro. Shortly after, Frémont's troops enlisted as California volunteers. Whatever Archer's good intentions, there was no way that California volunteers would be arrested for murder.

Initial resistance by the Californios had been hampered by their own divisiveness, with North and South split almost like warring countries. Military leaders and many men had fled to the hills when the Bear Flag Republic was declared. Workers disappeared from the ranchos. Confusion was rampant. Later, word came that New Mexico had fallen without a shot and that newly promoted General Kearney was on his way to California.

As for Rancho Los Palos, work almost came to a standstill. There were not enough workers to care for the fields. The Bacas' energies turned inward on their own sorrows and they barely acknowledged the changes sweeping across the land.

\*   \*   \*

Pedro Baca ran the rancho with the help of three of his brothers. Like many Californios, his youngest brother Andrés had joined the men fighting the Yankees. These hostilities followed the movement of U.S. troops. Where there were no Yankee troops, things were

peaceful. Where troops appeared, fighting broke out, sometimes pro-
voked by one side, sometimes by the other.

As of late, Pedro kept the rancho accounts without involving his
father, except to note how many bottles of brandy and wine from in-
ventory were consumed by the old Don.

"Things cannot go on like this," Pedro said one day after looking
at the accounts for the hundredth time. Bankruptcy was inviting itself
and he needed to take action against this unwelcome guest.

The next day he rode with a small escort into San José to talk to
John Archer. He had appreciated Archer's concern for his murdered
uncle and cousins. This was a man who saw that justice did not belong
to just one country but was a citizen of every nation.

"Señor Archer," he began. "The war has driven men from the ranchos. Los Palos is no exception." Archer nodded cautiously, his eyes
riveted on his visitor. "This will be a poor year for us. Although our
lands are worth a fortune, we have little money for day-to-day needs.
I understand, señor, that aside from your law practice you lend money
from time to time . . . or find sources for loans."

"Times are hard," Archer said. "And uncertain. My resources are
limited, although I hear of possibilities on occasion."

The man's cautious answer angered Pedro. "I need money now!"

Archer looked at him with more calculation than chill, silent in his
lawyer's caution while he thought. "How much?"

Don Pedro told him, increasing the amount because he did not expect to receive all that he asked for. But Archer only blinked as Pedro
sat trying not to appear as if he were begging.

"I need to look over your books and any papers describing your grant
before I can give you an answer."

"It's a Mexican grant. It may not conform to the legal practices of
the United States."

Archer nodded. "The United States may have claimed California,
but that claim is still being contested on the battlefield."

"Come to Los Palos at your convenience. I will show you everything
you want to see."

"If there is any agreement at all," Archer said, "it will have to be
satisfactory to us both."

In spite of the caution of the lawyer's words, Pedro rode home with
a feeling of hope that was rare these days. A satisfactory loan would
carry them through this year and next. This should give ample time
to put the rancho on a paying basis again.

But there was one more problem: his father. Although Pedro was in fact the manager of Los Palos, everything was legally in his father's name. What if the old Don should, for some reason, refuse to sign the loan? In a sense, Pedro had already overstepped his authority by seeking such a loan. He would hate to compound the usurpation by signing the papers himself. Yet for all practical purposes his father was incompetent. So he would have to speak with his mother. Surely, with the deference and respect children had for their parents, no matter what age, he could do no less.

That evening after supper Pedro sought out Doña Beatriz. He waited in the rancho office, going over the accounts and trying to decide how much to tell her without confusing her.

A soft knock announced her entrance. He stood and waited for her by the desk. She was uncertain, he could tell, partly in deference to his role as head of the rancho and partly to the learned role of her sex that the male was superior, even a son who had come from her own body.

"Mamá," he said, smiling affectionately.

Doña Beatriz waved a hand in annoyance. "Oh, these servants. They get more impossible every day. And now this — " she added, sweeping a hand around the office. "Business! I have no head at all for business."

"Sit down, Mamá."

Even her irritations had always amused Pedro. She was such a gentle woman that the servants did not respond to her scolding. Her impotence at this sorry state of affairs made her more endearing, as if she were a lovely child. And her small stature reinforced this childlike illusion. Unlike many Mexican women she had remained slender and did not show her age. Her skin was smooth and her hair still black and silky. Although she was nearly fifty years of age, she looked years younger.

"Well, son. What is this all about? Such important mysteries that we must have a secret council."

"I hate to burden you with business," he apologized. "But I need your help." Her eyes opened wide and round in surprise, as if to ask: How could I possibly be of any help? Poor, ignorant me?

"It's about Papá."

Her expression betrayed pain and concern. "He is not well," she said.

"As legal owner of the rancho, Papá has to approve any important steps that have to be taken. With his . . . sickness, I am not sure he would understand and agree, even if something were absolutely necessary. It is such a time now. I need your help to make Papá understand. So I must tell you about this . . . business."

The girlish aura with which Doña Beatriz faced the world faded. She sat with hands crossed on her lap, serious and uncertain, waiting to deal with matters with which she had never before concerned herself.

"What is it, hijo? Do not hold back. Fate has already burdened our good life with sorrow. Could there be more and worse?"

Pedro glanced at the account book and decided to show it only if necessary. "To put it simply, Mamá, we are spending more money than the rancho is making. What little savings we had have been used up these past months. With so many workers fleeing the rancho, our income this year will be a disaster. If this damned war would resolve itself one way or the other, Californio or Yankee, things would be better. As it is, we need to borrow a huge sum to keep going."

But when she didn't respond he knew that he shouldn't have mentioned the war. Immediately her thoughts focused there, and for a moment it seemed that she would cry. "Pobre Andrés," she sighed. "Why did he think he had to join the militia and fight? Why did he not listen to me? May God bring him home safely and soon." She crossed herself and sat distracted.

"He will be fine, Mamá. But we want him to come back to a prosperous rancho. That is why we need this loan."

Doña Beatriz turned toward him, but he could tell that her thoughts were still elsewhere. Pedro sighed and pushed the large account book toward her to break the spell. He leaned over and pressed a brown finger on a sum at the bottom of a page.

"Here," he said, tapping his finger until she looked, "is our income so far this year. With fields gone to weed and the hide and tallow business almost nonexistent because of the war, we will earn very little more the rest of the year.

"Here," he continued, moving his finger across the page to another column, "is what it has cost us so far this year to support the rancho."

"Oh!" She clasped her hands to her mouth as she stared at the numbers. "We spend more than we earn."

"Yes, Mamá," he said patiently.

"Does that mean I can't buy any new clothes? What about that lovely bedroom furniture that was shipped all the way from France? And your youngest sister's wedding? Will she and her young man have to slip into the small chapel at the mission and take their vows like barefoot Indians? Oh, my God, how have we come to this? We who own so much."

Pedro ignored her outburst. "We desperately need a loan until we can make the rancho pay its way again. I need you to convince Papá of that so he will sign the papers when the time comes. Will you do that, Mamá?"

"I could have the seamstress remake some of my old dresses. Then if we bought only the small French dresser and returned the other one, our bedroom would look nice without spending a great deal. Yes. We can certainly cut back on expenses."

"¡Mamá!"

She looked up in surprise. "What is it, son?"

"Will you speak to Papá?"

"About what?"

"About agreeing to the loan."

"Why . . . of course."

Then she lapsed into her monologue of ways that she would save money. All the inconsequential feminine thrift that would not affect their fortunes one way or another. To buy the silver-colored rather than the gold-colored shoes. To put her personal maid on a diet; she was too fat anyway. To add more water to the soup and pat the tortillas thinner so they would appear to be larger.

Finally Doña Beatriz reached across the desk and closed the account book, giving her son a warm smile. "There. See? Everything will be all right. We can live on half the income. All it takes is a little cleverness and self-restraint." She rose and kissed Pedro on the cheek. "Now I will see your father and settle it all."

As she left the office, he shook his head. Had she really heard him and understood? Or had she gone off, convinced that by using the less expensive material for her daughter's wedding dress the rancho would be saved?

Once again Pedro reopened the account book and looked at the sums. Yes, he thought. There was a good chance that all would turn out well. A very good chance. All they needed was that loan from John Archer.

\*   \*   \*

John Archer came to the rancho a few days later. Together with an escort of vaqueros, he and Pedro rode the boundaries of the property.

"There," Pedro pointed out, "at the bottom of the slope by the last old oak tree before you come to the bay. That is the northern line of Los Palos. Sight along that line just to the left of the farthest hill to the east. About three miles from here is a giant boulder, marking the northeast corner of the property." They rode along, Archer referring to the grant with its description and map and nodding as Don Pedro pointed out the landmarks.

Pedro made it an easy ride, stopping often to point out something of particular interest. Since they had started late that first morning, they slept outdoors and finished their tour the next day, covering the almost forty miles around the perimeter of the rancho.

As they rode back toward the two-story house and its complex of buildings, Pedro pointed out its features. "You can see the main casa, the bunkhouse and servants' quarters, the barn and storage buildings, the workshops. Not far from the cluster of buildings is the corral. Behind the main casa are the orchards and vineyards, with the cultivated fields nearby. Farther beyond is the open cattle range."

Archer nodded and scribbled in a small notebook. They proceeded to the ranchhouse to clean up and have a meal before returning to business. Later, as they sat in the office, they lit cigars and sat silently, taking easy luxurious puffs and staring absently into the air.

"How much was it that you wanted to borrow, Don Pedro?" Pedro told him. "Humph. A goodly amount."

"It is a fine rancho. If times were better, it would pay its way and more. It has in the past."

"No doubt. No doubt. There's no question that it's excellent property. Good collateral. Perhaps before we talk more about how much, we should talk about how long."

Pedro knew that most loans were for one year. "With things so unsettled because of the war it is hard to know when the market for hides and tallow will return to normal. The longer the loan the better."

"Yes. Yes. Of course. But a lender would draw the opposite conclusion from the same premise. Because of the war, a lender might prefer as short a loan as possible, and the interest would be higher than usual."

Pedro put down his cigar and looked at Archer's guileless mask of a face. What was the man thinking? He was a friend of Samuel Barker and Barker was an honest man as far as one could say that of a shrewd, profit-minded Yankee. Well, one must put it as honestly as one could. "I need two years."

"That . . . might be very difficult." Archer's eyes narrowed. He is thinking about money, Pedro thought. "What value, Don Pedro, do you put on your rancho?"

"I have never thought of it as so many pesos. It is much more than that. My family. The years that they have worked hard to make it what it is. Those who work for us . . . like family most of them. The products of the land that God has lovingly given us: horses, cattle, the peaches and apricots in the orchards. All the blessed things a nearly self-sufficient rancho produces.

"How does one put a number on something like that, señor? It is my life. Precious as life itself." Don Pedro pushed forward the account book, "As for monetary value, in a good year, after expenses, the rancho earns twice, maybe three times the amount of the loan. See for yourself."

The lawyer took the book and started at the beginning, slowly scrutinizing the records of past years. Occasionally his eyebrows would raise and a soft "Hmmmm—" would issue from his throat. Now and then he would jot something in his notebook, numbers no doubt, for he mulled over these jottings as if calculating.

Pedro sat quietly and let him take his time. The records were complete for the past ten years, ever since the acquisition of mission lands had doubled the size of their holdings. There had been good years and poor ones. But mostly good ones. There were inventories of not only land, but cattle, horses, trees, numbers of workers, buildings, equipment, seeds, hides, tallow, hay, wine—anything that the rancho produced or bought.

After a time, seeing how thoroughly Archer was examining the book, Pedro excused himself and sought Doña Beatriz.

"Yes, yes," she told him impatiently. "Everything is settled. Your father is resting and I told the servants not to serve him anything to drink. So be calm. There is nothing to worry about."

When Pedro slipped back into the office, Archer had closed the account book and was sitting with his eyes shut, an unlit cigar in his mouth. Archer looked up as Pedro settled into his chair.

"Everything seems to be in good order, Don Pedro. A few errors in arithmetic here and there, but nothing significant."

"Ah. Then what about a two-year loan?"

Silence. Then finally, "Certainly I think I can get you one year. Very few borrowers are getting such terms on large loans these days."

The disappointment showed on Pedro's face. "Perhaps we could make the second year subject to negotiation. That is, after the initial year, depending upon circumstances, we might renew the loan."

"But what if the circumstances are bad?"

"The loan would be called."

"And if things are good?"

"The loan would probably be renewed."

"I do not mean to be facetious, Señor Archer, but if we don't need money, you would be glad to lend it to us. If we do need money, you would call our loan. I'm sorry, señor. That sounds very crazy to me."

Archer's eyes flared. "The lenders have to protect themselves."

"The rancho — or that part that I put up as collateral — is their protection."

For the first time a thought seemed to cross Archer's mind and he stared at Don Pedro in mild surprise. "What had you planned to offer as collateral?"

"I would never mortgage the main casa and our central complex with its orchards and fields. If nothing else we could farm and support ourselves. The main business of the rancho is the range and its cattle. That would be my collateral."

"Not the entire rancho?"

"¡Señor! The rancho is worth many, many times what we seek to borrow. The southeast range and cattle alone are worth more than the loan even on today's poor market. But if I sell them, I sell what earns us our income."

Archer slid back in his chair, placing the fingertips of his hands together and peering over this steeple of flesh. After a long silence, Pedro felt drops of perspiration trickle down his back. Had he gone too far? After all, it was he who needed money. He who needed help desperately. He who was in no position to force demands, while the lender sat across the desk, the power his to grant or deny.

A light knock broke the strained silence. It was merely a warning and the door opened a crack.

"Pedro?" It was Doña Beatriz. "Are you ready for us yet?"

"Come in, Mamá." The men stood as Doña Beatriz fluttered in, preening herself. "Do you remember Señor Archer? From the funeral?" Then to Archer. "Doña Beatriz Baca, the lady of the rancho."

Archer's grim face relaxed into a smile and he bowed. "Don Pedro never told me that he had such a lovely sister."

A giggle escaped from her smiling lips. "Such charming flattery. I hear that you Americanos are better at it than Frenchmen."

"My mother," Don Pedro said stiffly. Then to her, "We're not quite ready for you yet."

Archer's smile held until Doña Beatriz looked away. "I don't mean to disturb you gentlemen. Call when you need me." Then she turned with a slight curtsy and left the room.

"She will bring my father when it's necessary. He is . . . not . . . well."

But Archer was staring at the closed door through which Doña Beatriz had left. "There will be much for us to discuss, many papers to sign over a period of time." Then he turned and looked at Pedro earnestly. "Is your father well enough to be bothered with business?"

Pedro had tried to ignore the electricity he had sensed between his mother and Archer. He had interpreted Archer's flattery as the business ploy of an artful gentleman. But a seed of suspicion had nevertheless been planted.

"The rancho does well enough without him now," Pedro said, ir-ritated by the unspoken implication.

"Might it be easier if your father turned over his power of attorney? It would save a great deal of trouble later."

For some reason the suggestion angered Pedro. "Perhaps."

"Who would he turn it over to? You? Your mother?"

Pedro turned and glared out the window. There was no hiding the anger on his face. He knew what the man was driving at: Where is the power on this rancho? With the old Don, Doña Beatriz, or the devoted son?

"We would have to discuss that," Pedro said coldly.

"Well. In due time." Pedro nodded, still angry over the question-ing of his authority. "You want two years," Archer said. "I can offer one. Your collateral is the southeast range and all your cattle. To lend you what you want, I would need the entire rancho as collateral."

"Impossible, señor."

"We might reduce the amount of the loan to match the collateral you are willing to pledge. I might be able to get you two-thirds of what you asked for."

Pedro repressed the joy that surged through him. He turned dull, impassive eyes toward Archer. Two-thirds would be about right. "Plus an option to renegotiate for a second year."

"I'd have to confer with the others who might put up portions of the loan. I think it's possible."

"Ah, Señor Archer. Then we are on our way."

"Don Pedro, it looks like we are close to a deal."

Pedro's smile masked the thought: How far can I trust this Yankee?

*       *       *

A week later lawyer Archer was back at Rancho Los Palos with two agreements to sign: the power of attorney to be shared by Doña Beatriz and Don Pedro and a loan as agreed upon by the two men in their previous meeting.

Pedro and Doña Beatriz ushered Señor Archer into the sunroom where the old Don sat dozing in his rocking chair. A servant had carefully shaved him and he had been given only a small glass of wine that morning. He stirred as the footsteps approached, opened his startled eyes, and cleared his throat. "Did you bring my medicine?" he asked.

"First we have some papers to sign, Papá," his wife said.

Don Pedro senior rose and tottered to the small table on which pen and ink were laid. He grunted at Archer's effusive greeting, then sat.

"This first," Pedro said, "allows Mamá and me to sign business papers so we won't have to disturb you when you're sick."

Another grunt as he took the pen his wife offered. She took hold of his hand, dipped the pen in ink, and guided the old Don to the proper space on the paper.

"Is my mark good enough or do you want my whole name?"

"Your name, Papá," Doña Beatriz said. "Here. I'll help you."

"About the loan," Pedro whispered to his mother, "there is no need for Papá to sign it."

"But he must. It is too important for him not to."

"Papá," Pedro said aloud. "We need you to sign this other paper so Señor Archer can give us some money." Again Doña Beatriz guided the old man's signature.

"Now," Archer said, "Doña Beatriz. Don Pedro." They signed, and then the lawyer added his name to the bottom of the agreement. "Don Pedro. Here is your copy. This one," he said, placing it in his inner coat pocket, "is mine."

Archer smiled now that it had been settled. "Doña Beatriz. Don Pedro senior. It has been a pleasure."

"Do not be a stranger," Doña Beatriz smiled. "We are almost partners now."

Archer looked deeply into her eyes. "I'll be here often looking after my interests."

Pedro watched him turn to leave. "Señor! The most important thing. When do we get the money?"

Archer turned abruptly, embarrassed. "I'll have a letter of credit for you next week when you come to my office."

"Until then, señor."

"Adiós."

As the lawyer left, the old Don shuffled back to his rocking chair. "My medicine," he complained. "Where is my medicine?"

"I'll bring it right away, Papá."

Doña Beatriz left the room and Pedro suddenly felt very alone.

# 13

"Leonardo! Le-o-nar-do!"

The scream broke the spell that José Antonio's words had cast. Leonardo looked up and sighed. For once José Antonio had not had to suffer through the boy's fit of yawning.

"Le — o — nar — do! You come home this minute!"

José Antonio waved hand past his ear as if swatting an insect. "That's enough for now. There will be more later."

"She sounds mad tonight. Maybe it's because Papá had to go to another meeting." The boy leaned forward to whisper, although there was no one to overhear. "She's afraid to be alone at night." A mischievous smile lit his face. "You wouldn't believe that, would you? The way she screams around."

But José Antonio was pondering this other meeting that Francisco had gone to. He had the uncomfortable feeling that something important was being kept from him. "What meeting?"

"Le — — o — — nar — — do! For the last time —"

"La política," the boy answered as he jumped to his feet. "I'd better go, Grandfather."

José Antonio watched the door close, thinking of Francisco closing off something from him. La política, he thought. He, José Antonio, was the chief party worker in the rural area. His son was involved only by the grace of José Antonio's years of faithful service and his term in the territorial legislature. There should be no meetings without José Antonio.

He sat in the flickering candlelight, brooding over this slight to his advancing age. It had to be that. Young men finally tired of being under their elders' wings. So they struck out on their own without the benefit of accumulated wisdom. Struck out to make the same mistakes that José Antonio had made as a young man. It was too bad that God did not put age and wisdom in bottles like wine. Then young men would gladly get drunk with it and leave undone all their stupidities.

"You look like you want to bite someone's head off." Gregoria had come in from the kitchen with a lamp.

He glowered at her in irritation. "When I was young," José Antonio said, "I was impatient to be older so stupid people would listen to me. Then as I got older I found that it still didn't make any difference. They were as deaf as ever, as if their ears turned inward and listened only to the sound of their own voices. Sometimes I despair of progress. We are too stupid to listen and learn and so we deserve whatever happens to us."

Gregoria sat in grim silence. He could tell what she was thinking: What is eating you, you old grouch?

"Francisco went to a political meeting tonight."

"So that's it," Gregoria said.

Her smug reply angered him. He clenched his fists, but resisted an outburst. He resented her words that tried but failed to sum up and explain something much deeper and more complex than she realized.

"What does Florinda say about Francisco's politics?" he asked.

"She does not speak to me; she complains. But she says nothing about politics except that Francisco goes to too many meetings. Like tonight."

"He's probably getting away from her to meet some of his friends at the cantina." But José Antonio didn't really believe that.

"I wouldn't blame him," Gregoria said. "Tercero, do you ever regret leaving the priesthood? People would have listened to you then."

He looked at her in surprise. "Don't be silly."

"You're sure?"

"Well—maybe under one condition. If you had been my mistress."

Her lips exploded a shock of air and she reached over and slapped him on the hand. "It's a lucky man who knows what he should be," José Antonio said. "I was never meant to be a priest. I am a husband, a farmer, a father, a grandfather.

"And you," he continued, "would you have given me up to the Church?"

"No."

He smiled, recalling an incident from years past. "Remember that time you met the young widow on the bridge when you were both on horseback?"

"Oh, shush."

"What had you heard? What was the gossip?"

You know as well as I, her look said, but she answered anyway.

"It was just after you had left the priesthood, and we had just married. First of all there were rumors about that. That I was pregnant." His loud laugh filled the adobe room. "Which wasn't true.

"The other rumor was that this young widow had her eyes on you. That she had gone to you for counseling when you were a priest and now that you were not, she was forcing her attentions on you. I had seen her at church one Sunday making a spectacle of herself."

"I had no idea."

"Men are blind. You're such trusting fools when it comes to women."

"So you met at the bridge."

"I was going to my Cousin Mathilda's across the river, thinking God knows what as I rode along. I heard the clatter of hooves and looked up to see the widow. The bridge was barely wide enough for two horses, so we stopped. She was as surprised as I.

"For a moment I didn't know what to do. I was overcome by anger. Then she shouted, 'Let me pass. I'm in a hurry.'

"I was so overwhelmed by my own emotions that I almost pulled my horse aside. Then my better sense took hold.

"'You've been making eyes at my husband!' I shouted. 'I saw you in church, and I hear what people are saying!'

"Her eyes widened in fear. 'Let me pass,' she said again, but her voice was trembling.

"'José Antonio Rafa,' I shouted, 'who used to be the priest, is my husband now! People say you've been throwing yourself at him! You had better stop!'

"A cold, haughty look came over her. 'Humph!' she said. 'He only married you because you were pregnant.'

"That did it. I don't know what possessed me. I lashed out at her with my riding whip. '¡Puta!' I shouted. 'Whore! If I see you even look at him again, I'll tear your filthy eyes out!'

"Terrified, she spurred her horse across the bridge, forcing me to the edge. But I turned my horse and rode alongside her, angrily whipping her. Once across the bridge, she broke toward the right, screaming at that poor beast of hers to run faster from this madwoman.

"I reined in and shouted, '¡Puta! If I so much as see you again, I'll kill you!'"

José Antonio shook his head in mock dismay. "That poor woman," Gregoria said. "I think she really believed me. I wish I could say she learned her lesson and lived happily ever after. But at least she left you alone and found some other husband to chase."

"And you felt no remorse?"

"None at all. Though for awhile I was afraid that we might meet again and I would be forced to make good on my threat. And you, Tercero. No regrets that you gave up the priesthood and the audience that hung onto your every word?"

"None about the priesthood. Some about the audience."

"So you are really upset about Francisco?"

He did not answer. He needed to think it over. To taste and savor the different and subtle flavors of what he thought about Francisco not telling him.

Francisco was thirty-four years old, old enough to strike out on his own. Maybe José Antonio had lived too long. Some old people had, so that grown men of forty and fifty still acted like children before their doddering parents. So that when old people finally died, their survivors were too dependent to take charge of their own lives, and they wasted away. Yet there had to be respect, like in the old days. Old people deserved respect for surviving if for nothing else. And above all there should be openness, like with the Yankees. Direct. Spit it out. No huddling in corners, whispering what this one said or that one said.

"You're upset," Gregoria repeated.

"Yes."

"You should speak to him."

"I will."

\*　　\*　　\*

Although the days were long and busy this time of year, there were days when little needed to be done. There were also days, usually church holy days, when it was almost a sin to work rather than to celebrate. José Antonio saw his son every day, yet waited for the right time to speak other than what was necessary for their daily work. Finally he felt the tempo slow, and he knew that the day would come soon.

Early the next morning they surveyed their fields with cautious eyes, deciding whether or not this was a day to rest. José Antonio rolled a cigarette and offered tobacco to Francisco.

"I hear," José Antonio said, "that there have been meetings about the election."

Francisco recoiled from the tobacco pouch. But then he took it and rolled a cigarette with his face red and angry. "Where did you hear this?"

"Oh, around."

Francisco peered through a cloud of cigarette smoke. "Well, there's an election," he answered lamely. "They were about unimportant little things. Things I didn't want to bother you with."

"What does Señor Smith think about these little things?"

The shot found its mark. Francisco's mouth dropped open, the homemade cigarette hanging from his lower lip. "It is no concern of Smith's."

"Señor Smith is the party patrón for Los Rafas. I am his delegated contact with our people."

"Damn Señor Smith!"

"Is there something you should tell me, Francisco?"

"No, señor."

"Are you, in these little things, considering the best interests of our party?"

"Sí, señor."

"What do the others say — those that you meet with?"

"Nothing, señor."

José Antonio inhaled deeply, then spit the cigarette butt onto the ground as he exhaled. Yes. No. Nothing. That was all he would get from Francisco. Perhaps he was being too sensitive about not being invited to these meetings. Unimportant little things, Francisco had said. All right then. He would accept that.

"Well," José Antonio said. "It looks like a fine day for a siesta."

Francisco nodded, anxiously studying José Antonio's face. "I thought I might go into town."

"I'm going to take a little nap. I'm getting old, Francisco."

José Antonio took out his tobacco pouch and offered it again. They stood silent in the morning sun, smoking, and eventually they smiled at this quiet pleasure.

## 14

Francisco Rafa masked his guilt with anger. Not anger at his father, on whom his guilt centered, but anger at the political situation and the toady candidate, Plácido Durán. And anger at his inability to influence events.

A few days after his evasive and short conversation with José Antonio, he sought out Pablo Griego. "Friend," he said as they sat in the shade of a cottonwood in back of Griego's house. "My father is suspicious."

"It was bound to happen. Eventually Don José hears everything."

"The fewer who know about our meetings the better."

"Other than you and me there are only Lucero and Armijo. None of us would even talk to our wives, would we? But, there's more to think about than this damned election. Have you heard about the Court of Private Claims?" Francisco shook his head. "They're convening this year. The Court is going to review the old land grants that have been in dispute for so long."

"But our grants are valid. They've already been recognized by the government."

"Those of us who are lucky. For every one of us there are three or four others who were robbed blind. Now they'll get a chance in court."

A cynical smile twisted Francisco's mouth. "Do you really believe that? Next thing you'll tell me that the archives in Santa Fe were destroyed by accident twenty years ago. What chance does a poor man have? Those who steal your land not only destroy legal records, but then they send their own judges to legitimize this thievery in the courts. It will be a whitewash unless we have our own judge."

"But first a sheriff. Judges come later."

Francisco scooped a handful of dirt, then suddenly threw it into the air and leaned forward, his voice low and intense. "All the more reason we need to elect our own sheriff. If we can't do that, we'll never elect a judge. Or influence the appointment of a governor. We need to do something about Durán before it's too late!"

"Something drastic?" Griego said apprehensively.

"There's no other way. And the fewer that know about it the better."

"But it will have to be done by men who won't be recognized. Unknown men." Griego's nervous eyes looked past Francisco toward the irrigation ditch, as if salvation might come floating on the muddy water from the river. "The more people involved, the greater chance of being discovered. It is a dangerous game."

"But absolutely necessary!"

Suddenly they stopped talking, aware of what it was they were saying. Francisco sat tensely and impatiently, Griego's unspoken fear shouting louder than the man's words. "Lord, Francisco. I wish I could help, but it's not the sort of thing I'm good at. I'm more likely to shoot myself than a target. I can't look at a knife without cutting my hand."

Francisco glared angrily. Just what he should have expected. It's well and good to bring up the idea as long as somebody else has to do it, goddamn it!

"Lucero is not the man for the job," Francisco spat. "Too nervous. That just leaves Armijo . . . or me."

Pablo sat silent, his fear hanging like low fog, enveloping them with its cold presence. "If need be," he finally said, "I'll help."

But Francisco knew that Pablo did not really mean it and the thought of the pompous Armijo in this delicate job infuriated him. He could see Armijo puff up with even more self-importance than usual. They would be in debt to him and he would never let them forget it. He would view it not so much as a necessary job for the benefit of all as he would a job for the glorification of Ignacio Armijo.

"We should only risk one man," Francisco said. "He will have to get help from others not linked to us."

"We should draw lots — you, Armijo, me. The one who loses . . ."

"No, Pablo — wins."

". . . gets the job."

"What if it's Armijo?"

A worried look crossed Griego's face. "Would you rather risk it yourself than leave it to that peacock?" Francisco nodded. "No," Griego said. "Fair is fair. We are in this together; you, me, Armijo draw lots."

Francisco stared at the frightened Pablo, thinking about Armijo and of the danger, and finally said, "So be it."

\* \* \*

It was not as easy as Francisco first thought. Armijo had balked, wanting to take on the task himself. When they explained why they had to draw lots, he became angry. Francisco had watched with apprehension as Armijo had stomped from the cantina. The man was not only pushy but hard-headed. They had not pacified him and there was an off chance that he might do something stupid and spoil their plans. Finally, after whispered discussion, they decided that Armijo would cool down. There was too much at stake for him to do anything but go along.

Then, of course, there was Francisco's father. Since the day of their conversation José Antonio had seemed his usual self, but Francisco could not forget that the old man had suspected something and he carried this wariness like a yoke hitched to his guilt. He knew that his father was shrewd and perceptive. He found it almost impossible to be natural in his presence and so wanted to avoid him. But how could you avoid someone who lived next door and with whom you worked every day? Just today the old man had suddenly looked up from one of the sluice gates and stared at Francisco with a strange, puzzled expression on his face.

"What is it, Papá?"

José Antonio shook his head, answering Francisco as well as seemingly rousing himself from a daydream. "How long before the election?"

Why had he asked that? He knew as well as Francisco. "Three months."

"Humph!" He closed off the gate and moved down the ditch to another.

That had been the end of it, although as the day progressed, Francisco became increasingly nervous. Tonight they would meet and draw lots. Better that José Antonio not know. Or if he did, that he not confront Francisco with his suspicions. The anxious day passed and they parted at supper time. Francisco made his muddy way home with relief.

\* \* \*

A week later the rumors spread throughout the countryside, parts of it confirmed by Plácido Durán. It was not so much what he said, for he said very little. But there was the bandage on his head that his new Stetson could not hide; his furtive, frightened aura, even with the increased number of bodyguards that followed him everywhere; and his brother's loose mouth.

"Los Hijos," someone said.

"Los Hijos de Libertad," another amplified.

Then absolute silence as Benito Durán led the way down the wooden sidewalk toward the railroad station where Plácido was attending a rally.

"Thieves in the night," Benito snarled. "Just wait."

It had been a still Tuesday night, the rumor went. A night when witches were abroad stealing small children and pet dogs. An unnaturally still night when even the sliver of a moon hid behind clouds.

One could hear the nightlife along the river: the croaking frogs, the chirping cicadas, a dog howling in the distance. The darkness seemed to cleanse the air so that sound traveled purer, cleaner, farther. The throbbing of one's own heart was like the pounding of a drum. The absence of human sound, of voices or footsteps, heightened one's senses to a tautness that reacted to the slightest sound as if it were a cannon shot.

Around midnight came the sounds of distant hooves. Later, the snorting exhalation of a horse warned whomever paid heed. Shortly after, the hoofbeats of several horses made their way through the darkness at an easy pace. Unusual that several horsemen should be riding the same way at the same time on such a night. Although the adobe farmhouse was quiet, there was a dim light in the window. Plácido was still working while his wife and children were in bed.

Half asleep, he barely heard the hoofbeats circle to the back of the house or those that slowly approached the front.

"Durán!" a muffled voice shouted.

"Durán!" the voice shouted again.

Puzzled at who would be visiting at this hour, Plácido answered the heavy pounding on the door. He cracked it open so the light from his lamp thrust its narrow eye into the dark. "Who is it?"

"Friends!"

He opened the door wider and his alarmed face peered out, the lamp in one hand and a pistol in the other. As he stepped forward for a better look, men with kerchiefs over their lower faces grabbed and disarmed him. Durán screamed in a strained voice, "Mamá! Bolt the door! My God —"

"Get him away from the house," one of the masked men growled. Another tied a gag around Durán's mouth, while others forced him into the open field. "All right. Stop here!" They gathered in a circle, the leader facing Durán, whose eyes bulged in fear and anger.

"Do you know who we are?" the leader asked. Durán shook his head. How could he see behind masks? "Los Hijos de Libertad. The Sons of Liberty." His grunt was muffled by the gag. "Do you value your life?" Durán started to tremble. "Do you?" the leader snapped, pounding a finger onto Durán's chest. The response was a fearful nod.

"Then listen to this," the leader continued. "You do not represent the interests of the people of this county. You are the toady of the special interests. The privileged interests. The money-grabbing interests. As far as you're concerned, the people can go to hell as long as you get yours.

"We cannot tolerate a sheriff like that. One who will not stand up for us. Therefore we are ordering you to withdraw from the election. The party will have to pick another man. One whose interests and actions are more in sympathy with the true needs of our Spanish-speaking New Mexicans.

"If you do not . . ." Durán could see a cruel gleam in the bandit's eyes. "We have no qualms in getting rid of a traitor to our people." The leader nodded to the men holding Durán. "Now," he said, "we're going to remove your gag so we can hear what you have to say. If you shout or try to run, that will be the end of you. What did you just hear?" the leader asked.

Durán rubbed the red streak across his mouth and cheeks where the kerchief had cut into them. He cleared his throat and swallowed hard. His eyes moved nervously around the semicircle of masked men trying to recognize them.

"You want me to withdraw from the election," he croaked in a hoarse whisper.

"And if you do not?"

"You'll kill me."

"You understand."

"But you won't . . ." The gag closed off Plácido's words.

"Now we're leaving," the leader said. He took Durán's pistol, which one of the men had unloaded. "A nice gringo revolver." He weighed it appraisingly, then with a sudden snap, smashed Durán on the head so he plummeted to the ground.

After a few minutes the door opened and a shaft of light pierced the dark. "Plácido?" his wife called. "Are you all right, Plácido?"

His daughters rushed from bed at their mother's scream. Together they dragged the bleeding Durán into the house and bolted the door, fearfully waiting for daylight. Then two of the girls rode off for Uncle Benito.

"The night riders mean business," the rumor went.

"Los Hijos," another said.

"Los Hijos de Libertad."

# 15

Gregoria peered through the kitchen window. The men were in the fields and her grandson Leonardo was with them. She could see her daughter-in-law hanging the latest of the constant flow of laundry from her five children.

Gregoria sighed. Now would be an ideal time to talk to Florinda. But Lord — She shook her head anticipating the difficult conversation with her daughter-in-law. Then Gregoria thought of other things to do in the house once she finished the kitchen, but she did not deceive herself. She knew that if she kept busy enough she would never have to confront Florinda.

Her two oldest granddaughters banged the door behind them as they carried another basket of laundry to the line.

"Watch out, Rosa! Gregoria! Pick up that basket! You'll drag something in the dirt for sure! ¡Válgame Dios! You're worthless! Both of you!"

Grandmother Gregoria closed her eyes and sighed. Those dear little girls, she thought. They went about their work as if they had not heard their mother's harangue.

"Over here!" Florinda screamed. "Don't you know anything? Now take the empty basket into the house!"

"All right, Mamá."

Gregoria took off her apron and hung it on a peg on the wall. She left by the back door, carefully descending the steps, then glanced quickly toward the shed. Pedro was quiet.

As she crossed the orchard, she picked a small green apple from the ground and wiped it on her cotton skirt after inspecting it for wormholes. The crisp, tart flavor pleased her, although it would taste even better baked with a sprinkling of sugar.

Gregoria dropped the core on the ground just before she called out, "Florinda."

"Ay, Mamá."

Gregoria picked up a piece of folded wash and made it ready for Florinda to hang. She was never comfortable initiating conversation with her daughter-in-law. Somehow she believed that if she started with the right words Florinda would respond cheerfully. As if what she said might calm the younger woman. But after years of effort, she decided that this belief was only vanity. It did not matter what she or anyone else said. Florinda's response would be true to her own nature. Yet Gregoria harbored this tiny hope in a corner of her heart. It made her hesitate before speaking, as if this time the miracle might occur.

As so often, Florinda spoke first. "Just look at these. There are more holes than patches and more patches than original pants. That boy!" She meant Leonardo. "I think the holes were worn from the inside by his knees and legs."

From someone else these words could have been amusing, even loving, but from Florinda they were impatient and blaming. As if the holes were put there on purpose to spite her. Another plot to keep her up nights, patching with stiff and weary fingers for someone who did not appreciate her sacrifice.

"My," Gregoria smiled, "he must be growing right through them. He'll be wearing Francisco's pants soon."

"He already eats more than his father. He will drive us to the poor house." Florinda hung up a pair of Francisco's work pants. "Look at this," she complained. "No better. One more scrubbing and the cloth will disappear. He never thinks that things wear out. That they have to be replaced. No. All he ever thinks about are his damned meetings and his drunken cronies down at the cantina. You don't know what I have to put up with. Men! You know how men are!"

Florinda stared accusingly into Gregoria's eyes, looking for confirmation. "No," Gregoria said. "I don't."

A loud guffaw was Florinda's answer, as if saying: After all these years, you've learned nothing? That husband of yours has you completely fooled or cowed. But they're all devils. I know.

"Mamá," she finally said. "You're a saint."

Gregoria bit her lip, telling herself to be quiet. She knew how easy it would be to quarrel with Florinda. The easiest thing in the world. Once the angry words started, it would be even easier to dredge up all manner of past offenses. Not just Florinda's shrewish tongue, but her nasty temper, her lack of warmth to Gregoria's grandchildren, her disloyalty to her husband. The list went on and on.

How? she thought. Just how did her son marry this shrew? How did her son with his own temper find his match? Was it that quarreling was so important to them that they sought in marriage not so much mates as opponents? It would drive her mad. Absolutely mad.

"Rosa!" Florinda screamed. "Gregoria! Where's the other basket? What are you doing in there? Hurry up!"

The door slammed and a patter of bare feet came around the corner of the house toward the clothesline. "Grandma!" Rosa's eager little voice piped. "Grandma!" her little sister echoed.

"All right!" Florinda said. "Hurry up with those clothes!"

The girls carried a full basket to their mother, picked up the empty, and hurried back into the house. Gregoria continued hanging clothes in silence until they were done.

"Come over for a cup of chocolate," Gregoria said.

Wiping a wisp of hair from her face, Florinda looked from the empty basket to the fully ladened clothesline and nodded. "Rosa!" she screamed. "You girls finish the kitchen! I'm going to Grandma's!"

Florinda sat at the kitchen table, enjoying the respite from chores and small children, enjoying the company of another adult. "Your house is always so neat," she said. Her manner implied that there was some kind of witchcraft to it, although Gregoria knew that two adults made much less mess than even one child, much less five. "I remember the old house. The really big one with the patio," she continued. "I was just a little girl. I had never seen such a grand house. It was the grandest house in Los Rafas. I think I fell in love with Francisco because of that house as much as anything.

"Why didn't you rebuild it after those Confederates ruined it? More than half of it was left standing. It would have been less work than building this new one."

Gregoria's feelings toward the younger woman softened. It was if as Florinda finally showed that she cared about something, even if it was only an old house.

"It was a lovely huge place," Gregoria said, remembering. "But after Francisco's grandfather died, there were just Tercero, his mother, and me. We only had the two small children then, Francisco and Carlos José.

"Tercero and I had talked of a smaller place. Especially after we sold some of the land to pay the lawyers for the work on our grant. The house was too big. We could no longer afford the work or the money to keep it up. And it was like there were ghosts in the old rooms.

"So when the house was almost destroyed, we leveled it and rebuilt in the center of what land we had left."

"Such a pity," Florinda sighed. "When I was a girl I dreamed that one day I would live in a beautiful house. Like a princess. Now look at me!"

Gregoria glanced at the pinched face, the hair falling over her forehead, the unkempt dress. She was certainly no princess. Yet Gregoria's heart could not help but reach out toward her daughter-in-law whose looks and actions hammered out her life theme: disappointment!

Some were born to disappointment and anger. Others to be placid or joyful. It had nothing to do with what happened in their lives. They could all live side by side in the same mud wallow, yet there would still be those who could be happy splashing in the mud, while another would rage at the injustice. Even a palace of gold, Gregoria thought, would be a disappointment to some princesses.

She patted the younger woman's arm. "You have a good farm, a fine family." Now was the time, Gregoria thought, to turn the conversation to what she had intended all along. "Your Leonardo is almost a man. When I see him I'm shocked. I keep thinking of a happy little child coming through the orchard to his grandma asking for 'tilla.' 'Tilla, Grandma,' he'd say, sticking out his little hand. He always liked his grandma's tortillas."

Florinda frowned, as if in some way this praise of Grandma's cooking demeaned her own. But Gregoria went on, not giving her a chance to comment. "I wanted to talk to you about Leonardo."

A sharp look, like a dog that did not know whether to growl and bare its teeth or to be submissive. Something is coming, Florinda's look said. Something I will not like.

"I have seen him with his cousin Ernesto lately."

"He is so much like my poor dead brother," Florinda answered warily. My family, was her unspoken message. Chávez! Be careful. What you say about him, you say about me.

"Did you know that Leonardo had been spending so much time with Ernesto?"

"That's none of your business!"

"I have heard things. Things you ought to know if you don't already." Florinda reddened, her hands clutching the cup as if they were trying to crush it. "But if you already know," Gregoria went on, "I don't want to repeat it."

Florinda took a last swallow of chocolate and slammed the cup onto the table. "Lies!" the young woman spat. "They are always spreading lies about us Chávezes. It's jealousy. The hell with them and their lies, the troublemakers. I don't believe a word of it."

"Of what?"

Florinda jumped up in agitation and paced the floor, thrusting her face forward as her voice rose to a shout. "It's jealousy! They can't leave a person in peace. We're as good as they are. I don't have to listen to these lies."

Gregoria sat calmly, waiting for this outburst to exhaust itself. As she paced across the small kitchen, Florinda's fury gradually subsided. Finally she stood beside the table, then abruptly dropped onto a chair, her face in anguish.

"It's because we are poor," she said in a broken voice. "That's why they say those things about us. We're the poor branch of the Chávezes. You wouldn't know about that. You — you Rafas are rich."

"I'm no more nor less a Rafa than you," Gregoria said gently. "That's only my married name, the same as it is yours."

"We are good people," Florinda insisted. "Those liars ought to be horsewhipped." She picked up her cup, sipped air, then put it down without realizing that it had been empty. "So Leonardo has been seen with that disgraceful Ernesto?"

"Yes."

A shudder. A sigh. Florinda's eyes filled with tears. "My poor sister-in-law. The pain she has gone through. There is a cell reserved in jail for that one. It's just a matter of time."

"I'm sorry."

"I had heard, but I didn't want to think that Leonardo might be up to the same craziness. He's just a child. That damned Ernesto! Leading him astray. Oh, God! What am I going to do?"

"Talk to him."

"Yes," she said angrily. "A fine thing for you to criticize us Chávezes when you have that crazy in-law of yours out there." She jerked a thumb in the direction of the shed.

The sudden attack surprised Gregoria. Who's crazy? she thought. Pedro or this erratic shrew whom I should love like a daughter? Lord, give me strength. Give me patience. Give me love. Give me forgiveness.

Mastering all of her self-control, she placed a hand on Florinda's arm. Her daughter-in-law did not shake it off as she feared, but let it lay. "Do you want Leonardo to do something with Ernesto that will get him in trouble?" Florinda did not respond. "Do you?"

"I'll tell Francisco to talk to him."

At last! Gregoria thought. How difficult it is for parents to talk to children. Not just Florinda and Francisco to Leonardo, but Tercero and me to Francisco and Florinda. Sometimes it's like talking to a fence post. Or trying to make a blind man see.

"Would you like another cup of chocolate, honey?"

Florinda nodded as if it took all her strength. A tear rolled down her left cheek, then a rivulet followed.

Gregoria placed her arms around Florinda's shoulders. "It will be all right," she said. "Believe me."

# 16

One of the workers from James Smith's farm brought the message to José Antonio, who agreed to call after supper. Now he was on his way, plodding along Rafas Road on his old horse, wondering what this urgent call was about. There were only two things important enough for such a request from Smith: money and politics.

Smith was one of the principal lenders to the farmers in Los Rafas. His holdings had grown when an occasional borrower could not pay his debt and had to forfeit a piece of land. Not that Smith was an avaricious man or a usurer. His terms were at least as generous as the bank's, sealed with a handshake, and based, if not on friendship, at least on acquaintance with his clients. It was just that events favored the lender whether he was anxious to acquire more land or not. A certain number defaulted because of poor weather or illness or unexpected bills.

Smith's holdings obeyed one of the natural laws of money: the magnetic attraction that one saved coin had for another. Almost as if coins were birds, where one would search the ground for worms and bugs, to be joined by another and another, until there was an entire flock scouring the countryside for food.

Sometimes José Antonio would also make loans to neighbors. Seldom cash; he had little of that. But a chicken or a goat or chili or corn. He himself, though, considered it a matter of pride to be indebted to no man, especially James Smith.

The other possibility, politics, was a three-ring circus in which José

Antonio and his Spanish-speaking compatriots participated with enthusiasm. Money was something many of them could be indifferent to, but the intrigues of local politics engaged them all. It was in their blood — the conspiracies, the flamboyant oratory, the risks. An exciting game with prizes of both power and prestige.

There had been secret meetings, José Antonio thought. At least he suspected so, even though his son had denied it. Something was up. Something important enough for Smith to want to see him as soon as possible.

He tied his old horse to a tree. The front door opened even before he had climbed the steps and Smith ushered him into the living room. There was a tightness to Señor Smith's manner. He walked quickly to the wine bottle and glasses that were already on the table and poured without asking if José Antonio cared for a drink.

José Antonio was surprised at this breech of Smith's usual cautious politeness. The man was too polite at times, perhaps aware of ancestral differences and exaggerating the normal Spanish courtesy to such an extreme that José Antonio felt annoyed at what could be interpreted as his patronizing manner.

"Please sit down, Don José. It's important that I speak to you. I won't keep you long."

In all the years that Smith had lived in Los Rafas, there had been only one other time that José Antonio had been summoned like this. Just before the railroads came when there had been that bitter negotiation for land. Smith had sought his help in convincing the landowners that their price was too high. That if they did not budge from their rigid position, the railroad would seek land east of Old Town and eventually Old Town would wither and die. José Antonio had tried but failed. Now, ten years later, the outcome was incontestable. New Town was now the center of activity, growing vigorously, while Old Town at best barely held its own.

"Don José, you know how important this election is. We've got to have a new sheriff and the party is making a major effort to elect Durán."

"We're all working hard."

"Now there seems to be a countermovement against our man."

A faint smile played at the edge of José Antonio's mouth. "We can't expect the opposition to bow to us and let us win uncontested. They have the incumbent. They plan to re-elect him."

Smith shook his head emphatically. "No," he said. "No. No. It's not the other party I'm worried about."

"You can't mean our own people?"

With a heavy sigh, Smith shifted uncomfortably in his chair and reached to pour himself another glass of wine; José Antonio had barely touched his. "I don't know," Smith said. "What have you heard, Don José? What is going on out there?"

What should I tell him? José Antonio thought. What about those meetings that my son went to and to which I was not invited? Were they really petty details that had to be attended to?

"Nothing," José Antonio answered. "At least no more than usual. Francisco and I told you all we knew when you said that Plácido Durán was to be our party's candidate. Nothing has changed since then. It will still be difficult, although we're talking to everyone we can about how important it is that we elect our party's man."

"How much do people really dislike Durán?"

José Antonio shrugged. "Dislike is too strong a word. Let's just say that there are other, more popular possibilities."

But Smith did not seem to hear and continued on his own train of thought. "Enough to . . . want him out of the way?"

José Antonio's mouth fell open in surprise. "Did someone threaten Durán?"

"You haven't heard?"

José Antonio shook his head, his brows furrowed. Savage things still happened in New Mexico. Two strangers in a cantina could start a discussion that ended in a gunfight. It happened all too often.

"Plácido Durán had some visitors two nights ago," Smith said. "An election committee." He gave his own ironic twist to the words. "Durán said there were six of them. Masked. Only one spoke. He didn't recognize the men or their horses. He wasn't sure about the leader's voice; he thought he had heard it before."

"What did this committee want?"

"For Durán to withdraw from the election."

"Wha-a-t? Do you mean that our opponents want him out? I don't believe it. Their man is favored to win. I don't understand."

"I don't believe it either."

"No one from our own party would—"

"It may have nothing to do with either party. Just a group that doesn't want Durán in the race. You said he wasn't the most popular candidate. Are there some who dislike him enough to threaten him?" José Antonio raised his eyebrows questioningly. "They said," Smith continued, "that they would kill him if he didn't withdraw."

"Madness."

"Does Duran have enemies?"

"Who doesn't?"

"I mean men who would kill him?"

José Antonio thought of Enrique Martínez and his followers, of his son, Francisco. There were others no doubt. But none of them, to his knowledge, would go this far.

"They spoke Spanish?" he asked. Smith nodded. "I don't know. I will quietly ask around."

Smith extended a hand in a gesture to halt. "Maybe you should just listen for now. Questions may just stir something up."

"What more could a question stir up? These men already threatened to kill him."

Smith sat silent for a moment, then nodded in acquiescence. "Find out what you can. Durán is our candidate. He won't quit. He and his family are being guarded." Smith drank the wine in his glass in a quick gulp, then refilled it. "Don José. Once you give in to a threat like this, you're lost. The next threat will be against a candidate for judge. Or territorial legislature. Any lunatic with a bandana and a gun could bring territorial politics to its knees. No! You can't give in. There's no alternative. We must move ahead as if nothing had happened."

"Of course."

"Go ahead with your work on the election. You see a great many people on your rounds. Listen to what they have to say." Then abruptly, "Do you know what these night riders had the audacity to call themselves? Los Hijos de Libertad."

José Antonio shook his head in wonder. The Sons of Liberty did not seem at all concerned about Plácido Durán's freedom. It was an upside-down world when bandits called themselves liberators.

"Should I say anything to those helping me?"

"Only that Durán will not be intimidated by sneak thieves in the night."

# 17

The corn was high and its sweet smell perfumed the air that was tinted by the faint pink horizon of twilight. A tired Leonardo walked along a furrow, hoe over his shoulder. Francisco waited.

As Leonardo approached, wiping his brow, Francisco felt a pique of irritation at his wife's anxiety. For God's sakes, he thought. How could she worry about the boy? If she had seen him working these past days, Florinda would have no cause to worry. Something had happened to him. He was trying to become a man. No more sneaking off to sleep in the shade. No more splashing in the ditch or hurrying off to the river when he should be in the fields. Poor Leonardo, he thought, as the sunburnt face smiled weakly at him. He does not have the energy or time to be off on any escapades.

"You did a good man's work today," he said.

"Thank you, Papá."

"Come. Let's sit by the corral." They crossed the ditch and trudged along the orchard to the shady side of the shed.

Francisco did not know exactly how to begin. He tried to remember himself at age fourteen. Only a little came. The endless fights with his brother Carlos, who had been two years younger. Their youngest brother, Blas, had only been five years old, the age of Francisco's youngest daughter. But he remembered the quarrels and his pervasive awareness of sex that led him furtively out at night to some accommodating girl whose name he had forgotten. And he remembered the heat and sweat of the fields that, in spite of his father's urgings, he preferred to school.

Francisco at age fourteen was not only dim in memory, but seemed an entirely different person from himself now. Like two strangers who at one time had shared he couldn't remember what and had parted to go their separate ways. Maybe it had been his parents and this farm that they had shared. These certainly were fixed as far back as his memory went. But if it had been true for Francisco, then it would also be true for Leonardo. This oldest son of his was already a stranger to the man he would soon become. Francisco's head ached at the thought.

Leonardo slumped, his head drooping between his knees, staring at the ground. A brown speckled hen clucked at them from under the huge cottonwood that shaded the back of the house.

"Tell me. How well do you know Ernesto Chávez?"

Leonardo slowly lifted his head and blinked as if he had not heard. Fatigue weighed him down and it took awhile for him to understand what it was that he had been asked. Even his look of surprise dawned very slowly. "Why . . . he's my first cousin."

"What have you heard . . . about him?"

A worried look dragged across Leonardo's face. "Nothing, Papá."

"When I was a boy," Francisco said. "I had a special friend, a cousin. Never mind his name." He's dead now, he thought with remorse. "We were together constantly when we were small. We were nearly the same age, the only boys among a swarm of girl cousins. We would go swimming in the river together. Tease our girl cousins. Rescue 'lost' melons in neighboring patches. All the things boys do without realizing that their fathers had been boys once and knew all about it.

"But when we got older, adults were not so amused anymore. What might have been a childish prank at eight years of age became lawbreaking at eighteen. By the time we were your age, well on our way to manhood, we had started to drift apart.

"My cousin could not understand how he could do an identical thing that people had smiled at in years past and be punished for it now. He 'borrowed' a neighbor's horse for a ride up into the Sandías. The only problem was that he hadn't asked permission of the neighbor. It was only after all sorts of promises that the horse-stealing charge was dropped."

"You think he would have learned from that, but no. A few months later he 'borrowed' another horse without permission. This time, though, it did not belong to one of our people but to an Anglo who, worse yet, was new to this place. It was a pony rather than a horse. A circus pony. My cousin was fascinated by the idea of the circus.

"As soon as the pony was missed, the Anglo went rushing to the sheriff. The next morning my cousin was on a flat meadow along the river trying to learn to ride this circus pony standing up. No matter how he tried, he could not stay on for very long. He didn't realize that the pony cantered in a circle the way he had been trained.

"On the last attempt he let the pony drift too near the river. When he fell off this time, he lost his footing and slid down the bank into the mud. He came up covered from head to toe; only the whites of his eyes shone through. And there on horseback was the sheriff aiming a rifle at him.

"They handcuffed him and led him to jail. This time the charges stuck and that began the long unhappy career of my cousin. After that it was as if he had entered into an unspoken agreement with the law to play tag. If he lost, it was the calaboose. If he won, he was free for awhile to enjoy his ill-gotten gains.

"He finally danced away his career at the end of a rope. In earlier times he might have started, as well as ended, his career that way. There has been many a man hung for stealing a horse. Or even thinking about stealing a horse.

"Now, Leonardo. Do you understand?"

The boy watched solemnly, thinking his own private thoughts. "Has Ernesto stolen a horse?" He asked.

"No. Not yet."

"Has he . . . been in jail?"

There had been stories. Whispers really. But even Florinda had slammed the door on discussion of such rumors. "I don't know. There has been talk, but you can't believe most of the talk you hear."

"Why do people talk about Ernesto?"

"Don't you know?" No answer. "There are things I know he's done. It's only by the grace of God that he hasn't been hauled off to jail. As he's grown older he's gotten worse. That's why I forbid you to see him! Understand?"

"Sí, señor." Leonardo sighed in relief. "Is that all, Papá?"

Francisco nodded. "I'm glad you understand. Ernesto is family, and one should be tolerant. But one must also choose his companions carefully. If you lie down with dogs, you get up with fleas."

Francisco rose and headed toward the house. As he approached he could hear Florinda screaming at the girls. Thank God she wouldn't be able to nag at him about Leonardo any more. He had done his duty.

*　*　*

Leonardo sat immobile against the shed. "I'll be in in a minute, Papá." He took the battered hat from his head and ran a hand through his matted hair as he stared at his dirty bare feet.

There was so much to think about. He felt that he had passed some kind of milestone. It was the first time his father had spoken to him man to man and it pleased and surprised him. When his father had waited for him at the end of the cornfield and asked about his cousin, Leonardo had felt like he had swallowed a stone that dropped to the bottom of his stomach.

"He has found out," he had said to himself. "Ernesto has told him because I did not meet him the other night."

But his father had not scolded him. Papá had treated him as an equal, the way Grandpa talked to Papá. You would never know they were father and son. They were just an old man talking to a younger man.

What had surprised him most was his father's calm. He was not his usual self, quick to anger. Even when he asked about Ernesto, it was as if Papá already knew that the answer would be no. That Leonardo was not involved. Papá trusted him. A sensible man, Papá seemed to say, would not involve himself with someone who would lead him to trouble.

This trust increased Leonardo's guilt. He thought of the sack of tobacco buried in the corner of the field that bordered their neighbor's property. His father trusted him and treated him like an adult, yet he had betrayed that trust by a stupid act. Better now to let the buried sack rot.

But it was Ernesto's fault, the child in him said. That bully of a cousin. He would never have stolen if it hadn't been for Ernesto. Now Ernesto was looking for him. Ready to — who knows what — if he didn't help him again. But he wouldn't! Not anymore.

What was still necessary though was some kind of penance. He owed it to his father, to the trust his father placed in him. So he would work hard. If he were truly conscientious, that would be enough. That and confession.

"Leonardo!"

His mother's voice startled him. "In a minute!" he answered.

18

Florinda's birthday had been Thursday, but because it was a busy time on the farm, the celebration was to be the following Sunday afternoon. After much consultation, Gregoria had agreed to hold the gathering in the big house. It would be a small affair. Family only. Which meant Florinda's eight brothers and sisters with their wives and husbands and their thirty-some children — her parents were dead. Plus Francisco's two younger sisters, Consuela and Andrea, with their husbands, who so far had only six children among them. Gregoria was not without a sense of humor. What, she thought, would I have done with a "big" party?

Sense of humor notwithstanding, Gregoria looked forward to the party with mixed feelings. She loved getting together with the young people; it made her feel young again. They were such a jolly group, especially if the men did not drink too much. The children in particular gave her pleasure. Eleven of them were her own grandchildren, of which Leonardo was the oldest and Andrea's new baby girl the youngest. It would be a festive time with food and drink and talk and music. There had not been a get-together like this in almost a year, and it was always a surprise to see all the children together and how they had grown.

In addition to the pleasures, though, there was the work. Not like in the old days when one could afford servants. Now the hostess could spend the entire day in the kitchen if she were not careful, cooking and serving and washing dishes while the others were having a good time. But Gregoria had learned long ago to avoid that mistake. She had each of the other women bring a dish, then had them take their turns in the kitchen so no one would be stuck there all afternoon. The men would bring whatever they wanted to drink. Usually beer or wine. While she and José Antonio would furnish the dessert, the house, and the hospitality.

When Gregoria and José Antonio returned from Mass, they made ready for the celebration. Francisco and Leonardo set up boards on wooden sawhorses under the shade of the trees. There were not enough chairs, so many would have to sit on the ground or stand. But there was ample table space for all the food for this "small" gathering.

The musicians arrived just after midday. The Nuánez brothers were distant cousins of the Rafas, two stately, white-haired bachelors dressed in their Sunday-, wedding-, funeral-best black suits. The younger brother, who sported a huge, drooping white mustachio, played the fiddle. His older brother, who was bald on top and let his hair grow long at the sides like white wings, played the guitar. They picked a cool spot in the shade and appropriated two chairs which Francisco placed on a raised pallet for them.

"Play a little something for us," José Antonio said. Nodding with shy smiles — the Nuánez brothers were quiet men whose vitality bubbled from their musical instruments rather than from their mouths — they tuned up and played a little polka for the workers. When the first guests arrived, it was as if the party was already underway.

\*   \*   \*

Gregoria supervised the kitchen, heating whatever needed to be heated before the younger women carried the platters outdoors to a table. Two women exchanged gossip as they patted and rolled flour tortillas, then cooked them on the hot stovetop while another woman stood over the stove frying eggs to top off the enchiladas, flat stacks of two or three tortillas like layered pancakes, with cheese and onion in between, and hot, spicy, red chili all over.

"¡Prima Gregoria!" She searched through the crowd for the source of the lisping voice. Across the kitchen at the entrance from the living room a black-garbed, gray-haired lady smiled, her eyes soft and moist, her long lashes fluttering.

"¡Prima Juanita! Such a surprise! Here," she said, handing her apron to one of the others. They embraced and kissed in the middle of the crowded kitchen. "I did not expect you," Gregoria said. "Let's find a place to talk."

Prima Juanita was Florinda's godmother in addition to being a distant cousin of Gregoria. As a godparent she was due particular respect, especially since Florinda's parents were dead. Yet whenever this short, heavy widow smiled in childlike innocence, she beamed a huge front snaggletooth that amused most people and repelled her goddaughter.

The two gray-haired women waved at others as they pushed through the crowd and made their way outside.

"Have you seen Florinda yet?" Gregoria asked.

"Oh, yes." Her bright smile was undiminished, though Gregoria suspected that the dear woman had been snubbed.

They sat on a bench away from the crowd and Juanita looked at the other guests, smiling pleasantly. People waved and smiled back, drawn as much by that beacon of a snaggletooth as by her friendliness. She watched the bachelor musicians with particular interest; they gave her a curt nod and looked away. But even this did not dim Juanita's smile. She beamed even more brightly, the way a puppy wags its tail to show that it is friendly and means no harm.

"How is Don Pedro?" Juanita asked.

Gregoria rolled her eyes. "He is around somewhere. You can see for yourself."

"He's better then?"

"Sometimes he's as sane as you or me. Other times—" She rotated a forefinger at her temple.

Juanita waved as her goddaughter danced by with Francisco. "She does not look thirty-three years old," Juanita said. "She still looks like a girl."

Gregoria laughed. "She *is* a girl. I haven't been thirty-three for almost thirty years. Válgame Dios."

Juanita's eyes narrowed. "You're over sixty, Prima? I had forgotten. I won't cross that border for another year." Gregoria smiled. She knew that her cousin was at least three years older than she. "Tell me. How is José Antonio's sister Andrea? She must be getting along in years, poor thing. It's so terrible living in Santa Fe so far from the family. But then," she said significantly, "she married that Anglo."

Gregoria sighed. Andrea was the only one of José Antonio's sisters still alive. Andrea was—yes, she was certain—the same age as Juanita, which made them both over sixty. Although Andrea had lived up north for many years and they seldom saw each other, Gregoria thought of her often. She, like Prima Juanita, was one of her favorites. Andrea was forthright and saucy. A cheerful woman who nonetheless would have her say. She was very unlike Juanita, whose gentle, ever-present smile masked sly barbs that amused more than angered Gregoria. Juanita had none of the grand passions of an Andrea, and if she had, she would have been intolerable.

"There are so few of us left," Gregoria mused.

"Oh!" The smile was transformed into an expression of shock. "Is Andrea gone? Qué lástima." Juanita crossed herself quickly, as if to ward off the fate that hung just over her head waiting for the right moment.

"Oh. No, no, no. Andrea is fine, living with one of her sons. I meant Tercero's other sisters. And so many others. At our age it's like watching petals drop from a flower, knowing that we are on the same blossom and it is only a matter of time."

Juanita's brave little smile looked more forced than usual. "With God's grace I am ready any time," she said in a quiet little voice.

Then the fiddle struck up a lively tune, and they caught sight of Don Pedro watching the dancers. Juanita jumped quickly to her feet, excused herself, and hurried to the old man. Gregoria watched in amusement as Don Pedro scowled, then turned sharply on his heel and hurried to escape.

"Keep that old hag away from me," Don Pedro hissed. "She's crazy to find a husband." Then he quickly disappeared before Gregoria could respond.

In a few moments Juanita returned, dancing a few steps to the music before she sat beside Gregoria. "Oh, me," she said, with an exasperated little sigh. The musicians played their lively fiddle and guitar, indifferent to the old impatient feet that danced alone for want of a partner.

*     *     *

Family gatherings were a bore to Leonardo. When younger he had enjoyed playing with his cousins. He could be their leader, decide what games to play, send someone for something to eat, awe them with stories or deeds.

Now that he was older, the younger cousins irritated him. He could not tolerate their company, their noisy, childish disorganization, their need for someone to tell them what to do. Yet he was not ready to join the adults, except perhaps to quietly hang around the fringe of one of the groups of men as they discussed something interesting. Like Indians. Or getting drunk. Or horses. Or even local politics. In times past he could at least have shared the company of his oldest cousin, Ernesto. Now, of course, he avoided him.

But there was food to eat. Plenty of tasty, hot, spicy food to be cooled with water from the pump. Until even his seldom-satisfied, growing

body was stuffed. Then he found a quiet place to rest, not quite dropping off to sleep as he kept one wary eye on the lookout for Ernesto.

In the distance he could hear his father's intense voice arguing about
the coming election. Then the soothing words of his grandfather. Occasionally, this orchestra of voices was punctuated by his mother's per-
cussive shriek.

Mamá would not tell anyone her age, grimacing in a tight little expression that on anyone else would be a smile. "A lady never tells. Just say twenty-nine." Of course, Leonardo thought ironically. When he became twenty-nine, his gray-haired mother would
still make the same silly claim. As if it mattered. As if it changed
anything.

"Leo! Leo!" His youngest sister, Juanita, ran up to him, rubbing
the tears across her dust-streaked face so they formed a thin layer of
mud. "Leo!" she screamed furiously. "Sister hit me!"

"Go tell Mamá," he grumbled.

"She told me to go away."

"Then Papá."

"He said he'd smack me if I bothered him again."

"Oh, for God's sakes. Go tell Rosa then."

"She told me to see you."

"Go away!"

"Le-o!" He rolled over, turning his back to her. "I'm going to tell
Mamá on you," she screamed.

He drifted into a torpor, into that state that was neither sleep nor
wakefulness in which he did not know where he was. The music and
voices played over him like the lapping of waves. The aroma of good
food, warm bodies, and the sweet scent of cornfields soothed him.

A kick in the flank shocked Leonardo awake. "You've been avoiding
me, cuz." Leonardo felt a chill and he forced himself to roll over toward
Ernesto. "You stood me up again."

"I've been busy. I couldn't get away."

"Don't give me that."

"No. Really. Don't you have to help at home?"

Ernesto shook his head, then moved his slender, agile hands as if
dealing cards. Leonardo rose and slowly walked toward the group that
included his father. His heart pounded as Ernesto followed.

"You heard what happened to Plácido Durán?" one of the men in
the group said.

Leonardo squeezed between his father and grandfather to listen.

*   *   *

There were six of them in the circle. A half-empty bottle of whiskey stood on the ground beside Armando Chávez, who took a swig, then passed it along.

Armando smiled benevolently. "Poor old Plácido," he said. "After all those years of kiss-assing the big boys downtown and knocking on doors to buy votes, they finally reward him with a chance to run for sheriff. Only trouble is, those so-called smart gringos don't seem to know that la raza won't vote for him.

"Did you see him in his new duds over in Old Town the other day?" Armando laughed as if that were the funniest thing he had ever seen. "He already spent a fortune on his 'Look! I won the election' costume. Damnest thing you ever saw. Like a gringo gambler-pimp from one of the casinos in New Town."

One of the men spit at the ground, then took a swallow from the bottle that José Antonio had refused and passed on. "Christ!" the man said. "Can you imagine that chicken as sheriff? If he didn't have that big, mean sonofabitch of a brother as a bodyguard, every little old lady in church would kick shit out of him. It's his brother Benito who should be running for sheriff."

"He's too stupid," Francisco said. "He thinks Benito is spelled 'X' because that's the way he signs legal papers. He can't understand why all those others sign 'X' when their names aren't Benito. He thinks the dumb bastards don't know how to spell." Everybody laughed.

"But did you hear the latest?" one of the men asked.

"They're registering the ghosts in the cemetery to vote," Armando said.

"What's the latest?" Francisco asked.

"Well," the man leaned forward and lowered his voice. "One night last week Plácido got a visit from los vigilantes españoles."

"Bullshit, man. Who could believe that?"

"I'm telling you, damn it. The midnight posse paid a call on Durán and told him to get out of the race or they'd kill him."

"Where did you hear this?" José Antonio asked.

"Well, Don José," the man answered respectfully. "I just heard it. I . . . I can't say from whom. I don't remember." He looked uncomfortably around the circle and reached for the whiskey bottle.

"More bullshit," Armando said. "Hell! Benito Durán has been going around trying to be secretive and asking a lot of questions. Was it Benito?"

"I can't say. I don't want to get mixed up in this."

"Then you should keep quiet," Francisco said. "You're the one who brought it up. Now you don't want to talk about it."

"So, is he out of the election?" someone asked.

"Hooo! Are you kidding? After spending all that money on those new clothes?" Armando shook his head and grinned. "Why do you think big dumb Benito is sneaking around asking question? Hell, the party won't let Plácido quit, even if he wanted to. Isn't that right, Don José?"

All eyes turned to José Antonio. "I hear there was a meeting with Don James Smith," someone said.

José Antonio had been listening to the banter, trying to learn what he could. He had known all of these young men for a long time, most of them since they were boys, so he knew how to weigh and judge what each one said. But now that they had turned to him, he would have to answer and he knew that he could not lie to them even if he wanted to.

"Plácido Durán is still the party's candidate," he said. "I'm still working to elect him."

"What about the meeting?"

"There has been no meeting about this among the party workers here in Los Rafas. Has there, Francisco?" José Antonio asked.

"No, señor. I have not met with Smith in a long time."

Francisco did not mention unofficial meetings over unimportant details. His response was too quick. Too glib. Without his usual irritation. It made José Antonio uncomfortable.

"I heard there was a meeting at Don James' last week," the man repeated.

In a small community like this, it was almost impossible to keep a secret. There was always someone who saw or heard something. The secret smile between a man and a woman. A recognizable horse along the road even on the darkest night. The missing light in the window where the light usually shone. The familiar bark of someone's dog.

Who had seen him leave Smith's house or ride to or from it? It didn't really matter. "I wouldn't honor it with the word 'meeting,'" José Antonio said. "I did see Señor Smith last week. But there was only him and me. We talked about Plácido Durán's visitors."

Now their eyes blazed intently at José Antonio. "What was the official word?" Armando asked.

"Plácido Durán is our party's candidate. I am still working to elect him."

"In a pig's eye!" Armando shook his head in dismay. "How much are they going to pay for votes this year? It's going to have to be a lot more than a shot of whiskey."

José Antonio froze, his face stern and unyielding. It always angered him to hear such comments. He would never do it himself, although he knew some who did. His son for one, though Francisco would never admit it. The young men probably laughed at him behind his back. How can you win an election without greasing a few palms? he could hear them say. Trust in God! he would answer. But they would laugh at that too.

"Now Armando," Francisco admonished. "You know our party doesn't operate that way. The opposition might. But nothing says a man can't collect his little tip, then go vote exactly as his conscience tells him."

But Armando was not satisfied. "Begging your pardon, Don José, but Jesus Christ! Do those big shots in New Town really think they can win with Durán? He should have listened to Los Hijos de Libertad. It would not only save his skin, but maybe give us someone decent to vote for."

José Antonio's ears perked at the mention of Los Hijos de Libertad. How did Armando know that? Who else knew it?

"Los Hijos de Libertad? Who are they?" Francisco barked in too loud a voice.

"That's what the midnight posse calls itself," Armando said. "At least so I've been told."

José Antonio looked with suspicion toward Francisco, then turned to Armando. "We have to work with the party," he said. "The party's candidate may not always be your choice, but no matter. Support him. That's the only way our voice will be heard.

"Tell me. Haven't we had good candidates most of the time? Once in awhile we get something like this sheriff's race. But for other offices there are candidates we support with enthusiasm.

"You should vote for Durán. The alternative is for the other party to stay in. Where does that leave us?"

There was an undercurrent of grumbling among the men. José Antonio knew that most of them would have preferred someone else. He hoped, by gentle persuasion, to minimize the number who would vote for the other candidate. Yet he was not sure. They would lose votes here and there. Even after he repeated his little pep talk to many more groups like this.

"Gentlemen," José Antonio said. "I'd better go have a dance with the birthday lady." He turned and sought out Florinda, tapping his hand nervously on his side in time to the music.

*   *   *

As the group broke up, Ernesto grabbed Leonardo by the shoulder and steered him away. "Look!" he spat. "I need your help tomorrow night and you had better be there. Otherwise — ?" He squeezed Leonardo's shoulder until it brought tears to the boy's eyes. "You understand?"

Leonardo fought back the tears and turned away. He was not going, but he dared not tell Ernesto. He would accept the consequences, whatever they were . . . later.

# 19

The next night Leonardo did not meet Ernesto but went instead to visit his grandfather. His mother had been so pleased about her birthday party that she had not screamed once at supper nor balked when he went next door.

"Thank Grandma for her kindness," she said as Leonardo left. His mouth fell open in astonishment.

Outside, he stopped to bask in the twilight, in that time that his grandmother called the golden hour. That pause between day and night when the last rays of sunshine bathed the sky in a soft glow. When the horizon was colored a spectacular rose. From things in the air Grandmother said — spirits. And when the clouds too exuded the same color, like dying flowers gasping out their final beauty.

As Leonardo watched the slowly changing colors of the sky, an unexplainable feeling came over him. As if he became more alive. Overcome by a heightened sense of himself and the natural world as unique and glorious.

After awhile the pinks and blues faded to gray. He sighed and made

his way through the orchard toward the big house. He picked up a
rotten apple and threw it at a tree, hitting the trunk square so the apple splattered and slid to the ground.

"Grandpa." The door squeaked as he stuck his head into the room.
"Grandpa?" José Antonio peered from the kitchen door. "You haven't
told me any of Don Pedro's story for a long time."

What puzzled Leonardo was Don Pedro's behavior at the party. He
had behaved like any normal old man: the two musicians, his grandfather. And though Leonardo had seen him in these spells of normality
before, he had never been so consciously aware of it. It was as if he
were seeing Don Pedro for the first time. Or seeing an entirely different
man. Nowhere was there a trace of the drunken madman. This new
Don Pedro was restrained in his drinking, polite in his talk, and gallant
to the ladies. The old rooster danced with the prettiest girls and avoided the snaggletoothed old hag who pursued him. This new side made
Leonardo realize how different Don Pedro must have been in the old
days in California and that it had taken something terrible to change
him.

"Tell me more, Grandfather."


                            *       *       *


Six months after the loan, the treaty between Mexico and the United
States was signed. The influx of settlers from the east brought a tremen-
dous demand for land. With the best land already parceled out in
Spanish and Mexican grants, an intolerable pressure built up that was
ripe for conflict.

Don Pedro mobilized the rancho to bring it back to paying status
as quickly as possible. His three younger brothers managed portions
of the rancho under his direction. Manuel and José Ignacio oversaw
the cattle range with their vaqueros. Rudolfo was put in charge of the
rancho's agriculture: the orchards, hay fields, vegetable fields, and
vineyards. Doña Beatriz ran the house. And Pedro oversaw the entire
operation from his office in the central complex.

One day as he reviewed estimates on the hides and tallow they hoped
to process, the high-heeled boots of one of their vaqueros echoed through
the hall, and Pedro followed the sharp sounds along the wooden floors,
until they were muffled by rugs as they turned toward the office.

"Don Pedro?" The vaquero held his sombrero in front of his chest with both hands. "There's trouble on the north range." Pedro dropped his pen on the desk and looked up. "Don Manuel asked that you ride out and meet him."

Pedro was irritable because the estimates that he had been checking for the third time showed that they would not earn enough to pay off their debt this year. The interruption increased his irritation.

"What could be so important on the north range? Rustlers? Cattle disease?" he grumbled. The vaquero shook his head. "I'm in the middle of very important work!" Pedro said angrily. "I can't be interrupted!"

The vaquero seemed to draw back, although he had not moved an inch. "Worse, Don Pedro. Covered wagons!"

"Why didn't you tell me, goddamn it!" Pedro grabbed his hat and stormed out of the house.

It was a hard, fast ride to the north range across the dark, rich land, fed by the creek that flowed toward the bay from the distant hills. If the range had been closer to the ranch house, it would have made ideal farmland, as rich as that near the central complex where their vegetables, orchards, and vineyards grew.

Up ahead Pedro saw Manuel approaching on horseback. Behind him, beyond the herd, puffs of light-colored canvas headed toward the creek.

Manuel shouted greetings and turned his horse toward a knoll that overlooked the range. "We saw them early this morning," Manuel said. "At first I didn't pay any attention. But later one of them rode to the creek and scouted it out. There's nothing to show the boundaries of the rancho. They must think it's open country, free for homesteading. Anyway, the scout finally rode back and the wagons turned toward that part of our land."

"Maybe they're just passing through," Pedro said.

"Maybe they're not."

Pedro studied his brother's face for a moment. Of all the brothers, he was the one most like Andrés, who had joined the militia. But Manuel was older and knew when a fight might be lost instead of won and he could control his temper.

"Eleven wagons. Two mounted scouts leading. If it came to it, you could drive them off with a few vaqueros. They're outnumbered, out-mounted, and outgunned."

"And they're Yankees," Manuel spat. "Land-hungry trash who probably cheered when the Bear Flaggers killed our people."

"They may only be passing through. If you need help, get the law to run them off."

"That Yankee would just as soon let them run us off."

"Then get the deputy. He's one of us."

Now that Pedro had surveyed the situation, his irritation returned. Eleven wagons? Preposterous! Manuel could have handled it himself. He had imagined an invasion of a hundred wagons. That would have been something to be concerned about.

"I'll leave this to you, Manuel," Pedro finally said. "Unless you think eleven Yankee wagons are too many."

"Damn it! No!" Manuel answered.

Pedro turned his mount and spurred it toward the rancho, shaking his head over this false alarm.

*     *     *

Pedro never knew exactly what happened afterwards. But he did hear from some of Manuel's vaqueros, and the rest he could imagine, knowing his brother.

As Pedro left, Manuel must have cursed under his breath. He was confused. On the one hand, his older brother had told him to let him know about anything important. On the other hand, Pedro had become angry when Manuel did as he had been told.

The eleven Yankee wagons were like scouts for a horde of locusts. The issue was not these eleven wagons, but those that would undoubtedly follow. All one had to do was to look at what had happened in the past ten years. Only a fool would ignore it. Spanish-speaking Californians were already outnumbered by these red-faced, twangy-voiced Yankees.

Since Manuel was only a year and a half younger than Pedro, he felt himself an equal in experience and knowledge. But the eldest son, the heir, was always elevated to a position only slightly lower than the angels, while the rest of the offspring were little better than hired hands.

"Well, damn it!" he must have said to himself. "I'll show him."

He watched the wagons the rest of the day until they finally reached the creek and camped. In the morning Manuel gathered a half dozen of his most experienced vaqueros. If he took more, the wagoneers might become alarmed and shoot as they rode into their camp. If he took fewer, they might be overpowered when they arrived.

As they approached, they saw a group standing around a campfire.

Two men, an older one and one not so much young as in the full maturity of youth, broke off from the fire, cups still in their hands, and walked out to meet them.

"Howdy!" the younger man said. Behind him, by the fire, the vaqueros saw the surreptitious moves that told them several had reached for their weapons.

"¡Buenos días!" Manuel said, dismounting. "My name is Don Manuel Baca. My family owns this rancho that you are camped on."

The man's eyes glazed over with a flinty grey look, cutting off whatever warmth and emotion had gleamed from them before. "I'm Elbert Travers," he said. "This is my father, Mr. William Travers. We're from Ohio."

"We saw you arrive yesterday. Where are you headed?"

There was an uncomfortable silence as the two Yankees looked at each other. "Well, we don't rightly know yet," Elbert answered. "We're looking, and we'll know when we find it."

Manuel smiled at his vaqueros. All the way from Ohio but they didn't know where they were going. These Yankees weren't even good liars. But what Manuel said was, "We hope you enjoy your short stay on Rancho Los Palos. If you should continue south, our casa grande is seven miles from here. We are more than pleased to offer hospitality to passers-through."

The older Yankee took off his hat and ran a hand through his grizzled white hair. He looked around, scanning the horizon. "Seven miles, you say?"

"The rancho is forty miles around, almost seventy-five square miles in area. A big rancho for these parts."

William Travers spat a wad of tobacco at the ground. "Seventy-five square miles? That's a lot of land for one family and a few cows."

It was hard to ignore the judgment in the older Travers' words. So much for your family while mine has so little, he seemed to say.

"It is killing time," Manuel said. "We round up the cattle and herd them to the rancho where they are slaughtered for hides and tallow. We handle several hundred a day."

"A waste of beef," the man answered. "Not very good beef but meat nonetheless."

Manuel's face hardened as he remounted. "I will send a vaquero to your camp with a beef. It might be a welcome change. Adiós, Señores Travers."

As they rode off, Manuel and the vaqueros heard the questions as the Yankees returned to the campfire. "What do they want, El? What was it all about?"

"The older one bears watching," Manuel said. "He is the trouble-maker."

\* \* \*

Two days later the visitors from Ohio were still camped on rancho property. Pedro had not heard from Mauel, but he was certain that his brother watched the interlopers closely. Meanwhile, the slaughter progressed, although Pedro's greatest concern was for Don Pedro senior.

The old Don had degenerated noticeably since the death of his brother and nephews. Doña Beatriz tried to cheer him by increasing her natural gaiety almost to the point of mania. Meanwhile, Pedro tried to cut off the supply of liquor to the old Don before he drank himself into the grave. But between the servants and Doña Beatriz, it was almost impossible unless he stood guard beside the old man day and night.

One day, as Pedro sought relief from the office in the orchard, a stranger rode toward the house. The dusty young man was dressed in what once had been a uniform, mounted on a bony horse that looked as if it had been ridden far and hard.

The horseman called out as Pedro stepped from behind a fruit tree; he wanted to know if this was Rancho Los Palos. When Pedro answered, the horseman asked for Don Pedro Baca. He had a message of grave importance for him. The stranger's eyes flashed skeptically when Pedro told him that he was Don Pedro Baca. He had expected a much older man.

My father, Pedro thought. When he explained, the young man, whose name was Miguel Barrio, nodded. He was seeking the father of his closest friend in the militia, Andrés Baca.

Although it was a sunny day, an icy premonition chilled Pedro. Barrio dismounted and wiped his dusty hand on his trousers before taking Pedro's hand. Even through the fatigue you could sense his gloom. Their father was very ill, Pedro explained. When Barrio asked for Señora Baca, Pedro told him that she was not much better. These had been difficult times on the rancho.

The young stranger stared as if trying to understand. Sensing his fatigue and reluctant to pursue the ominously urgent business that brought the young man to the rancho, Pedro invited him into the house to rest and eat.

Young Barrio shook his head as if shaking off lethargy. "I need to speak to the head of the family." Pedro told him that he was acting head. "I'm sorry, Don Pedro. He—Andrés—your brother is dead."

Pedro was stunned. It took all his willpower to maintain his composure and show the man into the house. He hardly realized that he was speaking when he asked Barrio to tell him about it, warning him to please not tell anyone else in the family. It would kill the old Don.

Pedro ordered a servant to prepare a bath. Then he sent one of the maids for something for Barrio to eat. All thoughts of work vanished. A numbness overwhelmed him and he walked aimlessly while his guest bathed and ate. He found himself in the corner of a grove of oaks where three white crosses reached out as if waiting for more. He dropped onto the center grave and crossed himself, praying silently.

Why us? he thought. Oh God, why us? Couldn't you leave us alone? Let others share this dreadful sorrow? But the mute oak trees and the orchard beyond answered with silence.

We who have been given much have much that can be taken away, Pedro thought. Those who have little have little to lose. So how can others share our sorrow? We can only share it with ourselves. Without sorrow there would be no joy. With much joy there is much sorrow.

A great cry burst from his lungs and he fell face down on the earth, striking it with his fists. "It is not fair!" he shouted. "IT IS NOT FAIR!!"

Exhausted, Pedro finally wiped his face and somehow found his way back to the office. He left word for Miguel Barrio to join him, then sat at his desk with eyes closed, praying.

When the door quietly opened, Pedro pointed the young visitor to a chair. Barrio placed on the table and pushed toward his host a Bible, a gold chain with crucifix, and the pocket watch that Andrés had received on his eighteenth birthday. It was a pitifully small collection to show for twenty years of life. What it did not show were the important things: the sly smile, the ready laugh, the penetrating dark eyes.

Andrés had been buried in the only clothes he had. Near Los Angeles where he fought his last battle.

Pedro admonished the young man once again not to tell anyone in the family. He would tell them in due time, but for now he wanted to keep the news from his father and mother. Let them hope a little longer.

Barrio nodded. Pedro wondered how he could sit through supper with the family tonight, carrying this burden and not letting it show. I have to, he thought. I must!

He dimly heard as Barrio began to tell of Andrés Baca's last battle.

\* \* \*

On the third day the Ohio caravan was joined by another group of wagons. The camp doubled in size. On the fourth day they were still there, immobile, perhaps unmovable, almost as if taking root rapidly and permanently in that piece of earth. They gave no sign of moving on. Or they may have been waiting for more wagons to join so they could — So they could what? Manuel must have thought. So they could stay and be harder to drive out.

The next day, when one of the vaqueros galloped into camp with the hides and hooves of several butchered cattle, Manuel decided it was time to act. Now they were stealing the rancho's livelihood.

By the time he had ridden into San José and returned with the deputy, still more wagons had rolled onto Rancho Los Palos. This time Elbert and William Travers met them with two other men, all noting with wary amusement the badge on the stranger who accompanied Manuel Baca and his armed vaqueros.

"Howdy, Sheriff," William Travers said.

"Deputy United States Marshal," came the terse reply.

"What can we do for you, marshal?"

"You are trespassing," Manuel answered. The men looked at him with amused disdain, as if not giving authority to his words or his presence. "Trespassing beyond the bounds of a guest's good manners toward the hospitality of his host."

The four Yankees exchanged looks. In the background a quiet, surly crowd of squatters gathered.

"I've been told," the deputy marshal said, "that some of Don Manuel's cattle have been slaughtered."

"Well, I don't know," William Travers said. "This gentleman," he nodded toward Manuel, "sent one of his men over with a beef for us. A gift. That's all the cattle slaughtering we know about."

"Then, of course," the deputy marshall said, "there is the problem of trespassing."

Now the Yankees looked at each other uncomfortably, then toward Manuel. "This gentleman here," Elbert Travers said, "Don Manuel, let us camp here for a few days."

"That was five days ago when there were only eleven wagons," Manuel said. "Now there are twice that many and who knows how many more coming."

William Travers blinked his serpent eyes. "We couldn't very well go off without our companions. It just took them longer than we thought to catch up."

"How many more are you waiting for?" Manuel asked. The men shrugged. "There are other places to camp that are not on private property."

"Now see here," the older Travers said. "We didn't know this was private property. There are no signs. No fences. One of our party went into San José to find out exactly where the property lines are. There seems to be some question that we're on your property at all."

Manuel's face grew red with fury. He was overcome by such rage that for a moment he could not speak. He could only stare in murderous anger at the interlopers.

"I want you off rancho property tomorrow!" Manuel shouted. "If not, the authorities will drive you off!"

William Travers spat on the ground near Manuel's feet, then turned abruptly and strode back to camp. The other Yankees nodded at the deputy marshal as if agreeing to Manuel's ultimatum.

"Tomorrow," the deputy said.

They turned slowly and strolled back to the gathering that stared at the Californios with grim hostility.

"I will have to tell the marshal," the deputy said as they rode away. Manuel grimaced. He had no desire to involve the gringo marshal, but the mess had grown too big. There might be a gun battle tomorrow and he wanted the law with him.

"My vaqueros will be ready when you come."

"Until then," the deputy said, "keep them calm. Give the Yankees enough time to break camp and move peacefully. Don't approach the camp without me. We'll be back midmorning to see how it goes."

He would have preferred to ride into camp immediately, shooting the arrogant interlopers, but Manuel nodded to the deputy. "Until tomorrow."

\* \* \*

Not only was the American marshal with the deputy marshal the next morning, but there was another man too. Another gringo. And when they came closer to the vaquero camp, Manuel and the vaqueros saw that it was the lawyer, John Archer.

"What is he doing with them?" Manuel said. "Did Pedro have something to do with this?"

But the marshal had sought out Archer on his own. Not only was he a lawyer who knew the land laws and boundaries, but he had a valid and substantial interest in Rancho Los Palos. Finally, he was an American, which would be of some advantage with these wagoneers from Ohio.

Manuel's stony face did not show what he must have felt about this absurdity. Like must talk to like. Ohioans would not talk to Mexicans. At least would not accept them the way they would their own countrymen. While he acknowledged the reality of this, it still offended him. But being a practical man, he let the marshal, deputy marshal, and lawyer make their way to the covered wagon camp while he and his vaqueros remained at a distance.

The camp itself was in a state of disarray. It was difficult to tell whether or not they were preparing to leave. From the knoll overlooking the camp, the onlookers could see the broad gestures and the mouths moving with talk that they could not hear. Manuel glowered, no doubt suspicious that the gringo marshal and gringo lawyer might not truly represent his interests. He should have gone, he grumbled. Should have insisted. It was his family's property. This part of the range was his responsibility. He cursed for letting them talk him into staying behind.

The lawyer, Archer, reached into his saddlebag, then carefully unrolled a large sheet of paper, anchoring it flat on the ground with a rock at each corner. The Ohioans clustered about and looked where Archer pointed. Then the Ohioans stood and nodded at each other, all except that gray-haired old serpent, William Travers. "That," Manuel said to one of his vaqueros, "is a man I would gladly kill."

As Archer rolled up the map and replaced it in his saddlebag, the marshal talked. Again the Ohioans nodded and led them into the center of camp where the marshal spoke to a general gathering of the homesteaders. There was much talking and hand-waving. Raised fists. A few men left the group abruptly, as if in anger. Still the talking went on until finally a few made a break toward their wagons and started to load.

"They did it!" Manuel said to his vaqueros. "The goddamned Yankees are leaving!"

He waited impatiently as the negotiators rode back. "They're leaving!" the marshal said through the tight smile on his harried face.

"Gracias a Dios," Manuel sighed.

"God had nothing to do with it," Archer said. "I showed them the plat of the rancho. There was no question that they are trespassing. As the mortgagee to part of the rancho, I told them that I would go to the United States Supreme Court if necessary to protect my interests. When the marshal explained the folly of a fight, especially with your vaqueros up on this knoll, they reconsidered."

"They'll be gone by tonight," the marshal said. "Heading south for open land."

"Or to a grant that someone can't prove is his in court," Archer said. "Until this mess is settled by the government, there'll be squatters on all the ranchos in California. This caravan is just a straw in the wind."

"But they're going," Manuel said.

"Without bloodshed," the marshal added.

\* \* \*

Two days later at dusk, while riding from the range to the central complex, Manuel Baca was ambushed and shot dead. His saddlebags and the pockets of his clothing were rifled, but his valuable horse and saddle were not taken. His clothes were left intact. It was either a hasty and clumsy robbery or an attempt to make it look like one.

The Ohio caravan was two days travel south, heading toward Monterey. Though he could not explain why, Pedro knew that Manuel's murderer rode among those supposedly peaceful settlers. But there was no proof, and all he could think was: The Yankees have murdered another Baca. That makes five.

A few weeks later there was a sixth Baca death. The old Don, drinking more than ever after Manuel's death, did not wake up one morning. Whether from overdrinking or a broken heart no one knew.

## 20

"Oh, Grandfather," Leonardo pleaded. "Don't tell me any more."

José Antonio saw his wife's angry glare. I warned you, that look seemed to say. Why must that poor boy listen to such horror stories? What good will it do?

"I'm sorry," he said. "I should not have started this."

"No, Grandfather. If you think I should hear it, I will. But not now."

"Remember," Gregoria cautioned, "there are good things that came with the Americans. Sometimes we forget how hard it was before. The constant wars with the Indians. The lack of tools, of clothing, of food. Of much that makes life pleasant. The state of our churches and our schools. Life is better than when I was a girl."

"Grandfather, why was it so bad in California? Was it like that here?"

"The end of the Mexican War opened the floodgates to California. There were only a few thousand of our people there before the war. Great ranchos existed because there was so much land for so few. Then came the avalanche of Yankee settlers. In just a few years, for every Mexican there were suddenly thirty, forty, fifty, a hundred Yankees. The Californios were like a tiny boat inundated by the entire ocean.

"Suddenly people who did not know the language, or the customs, or the old laws were there, seeking to make their fortunes without regard for the Mexicans whom they so greatly outnumbered. And outnumbering them so much while understanding them so little, most Yankees considered the Mexicans insignificant. A source of cheap labor. Or ignorant low-lives who somehow lucked onto great land holdings that were fair game by any means, no matter how devious, immoral, or illegal.

"Here in New Mexico it was not the same. We did not have the riches that lured so many Yankees to California. There are still more Spanish-speaking New Mexicans than Anglos, so we have more to say about our destiny. We were not outnumbered and in numbers there is safety."

"Do you mean that if so many Yankees hadn't gone to California it would not have turned out so bad for Don Pedro?"

"Sí, hijo. For Don Pedro and many others."

"I will never go to California," Leonardo insisted. "I will always live here where it is so much better."

"By the grace of God," Gregoria murmured.

"Tell me more some other time," Leonardo said. "I've heard all that I want to hear tonight."

More than you need to, Gregoria's expression seemed to say, while José Antonio placed a hand affectionately on his grandson's shoulder.

\* \* \*

A few days later José Antonio called on James Smith. As he approached, Smith's old hound and three dogs that he had never seen before barked hysterically, baring their fangs as they pulled their ropes to the choking point.

José Antonio walked cautiously around them. Only the old hound calmed down and wagged his tail. Before José Antonio reached the porch, Smith came to the door and shouted the dogs down to a reluctant and hostile undertone.

"Those curs are enough to drive you crazy. They bark at friends and hide in silence from thieves. Come in. Come in. Thank you for coming, Don José."

"I was on my way to Los Griegos," José Antonio said as he sat on the Chicago mail-order chair. He was never comfortable in this house with its store-bought furniture. It and everything in it seemed temporary. Wood frame. Peaked roof. Paint that alienated the house from its natural surroundings. Foreign. The way American words sounded as they tumbled from his lips.

Every once in awhile José Antonio would hear the American language from his own lips as if he were listening to a stranger, a not very intelligent stranger whose limited vocabulary placed him at a disadvantage among Anglo foreigners. In his heart he knew that in his own language, his own Spanish, any advantage would be his. For in his own language, he had the ability to use subtle words, to twist and shape propositions to his own best interests, to shade a phrase, to mask an attitude with virtue where virtue did not exist.

Yet power was reckoned in more than language. This power — the lands a man owned, the votes he controlled, the money he had in the bank — all these could overwhelm language so that people like José Antonio had to speak a foreign tongue in their own land. Had thereby to play the fool, the ignoramus, while inside seethed a man as intelligent in his own way as the man with power. More intelligent perhaps, since he had to have the intelligence to acquiesce in order to survive. It was more difficult to be a gracious loser than to be a gracious winner. Took more to accept the domination of men fewer in numbers, but numbers multiplied by the power they wielded.

Of all the locals, Don José, the patrón of Los Rafas, was the one man who was Smith's equal. But a standoffish pride stood between them. Perhaps, José Antonio thought, if Smith did not believe so much in money, things would have been different. He saw that as the chasm. A difference in wealth was the wedge that split apart otherwise equal men. As for José Antonio, he countered with the pride of the less well-to-do who could tolerate no favor. Pride that resisted even the appearance of charity, that spurned a charitable thought.

"Thank you for coming, Don José," Smith repeated. "It's about a personal matter. Not la política. Nor about water rights or any of the countless other things that plague the life of a farmer."

José Antonio's face relaxed into furrows that more truly showed his age. What was coming? he thought. Could that fool Pedro have assaulted one of Smith's nanny goats again? But no, he answered himself, his California madman had been at his most sane these past few weeks. He had not wandered off the farm unattended for some time.

"You saw the watchdogs?" Smith asked. "I turn them loose at night. They can tear a man's leg off if someone is foolish enough to trespass."

"I've been missing things." His manner seemed to imply that Don José should know what was missing. Important, valuable things that only another man of substance would recognize. "My old hound is no help. If Mrs. Smith hadn't interfered, I'd have shot him. What use is a hound who wags his tail at every stray Mexican in the area?"

José Antonio's eyes hardened into opaque brown stone. "Did you call the sheriff?" he asked, knowing damn well what the answer would be. He had asked the question not for knowledge but for spite.

"How would that look, asking the sheriff to meddle into a minor theft when we're trying to kick him out of office? Murder, yes. You'd have to call him on a murder. But petty theft?" Smith shook his head. "The voters would laugh us out of the county."

"It's his job."

"If we're going to accuse him of incompetence in the campaign, we'd be fools to ask him to help us now. That's why I called you."

José Antonio grunted. Why do the sheriff's work for him? Good God, why elect a man to office if you weren't willing to ask him to do his job? But he grudgingly admitted that Smith was right. You couldn't ask the sheriff to find a thief, wishing that he would succeed, then denounce him a month later as an incompetent who needed to be replaced. Stupid business, the whole mess.

"I found this by the shed." Smith held up a hunting knife with a handle shaped from a piece of bone that looked like deer antler. The end of the crude blade had been snapped off. "Someone used it to force the lock, then dropped it when the dogs raised a ruckus."

José Antonio's eyes narrowed. It looked vaguely familiar. He reached for it and studied it more closely. "What did they take?"

"Tobacco. Only tobacco."

"Tobacco?" Why would someone only steal tobacco? he thought. If someone were going to steal, there were many more things worthwhile. One of Smith's goats. Or chickens. A sack of beans. Chili. A horse for God's sakes.

"This is the second time in the past month," Smith said.

"And tobacco both times?" Smith nodded. "Somebody is doing a lot of puffing. All we have to do is look for a giant cloud of smoke." Smith's forced laugh did not mask his scowl. "What do you want me to do?" José Antonio asked.

"See what you can find out about that knife. If you find the owner, we can deal with him ourselves."

José Antonio turned the knife over and weighed it in his hand. Homemade, but not too skillfully. There were many such knives owned by a great number of men in Los Rafas.

This request was different from the usual missions he undertook. Like settling quarrels between neighbors, one of whose cows had knocked over a fence that separated one field from another. Or helping patch a lover's quarrel on the eve of their betrothal. Problems that people wanted settled out of court since in court the only ones who ever received much satisfaction were the lawyers, who got their fee no matter what.

But to be a snoop? That was the sheriff's job! It was bad enough having the parish priest harangue him because people consulted him instead of the priest. People could consult whomever they wanted. The church had no monopoly on advice. But the proper person for solving a crime was the sheriff. It was not José Antonio's job. He did not want it.

"There are many such knives in Los Rafas. When men can't afford to buy a fancy one in town, they make their own." He punctuated his comment with a shrug that spoke more loudly than words: This is foolish. Forget it.

"These thefts have to stop!" Smith's voice was uncompromising, his face rigid and hostile.

José Antonio looked away, not wanting Smith to see on his face what nonsense he thought it was. The watchdogs had already solved the problem. Only a fool would come back.

"I'll do what I can," José Antonio said.

"That's what I want to hear." Smith's smile came easy, but José Antonio sensed its falseness. He half expected a hearty slap on the back and he was prepared to flinch.

He sat a moment, waiting to see if there was more. Finally he rose. "I'd best be going, Señor Smith."

"Thank you for coming, Don José."

# 21

José Antonio pointed his old horse toward Los Griegos and urged him on. After trying to turn around and head for home, the horse shook his gray mane and moved forward. José Antonio let him amble at his own pace along dusty San Ysidro Road, named for the patron saint of farmers.

The slow rhythm of the horse and the warm sun lulled José Antonio. His irritation at Smith's request faded and he mused on the Spanish saint, the native of Seville, for whom this dusty road was named. Every year they celebrated San Ysidro's Day in a time-honored ceremony. The parish priest blessed the acequias, the irrigation ditches, that brought the lifeblood of the fields from the river. Then their season of work began with the communal clearing and repairing of the ditches under the direction of the mayordomo of the acequias.

Well, good San Ysidro — Saint Isidore as our Anglo neighbors would say — bless these lands and grant us God's grace, which for a farmer takes its shape in green splendor reaching out from under the ground toward heaven.

The old horse stopped in the middle of the road to drop a load and José Antonio smiled. Bless our animal friends too, he thought, for their less than heavenly droppings that encourage our plants to grow.

Up ahead the road rose straight north over a main irrigation tributary, then continued until it dead-ended at Los Griegos Road. Just behind, San Ysidro Road started its short journey where it dead-ended at Rafas Road. A saint hemmed in by two farmers.

"All right," he said, "now that you've fertilized the ground it's time to move on."

The old man smiled with a sense of well-being. Whenever he was burdened by too much of humans and their petty irritations, he had but to go outdoors for awhile and all was peace again. Animals did not worry about stealing tobacco. Wasn't there enough for all? Plants did not argue over which one was going to be picked and eaten first. It was all the same to them.

Somehow these lesser creatures had more of God-sense than the bickering humans who — made in the image and likeness of the Almighty, or so they thought — acted more like warring devils. No, God could not be a superhuman. Not from all that José Antonio had seen on earth. If anything, God was a super chili or a magnificent horse or even a giant, bearded billy goat. Anything but a petty human.

He inhaled deeply, savoring the faint, sharp aroma of growing chilis. Then a strange thought struck him. He had breathed in the essence of those growing plants and that essence had gone into his body and become part of him. So that as he moved along the road whatever he inhaled would become part of him: the aromas of beans, corn, tomatoes, cottonwood . . . and in the mountains, piñón.

In the same way, every breath he exhaled joined these other essences which were in turn inhaled by others. This old horse over the years must contain a great quantity of José Antonio. The same for the plants in the fields and the people who ate them, as well as the birds in the air and the beasts.

We all partake of each other. All, in a sense, are one another. The amazing thought made him laugh in astonishment. A farmer working in an adjacent field looked up, his eyes narrowing. José Antonio could see, in his imagination, the farmer raise a forefinger to his temple and rotate it slowly.

"Buenos días, Don José."

José Antonio waved, still smiling, unable to keep his astonished joy from bursting forth.

\*   \*   \*

The few horses were grouped around the giant cottonwood, swishing their tails at flies. Those who lived close by would have walked.

A dark face peeked out of the half open door and nodded abruptly, "Everyone is here, Don José." Griego's voice was hurried, his forehead wrinkled over solemn eyes.

Normally, Cipriano Griego was the most affable of men, his tooth-gapped mouth beaming at everyone. José Antonio almost asked what was wrong, but as he entered the house, he saw Armando Chávez with an unnatural glumness; then as his eyes swept the crowded room, he understood.

"Greetings, Don José." Eyes focused on the giant who seemed to fill half the room by himself.

"Señor Durán." José Antonio looked around the room but only saw this hulk of a Benito. "I'm disappointed that Don Plácido is not here."

Benito guffawed. "He has more important things to do. The Anglo big shots in New Town wanted to see him."

The others exchanged glances, but no one spoke. Neither Plácido nor Benito had been invited, so it was not a snub by the candidate but an intrusion by his brother. As long as Benito was here, much of what they planned to discuss would go unsaid.

"What brings you here?" José Antonio asked.

"I have to watch out for my brother's business." Benito looked around the room at the glum faces that failed to return his smile.

"Señor Durán is conducting a little investigation," Cipriano Griego said. He pronounced "Señor Durán" with an exaggerated politeness that gave a twist of irony to it. "About the threat to Plácido Durán."

"Los Hijos de Libertad," Durán said. He looked down at his dirty, worn boots, then glared at José Antonio, his eyes narrow and hostile, his mouth tight and strained. "The sons of bitches threatened to kill my brother, the sheriff." He looked from face to face, as if each man was somehow responsible. Or as if to dare them to disagree with calling his brother the "sheriff" when he was only a candidate and not the favorite either.

"I can't stand that shit!" Durán said. "When they threaten my brother, they threaten me. And I don't take threats."

José Antonio sat on the empty chair, the good chair, that had been reserved for him. He knew that after a few more grumblings, Durán would shut up. What amazed him was the Durán should be investigating here. These men were all loyal party members. Not men given to violence. Hardworking men of the soil, who might not be above dominating their families, but certainly not prone to bullying their neighbors.

"I want to see the horses!" Durán snapped. "Don José is here now. I demand to see the horses!"

"We've been waiting for you," Cipriano said to José Antonio.

José Antonio smiled at Durán. "If you make me a good offer, I might sell you my old nag."

Durán's face reddened. "This is no joke, Don José."

"You think my old horse had something to do with your brother's midnight visitors? Tell me. Who would have ridden that broken down old nag?"

"Certainly not you, Don José."

"Perhaps one of these other men?" Durán did not answer. "If I were committing a crime and wanted to escape, that's the last horse I'd choose. Better my pursuer was on him; he'd never catch me. But— You're welcome to inspect him. Ride him if you want. Only not too far. You're a big man, Benito, and my horse has a weak back."

A few of the men smiled. Benito stood and stomped from the house, muttering under his breath.

"Stupid bastard," Armando Chávez said. *"My brother has more important things to do,"* he added, mimicking Durán's speech.

Cipriano peered out the half open door. "He's looking at the horses' hooves."

"If I were the candidate for the other party," Armando said, "I'd send Benito out to visit all the people he could. He loses votes every time he opens his mouth. Jesus!"

José Antonio sighed. He was here with the key men of Los Griegos to discuss how to hold on to their own votes. He looked around the room and wondered which ones might defect. Possibly Armando Chávez. But then— No. Trying to guess what other people would do was madness.

He turned toward Griego. "I'm going out to talk to him, Cipriano. I don't want him coming back into our meeting."

José Antonio left the house, feeling an invisible wall close behind his back. It would have been difficult enough to persuade these men to hold fast under the best of circumstances, but now . . .

"Benito!" he called. Benito dropped a horse's leg and looked up at him.

\* \* \*

Even the ride back down San Ysidro Road did not calm him. José Antonio patted his horse as he rode along, muttering to himself. The horse had turned left at Rafas Road and picked up speed. "Almost home," José Antonio said, patting the horse again.

As he approached a shout greeted him. "Grandfather!"

Leonardo waved at him from across the field. José Antonio waved back. When he had been that age, he and his twin brother — God rest his soul — would wrestle in the dirt when their father was not watching them. Then there had been servants to do the heavy work in the fields and boys had time to play. How times had changed. When you no longer can afford servants, you become your own servant.

Francisco looked up and shouted at José Antonio. "Consuela's here!"

What was wrong now? They only saw their eldest daughter when there was some tragedy to relate. He could see her now, sitting in the kitchen, her long face with drooping mouth hissing out the latest gossip.

There but for the grace of God go you! she seemed to imply. But me? I lead the good life. Church every Sunday — and here her eyes would shift toward her brother, Francisco. Obey my husband — and she had the audacity to glare at her own mother. And speak lovingly to God, not as to an earthly acquaintance but as to the Almighty. This last was always for her father.

"Oh, Christ," José Antonio would say to Gregoria. "How did we give birth to that woman? She's from another world."

"She only wants us to know she's good because she loves and respects us."

Silence would show more love and respect, José Antonio thought. And a tender smile for that beaten dog of a husband of hers. When a woman rules the house, the devil hides under the bed.

As he approached, the excited laughter of the youngest of his two granddaughters, Consuela's children, greeted him.

"Mamá got a letter," the younger squealed.

"Hello, Grandpa." The older girl's solemn face resembled her mother's.

He dismounted and tied up the horse. "Hello, hijitas. Come kiss your old grandpa."

Hand in hand they walked to the house, his younger granddaughter chattering happily. "Out!" Consuela shouted when she saw the girls. They let go of his hand and retreated.

"There's a letter from José Blas," Gregoria said.

"You can't guess what she's up to," Consuela said. "But then, knowing Blas, you might." Consuela nodded at him as if she knew great secrets. "A woman," she said, her lips pursed. "Can you imagine?"

"He's twenty-seven," Gregoria said. "It's about time he got married."

"He's in the army," José Antonio said. "What time does he have for a woman?"

"You know how it is in California." Consuela nodded as if everyone knew. "And the army," she added. "There are always those women. Either following them around or working in the cantinas."

"Blas said her father is a rancher." Gregoria handed the letter to José Antonio.

He read it thoughtfully. This was from their youngest son, the quiet one whom Mamá loved best. The one that José Antonio felt most at ease with. Who would have ever thought he would become a soldier?

The letter was terse like Blas' speech. He was fine. Gaining weight on army food. He had the second finest horse in his troop. Of their sons, only Blas would have said second finest. His brothers would have loudly claimed the best. The magnificent. And if you did not agree, they would likely have fought you about it. But when Blas said second finest, José Antonio was certain that it was true.

Blas had met a young woman. At church. Where else? Her father was a rancher and had invited him to help break horses. It was a lovely family.

José Antonio raised his eyes from the letter for a quick glance at his daughter. There was no mention of marriage nor of any relationship at all. Blas ended the letter with the news that his troop might be transferred soon. Where, he did not know.

Gregoria looked at José Antonio with anxious eyes. It irritated him, though he had never told her so in all the years they had been married. Are you going to quarrel with her? Gregoria's look seemed to ask. Are you going to be angry?

But he was more apt to be angry at Gregoria's concern than at his daughter. He had long ago given up being angry at Consuela. It served no purpose. She was the way she was. If anything would have changed her, certainly Gregoria's and his attempts over the years would have helped. She had skipped back a generation and taken after an aunt of Gregoria's. Nature and temperament reincarnate, fixed and constant since babyhood.

"It seems that she is a gentle young woman," he said. "If he is to be transferred, nothing much will come of it."

"Well, now," Consuela said, "I don't see —"

The kitchen door slammed. Leonardo rushed in, breathing heavily, wet with perspiration. "I came for the dipper. Papá wants a drink."

Consuela turned toward him, her eyes brightening, her voice coy and teasing. "Well. Who is this handsome young man? Let me see you, honey. My God, how you've grown." Leonardo's red face deepened in color and he looked down at his bare feet. "You'll be ready to get married soon," she said. "Do you have a sweetheart?"

"No, Aunty."

Meanwhile, José Antonio had removed the broken knife from his pocket and laid it on the table. "Look at him," Consuela said. "Look at him. How handsome. He's my favorite nephew. But don't you dare tell my sister."

Leonardo averted his aunt's gaze. As he turned to leave, he glanced at the table and gave a startled gasp. "Where did you find Ernesto's knife?"

José Antonio quietly picked it up and motioned to Leonardo. "Let's go outside," he said, "so we can talk."


# 22


Francisco sat in the shade of a tree wiping his face with a worn and stained old handkerchief. He could have gone into the house for a rest, but Florinda was in a vicious mood. At his parents' house his sister Consuela was no doubt carrying on as she usually did.

Here in the orchard the quiet lay gently under a hum of insects that was so low it could have been the buzzing in one's own ears. After a few minutes his son and father came out from the kitchen of the big house and stood by the woodpile talking softly and looking over their shoulders. Then, just as quietly they separated. Leonardo walked toward the orchard with the dipper while José Antonio watched.

"Don't spill it!" Francisco warned when Leonardo started to hurry. By the time he arrived, José Antonio had re-entered the house.

"What does your aunt have to say?" Francisco asked.

"Nothing, Papá."

"She takes a long time saying it."

"She has a letter from Uncle Blas."

"Borrowing money again I bet." He handed the empty dipper to Leonardo. "Just put it on the stump by the woodpile. If you go inside, they'll jabber your ears off and we won't get done." Francisco stood and wiped his brow before donning his hat. "Let's go."

He turned to his work mindlessly, wielding the hoe without a thought. A machine that sweats. Indifferent to the sun. Thinking of nothing except what must be done. Endlessly. Each slash of the hoe ruthless and efficient as he made his way across the field. Indifferent even to his son, who tried his best to keep pace.

After the day's work and before it was time for their dinner of frijoles and chili and tortillas, Francisco sat quietly in the fading sun smoking a homemade cigarette, softly blowing smoke in the air. Only now did thoughts other than of this field intrude themselves.

Saturday, he thought. The dance. The big fiesta for that incompetent Plácido Durán. Music. Food. Lots to drink. The first rally to make sure the voters turn out on election day.

Before then he would have to visit old man Smith. It was time to arrange for the fund to buy votes. Free food and drink at the rally were only part of it: the down payment. The real price came at election time and it would require a bigger fund than usual.

Plácido Durán, he thought as he spat into the dirt. The stupid bastard was more intent than ever on running. The midnight riders had only hardened his resolve and stirred up the hostile suspicion of his brother Benito.

Well. Benito was too dumb to find out anything about Los Hijos de Libertad. But then that midnight ride could not be repeated. Durán and his people were on the alert. And that stubborn Plácido kept on campaigning. It figured. Anyone who was stupid enough to think he could win would be stupid enough to ignore a threat.

But, he thought with chagrin, the next move was up to Los Hijos de Libertad. He did not see a next move that had a chance of succeeding. Unless they shot the stupid bastard. But electing a sheriff wasn't worth a killing. Honor might be. Or protecting one's family. But not an election.

The thought of the bluff that failed settled like a hot lump in his gut. He could feel the burning radiate until he was flushed with frustration and anger. But he was tired from his day's work. All he had the strength to do was sit and let his anger dissipate.

Anyway there's Saturday, he thought. At least I can get good and drunk on Durán's whiskey.

\* \* \*

Francisco could hear the watchdogs still barking outside. He lounged comfortably in one of Smith's new chairs, surveying the living room with more pleasure than envy. This was the way to live. Store-bought things from some fancy place back east. With nice pictures on the wall in place of those wretched, homemade santos that one saw in every little adobe shack along the Río Grande. And good whiskey, he thought, hearing the tinkle of glasses.

"Well, Francisco?" Smith lifted the bottle and winked at him.

Francisco held a thumb and forefinger close together. "To rinse out the dust from the road." His voice was polite, almost obsequious, as if asking for a small favor while hoping for a large one. Smith smiled and poured a good portion into a tumbler.

"To our new sheriff," Smith toasted.

The forced smile was automatic, but the first swallow of whiskey dispelled whatever sense of hypocrisy Francisco felt. "To the new sheriff," he echoed.

This is the way, Francisco thought. These rich Anglos really know how to live. Soft chairs. Good whiskey. Vicious dogs to keep out the riffraff. And the women in the kitchen where they belong.

Occasionally one of them would sigh after a particularly satisfying sip. Minutes passed before they began to talk.

"You know, Francisco. I mean no disrespect. But I wish your father was as easy a man to talk to and work with as you are." Francisco looked up warily.

"You Rafas have known me ever since I settled here right after the War between the States. Almost twenty-five years now. You were just a small boy then. I remember. Hardworking and ambitious.

"We've been neighbors all those years. Your father even sold me part of the land that I own. You and your brothers helped work my fields. We've been on the same side politically from the very beginning." Francisco nodded. "Yet in all those years I've never dealt with Don José on this matter that you and I have to settle today."

"True." Yet, Francisco thought, even you, Señor Smith, cannot quite bring yourself to say "buying votes." It is always something like "helping the poor" or "rewarding our friends."

Smith shook his head. "I've never understood. Surely Don José must know?"

"He prefers not to know. Deep in his heart he believes that it really doesn't happen. That all his friends and neighbors and relatives turn out and vote for us because it is the right thing to do, not because someone is pouring whiskey in the cantina or handing out silver dollars when they come out of the voting booth."

"Yet he knows!"

"He believes in heaven though he has never seen it. Yet he has seen men come out of the voting place with palm extended and a silver dollar in it, but he chooses not to believe what he sees."

"Strange. It's as if he doesn't believe in the power of money. Yet he's a man of power and influence. I don't understand."

Francisco had never really thought about this before. He had always looked at power in the way that Smith did. Money. Political position. Even physical force when you could get away with it. But then there was the contradiction that was his father.

"My father's power does not come from money; therefore he ignores the power of cash. His power is a relic of the old days. He was a priest at one time, you know. Until he left the clergy to become a farmer and raise a family. In the old days, before we became Americans, the priests had great power — more than the government — because all were convinced that their power derived from the ultimate source."

Francisco raised a forefinger toward the ceiling. It was hard for him to hide a slight trace of contempt in his voice. Ghosts, it seemed to imply. Boogey men. Witches. Nonsense. Yet the contempt was tempered by respect for his father, whom he did not quite understand.

"But it's more than that," Francisco said. "He is a very intelligent man, a leader by inheritance. They named this area for our family. Until you came, Don José was the largest landowner in Los Rafas. He was the patrón. The boss.

"His power derives from three things. His aura as a man of the church. His intelligence. His former wealth. Among many of our people these things are more powerful than money. In addition, of course, he is an old man. We still respect age and the wisdom that goes with it."

"His influence is a very personal and individual thing," Smith said. "When he is gone, his influence will be gone." Francisco understood. Don José's power could not be passed from one generation to the next. He, Francisco, would not inherit his father's influence and he should not expect to.

"But money," Smith continued. "Or land. Now these things last even after all that remains of a man are his bones in the ground. You can pass these things on to the right people, to the people of your own choosing. That way you know that the right things will be done even after you're gone."

How true those words were. Their truth illumined the dark corners of Francisco's mind where lurked the dread that he would never have money or land. That he was on this earth but once and it really didn't matter much. His father would not have much to leave him and Francisco would have even less to leave his sons. The truth of Smith's words depressed him.

"America is still the land of opportunity," Smith said. "There is no reason that we should be bound by what our fathers were and what our fathers had. Change is inevitable. One must change or be left behind. Like the dinosaurs. Opportunity? One must seize it by the throat and give it a rattling good shake until its teeth chatter and it hands over its purse."

"To make money one needs money."

"Not always. Sometimes one just needs to know something a little before the crowd knows it."

What did all this have to do with buying votes to win an election? Francisco thought. What did it have to do with him?

"Even so," Francisco said, "it would still involve some risk."

"Naturally. But to borrow for a sure thing is an investment. At least for the insiders."

Francisco became suspicious. Unlike some of his neighbors, he had never had to borrow money to make ends meet. He had always managed to take care of his needs. To even have a little left over. How many unlucky paisanos had borrowed money because of a poor crop? Or when someone in the family became sick? Or after they had lost at cards when they could not afford to lose? And how many of these had gone with hat in hand and a penitent expression on their faces to Señor Smith, then rued that foolish day after they lost house, corral, and fields for failure to repay their loan? Was that what was happening? Francisco thought. Was Smith trying to press a loan on him in hope of adding more land to his holdings?

Smith's eyes gleamed as he leaned forward in his chair. "A man could get rich," he said. "All we need is to win this election."

Francisco was tempted to laugh. What foolishness. The most the sheriff ever did was arrest a few drunks and break up an occasional barroom brawl. There was no fortune in that.

"You don't believe me?" Smith said. "There is money yet to be made in New Mexico. Land waiting to be developed. Fortunes ripe for plucking. With our own sheriff we could straighten out a few legalities and get some of this choice land. We could buy it for ten cents on the dollar, then turn around and sell it for twenty, thirty, fifty times that. If our man were sheriff. I can say no more than that."

Yes, but why me? Francisco thought. He could see this opportunity being shared with the Anglo big shots in New Town. The land developers and the railroad men would know what to do with a new, large parcel of land. He did not have money to contribute to such a coup. It was not his land that was in the way of any such development; his farmland was too distant from town, and progress was moving in the other direction.

"But we need to win the election," Smith said.

He has more faith than I do, Francisco thought. But the urgency with which Smith spoke, his intensity, told Francisco what it was that he must do in order to share in this coup.

"We always deliver the vote in Los Rafas, Los Griegos, and Los Chávez. There is no reason to think it will not be the same again."

"That's what I want to hear." Smith slapped him on the shoulder. "I have heard much talk about Durán," Smith said. "That la raza would not vote for him. That there are better candidates. But there are factions in other areas that are solidly behind him. Of all the candidates that we might have chosen, he is the one who can make this land development thing work without causing an open scandal. I'm glad that you can deliver."

"But it will cost money," Francisco said. "More than usual."

Now finally, after their quiet drink and their talk of fortunes to be made, they arrived at the heart of the matter. How much for how many votes? Smith poured another drink, a business-like, small one this time, while they talked about how to get the votes they needed.

# 23

Election campaigns were just one of many excuses for having a party. Although these usually took the form of daytime speechifying in some convenient open field like the fairgrounds, with something to wet the whistles of the listeners as much as of the talkers, party leaders agreed that something special needed to be done to bolster Plácido Durán's candidacy. Although only men were eligible to vote, the swelling tide of sentiment for women's suffrage showed the influence that non-voting wives had on their voting husbands. So it was to be a family affair. All the more appropriate for the family-oriented, predominantly Spanish-speaking citizenry.

What better way to encourage good will than with a baile, that is, a dance, with lively music and a flow of refreshments, both liquid and solid? And what better place to have it than in Old Town?

They came from the little farms for miles around. Entire families rode unpainted wooden wagons drawn by tired, underfed old horses. Young men in their finest clothes rode the one good horse that the family owned. Others came on foot, walking slowly but cheerfully on dusty dirt roads. Greeting old friends and distant cousins as they walked along. Looking forward to a quiet rest before the dance in the adobe-cool church of San Felipe that was on the plaza across from the hall.

"Hi, cousin. Going to the baile?"

"I hear they invited that old fiddler from Alameda. You know? The one with the wife who has one arm and sings dirty songs."

"Durán really wants to get elected, doesn't he? The best fiddler for miles around. Enough drink to get half the town drunk."

So they came. Cheerfully. Not only looking forward to the festivities, but looking forward with almost as much eagerness to the oratory. Speeches, especially important speeches from important people, were public spectacles that were often as enjoyable as fiestas. Since the written word, the printed word, was not a deeply ingrained local tradition — only the more affluent could read and write — the spoken word assumed a more prominent place in their daily lives.

After all, wasn't it more human, more friendly, more fun to exchange news, gossip, history on a personal level? Much better to deal person to person than to sit alone in a room with a lamp or candle, a newspaper or book, like those crazy Anglos. As for politics, one had to see and hear the candidates rather than just read the lies someone had written for or about them in a newspaper. Otherwise how could one take the measure of a man?

\*　　\*　　\*

When Francisco and Florinda arrived, the fiddler had already tuned his instrument and struck up the music. The two guitar players who accompanied him were sweating and smiling from their first efforts.

The dancers moved from the floor as the musicians laid down their instruments to take a break.

"We already missed some of the dancing," Florinda complained.

"Whose fault is that? You didn't have to change your dress at the last minute." But she was looking around the hall searching for one of her sisters he was certain. She hadn't even heard, damn her. She could complain well enough about others, but she never listened when it came to herself.

Her eyes lit up and he knew that she would leave in a moment to go gossip with one of her sisters. So much the better. He had his own business to take care of. Across the hall he saw his father in the center of a group of family patriarchs talking seriously, intently, as his listeners nodded. Don José was using his powers of persuasion on the important old men who swung the vote in the rural area.

"I have to go see Beatriz, Francisco."

"Don't you want to dance?" She shook her head and threaded her way across the crowded hall. Well, he had offered. She had had her chance.

Francisco continued to survey the crowd, weighing Durán's chances by who was or wasn't present. Although the old men with Don José represented all the important families, few of their sons and grandsons were here. A bad sign.

He saw Señor Smith by the speaker's platform with two well-dressed Anglos who smiled and nodded at the passersby. Mr. Railroad and Mr. Land Developer, Francisco noted. But where were Mr. Lawyer and Mr. Merchant? Together these represented the power in the town. Maybe that was as much as they thought of this gathering, a two big-shot rally. The four big-shot rally was for other offices or other parts of the county.

Smith beckoned as Francisco walked toward the platform. Introductions all around. More Anglo smiles.

"We'll want to have the speech before too long," Smith said. "Before they drink too much and can't hear." Plácido Durán worked his way through the crowd toward them, smiling and waving. "The candidate is ready," Smith continued. Durán was among them now, nodding. "But where is the priest? He is supposed to give the invocation."

"Nobody told you?" A shake of the head. "The priest isn't coming," Francisco said. The smiles on the Anglo faces froze. "It's these damned foreign priests they keep bringing here. They can't abide the dancing. Sinful they say. And all but the Irish priests think the drinking is worse. If we had made a donation to the church, the padre might have come in spite of the drinking and dancing."

"Damned stupid mistake," Smith said.

"God is on our side, anyway," Plácido said.

Jesus Christ! Francisco thought. "Our priests are erratic," Francisco said. "If it pleases them, they come. If it doesn't please them, they stay away."

"Well, damn it. We have to open the meeting with a prayer." Smith looked around the hall in frustration. "You can talk all you want about separation of church and state, but if the priest doesn't give us his blessing, some of these people might not vote for us."

"What about Don José?" Plácido asked.

The men from downtown looked at each other, then Smith turned to Francisco. "I can ask him," Francisco said. "But I can't promise. You know how he is."

Smith turned toward another man and quietly told him to hold the crowd's attention for a few more minutes until they could start the program.

"¡Señora Corrido!" someone shouted.

"The fiddler and his wife!" another echoed.

As Francisco walked toward his father, he saw the fiddler and his wife, who had a shawl over her shoulders and around her arm-and-a-half, smile and head for the platform. Behind them he saw Benito Durán watching the proceedings as if the enemy were everywhere and only his constant vigilance would protect his brother.

*       *       *

As the fiddler tuned his instrument, his wife wobbled from spot to spot, testing each to find the right one at the front of the platform. She turned around at each place, circling cautiously, pressing a foot as if to test its support, then looked with a blank stare out over the hall.

José Antonio arched his brows; he knew the sign. She had been drinking too much. And he was supposed to lead a prayer after a song or two. God forbid. When Señora Corrido was drunk, she would more likely sing obscenities than not. It was if he had been asked to lead the rosary in a brothel.

"¡Señora Corrido!" several in the crowd shouted, applauding in anticipation.

The señora was one of those rare singers, sharp-tongued and witty, who made up verses as she sang, inspired by the sight of someone on the dance floor. With that gift, José Antonio thought, she should have been a priest, haranguing her congregation to abandon sin and increase their donations.

He glanced toward Francisco, who had rejoined the políticos from downtown. It was not that he objected to praying in public. It was not even the surroundings. What places needed prayer more than dance halls and barrooms? It was really the hypocrisy of the occasion. Praying to God so our candidate would win. As if God cared. Or could be cajoled or bribed by prayer.

José Antonio turned back to the patriarchs with whom he had been talking. The fiddle struck up a lively tune. There was shuffling on the floor as couples began to dance. Señora Corrido stood bolt upright, her wobble suddenly gone, as a few in the crowd applauded. Then her voice rang through the hall, clear, sassy, insinuating.

> "With public beads and pious face
> There goes old Widow What's-Her-Name.
> The men that visit at her place
> All revel in her private shame."

Snickers rippled through the crowd and a few curious eyes looked around for the target of Señora Corrido's verse.

> "The old señor with trembling hand
> Sits next to you at early Mass.
> But one thing you must understand:
> Watch out or he will pinch your . . ."

The roar started before she finished the verse. The old señor was not in the hall, but several of his victims were and many knew about him.

> "They say she gives her husband horns.
> She sneaks out here and there to play.
> While in the field he gathers corn,
> She's in the bedroom making hay."

Hoots from the audience. José Antonio turned to his companions and shrugged. What could you do about Señora Corrido? Besides, the audience loved it.

> "It takes more than a flashy coat,

> A Stetson hat, and gringo's gun.
> You first must have the public vote
> To wear the badge, see justice done."

Now she's done it, José Antonio thought. But there was little reaction from the crowd. It was as if political ambition could not compare to earthier subjects for the verse of a song, although the crowd around Benito Durán suddenly drifted away, leaving him conspicuously alone at one end of the hall.

José Antonio excused himself and pushed his way to the platform. It was time for the invocation. Too late actually. But it was time to stop the singing before it got any worse.

*     *     *

The crowd gathered around the platform. The words of invocation had faded and the last bowed head had raised. Señor Smith introduced the big shots from downtown, each of whom fumbled through a few words of butchered Spanish before Plácido Durán was introduced.

Plácido smiled and waved at the applauding crowd. He graciously acknowledged the honored guests who had come from New Town to this historic plaza that for almost two hundred years had been the center for the Hispanic peoples of Albuquerque.

"Raza de Nuevo Méjico," he shouted. "Friends. Brothers. Cousins. People of the Spanish race. Are you having a good time?"

The crowd cheered.

"Has the other political party ever done such a thing for you?"

"No!"

His smile beamed at them. "Raza! There is only one true party like there is only one true God. That is our party. The party of the people from which all good comes."

Cheers. Applause. A shout from someone hidden in the crowd. "How much are they paying for votes this year, Plácido?" A ripple of laughter.

"It's time," Plácido went on, "for us to have a new sheriff. A man of the people. A man who speaks for and to la raza. Who can get things done downtown and take care of his own.

"Not a man who serves only the special interests in this county. But a man who serves all of you. Not a man who toadies to the Anglo minority, the Johnny-come-latelies, the newcomers, but a man who is rooted in the great tradition of this great country. A man who calls you brother. Who has plowed the fields with you. Waded in the mud of your ditches. Bent his back over your hoes. Eaten frijoles a mano with you. A man who understands and knows your needs."

Francisco drifted slowly toward the edge of the crowd. He was not interested in Durán's speech. He had heard it before. Many times. Given by many different speakers. In jesting moments he and his cronies referred to it as "The Speech." Covering, in one glorious oration, God, country, the Territory of New Mexico, la raza, and the common good. "Vote for us," The Speech went, "we will give you more." Francisco knew that he could recite it in his sleep. Yet from the mouths of some it inspired him to belief. While from others, like Durán, it only fed his cynicism.

He strolled to the bar, helped himself to a drink, then breathed deeply of the cool night air that flowed through the adjacent open door. He heard scuffling and a muttered curse from outside, but it barely registered. The usual stuff. Then a woman's scream pierced through his indifference.

"¡Demonio! ¡Cabrón!"

Curious, Francisco peered out the door into the dark plaza. Probably some drunk and his wife having an argument.

"You shouldn't have sung that about my brother!" the great hulk of a man snarled. "It's disrespectful!"

"Oh, come on," the smaller man said. "We were only having a little fun. No harm meant."

"You son of a bitch," the woman screeched, "picking on a crippled woman! You're the kind who would use your own mother!"

"Shut her up!" the big man warned. "Keep that wife of yours under control, or I'll do it for you."

The bartender rushed past Francisco into the dark. A few others followed. Francisco glanced to see who had gone past, then glanced outdoors at Benito Durán and the Corridos. The blow had already been struck. Benito held the broken fiddle in his huge hands.

"Bastard!" the woman screamed. She threw herself at him, clawing at his face with the fingernails of one hand and beating at him with the stump of the other.

"My fiddle!" Señor Corrido cried. "You . . . you . . . name of a name! Fiddle-killer! Unspeakable low-life!"

Francisco set his drink on the bar and rushed out. "Stop it, you fool!" he shouted at Benito.

The big man hesitated, his ham-hand raised to strike the señora, when Francisco grabbed his arm. Meanwhile the fiddler had picked up the neck of his broken instrument from the ground and rushed at Durán, swinging it at his head.

"Grab him," Francisco grunted to one of the others. Then to Benito, "You damned fool. You can lose more votes for your brother with this brawl than he can gain inside with a dozen speeches."

The taut arm, thick like a tree limb, relaxed, and Benito turned to Francisco, ignoring the Corridos, who were dragged off cursing. Benito stared at Francisco. "I won't forget this," he muttered. But Francisco did not know what he meant.

# 24

Leonardo had been in a deep, dreamless sleep. Then, in the very next instant, it seemed that he was immediately awake, his eyes peering into the dark. He focused on the ominous silence that was but a pause before something else — he knew not what.

His little brother Carlos lay on the pallet beside him, his legs crosswise, heavy and motionless, crowding Leonardo. The smaller boy twitched with an abrupt snort, then it was silent again.

Not too long ago it seemed — or had Leonardo dreamed it? — his mamá and papá had stumbled in with whispered laughter. Then there had been the sighs and moans and body shiftings in the next room that told him they were doing it again. That nasty thing. But it did not stop them from doing it anyway.

Leonardo remembered his mother's hysteria one cold winter morning when his little sisters had crawled into the boys' pallet, huddling between them to get warm. "Nasty!" their mother had screamed at them. But there had been nothing nasty about it. They had done nothing. Certainly not what the horses did to each other in the fields. Or the dogs out in the dirt. In fact it had been nice, all of them huddled warm and cozy, while the layer of gray snow lay on the ground outside.

But now — silence. From his little sisters on the other pallet in the corner. From the next room where his parents lay asleep. Even from outside. Until the something else came from out there. Low like a warning growl deep in the throat of some wild beast. Growing in intensity until it broke into the wild howl of a coyote that seemed to last forever.

The hair stood up on the back of Leonardo's neck and he wrapped his arms around his chest and shivered. Then silence again. More frightening now that he knew that something really was out there. Wondering if it would come closer next time — closer and closer until the moist breath wet his face and the suffocating smell of putrid meat overwhelmed his nostrils.

When it seemed that he could not bear the silence another second, the deep-throated growl started again, and he did not know what was worse, the silence or the animal howl.

His littlest sister, Juanita, cried out in her sleep. Carlos groaned and rolled on his side, grasping Leonardo's arm. By the time the animal cry was at full power, there was a low curse from the other room and he heard his father walk barefoot through the bedroom to the door.

"Goddamn it! The loony is at it again. It must be full moon."

Then Leonardo remembered Pedro Baca locked in the storeroom. He was not irritated for once. His curiosity about Don Pedro had been slowly growing and he saw the old man in a different light. What would make a man behave like an animal? Especially an old man, old as his grandfather. What was it that could so overpower a man that he lost his reason?

He lay quietly, hearing his father return from the shed while the howl degenerated to a low whimper. Yet, Leonardo thought, through all of old Pedro's animal craziness, there was something human that responded to his father's scolding. He would have to ask his grandfather. Try to find out what it was that drove a man to lunacy.

\* \* \*

"Sometimes," his grandfather said, "there is too much to bear. So one has to hide until it is over. For some that hiding place is in their mind. It's like when the Río Grande floods. The water can no longer be contained. It overruns its banks and flows every which way, apparently without reason. Except that water has its own reason, which is to flow downhill. So it must be with the mind."

Leonardo and his grandfather sat in the cool of evening under a

tree in back of the big house. The boy listened with a puzzled look
on his face.

"Are you sure," José Antonio said, "that you want to hear the rest
of the story?"

"Sí, señor. I want to understand."

José Antonio settled against the tree trunk and placed a gnarled
farmer's hand on his grandson's knee. "Where were we?"

"The wagon train from Ohio had come through and the old Don
had died."

\*　\*　\*

That wagon train was just the beginning of the great invasion. An
invasion not by armies with rifles and cannon and a thirst for blood
and victory, but a non-military army armed with hunger and energy
and greed for land. Like the Biblical locusts, they overwhelmed
everything in their path, not realizing that there were people who had
lived there first. In a way it was a retribution. What the Spanish had
taken from the Indians, the Yankees took from their Spanish-Indian
descendants.

Then, less than a year after the old Don had died, gold was
discovered in Northern California. The horde of locusts multiplied ten-
fold. The invasion became an inundation. Not just of farmers hungry
for land, but of all manner of rapacious and desperate characters.

At Rancho Los Palos they would see them heading north toward
San Francisco, from where they would turn east toward the big strikes
being made in the Sierras. But gold fever did not infect the Bacas,
although a few of their workmen succumbed. Debt was their disease.
Their one-year loan would be due soon and the rancho was still not
producing as Pedro had expected.

One day Don Pedro rode to consult his brothers about the state of
affairs. He set out first for the southeast range to talk to José Ignacio
who, since Manuel's murder, oversaw the entire range with the help
of a hired foreman.

"It doesn't look good," Pedro said, as they sat on horseback side by
side, looking across their dwindling herd toward the mountains.

"Surely they will extend the loan."

"Why should they?"

"Archer is a friend. He has been very attentive to Mamá."

"For a Yankee a loan is business. There is nothing personal in it. We pay or the lenders foreclose."

José Ignacio shook his head solemnly. "But we are friends," he insisted.

"There won't be much profit from the herd," Pedro said.

"I can't believe that he would not help us. I'll ask the señora to plead our case. Surely he will listen to her."

"Perhaps we could find gold on our own land. But no such luck. The gold country is north and east of here, drawing Yankees like fresh meat draws hungry jackals. Good riddance. Let them go. There will be fewer to plague us here."

"I'll talk to Mamá," José Ignacio said. "There must be a way."

Pedro urged his horse toward the herd for a closer look. Not many, he thought. Not fat. And not a very good market.

He forced himself to stay awhile, resisting his impatience to be off to his other brother, Rudolfo. Finally he waved adiós and rode toward the fields near the main casa.

Rudolfo, the youngest of the brothers, sat morosely under a peach tree at the edge of the orchard. Pedro dismounted and walked toward him. He lowered himself to the ground beside Rudolfo, who acknowledged him with a nod. Then he sat quietly, waiting until his brother was ready to talk, watching the bees buzz from one tree to the next.

At last Rudolfo said, "We'll never make it. Now my foreman, Juan, has left. There is more money in gold than there is in farming."

"He went prospecting?"

"He hired out to teach some gringos. They'll pay him whether they find gold or not. If they make a strike, he'll get a share."

"He has this in writing?"

"No."

"Fool! Once they have learned all he has to teach, what's to prevent them from dumping him down some mountain?"

"Nothing. Meanwhile—" Rudolfo's hand swept an arc toward the fields. "There is too much to do. It will rot in the sun for want of harvesting."

At least, Pedro thought, we will not starve to death. But how much they could sell depended upon how much they could pick. Sometimes nature was too generous while man was not generous enough.

"Our loan is due in less than three months."

"I've been thinking of that," Rudolfo said. "Everything has turned against us. We will lose it all." Again his hand described a loose arc that included the fields, the complex of buildings, the main casa, and further beyond the range.

His youngest brother's lack of spirit irritated Pedro. It reminded him in its exaggerated way of his own worst moments. Yet he knew it would do no good to try to cheer him up. That would only make Rudolfo all the more depressed. In temperament and spirit he was like their father, old Don Pedro, while José Ignacio had the sometimes naive and ever hopeful outlook of their mother, Doña Beatriz.

"We'll do the best we can." Don Pedro rose and brushed the dust from the seat of his trousers. "We'll find a way. The fruits of our labor are here. All we need are a few more hands to harvest and sell it."

Mute, unbelieving eyes watched as he mounted his horse and headed back to the main casa. Pedro kept his irritation to himself, but that did not prevent dark thoughts about his youngest brother, who remained brooding under the tree.

\*      \*      \*

"What happened next," José Antonio said, "no one knows for certain. But Don Pedro swears that it must have happened this way."

\*      \*      \*

One afternoon the ex-foreman, Juan, came to see Rudolfo. He spoke excitedly about the rich claim that his Yankee employers had staked. Juan was helping them gather equipment and supplies for their trek into the gold country. They were going to be rich.

Rudolfo looked at the fruit ripening on the trees and at the eager Juan, whom he considered a deserter. It was lucky that his overpowering frustration paralyzed him into inaction. Otherwise he might have thrown Juan off the property. Why had he come? Rudolfo wondered. The ex-foreman was not given to braggadocio.

There was one thing, Juan finally said, in which Don Rudolfo could be of service. For old times' sake.

For old times' sake? Rudolfo thought. Or for goodness sake, if one felt like being good. Or for one's own sake, he thought, wondering what it was that Juan wanted badly enough to dare return after leaving them in such a difficult situation.

Did the family still own that property south of San José? The one in the hills where in years past Indians used to dig the red earth for painting their bodies?

Yes. As far as he knew. But he would have to ask Don Pedro to be certain.

Could he and his partners dig up some of that dirt? They would even pay for it. At least a little.

Rudolfo had to smile. "You're going to paint yourselves like Indians and rob the miners in the gold fields. That's how you're going to get rich. All the time I thought you were going to be miners."

Juan laughed. "Sí, señor. You have found us out."

"Tell me. What will you really use the dirt for? To fill gold sacks after you've secretly emptied them of their treasure? For that any dirt would do. Or will you truly paint yourselves red and play Indians?"

"I have been told by my Yankee patrón that it has certain curative powers. Our claim is on an isolated and distant place, so we must take certain precautions."

His serious bearing convinced Rudolfo. Juan was just superstitious enough and ignorant enough to believe in magic dirt. "Take what you want," he said. "What are a few sacks more or less. That place must be full of dirt, down to the center of the earth — down to hell itself for that matter."

Only later did he wonder why anyone needed a sack full of magic dirt. A pinch would be enough. Since he knew little about that isolated piece of property, won by Pedro in a horse race some years past, he thought it best to ask in case he had blundered.

When José Ignacio next rode back from the range, Rudolfo spoke to him. The older brother's eyes brightened. "Quicksilver," he said. Rudolfo realized that a way had been shown to them.

## 25

"I have not been there for two years," José Ignacio said. "It is Pedro's property, separate from what belongs to the rancho and the family."

"You mean to Mamá?"

"To the family! In her name as with all widows. But really in trust for the family." Then, as an afterthought, as if it were of little consequence. "And how goes it with the Yankee lawyer?"

Rudolfo shrugged. "When do we go see the quicksilver mine?" he asked. He knew that José Ignacio was avidly curious about John Archer, but what was there to say? He could not spy on their mother while he was supervising the work in the fields. Archer came and went, seeing Pedro on almost every visit. When and how often he saw Doña Beatriz was incidental. Besides, José Ignacio had always been more attached to their mother. It was jealousy that prompted his question. Let him find his own answers.

"When?" Rudolfo repeated.

\*     \*     \*

Two days later they rode across the valley toward the foothills beyond San José. The day grew warmer as they progressed south. All they had told Pedro was that they had business in San José and were then going to inspect their property in the hills.

"Quicksilver," José Ignacio repeated. "These goldminers will want it. Pay dearly for it. Once they have found their gold-bearing rock and dug it from the earth with sweat and drill and pick, they'll need to crush it and extract the gold. For that they'll need quicksilver. Where else could they get it unless they brought it across the continent in wagons or around South America in ships? My God, little brother. It could make us a fortune."

"Won't Pedro be surprised?"

They stopped in San José at lawyer Archer's office, knowing that he was not there but repeating their names with emphasis to the clerk. Then they went into the nearest cantina for a drink. In a short while they were on their way south again, across the flat terrain toward the hills.

José Ignacio shook his head and laughed. They would show that elder brother of theirs. Wouldn't Pedro be jealous when José Ignacio and Rudolfo saved the rancho? And wouldn't he be grateful? He and Mamá both. By God! They would show that gringo Archer, too. Maybe then he wouldn't be around so often, rubbing his hands, his mouth juicy with desire for their property. Maybe then he would not try to ingratiate himself with Doña Beatriz by his obvious flattery and attentions.

"Won't Pedro be surprised?" Rudolfo repeated.

They veered toward the Guadalupe River, sauntering through broad fields of wild flowers splashing the landscape with bright oranges and blues and reds and yellows. They rested alongside the river, watering their horses and eating what they had packed in their saddlebags. Then they continued on the trail that rose gently toward their destination.

Halfway up the slope where the grade became steeper, they approached an adobe hovel. A white-bearded old man sat on the ground, watching them. "Buenos días, señores."

"Buenos días, Grandfather."

"Do you gentlemen go up to look for timber?"

José Ignacio and Rudolfo smiled. "Do we look like woodcutters, Grandfather?" José Ignacio asked. "No. We go up to dig dirt."

The two young men chuckled, expecting surprise and bewilderment from the old man. But it was they who were surprised. "The red dirt. I don't see why so many want it. We have more than enough dirt here. All colors. But them—" He shrugged. Why not? he seemed to imply. God made all kinds. Even fools.

"Who else?"

"Nobody much. A few days ago a paisano with gray in his hair. With a Yankee." That must have been Juan. "Then sometimes other men come and go. But then I do not see them all."

"What do they say, these men?"

The old man broke into a toothless grin. "¡Buenos días! Then: ¡Adiós!"

José Ignacio scowled in irritation. "Is there anyone up there now?"

"I don't know, señor. They come and they go."

"Well, Grandfather. We must be on our way, too. Adiós."

They rode off, speaking in undertones. "What do you think?" Rudolfo asked.

"I wish Pedro had not ignored this property for so long."

Their progress to the top of the hill became slower as the way became steeper. The few trees near the summit thrust up conspicuously from the low underbrush. "Look for timber?" Rudolfo muttered. "That old man was a fool."

The tree furthest up the hill, a giant oak on the right, seemed to stand guard. The air was still, too early yet for the afternoon breeze that cooled the valley below even on the hottest days.

"José Ignacio," Rudolfo whispered, reining his horse to a stop. "There's something in that oak."

They drew their pistolas and peered cautiously up the slope. "See," Rudolfo whispered, pointing with a short thrust of his pistol. "Just behind the trunk. Something moved."

Motionless, necks thrust forward, they stared intently. "Surely they have already seen us," José Ignacio said in a low voice. "If they mean us harm they would already have done it." He motioned to Rudolfo to approach from the left while he circled from the right. Only the slow clop of hooves and the chatter of squirrels in a nearby tree broke the silence.

"Hello!" José Ignacio called as they approached the oak. "Hello! Who's there?"

Rudolfo, circling from the left, had the first clear view. "Oh, my God!" By the time José Ignacio had reached the tree, Rudolfo had drawn his knife and cut the rope. The body dropped stiff like a piece of lumber. "It's Juan," Rudolfo said.

"We'd better go for the sheriff."

"Who could have done this? Juan was no saint, but he didn't deserve this."

"What happened to the Yankee? Did he kill Juan and run away?"

"A man alone does not hang another man," Rudolfo said. "He uses a gun . . . or a knife. I say the Yankee's body is somewhere around here too."

José Ignacio stared grimly at his brother. Juan had probably been dead a few days. It was not likely that his murderers were still around. Yet he felt wary of what might await them at the summit, wondering if hostile eyes might already be watching them from some hidden place.

"Do you think we should go all the way up?" Rudolfo asked. "Maybe we should go for the sheriff first."

"It's ten miles to San José. We came to look at the mine."

They carried the body away from the tree and laid it alongside the trail, covering the purple face and twisted neck with the dusty sombrero that they found on the ground. Then, leading their horses by the reins, they cautiously walked toward the summit.

\* \* \*

Only someone who knew where to look would have seen the opening into the interior of the hill. It faced away from the trail and was just large enough for a man to slip through.

They tethered their horses to a burned-out stump, then picked their way cautiously over loose rock and dirt. An empty canvas sack lay on the ground, red dirt spilled from its mouth and scattered across the front of the cave. They stopped, exchanged glances, then squeezed through, lighting a piece of dried wood that José Ignacio had picked up.

"There couldn't be anybody here in the dark," Rudolfo said.

José Ignacio raised the torch and slowly turned, illuminating the area that widened and led down into the earth. A pile of bones lay in a heap beside the wall.

"Indian skeletons," José Ignacio said. "They buried some of their braves here. Though God knows it must have been hard work carrying the bodies up the hill and through the opening. There are more bones farther down."

"Maybe they died digging out the red dirt."

José Ignacio turned to the right, slowly illuminating other parts of the cave. Blank walls. A floor that twisted and turned as it sloped down. Again José Ignacio turned. A white face stared at them through wide, dead eyes. The body sat on the floor, its back against the wall, the shirt front dark and stained.

"¡Jesucristo! For a moment I thought it was alive."

"The missing Yankee," José Ignacio said.

"I think we'd better go for the sheriff."

José Ignacio continued circling the torch toward the last unseen part of the cave. Seeing nothing, he glanced over his shoulder at Rudolfo whose eyes gleamed like a cat's in the flickering light.

"We'd better go," José Ignacio said. He propped the torch on a ledge near the exit. "Let's take the body."

Rudolfo grabbed the feet and José Ignacio the shoulders of the dead Yankee, then they made their way to the narrow exit.

"Wait," Rudolfo said. "Just this last leg. Hold it. Don't pull. I have to make it past this sharp turn. He's stiff as a rock. All right. Now I'm clear."

They made their way into the sunlight, blinking as they lowered the body to the ground. Only then did they see the four Yankees who emerged from behind cover. Grizzled, hard-looking men with cold, flinty eyes and weapons in their hands.

"What'd I tell ya," one of them said. "Greasers."

"Back in Texas we string 'em up just like them chili peppers they hang on the outside of their dirt houses. Hell! We string up more greasers in Texas than they do niggers in Mississippi."

José Ignacio glanced at Rudolfo. We should have left the body inside, he thought. Then at least we would have had our pistolas in our hands and made a fight of it.

He glanced at the Yankees cautiously. He knew what might happen if he stared. Even the slightest hint of antagonism could cause a reaction. Even death. For that was the one thing he saw in common on the four faces. A grim hostility that needed little excuse for violence.

One of the Yankees put out a hand to silence the others. Then he stepped forward to peer at them through narrowed eyes. "You're on our claim, greasers. What're you doing here?"

"Aw, for Chris' sakes, Jake," the one with red hair said. "What the goddamn hell you think they're doing? String 'em up, and let's get on with our work."

"I think there is some mistake," José Ignacio said.

The Yankees exploded into laughter. "That's just about the smartest thing I ever heard a greaser say," the red-haired man said.

"It's our property," Rudolfo protested. "It belongs to my brother Pedro."

"Sure. And your sister takes in washing on Saturday night." The Yankee punctuated his words with a leering wink.

"Come on, Jake. What the hell're we waiting for?"

"This property belongs to our family," José Ignacio said. "We came to inspect it."

"Next thing you know," the red-haired man said, "they'll be up in the gold fields trying to get rich like white men."

"Right to the cave," another man said. "Did you see that? Just like they knowed something."

José Ignacio realized that nothing he said would be believed. The more he said the more likely he was to anger these men. "It seems that we have been trespassing by mistake," he said in a conciliatory voice. "We should be on our way."

His eyes followed Jake's glance to the cave entrance and the body of the dead Yankee. "I don't think so," Jake said. "Another dead greaser or two won't matter. But a dead American will bring the law out." He nodded to his men. "All right! No sense wasting bullets or dirtying knives. Rope can always be reused."

Rudolfo broke for the tethered horses. Before he ran half a dozen steps he was struck on the head with the butt of a pistol.

"We'll have to wake him," the red-haired man said. "I hate to string 'em up when they're unconscious. There's no sport to that."

José Ignacio looked with fear at their leader, searching for a spark of human feeling. Seeing none, he began to pray silently.

## 26

A knock interrupted the story. Leonardo heard his grandmother move from the kitchen to answer it, then the voices in undertones before footsteps stopped at the door to the room.

"Auntie Rosalía!" Leonardo said.

Gregoria waited for José Antonio's nod of recognition. "Rosalía would like to talk to you, José."

The short, skinny woman stood with her arms folded across her chest, her rebozo tight around her head and shoulders. She was hunched over so that she seemed to be staring at the floor. Her lips, though pressed tightly together, moved in quick and incessant motion as if she were silently talking to herself or gnawing thoughtfully on the marrow of some important concern.

Suddenly Rosalía looked up, the whites of her eyes in startling contrast to her dark skin. "Don José," she whispered. It was the whisper of a woman who mumbled prayers in church, huddled over her beads, on the verge of tears, asking God to live life for her because she could not handle life by herself.

Leonardo looked from face to face in panic as the realization struck him. Auntie Rosalía was Ernesto's mother, widow of his own mother's oldest brother, Tomás, who had been killed at a gambling table when his knife had been outraced by a bullet.

He barely remembered his Uncle Tomás. Perhaps what he had heard was more rumor than truth, since his uncle had been dead almost ten years. Tomás Chávez had been the most quarrelsome of the quarreling Chávezes, a drinker and a brawler whose son Ernesto was but a pale copy.

The boy searched his aunt's face, trying to read her intentions. She's going to tell him about Ernesto and me, Leonardo thought. His heart began to pound so loudly that he was sure his grandfather heard.

"All right," Don José said to Rosalía. He rose and placed a hand on his grandson's shoulder. "That's all for now, Leonardo. We'll talk some more tomorrow."

Leonardo sat immobile, overcome by the desire to stay and listen even if it turned out to be the worst, yet with almost equal strength wanting to run and hide before the truth came out.

"Go on now," Don José said.

The boy bolted from the room, almost at a run as he hit the door and slammed it behind him. Then, as if that had been a signal, he stopped short and sneaked to the window where he leaned, listening as best he could.

The voices were murmurs of different pitch, muffled by the adobe walls. Leonardo closed his eyes and strained to hear . . . nothing.

\* \* \*

José Antonio saw his wife's expression and knew what it meant: Be nice to the poor old widow. She needs all the kindness she can get. Then Gregoria disappeared into the kitchen.

"Sit down, Rosalía," he said in that quaint, formal manner he used with women whose tears he was trying to forestall. He held a hand out toward the rude bench, still warm from his grandson's body.

"Thank you." The words were barely audible. "Thank you, Don José."

Rosalía Chávez' nose was red and shiny, her eyes aggrieved and threatening tears. Her pinched face had the look of statues of martyred saints. It made José Antonio uncomfortable, aware of his satisfying paunch and the smug contentment of his life.

The instant she sat on the bench the tears started. Perhaps the warmth that her nephew had left was more than she could bear. One son reminded her of another.

"Oh, Don José." The words struggled through the tears, past the twisted, unattractive mouth that even the kindest heart must force itself to listen to. "My life is so miserable. A poor old widow. If only my Tomás were here to help. Oh, Lord, why is my life such a trial? I'm a daughter of Job if ever there was one."

He looked at her, thinking that she was not yet forty years of age, young enough to be his daughter. But then people like Rosalía Chávez were old at twenty. One's age was what one took it to be. Old age was locking one's mind and heart and burying the key. Poor old widow was right. Poor in more, much more, than worldly goods or not having a husband.

"How can I help, señora?"

"Some of us were put on this earth to suffer. I've been to the priest. I've prayed. Said my novenas. But God does not hear. Like people in Los Rafas, He, too, is against me. How can one cope when God is against you?"

"What happened, señora?"

Her tears gave way to irritation. Her voice rose to a whine. "I do my duty to God and to my neighbors. Better than most. There are some I could tell you about. Some that would shock you. The pious faces they show to the world, while inside . . . maggots and scorpions. I could tell you— But then, nobody would believe me. They'd say I was lying. They'd say there goes that crazy old widow with her stories again. That's what they'd say. No one wants to hear the truth. No one wants to look at what is really happening."

José Antonio leaned back and rolled his eyes toward the ceiling. Lord, give me strength, he thought.

"The priest," she spat. "That old hypocrite. Told me to go home and mend my own fences. 'Beware of throwing the first stone,' he said, wagging that big, pink, well-fed finger of his. 'I don't want to hear gossip.' How is he supposed to serve God if he doesn't want to know the sinners in his parish? That's what happens," she leaned toward him confidentially, "when you have Anglo priests. They don't understand. That's why I came to—"

José Antonio's patience was at an end. He did not know which was worse, tears or spite. It didn't matter. He had had enough either way. "Señora!" His voice was sharp and stern. She stopped in mid-word, mouth open, and drew back as if she had been struck. "I am not a priest. I, too, do not want to hear gossip. If you want a priest, you've come to the wrong place. Now, what is it you want?"

Her mouth closed abruptly and the tears started again, huge drops flowing from those miserable eyes, down the gaunt cheeks and under the quivering chin into the hollow of her thin, dark neck.

A tinge of guilt softened José Antonio. "What is it?" he asked in a more gentle voice.

"My son!"

Immediately he recalled the broken knife. He had not yet talked to Ernesto about it, perhaps because he did not think it would do any good.

"That miserable gringo sheriff has him in jail," she said. "And he didn't do anything—" Her voice rose to a wail.

"What is it that he didn't do that they put him in jail for?"

She stopped in mid-wail and flashed him a questioning glance. Was he teasing her? Baiting her? "They say he's been stealing. Not just once, but many times. Not just in Los Rafas but all over the county. To hear them talk it would take six boys—he's only a boy, just a baby—to do all the things they accuse him of."

"So he's in jail. What do you want me to do?"

Her mood, her manner, shifted again. Now with a fluttering of her tear-drenched eyelashes and a smile on her twisted mouth, she was half supplicant, half coquette. "You're the patrón of the Spanish people here in Los Rafas. You know all the politicians and bosses in New Town. All the big Anglos. You could talk to them. Talk to the sheriff. You could tell them that Ernesto didn't do it. That it was a mistake. Then they'd let him go."

That's what patróns are for, José Antonio thought. To get jailbird sons out of the calaboose. To lend money to destitute farmers. To comfort wives whose husbands have beaten them. Or comfort husbands whose wives have beaten them. Reunite estranged parents and children. Beseech God for rain during droughts. Cure sick goats, cows, and burros. Forgive those whom the priests will not forgive. All manner of miracles.

"Please, Don José. Only you can do it."

He wished he had as much faith as she did. "I'll do what I can. But I cannot promise anything."

"Oh, Don José. Thank you. Thank you." Her face brightened, and for a moment he was afraid that she was going to kiss him. Then her face hardened and she sat back. "And, if you would, talk to him."

She shook her head, one exasperated parent to another. "That ingrate. That wretch. Just like his father. Why is he doing this to me? I don't need all this. The shame of it. The sheriff. Jail. All of Los Rafas looking at me and whispering behind my back. Oh, Don José, what are children coming to when they do not listen to and obey their parents?"

José Antonio did not know how to answer. There was some truth in what she said. Look at his own three sons. Only Francisco had stayed home. Blas was a soldier, off God knows where, because: "I want adventure, Papá. This beanfield desert bores me to tears." And Carlos, overly sensitive to the new Anglo world of New Mexico, ran away to Old Mexico. To prospect for gold, he said. But really, José Antonio thought, to escape from Anglo encroachment. Anglo assertiveness. Anglo competition.

Yet none of his sons had ever been in jail. Or ever would be, he hoped. None of them would ever have Ernesto's problems. With a mother like that, he thought, and a father like Tomás Chávez, what would you expect?

"Talk some sense into him," Rosalía continued. "Give him the tongue-lashing he deserves. He'll listen to you. You're the patrón."

Of course, José Antonio thought ironically. All I have to do is say: "No more, Ernesto. Think of your poor mother. Think of your eternal soul." And the wretch will change overnight.

He had been a priest long enough, heard confessions from too many, to really believe that very many people ever changed. It was the exceptional person who experienced such a miracle. Sometimes only when struck down by God, like Saul of Tarsus.

"I'll do what I can," he said again.

She stood, face beaming. "Now I can go to my poor little home happy. Now I know that my son will be all right. All that's left is to find something to eat until Ernesto can go to work again."

José Antonio sighed; he knew that he would go to the storehouse and drag out a sack of beans for Widow Chávez. He might even have to haul it to her adobe hovel with the widow riding alongside him in the wagon. Unless— Perhaps his grandson could do that little favor for him. Please God, just one little favor.

## 27

Town was five miles south of Los Rafas. As José Antonio rode along, he remembered when there was no New Town. There had been only Old Town with its plaza, its church, and its adobe buildings.

The morning train shattered the silence, its assertive whistle reminding him that the Santa Fe Railroad had fathered New Town. Progress out of technology through profits.

The old horse shook his head as if rejecting the thought. Iron horses may make more noise, belch fire, and haul more goods from manufacturing centers back east, but there were things they could not do. Their paths were limited by the shiny metal rails that stretched undeviating toward the horizon. No man would ever pat old Santa Fe on the neck in appreciation and affection. Not unless he wanted a burnt hand. Iron horses were as cold in feeling as they were hot in operation.

The train roared past. Its whistle fell in pitch as it sped away. José Antonio was grateful for the quiet as they plodded past cornfields, approaching the sparse settlements on the edge of town. Just a short ride now and they would be in the center of New Town with its complex of buildings and offices, and the jail.

Sheriff Davis was at his desk as José Antonio entered. "Don José."

"Good morning, Sheriff."

"Who do we have locked up from Los Rafas today? It's not Sunday, so you can't be coming for the Saturday night drunks. It must be something special. You wouldn't be here to buy my vote for the upcoming election, would you?"

José Antonio forced himself to smile in spite of his irritation at the mention of buying votes. "We won't need your vote, Sheriff. We already have more than enough." The sheriff knew that it was not true and he was confident enough to let the comment pass. "I would like to see Ernesto Chávez."

The sheriff took a ring of jangling keys from his desk and headed toward the cells. "His mother was here yesterday. He didn't want to see her."

"I don't blame him."

The sheriff laughed. "He might not want to see you."

"So be it."

Ernesto stood staring out the high, barred window of the end cell. He did not turn around even though he must have heard them coming; his back was arched in silent reproof.

"Here's a visitor for you, Chávez." The sheriff unlocked the door, then relocked it after José Antonio had slipped in. "When you want out, Don José, just give a yell. And you," he said to Ernesto, "Behave yourself."

José Antonio stood waiting for a sign of recognition, but the young man did not move. It became a war of silence and immobility, for José Antonio was determined to be acknowledged by this insolent pup before he spoke. In the charged stillness, Ernesto's silent reproach slowly weakened. Finally, he whirled around and thrust his angry face forward.

"She sent you, didn't she? She told you to come."

"Is it true that you're in jail for stealing?"

"She thinks you can get me out like I was just another Saturday night drunk sobering up in the jail. Hah!"

"All over the county I hear, Los Rafas. Los Chávez. Los Martínez. Old Town. I didn't hear New Town so maybe you'll be lucky. As long as you're just stealing from your own people they might show a little mercy. Otherwise they'll send you to territorial prison."

Ernesto stood with heaving chest, almost as if he were panting. There was a pained look in his eyes, and his chin began to tremble when José Antonio said "territorial prison." But that passed quickly, and he bristled with hostility again. "They've got nothing on me. As God is in heaven, I didn't do it." He spoke earnestly as he looked José Antonio in the eye.

"Then they will let you go."

"I want out now. They've got no right. Someone is just trying to get me."

José Antonio almost asked: Who? What for? But that way lay an endless swamp of accusation and recrimination. A pointless exchange. He was neither judge nor jury and he did not want to be. Yet his hand was thrust deep in the right pocket of his trousers, wrapped tightly around the broken knife that he knew belonged to Ernesto. When he brought it out, when he asked the question, what would he be if not judge?

But being the target of the young man's antagonism, hearing the false sincerity of his lies, made José Antonio more angry than sad. He pulled the knife from his pocket and thrust it out in his open palm without a word.

Ernesto blinked, then turned away with an expression at once trapped and fearful. "Where did you find *that*?"

"Señor Smith found it."

The young man's mouth dropped open as if he were about to speak, but he caught himself. His eyes spoke, though. José Antonio saw a recognition, an admission, as surely as if Ernesto had said: "Yes. I lost it there. The dogs started a ruckus and the light went on in the house."

"I lost it," Ernesto said. "A long time ago. Up by the river. I made it myself. It's my favorite knife."

José Antonio thrust it back in his pocket. "You lost it the way you haven't been stealing." No answer. Only a sullen glare.

Why had he come here? José Antonio thought. There was nothing he could do for this young man. Son of his father. Son of his mother. Although he felt compassion for people in trouble, especially the young who might not know better, when confronted with hostility like Ernesto's he would gladly be the jailer who turned the key. Let them stay locked up and think about it. Maybe some dim light would eventually come through and show the way.

As a priest, José Antonio had seen much of life as sin and redemption. When one sinned, one must admit that he had done wrong and resolve to do better. Only then could one's penance have meaning. Only then would there be forgiveness.

Ernesto had regained his self-possession. "I did nothing. They can't prove it." Then he turned his back and stared out the cell window. He cleared his throat and spat through the bars.

José Antonio almost said: "Don't lie to me." But he realized how futile it would be. He almost said: "What about your mother and what she's going through?" But he knew what this ingrate felt toward his mother.

José Antonio could not keep his increasing anger under control. "You have no pride!" he spat. "You wallow in deceit! You care nothing for anyone else! May God have pity on you! I don't!" Then he turned to the door. "Sheriff!"

They stood, back to back, silent, seething, as footsteps approached. José Antonio wanted to be clear of this place. To be free of the petty stench of a small, miserable mind. Perhaps in time the wretch would learn. Perhaps— But he would not be around to see it. The door opened and he left the cell without a backward glance.

"They'll fix him good," the sheriff said. "I know he's one of yours—" Meaning from Los Rafas. "But you can't save them all."

Well, there's one thing, José Antonio thought as he mounted his horse. I can truthfully tell Smith that there shouldn't be any more stealing.

## 28

As he worked in the field, Leonardo kept a lookout for his grandfather. He knew that Don José had gone to the jail to visit Ernesto. Leonardo knew too that Aunt Rosalía had said nothing about him or that if she had, Grandfather had decided to keep it to himself. More likely, Aunt Rosalía did not know about him because Ernesto did not speak to her of such things. So the remaining dread was that in a fit of pique his cousin would tell his grandfather. Perhaps to show, in the way of the Chávezes, that Ernesto was not the only one who did bad things.

Leonardo worked distractedly, hardly listening when his father scolded him. Late in the afternoon the old horse plodded along Rafas Road toward the big house. A few minutes later, Don José walked through the orchard and crossed the ditch toward them.

Francisco straightened up and leaned against his hoe. "What did you find out?" he asked.

Don José told them. "I'll stop and see Florinda. Then I'll see Rosalía after supper."

"You see why I always warned you about that one," Francisco admonished his son. "You lie down with dogs; you get up with fleas."

Leonardo felt his grandfather's roughened hand on his shoulder. "You don't have to worry about this one," José Antonio said.

The boy's face reddened in shame. He looked at his grandfather uneasily, relieved that his cousin had not betrayed him.

"Let him come with me to see Rosalía," Don José said. "I was telling him a story."

* * *

José Antonio left Rosalía Chávez' house with relief. Everywhere he
had looked he saw things that disturbed him. Why did the statue of
the Virgin look so new? In what church was there now an empty niche
where such a Virgin once nestled? Did Rosalía know?

"Couldn't you help her?" Leonardo asked.

"Sometimes there's nothing you can do. You just have to accept
things as they are."

He could still hear Rosalía wailing inside the small adobe house.
In his mind he could still see the distraught woman tearing at her hair.

Beside him, Leonardo shivered. He had thought about continuing
Don Pedro's story on their walk, but he decided to wait until they got
home. It was dark and now that the Chávez house was behind them,
the quiet was broken only by the occasional bark of a dog.

* * *

Don Pedro had barely paid attention when one of the servants told
him that Rudolfo and José Ignacio had ridden into San José. As on
most days, he locked himself in the rancho office and pored over the
books. Perhaps there was an error that he hadn't found. Some income
subtracted instead of added. An expense recorded more than once.
But nothing. Only the irrefutable, cold numbers that whispered in-
sistently: "Not enough. You will lose your land."

At times he was tempted to drink, his trembling hand reaching out
for the glass that wasn't there. For a moment he thought that he had
sent a servant for a bottle of brandy. But no. It was his imagination
playing tricks on him. He realized that his silent brooding did not solve
the problem, but dragged him closer to a different one. He thought
of his father, the old Don, drinking himself to death in this very office. Unable to bring order to his life. Able only to search for relief
in drink.

It was in such a mood, in such depths, that he heard laughter outside. Puzzled, he strained to hear who it was that would dare feel joy
while he was suffering so. Then once again the laughter stole insidiously

through the closed door and window, and he recognized in shock that it was his mother.

The laughter floated away lightly, following the sound of footsteps on the stairs. Were they going up or coming down? If coming down, he would surely have heard them ascend earlier. Whose was that other voice he heard? A deeper, masculine voice. Or was his mind playing tricks again?

It's stuffy in here, he thought. The warm air makes me drowsy so that I am half asleep and half dreaming.

A simple matter to cross the room and open the window. Pedro stood there a moment. His hearing was acutely alert as the footsteps faded upward. He breathed deeply, inhaling the faint aroma of a cigar.

"I'm so delighted that you were waiting for me, Doña Beatriz." The voice was John Archer's.

How could I have been such a fool? Pedro thought. How long has it been going on? The signs have been there for months. Longer. Almost the entire year that his father had been dead. Had he really believed that all those visits of Archer's had been necessary? The papers delivered and papers to be signed that could have waited for some other time or could have been delivered by another person. A clerk. A servant. Anyone.

Locked in his office, Pedro never knew when Archer arrived or when he left. Had they been meeting secretly like this before or after the so-called business meetings that in retrospect had seemed so frequent? What of the other women in the house? His Aunt María, widow of his Uncle Ignacio. Or his brother José Ignacio's wife. The servants. *His own wife.* Had they seen nothing? Were they so blind? Or was it all part of a conspiracy of silence, women protecting one of their own?

Pedro cautiously opened the window wider. He heard but could not see them. "You can see most of the rancho from here," Doña Beatriz said. "The rise gives you a view for miles. If we walk on the other side, we can see the rest. I make my little tour by walking around the balcony every day. That way I am not lonely when the men are out working."

"What will your sons say when we tell them?"

"Over in that direction is Mission San José."

"You have told them, haven't you?"

"Oh, my dearest. Do not worry." Then once again in the tone of a hostess showing a guest her treasures. "And beyond, west of there, the other mission. We are so fortunate to be near two. Twice blessed as the padres would say."

The answer was an impassioned whisper whose force carried it clearly to the open window. "I can't wait any longer. I love you." Then a silence that seemed to last forever, followed by a whispered sigh and heavy breathing.

Finally: "It is not a year yet, John dearest."

"Damn convention!"

Then the footsteps again, moving around the balcony to the other side of the house.

"¡Demonio!" Pedro cursed. Behind his back. In his own house. And already gone so far. Not that he disliked Archer. It was that he did not trust the lawyer. Some instinct of Pedro's saw through the polish and suavity, felt uneasy at the intelligence lurking behind the geniality. The gringo made him uncomfortable. He did not fathom his motives or his methods, yet he knew that the man was getting rich, not only from fees from clients but also from treasures when clients defaulted.

But another thought, a hopeful thought occurred to him. Since Archer was the principal in the group that held the mortgage on Rancho Los Palos, having Archer in the family really meant that the property stayed with the family even if they could not pay back the loan when it was due.

Damn the numbers that he had been poring over. That was not the answer. The answer was upstairs in the whispered words between two older people. Upstairs was their salvation.

Pedro returned to his desk and slammed the ledger shut. He strode from the office with a lightness he had not felt in months. Strode resolutely out of the house toward the orchard. Here was where he belonged. Among the trees and fields and open air. Not in that damned bookkeeper's den that narrowed one's outlook to a column of numbers on a sheet of paper. Life was more than that. Much more.

He inhaled the fragrance of blossoms, then walked carefree toward the corral where he watched the young colts frolicking. What did his damned ledger have to say about this? Two sterile entries: "Two hundred fruit trees bearing so many bushels." "Eight colts added to stock this past year." You could not smell a number in a ledger nor taste it. Nor ride it exuberantly across the "so-and-so many acres of grazing land."

With a wave at the groom, he turned toward the main casa refreshed. Up on the balcony he saw Doña Beatriz and Señor Archer circling slowly. A betrothal dance. A dance of salvation. He shouted and waved to them as he approached the house.

\* \* \*

For the first time in days, Pedro went for a ride. He let the horse go its own way, wandering toward the eastern range. He kept his distance from the vaqueros, wanting to be alone, not really thinking, just letting the day pass over him.

On the way back to the main casa, Pedro stopped at the family burial plot, a growing scar on what was once their Eden. That mound his Uncle Ignacio. Beside it his two cousins. Then his own father and namesake and his brother Manuel; next to him the empty plot for his brother Andrés, whose remains were buried somewhere near Los Angeles.

He cleared away the weeds that had newly overgrown the graves, then knelt to pray. It was his father whom he had especially come to visit. That old man whose body probably lay in a state of preservation, pickled by all the brandy he had drunk, while the others had surely rotted away as was the usual fate of flesh.

"She is still young, Papá," he said. "You would not want her to live alone for all the years she has left. But could you forgive her a gringo husband? I see you there, with your brother and nephews and son beside you. All victims of Yankee avarice. Of Yankee hate. I can't help but wonder if God has reconciled you to this. Helped you to forgive. He has not yet succeeded with me. I am still bitter, even with a friend like John Archer. And while I know that one should forgive, I find it difficult. No — impossible!

"Yet how ironic that the rancho might be saved by the marriage of your widow to a Yankee. It is because of the Yankees that we are in debt and in danger of losing it.

"So do not fear, Papá. Wherever you are in heaven, or in purgatory if God demands the fire for a time, rest assured that we will keep your rancho in the family . . . one way or another."

Then he addressed himself to his father's Father, the Father of all, with a rote prayer that he had learned as a child.

When he returned to his office, Pedro was surprised to see his mother sitting beside the window waiting.

"You've been gone a long time," she said. "I need to talk to you, Pedro." Her hands fluttered nervously, her fingers moving as if she were playing the piano or rapidly running over her rosary beads.

"You are the man of the house. The manager of the rancho." Pedro was taken aback, but almost immediately realized that what she said was not only true but was also the proper way of things. The male was the head of the household, whether grandfather, father, uncle, or eldest son. It was to him that others of the household came for advice and permission.

Doña Beatriz seemed uncertain, her nervousness betrayed not only by fluttering hands but by her incessantly blinking eyes that avoided looking directly at Pedro.

"There is something important I must ask you." Yes, he nodded, saying to himself: On with it, Mamá. Why the hesitation?

"You do not think," she said, her voice faltering, "that Señor Archer is too young?"

"Too young for what, Mamá?"

Her agitation increased and her face flushed a deep red that was both becoming and youthful. "For me, Pedro."

How could anyone say yes to a question put so timorously, so beseechingly? "Of course not, Mamá."

She beamed. "Then you approve! Oh, I was so worried."

Approve? he thought. Approve of what? She had not told him and he was sure that she was not about to tell him directly. She assumed that he knew what she was talking about.

"What do you know about this man?" he asked.

"Why—he's gallant and handsome. And he's forty-two years old. Only three years younger than me." The bookkeeper in Pedro was automatic. He was twenty-nine. That would have made Mamá sixteen when he was born. He tried not to show his disbelief.

"You sound like a young girl in love." The moment he said it he wished that he had not.

She reacted, flashing an anguished look that seemed to ask if he were ridiculing her. Or perhaps his answer held up a mirror to her and she saw reflected what she did not want to see. Was she behaving foolishly?

"He is a widower," she said. "From Baltimore, Maryland. His wife died in childbirth five years ago. Their only child, a young man, attends law school back east. When John came to California to start a new life, his son told him that he wanted to remain and go his own way."

"What can I say, Mamá? You are certainly of age and free to make the choice."

Her exuberance had given way to pensiveness. Do you think I'm foolish? she seemed to ask. But Pedro knew she would never say the words aloud. Was she looking to him for a reason not to accept John Archer?

"What would your father say?"

"If it were me speaking from heaven, I would say marry again. Everyone needs a mate. It's a lonely life without one, even in the largest and happiest of families."

A slight smile brightened the corners of Doña Beatriz' mouth. "I'm sure," Pedro continued, "that Papá would also say: 'If by marrying, you save the rancho from its creditors, then your marriage is doubly blessed.'"

"Why . . . that never occurred to me. The very thought repels me. As if I set after this man only because of our property. Oh, my God—"

Her naivete surprised him. But then, "Honor thy father and thy mother" allowed him to credit her with attributes that she did not possess. When he looked at her dispassionately, he saw that she was a childish, silly woman.

He could not help teasing her. "All the time people were saying how shrewd you were, making such a wealthy catch."

"People? What people? What are they saying? They have no right to gossip."

"Nothing, Mamá. I was only making fun of you." She looked at him as if she didn't understand. "The match is your choice. I only want the best for you. But before the marriage, you should sign an agreement so there is no misunderstanding about the rancho."

"Oh, I don't understand." She shook her head fretfully. "Business is beyond me. The whole idea makes me feel tarnished. As if I were selling myself for a few acres of dirt and a few head of cattle."

"The rancho belongs to the family. You have three sons and a great many grandchildren. This is their home, too. You must protect it for them."

"But you are the man of the rancho, the business manager. Why don't you take care of it? Protect it from what? From the man I plan to marry?"

"The rancho," he said in exasperation, "was left in your name. As far as the law is concerned, you are the owner of Rancho Los Palos."

"That's crazy. I know nothing about business. You are the one. The whole thing is nonsense."

"Sign an agreement before the wedding," he insisted. "It is very important. I will help you."

Doña Beatriz sighed. "All right." Then she sighed again and looked out the window as if it were all too much for her.

## 29

No one at the rancho missed José Ignacio and Rudolfo that first day or the next. The young patróns would occasionally go off on business and not return for a day or so. But on the third day Pedro sought Rudolfo on some question about the orchard. No one had seen him nor could anyone tell Pedro where he might be, except some vague reference to San José. Later that day a deputy sheriff rode to the rancho with the news.

An old man who lived halfway up the hill saw them, the deputy said. They had gone up three days ago, but he had not seen them come down. He hadn't thought much of it. Sometimes men went up one way and came down another. Or passed by and the old man did not notice. But he had gone up to the summit early in the morning to look for a pig that had broken out of its pen. That's when he saw the three of them, swinging on a giant oak tree.

Pedro broke into a chill and started to tremble. The deputy faded from view. His shocked eyes did not see and his shocked mind could not comprehend. In what seemed like hours, though it was only seconds, his vision returned and his trembling ceased. He leaned forward, put his hands to his face and began to weep.

"I'm sorry, Don Pedro," the deputy said.

"Who could have done that to my little brothers?"

"When you're up to it, I'd appreciate it if you would come into town to identify and claim the bodies."

"Oh, my God!"

The deputy took his leave and Pedro mumbled goodbye. It took some time before he truly comprehended what he had been told. There had been three of them. José Ignacio, Rudolfo—but who else? Up in the hills west of San José. What were they doing there? It had been years since anyone had been to that property.

The next day a grief-numbed Pedro led a contingent from the rancho to San José. The empty wagon bumped along behind the slow-riding horsemen. During the ride Pedro heard the ghostly voices of his brothers. There was laughter and family jokes. Then the voices faded, and he stared into the emptiness, hearing nothing.

The entire day was a blur. The silent ride to San José. The pained viewing of the bodies. Yes. Yes. Those were José Ignacio and Rudolfo. The two cold hunks of meat on the left. The other? Juan López, who had been a foreman under Rudolfo. But he had left the rancho and gone prospecting. What was he doing here?

They loaded the bodies onto the wagon and rode back to Rancho Los Palos in slow procession. That night there had been a rosary. Then a wake. Pedro found his solace in drink. He numbed himself so he could not see. So he did not hear voices from the past. So his mind went blank, registering nothing, thinking nothing. Neither grief nor revenge. Neither anger nor hate.

The priest rode up from the mission the next day. It was a grim funeral, with friends and neighbors from miles around gathering to pay their last respects. The prayers like the buzzing of flies. Other words unspoken but on the minds of many: "More gringo violence. To be followed by more neglect from the law." Silent eyes glanced warily at Doña Beatriz, who was flanked by her remaining son Pedro and by that gringo lawyer, Archer.

"Dust thou art and unto dust thou shalt return," intoned the padre, while unspoken thoughts answered: "Until the gringos steal all our land — even our dust — and leave us nothing."

Doña Beatriz slumped as the first handful of dirt fell into the open grave. Feebly, flutteringly, she tried to push aside Pedro and Archer, who caught her. Finally, the service over, she let herself be half-carried to the main casa. Don Pedro received the condolences of friends and neighbors alone, while Archer and a maid hovered anxiously beside Doña Beatriz, who had been carried to her room.

Only later, when the crowd thinned, did Pedro take to heavy drinking.

\* \* \*

"Murdered by person or persons unknown" was the way the sheriff recorded the foul deed. "José Ignacio Baca, aged twenty-five. Rudolfo Baca, aged twenty-one. Of hanging. On or about the third of May. Township of San José. State of California. United States of America."

Once recorded, it seemed to Pedro, the event acquired a life of its own, a shape and character that allowed law officials to repeat the words: "Person or persons unknown" and go about other business. What could they do, they said with a shrug, about person or persons unknown?

More than the death of his uncle and cousins at the hands of the Bear Flaggers; more than Manuel's death at the hands, he was certain, of land squatters; or of Andrés' death at the hands of Yankee troops; these deaths gnawed at Pedro. The pain was deeper and more pervading. The loss greater. Now only he was left of all the men in the family. He was the last of the male Bacas, who must protect the fragile thread that carried the Baca line onward. These murders must be avenged! There had to be justice. Against person or persons unknown.

The deputy sheriff helped Don Pedro as best he could. But even the ride into the hills to where his brothers had been killed only served to deepen his agitation. Beyond the huge oak lay the old mine that he had won in a bet. He had seldom been there since winning it; the rancho had demanded all of his time and energies. He had no interest in mining.

There was evidence of recent work in the cave. Was this a coincidence or was there a connection to his brothers' deaths? Even if not, he thought, someone had been trespassing on his property.

He gave little thought to the mine until one day, going through some papers in his office, he found a scribbled note attached to what he assumed was a deed to the property. The date was 1845. A pre-Yankee deed. Unimportant heretofore. It was the rancho he was concerned about. The rancho over which he had already gone to court, hired lawyer Archer, proven to the United States government that it was truly Baca land. Free and clear. Mexican or American government notwithstanding.

Now that he thought about the mine, he realized that the note and deed seemed feeble claim. He had never registered the deed. No one at the time had been much interested in quicksilver. The mine had merely been a medium of exchange over something more exciting—a horse race. It changed hands the way money did, or land, or cattle. But now another price had been paid, his brothers' lives.

Some weeks after Pedro gave the mine papers to John Archer, the lawyer rode to the rancho. Don Pedro brought out the brandy, to which he had become more partial in recent months. They lit cigars and sat enclosed in the office.

"There's a conflict about that quicksilver mine," Archer said. "First of all, it was never registered with the Mexican government so there is a question whether it ever belonged to the gentleman who gave it to you."

Pedro refilled his glass and heaved a sigh. He was beyond anger.

"There's another claim on the property. One to which there seems some validity. It has been registered and, without reference to any prior claims when California was part of Mexico, seems proper enough."

"By a Yankee?"

"A man from Missouri," Archer said.

Pedro gulped down the brandy and set his glass on the desk. "Then," he said in a soft voice, "we will have to go to court."

"I can't assure you that we'll win."

"I want my day in court."

"Even if you had a strong claim under Mexican law, which you don't, American land laws are different. To all intents and purposes you had abandoned the property or, at the very least, ignored it so that there were no signs of prior ownership."

"I will fight in the courts."

"The current claimants have invested money and labor to make it a working mine."

"Stop! It belongs to me. These latter day usurpers are just that. Usurpers. By God, I'll demand justice in court. My two brothers, hung to death on that property, are a more just claim than any piece of paper signed by any government. You're my lawyer. Push the matter into the courts!"

Archer puffed silently on his cigar before he answered. "If that's your wish."

"That is my wish."

Pedro turned to his brandy, a close friend who sympathized with the cruel blows that unkind fate and the gringos had brought upon his family.

\* \* \*

Pedro felt his legal adversaries before he saw them. Heard about them before he felt their presence. The claimants were a partnership of gringos, of which the chief partner was the man from Missouri,

Jacob Schloss, and it was in his name that the suit was brought to court.

Like many gringos who had followed the Lorelei's call west, they were a group without a past. Sprung full-blown where there were riches to be had for the least effort, propelled by hope and some shiny dream that enough money would solve all their problems.

They were a rough crew, Pedro heard, come together in that random way that made bosom friends of strangers met just yesterday. Jacob Schloss, Jake he was called, and those others whose names Pedro did not care to know. The man from Texas with the outspoken attitudes of white Texans toward Mexicans. The redhead with the furtive eyes and the jumpy hand that only became still when embracing a weapon. And the fourth, a quiet man with one eye half-closed, the eye itself opaque and staring out as if on guard, and unquestionably hostile, even though there was little that the opaque eye could see.

In court that first day Pedro was sitting quietly beside John Archer when the door behind them opened with more noise than necessary and slammed shut with an even louder sound. The aggressive stomping of boots thrust its way toward the front of the courtroom. There was no question in Pedro's mind that these had to be his adversaries. He did not need to turn and look. The hair on the back of his neck bristled and the whispered words leaped to his tongue without a thought: "Thieving gringo bastards."

"What was that?" Archer asked.

A silent shake of the head and Archer sat back, shuffling through his papers. Then the stomp of bootheels stopped, the quiet more intense now in contrast. When Pedro looked up, the animal eyes of Jacob Schloss were staring at him as if trying to decide how he would do away with this enemy.

Pedro's nod of acknowledgment broke the stare. As he looked away, what had only been a vague suspicion, a gnawing question, became a certainty. *He knew.* As certainly as he knew his own name. He gazed back at the men, watching the other three as they followed Jacob Schloss along a row of empty seats. *These were the men.* His brother's murderers. Immediately, the court case, the judge, his lawyer, the whole civilized hypocrisy gave way to his desire for vengeance.

The lawsuit dragged on that day, with its interminable paper shuffling, objections, counter-objections. The judge sat, solemn and expressionless, nodding his head at points made, not so much in agreement as in acknowledgment that he had heard and understood.

The next morning the court sat quietly, waiting for the vicious, hard bootheels to announce the entrance of Schloss and company. The time for court to convene came, with silence now transformed to whispered agitation. The court rose as the judge made his entrance. But still no sign of Pedro's adversaries.

"Maybe they think they've already won the suit the way things went yesterday," Archer said softly.

There were whispered gatherings of the officers of the court. Concerned glances were cast across the room toward the door, which remained shut.

"Maybe they see that right is on my side," Pedro responded, "and decided to default."

Finally, after some minutes, the door to the courtroom opened and quick, light footsteps moved down the aisle to the bench. The newcomer leaned over and exchanged whispers with the judge.

The buzz of voices in the courtroom increased in volume. After a few more whispered consultations, the judge gaveled for silence. "This lawsuit," he said in a rasping, low voice, "is postponed until further notice. Will the attorneys for the plaintiff and the defendants please come to the bench."

Archer shot Don Pedro a questioning look and walked toward the judge. The exchange was brief and decisive. Archer came back, his face grim and bloodless.

"They're dead," he said. "All four of them. Shot down last night by person or persons unknown."

Pedro could barely restrain a smile. His words, "It serves them right," were drowned by the pounding of the gavel.

"Court dismissed," the judge rasped.

"Shot?" Don Pedro asked Archer. "You're certain they weren't hung?"

"Shot," came the reply.

As they made their way across the courtroom, the deputy sheriff approached them. "Gentlemen," he said. "The sheriff would very much like to talk to Don Pedro in his office."

## 30

Gregoria sat in the kitchen mending clothes in the small, dim island of light from the oil lamp. When her eyes tired, she stuck the needle into the torn work pants, closed her eyes, and rested. If she sat very still, she could decipher her husband's muffled monologue from the next room.

She shook her head in exasperation. That boy does not understand half of what his grandfather is saying, she thought. But that old fool does not realize it. Why does he tell Leonardo things that the boy is better off not knowing? What purpose does it serve? Thank God it either bores Leonardo or is beyond his ability to understand. If I wait long enough I will hear the yawns and know it is time to offer them chocolate.

After a short rest, Gregoria took up her mending again, turning her attention from the drone of her husband's voice to the details of her work. When she next rested, she shook her head at José Antonio's new revelations, most of which she had not heard before.

Why has he never told me that? she thought in surprise, hearing a particular anecdote. It's just men's talk, she finally concluded irritably. They are our protectors and therefore cannot tell us certain things — so they think. Those damned men! Whose bodies do they think they came from? All their talk, their insufferable egos, see only the maleness of their heritage: sons and inheritances and family names. Male family names.

At least in the old country, she thought, the old, old country, Spain, children took both the family names. Perhaps because way back, Isabella was queen on her own. When she married Ferdinand, who was king of a different country, she saw no reason to bow to him. She was his equal. Their property was half hers, half his. But here on the frontier only maleness counts. Muscles. Guns. Force. Well, let them do without us and see how far their maleness goes. One generation, that's all. Then no more heirs, male or female.

She attacked her sewing with renewed vigor. Why had her husband chosen this grandchild as his favorite? There were others. Children of their daughters, Consuela and Andrea, who were no longer Rafas. That's what the old fossil would say. Not Rafas! But what about Francisco's darling little daughters or his younger son Carlitos?

Why was it that some were favored while others were not? Even among the five of her own children who had survived, she had her favorites. One must love them equally, and she did, yet she preferred Consuela and Blas to the others. If Carlos José had been a stranger, she might never have spoken to him. Never sought him out. Perhaps even avoided him. She was drawn to Consuela and Blas not by blood but by something deeper. A kinship that let them see the world almost as if through her own eyes.

Maybe that's what it was between José Antonio and Leonardo. Even across the generations there could be this bond when you discovered a kindred soul. You wasted no effort in understanding each other because you already did, and you could go on to more important and deeper things.

Like it had been with her sister Rebecca all those years ago when she had been a girl and before Rebecca had married and gone to California with that poor loco out there in the shed. She had never had another friend like that in all the sixty years of her life. Her eldest daughter Consuela was almost like that, but not quite. Even there she had been luckier than her husband, who had found no such relationship with any of their sons. Only with this one grandson.

She could still remember when Rebecca had left. "Listen carefully," Rebecca had said. "Now you will have to be Mamá's helper. You must help cook and care for Papá."

Looking back from the vantage point of maturity, Gregoria realized that Rebecca must have tired of her own role as helper and married the first man who would take her away from Papá and New Mexico. It didn't have to be California; it could have been Texas or Arizona. What had Rebecca known about Pedro Baca except that he was eligible and could take her away to "his riches, his rancho," which no one really believed that he had?

But Rebecca had been more than beautiful, that she knew. She had been like a second mother to her, teaching her all those things a dutiful mother passed on to her daughters. How to make good tortillas. How to peel the roasted chilis without getting the fire-hot seeds or juice onto your bare hands so they would not sting for an hour afterwards — God forbid if you had a cut on your fingers or rubbed your eyes. How

to sweep and clean a house made of earth so that it was cleaner than
any house made of wood. How to sober up a drunk father in time
to get him to his job in the patrón's field. Or how to lie to the patrón
when Father could not sober up.

It had been fifty years since Rebecca had gone. All that remained
were a few memories captured in the ten-year-old girl Gregoria used
to be, a girl who would be a stranger to her now, like a child Gregoria
might see crossing the dusty fields, a child she would not recognize.

Rebecca was now only those memories and a thin stack of letters
that had come infrequently over the years, then stopped altogether.
Letters that Gregoria could recite as unerringly as she recited her
prayers.

"Dear little sister. The bad times are upon us here in California.
The Yankees are like a plague of locusts devouring the land. It all
falls on Pedro. I hardly see him now, only feel him beside me in bed
late at night, stiff and restless, no doubt wondering how it will all end.

"More and more I take over household duties from his mother. She
is like a child overwhelmed by it all. Now that her husband, Pedro's
father, has gone to the Great Beyond, she seems to cast about like
a leaf blown by every breeze, looking for a tall, strong tree to light upon.

"It appears to me — please forgive me for stating the truth which may
seem more like spiteful gossip which it is not — but it appears to me
that she has found a tree. A widower, a Yankee lawyer who comes
to the rancho to help Pedro with his affairs but who always has time
to look after his own affair, Doña Beatriz.

"Pedro does not notice. He is consumed by numbers. He sees cattle
and horses and fruit on the trees not as beauties of nature, but as things
to be transformed into money to pay off the loan on the rancho.

"That is the way it is with all the ranchos. What is not stolen outright
by these Yankee locusts, these cutthroats that invaded our beautiful
land, is lost for failure to pay the debts we foolishly incur or the taxes
that the government demands.

"I do not know how it will all end. It is not the paradise it was when
I came to California as a young bride almost ten years ago. It's as
if God had abandoned Eden and Satan had taken over.

"I realize that you are now about the age I was when I married and
left New Mexico. It will be your time to marry soon. Perhaps you
already have someone picked out. Don't let him entice you to California. And as for Texas, you know what horrors have gone on there
for years and years. Stay where you are. The riches that other places

promise are but fool's gold. Better a poor ranchero in New Mexico than the richest Don in California.

"And choose your man carefully and wisely. I see from time to time how much my dear Pedro is like his father. The old Don drank himself to death, to the very end a slave to the grape. I worry that all these troubles will drive my Pedro to the same sickness. What a cruel trick life has played on me if it happens. I leave our own drunken father, God rest his soul, and escape to a family where I have escaped nothing at all. Here they just drink better brandy . . . and more of it.

"But enough. The children are well and seem to take it all much better than their parents and aunts and uncles. Panchita is learning inglés and can chatter like a little gringo when she wants to show off. I hope all is well with you and pray that God bless you and keep you.

"Your loving sister, Rebecca."

There were a few more treasured letters that Gregoria kept stored in a jewelbox. Had there been so many horrors that the incidents in this one reflected but the major tragedies, like the larger beads on a rosary? Had there been so many horrors that one only felt the larger beads as one's fingers moved blindly along through life? Something monstrous had happened. Can you not sense the size and shape of it? Are you so numb that even this does not rouse you to anguish?

Abruptly she came to the end of her mending. She looked at the faded gingham of her granddaughter Juanita's dress, knotted the thread, and cut it with a sharp snap of her front teeth. From the other room she heard her husband's monotone interrupted by a boyish yawn. She put aside her mending and called out, "Chocolate anyone?"

# 31

It was two nights later before José Antonio continued the story. "It was California gringo justice," he began. "A twin of Texas gringo justice. For when one makes the law as well as administers it, one can do as he pleases legally. All things can be made to seem reasonable. One can even be arrested on suspicion, whatever that means."

\*     \*     \*

Don Pedro, accompanied by John Archer, made his way from the courtroom to the sheriff's office. The sheriff stood waiting, a frown wrinkling his sun-beaten face. He grunted and then, as if propelled by their appearance, strode quickly behind his desk and dropped onto his chair.

"This does not look good, Don Pedro."

"Especially for the deceased," Don Pedro answered. When the sheriff looked up, Pedro challenged him with a stare that was not so much belligerent as self-confident.

"What is it you want?" Archer asked. "My client and I have had a difficult enough time with this lawsuit without it ending like this."

"Who had good cause to ambush these men?" the sheriff asked.

Don Pedro turned to Archer and scoffed, his lips compressed in a tight, painful smile.

"Sheriff," Archer said, "my client never saw those men until yesterday in court. He knows nothing about them or their activities. You're asking your question of the wrong man."

"Who had most to gain from their deaths?"

"Their heirs," Don Pedro answered.

"That disputed mine," Archer said, "is but a small part of Don Pedro's holdings. Don Pedro has nothing to gain from their deaths. The lawsuit is merely postponed. The title to that mine is still in dispute."

"Sheriff," Don Pedro said irritably, ignoring Archer's hand outstretched in warning, "just what is it that you are trying to ask me? If I shot those four men?" The sheriff grunted and shifted in his chair. "What I heard in court was that they were killed by person or persons unknown. Exactly the same as my brothers who were found hanging in a tree outside of the disputed mine. Did you ever question Señor Schloss and partners about that?"

The sheriff's face reddened and he turned away from the two men. Before Pedro could say any more, Archer put a hand on his arm to interrupt. "Sheriff, we're very willing to cooperate in bringing to justice whoever committed the outrages to Schloss and company as well as to Don Pedro's brothers. I'm certain Don Pedro will answer any reasonable questions. But damn it, I won't have my client treated like any peon walking the street. Don Pedro is one of our leading citizens. A man of property and propriety. I'm here to see that he is treated accordingly."

"If I had treated your client like any peon I'd have had him arrested and interrogated in jail," the sheriff said stiffly. "We're just having a friendly conversation here. I'm telling you, with all due respect, Don Pedro, that people of your race are very vulnerable to public opinion. You know what's happening in the goldfields. I just want to clear away any hint of suspicion before these killings become general knowledge."

Pedro found it difficult to control his anger and his voice quavered as he spoke. "We are more sinned against than sinners," he spat. "The law is here to protect the innocent as well as punish the guilty, regardless of their so-called 'race.'"

"I don't think this conversation is going very far," the sheriff said.

"I must repeat," Pedro said, "that I never met nor saw Señor Schloss and partners before yesterday. After the court session I returned to my rancho. There are at least two dozen witnesses who will testify to that in court, including the padre from Mission San José who is a guest of my wife. I did not shoot those men and consider the dispute over the mine, while a business matter, not worthy of men's blood."

"But is revenge a strong enough motive?"

"Revenge?"

"For the killing of your brothers."

"How could that be when you yourself never questioned Schloss and company about those murders? It appears that they were never under suspicion. Would I have knowledge that the law did not have?"

Irritation showed on the sheriff's face. He compressed his lips and peered from half-shut eyes beneath furrowed brows. "No more questions. But I want you available in case I need to talk to you again."

"With pleasure, señor."

The sheriff turned his back on them abruptly. Don Pedro shrugged at Archer and they left. "Stupid bastard," Don Pedro mumbled to himself. "Stupid gringo son of a bitch."

\* \* \*

Back at the rancho, the unsettled status of the lawsuit added to the gloom of their daily lives. Pedro was weary of the unrelieved black of the women's mourning clothes. It was as if the rancho had committed some grievous, mortal sacrilege for which their punishment, like that of souls in purgatory, was an eternity of penance, in this case the wearing of black. Most aggravating of all, this damning grievous sin was merely to be themselves.

Doña Beatriz went into seclusion, seeing only close members of the family, her personal maid, and John Archer. She did not speak to Pedro of her planned marriage. When the loan on the rancho came due, it was extended for another three months through Archer's intercession. For what? Pedro thought. He would be as unable to pay it in three months as now. He settled into deeper gloom, as if his mind had taken on the permanent hue of the women's mourning clothes.

A younger brother of Jacob Schloss returned to San José from Sacramento where he had gone on business relating to the quicksilver mine. After a delay for the burials and settling of estates, the lawsuit began again.

During the interim, members of the Baca family avoided each other, perhaps so they could avoid discussing what lay heavy on all their minds, their future and their very lives. Each seemed to take solace in being alone. Doña Beatriz remained cloistered in her room sewing things for her forthcoming wedding, though no one knew when it would take place. Don Pedro searched endlessly among his account books for the miracle that would save them. Not finding it, he began to seek the answer in the bottom of a bottle, where his father had looked unsuccessfully for signs.

Pedro's distrust of John Archer grew, fed by his brooding on the cause of all his family's misfortunes, the cursed Yankee conquerors: an endless, depressing assault as if God had chosen them to suffer for reasons Pedro did not know.

It was not only their lives, but also their property that was in jeopardy. The rancho mortgaged to a syndicate headed by Pedro's lawyer. Their mine stolen by gringo interlopers and still in litigation, with Pedro's interests represented again by his lawyer. He felt caught in a tangle of laws, like a puppet whose strings were on the fingers of John Archer.

He watched Archer's comings and goings with increasing suspicion, the footsteps creaking up the stairs to Doña Beatriz' room in frequent visits. What are they doing up there? Pedro wondered in anguish. What is that gringo up to? Then, perhaps an hour later, the footsteps creaked down the stairs, and Archer would come into the office for a few minutes consultation.

Pedro hardly knew what the lawyer said to him. He did not listen to the words so much as to the tone of voice: dulcet, persuasive, with a kind of insincerity that he had never noticed before. The man was not real, he thought. He is playing a role like an actor on the stage.

Like a much younger man courting a girl and trying to make a good impression on her family.

At times there would be papers to sign at which Pedro would arch a jaundiced brow, wondering what gringo chicanery lay embodied in the slippery, dodging words that defied accurate communication. "Therefores" and "whereases" and "on the other hands" that left him more confused than when he began. Pedro would glance at the papers, then put them aside for careful reading after Archer had gone.

He would offer the lawyer a drink, hear the polite but firm refusal, then realize that he did not trust men who did not drink. Especially gringos. More epecially, lawyers. As if they sat, sober and expectant, waiting to pounce on some advantage from what should have been a joining together in good fellowship.

"Tomorrow," Pedro would say when the papers were offered again while he drained his second or third glass of brandy. "That can wait until then. In the meantime—" He poured himself another glassful.

In his dreams everyone spoke English which he did not understand as well as he did when awake. His mother, whispering to Archer from behind a cupped hand while keeping her wide eyes on Pedro. The ranchhands, who watched him warily while breaking horses or rounding up cattle. The padre, whose mass in inglés was as unintelligible as it had been in Latin.

Everywhere in his dreams people were looking at him. Pointing at him. Mumbling indecipherable cluckings and admonitions and accusations. He imagined what it was they muttered. "Is it true that he killed those mine stealers?" "His mother's being screwed by that gringo." "We are going to lose the rancho and our jobs. Our livelihoods. Because of him."

Then one night the dead men in his family rode their silent, ghostly horses into his bedroom and surrounded him. There was his father and his uncle. His two cousins. His four brothers. All looked sadly at him, shaking their heads and whispering one ghostly word over and over again: "Gringo. Gringo, GRINGO." Their insistent chorus demanding an answer.

"Yes!" he shouted in his sleep. "They're out to get me! You cannot trust any of them! Especially those thieving lawyers. Agh-h-h-h—"

A hand on his shoulder shook him awake. "What is it, Pedro?" his wife asked in a frightened voice.

He stared unseeing, the cry stuck dry in his throat, the fear chilling him to the marrow. "Nothing," he muttered in a thick, sleep-laden voice. "Just a dream."

But when he awoke the next morning, he was convinced that there was more truth in his dream than there was in real life.

\*   \*   \*

The judge had heard the summations from the opposing lawyers. Across the sparsely filled courtroom Pedro saw young Schloss look up with confident eyes, glancing briefly from the judge to the two lawyers before his glance fell on Pedro, hardened, and turned away.

"It doesn't look good," Archer whispered. "We should have accepted the offer Schloss made and dropped the suit. This way we will probably get nothing."

Pedro did not take his eyes off young Schloss. "Why would he offer to pay unless he thought we had a just claim? Men like that do not give unless they are forced to. They are takers, not givers." But silently Pedro thought: I pay this lawyer to protect my interests. Yet he wants to give up my claim and accept a pittance in return. Conscience money. Damned little at that because there is so little conscience to buy off. And Archer's pleadings to the judge were half-hearted. As if he didn't care. As if, when I refused Schloss' offer, Archer had gone ahead and accepted it in secret, surrendering my claim by his legal flabbiness.

"Young Schloss is a different breed from his brother. He doesn't want to stay in California a minute longer than he has to. He has a fiancée in St. Louis and he'd like nothing better than to settle the suit, sell the mine, and hurry home. We should have taken his offer."

Across the courtroom Schloss turned toward the judge whose polite gavel was the only sound in the already quiet courtroom. Pedro looked up, expectant. This will be it, he thought. Now I will have my vindication.

"Señor Baca. Mr. Schloss," the judge said. "We have spent more time on this lawsuit than it would normally justify due to unfortunate and tragic circumstances, plus the desire of the court to be scrupulous and fair to one of our prominent citizens." The judge inclined his head toward Don Pedro.

"We have heard witnesses," he went on, "for both the plaintiff and the defendant. Witnesses whose knowledge goes back a number of years into the history of the disputed property. A key witness for the plaintiff, one Pablo Romero, was not available. Word is that he left Northern California for Mexico, where he subsequently died. We did examine a note signed with the name Pablo Romero, which the plaintiff testified he had received as payment for a gambling debt, this note giving title to property that Señor Romero claimed to have owned.

"We have also examined witnesses for the defendant, including one Octavio Sánchez who held a grant given to him by the Mexican government for the property in dispute. This property he in turn sold to Jacob Schloss and partners who had intended to finance mining operations and furnish for sale quicksilver for use in processing gold ore. All of this has been duly transacted and legally recorded here in San José.

"The crux of the dispute revolves around the relationship and negotiations between Señor Pablo Romero and Señor Octavio Sánchez prior to the time that Señor Romero gave his note to Don Pedro Baca and prior to the time that Señor Sánchez sold his property to Mr. Schloss.

"There is no question about the legality involved. Señor Romero never legally owned the property according to the records filed with the township of San José. The question is, rather, whether there was any verbal agreement between Señores Romero and Sánchez to turn over the property to Señor Romero for certain considerations. If such existed, then the question is: why was it never legally acted upon?

"The plaintiff has been unable to show that Señor Romero ever owned the property in dispute. Señor Sánchez, who would have been a party to any such transaction, emphatically denies that any such transaction ever took place. Señor Romero, who had earned his living in Northern California buying and selling horses, had in fact been a miner in Mexico. He approached Señor Sánchez about managing the mine. The horse business had been going poorly. Señor Sánchez had been unable to help Señor Romero since the mine was inactive. He did not have the capital to work it and at that time quicksilver did not have a strong demand nor was any foreseen. Only later, after the discovery at Sutter's Mill, did its use in processing gold ore create a demand that made the mine economically viable.

"Perhaps it was this discussion about a job in the mine that gave Señor Romero the inspiration to become a mine owner. That is sheer speculation. What is known is that Señor Romero and Don Pedro Baca entered into a wager on a horse race between one of Don Pedro's horses and one of the horses Romero had for sale, ownership unknown. Being as unfortunate in racing as apparently he was in selling horses, Romero lost and offered this piece of paper in payment. We have the sworn testimony of Don Pedro and other witnesses to that fact.

"What is also certain is that the mine was not Señor Romero's to assign. The piece of paper, which Don Pedro accepted in good faith, was worthless.

"In the light of such evidence, carefully and painstakingly reviewed, we cannot but reach the conclusion that the plaintiff's case has no substance in law and the court must rule in favor of the defendant.

"Case dismissed!"

Stunned, Don Pedro stared in astonishment at the three gringos who had done him out of his mine. The judge, all business, put down his gavel and turned toward a member of the court who had come up to him. *Curses to the stupid judge!*

Across the room young Schloss looked up from his shoetops and smiled at no one in particular. *Bribing brother of a murdering son of a bitch!*

Beside him, Archer sighed, his face impassive. *Shyster! Betrayer! Accepter of bribes!*

Pedro stood abruptly and stomped from the courtroom, while the aftermath of the decision, a mild buzz of discussion, filled the room. He was the first to leave, slamming the door behind him, burning inside at the injustice, the perfidy, the outright thievery.

\*    \*    \*

From one who had once been an admirer, a friend, and a welcomer of Americanos to California, Don Pedro made a complete change. His life had been assaulted by a large, black bird of prey perched on the shoulders of immigrant gringos. Soft words and smiles were the gringo smokescreen behind which the destructive bird selected the flesh that it would pluck clean.

He spoke with impassioned urgency to Doña Beatriz about breaking relations with her gringo fiancé. Again and again she refused, teary-eyed, her trembling little hand reaching for but not quite grasping Pedro's arm.

"I'm alone," she repeated. "A lonely woman with just a few years left. I want them to be happy years."

"I'll fire him!" Pedro shouted. "I'll find another lawyer. One who has our best interests at heart."

But his mother's intransigence and the relentless march of days to the due date for the loan reduced him to impotence. Even the bottle did not help. And the rancho suffered from his inattention. If ever there had been the slightest hope of showing a profit and paying off the debt, it disappeared like the bottles of brandy with which Pedro nursed his hatred and frustration.

One day, riding half-drunk and angry into San José, he heard in a local cantina that the quicksilver mine had been sold and young Schloss had returned to St. Louis. The bartender tried to hush the loudmouth at the end of the bar, all the time watching Don Pedro with quiet, sad eyes.

"What's that? What's that you say?" the drunk asked in a loud voice. "What do you mean shush?" Then, after a few minutes at lowered voice, the man laughed aloud and spoke out again. "That lawyer has got to be the slickest article in these parts. Lost the case for his client, then bought that mine for next to nothing because that young feller had to get back east to wed and bed that young woman of his. By God—"

But Pedro heard no more. He did not even finish his drink, which signaled the depth of his rage. Grimly he walked from the cantina, crossed Market Street, and entered the law office. John Archer looked up from his desk and smiled. As he started to rise, Pedro drew his pistol. Two shots shattered the quiet.

"Somebody go for the sheriff!" he heard someone shout as he walked from the office toward his horse.

"Was anybody hurt?"

"That lawyer, Archer, got it!"

That was the last that San José, and almost the last that Rancho Los Palos, saw of Don Pedro Baca.

# 32

José Antonio let his story hang suspended in silence. For a moment he thought that the questions were coming: Did Don Pedro kill the lawyer? How did he get away? But his grandson only blinked himself awake, mumbled "Buenas noches," and stumbled across the room and out the door.

The next day was José Antonio's duty day, a throwback to the time he had held political office and assumed the role of unofficial patrón of Los Rafas. He would seat himself on a rocking chair in the front room with the door open and only the screen door separating him from outside. Here he would rock, waiting for those visitors that he knew would come.

All Los Rafas knew that this was his day to be "at home," and many of the old-timers would come to him with problems that they hoped he could solve. As for the younger people, who knows where they went? Not to the priests at San Felipe Church, that was for certain. But their parents, their aunts and uncles, came to see the patrón much the way their grandparents had come to see José Antonio's grandfather back in the old days when the Rafas were the richest landowners in the area.

"Don José?" The whispered call was followed by a light knock on the screen door.

"Come in."

"I don't want to disturb you, Don José." The hinges squeaked and footsteps approached.

"Señora Luján. Come in. Sit down."

The señora dropped the rebozo from her head to her shoulders and sat cautiously. "I do not want my husband to know that I came. He would skin me alive." José Antonio nodded as if this were the most usual request in the world. "He gets angry when he thinks I interfere."

He smiled. When did wives not interfere? And what husbands were fool enough not to know?

"I need your advice, Don José."

"Sí, señora."

They sat facing each other, ramrod-straight and formal; their choices of words, their tones of voice formal in the extreme even though one of each of their grandparents had been brother and sister, and they had known each other most of their lives.

"It is all this politics," Señora Luján said. "All of this election business. One person says vote for this one, he'll do such and such. Another person says vote for that one, he'll do more such and such. My head is spinning from all this tugging and pulling. Especially about the office of sheriff. We don't know what to do with our vote."

José Antonio's smile faded. We don't know what to do with our vote, he thought with annoyance. *Our vote.* "Señora. It is your husband's vote. It is up to him to decide. It is the man's privilege, no—duty— and women should not interfere."

Her face hardened. The docile mask disappeared. The firm, tight mouth and glaring eyes of one who usually got her way bore into him. He remembered that look from years past. From his boyhood, from her girlhood, from more recent disagreements with his own wife. Yet there were times when one must shout advice against all deafness. Appeal with honeyed tones against all stubbornness. Resist giving in to one's own anger against all the furies of another's assault.

When she did not answer, he spoke again. "Did your husband send you because he is too busy to come himself?"

No answer. Yet she did not move to leave. He was tempted to usher her out. He stared at her in annoyance. What did she want? There had to be more to it. Then he realized his mistake. He had reacted to her first superficial statement. Women were deeper than that. But as so often happened, he heard only the words and did not seek what lay hidden behind them.

In that instant he clearly saw the stubborn woman who would not be driven away by insult or anger. Who would not leave until she got what she came for or until she had irrevocably given up hope that she would ever succeed.

He saw the rebozo with the frayed edges and a rip beneath the fold where it lay over her shoulder. He saw the bare feet, trying to hide beneath the long skirts. The gap in the seam under the left arm of her dress. There was about her the look and odor of earth and work and hunger that manifested itself in the rough, thin fingers and in the pinched cheeks. Yet there was a defiance about her, a toughness underneath that demanded his admiration,

It was women like her, her mother's mother's mother generations back, who had followed their men to this new land. To this "New" Mexico. Sharing hunger and thirst on the trail, the depredations of the Indians, the fickleness of sun and rain.

The gringos talked with pride about their pioneers crossing the American continent in their covered wagons. Yet when they got here, women like Señora Luján were already waiting to greet them. Had been here for two hundred years. Even before that their red-skinned half-sisters had not only survived but thrived in this arid land for thousands of years.

"I don't know," she finally said after long thought, "if we can bring ourselves to vote for Plácido Durán. He is a fool and his brother is a brute. But then the current sheriff—" She made a sour face. José Antonio knew what she meant. More than once he had gone to the jail to see about one or another of her sons who had either been in a brawl or overindulged in cheap liquor. "Well," she went on, "at least he does his job honestly. Even if he is an Anglo."

Her mood shifted. There was an expectancy in her voice, in her

manner. José Antonio finally knew what it was about. In her own way
she was selling her husband's vote. What she was waiting to hear was
the price.

He clenched his teeth and took a deep breath. Looking at this poor
woman, he could not be angry at her.

"As you know," he said, "Plácido Durán belongs to the political party
that has always done the most for us. Whether it's jobs for those who
need them or something like the irrigation system or schools that benefit
all of us. So, I feel that the people of Los Rafas owe some loyalty to
the party that has been loyal to us.

"I respect your opinions about the party's candidate. Some of our
canidates are better than others. But we cannot let personalities blind
us to what is really important and in our best interests, the party itself.

"What I suggest is that your husband vote for the party that has
taken care of us in the past and will take care of us in the future."

Her dried old face cracked a smile and he could tell from her bright,
expectant eyes that she was waiting for what would come next. She
opened her mouth to speak, and José Antonio was certain that what
he dreaded was coming, the question: How much will we get for our
vote? But to his surprise, she said, "You mean vote for Durán?"

He responded with a quick nod. They sat silently a moment. Each
reluctant, for different reasons, to say what had to be said. José Antonio because he would not pay for a single vote. Señora Luján, he
knew, because of some innate sense of propriety, some sense of pride
in not wanting to openly sell something that should have been private,
personal, and unsellable, some sense of not wanting to acknowledge
prostitution although skillful seduction would be tolerated.

José Antonio looked again at her clothes torn in places where thread
would no longer hold the pieces together, saw the thin, nervous hands
trying to be still and not quite succeeding.

"How is Señor Luján?" he asked. "Is he better able to work these
days?" Her eyes narrowed and she looked away from him as she shook
her head. "Are your sons able to help much?" A tighter, shorter, but
more violent shake of the head. "Your husband has helped me in the
past clearing our section of the acequia and during harvest. I have
never fully repaid him. He is a proud and generous man. If you would
not tell him, perhaps we could give you some beans and corn until
things get a little better."

"I . . . I thought there might be some money."

"I cannot do that, señora."

She sat pondering, the dilemma showing in her eyes and puzzled brow. "Yes," she finally said. "We will keep our secret from Señor Luján. The beans and corn would be very welcome. God bless you."

With the formal elegance of a duchess, she lifted her tattered rebozo over her head, stood, and glided out the door.

*　*　*

He could smell the next visitor long before he heard the feeble rattle on the screen door. There had been a pause between the aroma and the sound, as if whoever stood there had hovered indecisively before laying an unsteady knuckle onto wood.

José Antonio's jaw and neck tightened. He resisted the urge to shout that he was not in. It was the local drunk, he was certain, and the especially pungent smell of cheap liquor told him that the man was farther gone than usual this morning.

"Don José." The voice was hoarse and rasping, almost impossible to understand. "Compadre. It's me."

José Antonio stopped rocking and remained still until his conscience shamed him for trying to ignore this miserable creature. "The door is open."

The shuffling of unsteady feet, the tilt of an unsteady body, and old Sánchez leered at him from behind blinking eyes. "I was just passing by, Don José. God bless you, Don José. It's a beautiful day, Don José." Sánchez slobbered a twisted smile, then wiped the saliva from a corner of his mouth with the back of a filthy hand.

José Antonio shook his head continually, indicating that the answer was no. "Not today," he said.

His visitor cocked his head like a dog listening to a high-pitched sound. "Just a centavo," he pleaded. "God will love you for helping an old sinner."

The shaking head persisted. "Not today."

"Just enough for a tortilla and some frijolitos."

"Go to the kitchen. Señora Rafa will feed you."

The drunken eyes blinked in momentary confusion. "No. Not tortillas. I mean tobacco. Yes, tobacco. I need to get it from the store." The twisted smile beseeching sympathy until Sánchez' eye twitched and one corner of his mouth followed suit.

"Not today."

Sánchez stood there, head hanging so his chin rested on his chest, his face full of disappointment. The foul stench of his breath seemed to fill the tiny room and José Antonio wished that he would leave and shuffle his drunken way down the road toward the cantina, where his extended palm and beseeching face were much more familiar than the sight of his money.

After a few minutes, Sánchez shuffled his feet to remind José Antonio of his presence. José Antonio ignored him and continued reading his Bible. Finally the footsteps shuffled off, yet he dared not look up until the door slammed and the shuffling faded along the dirt path.

*     *     *

"I thought I would wait until dark," Ignacio Montoya said, his dark furtive eyes peering intently into the corners of the tiny room. "But then I said the hell with them! Let them see me. Let them stick their heads in the window and hear every word I say."

Ignacio Montoya, a tall, skinny man with stooped shoulders and a full lower lip that protuded and in some strange way matched the thrust of his dark eyebrows, ran a nervous hand through his hair that showed a few streaks of gray.

"It happened this spring when the river flooded," Montoya went on. "It changed the channel of the mother ditch that borders my property, moving it into my land so that my north boundary was on the wrong side of the acequia. That's when Archuleta and his sons quickly dug the new channel deeper and filled the old channel with dirt and claimed that the island of my property on the other side of the ditch was now theirs. To add insult to injury he has fenced it off and grazes his cow there. I'm going to kill that goddamned cow and have a barbecue!"

"You could go to court," José Antonio said.

"I don't have the money. I would have to sell that disputed piece of land to pay the lawyer and whether I won or lost in court, I will still have lost."

José Antonio sighed. Every year or so it was one thing or another between Montoya and Archuleta. A cow knocking down a fence and trampling a cornfield. One or the other leaving the sluice gate to his field open longer than was decreed and using more than his share of irrigation water. The Archuleta sons beating one of the Montoya boys foolish enough to be out alone at night near Archuleta property.

"What do you want me to do?"

"Talk to old Archuleta. He'll listen to you."

Wearily, José Antonio nodded in assent. He could see old Archuleta with his meek smile and bland, innocent face. "Who? Me? Oh, no, Don José. Someone is telling lies again. Who would tell lies about me? I mind my own business. Go to church on Sunday. Love my neighbor—" The old liar.

"Thank you, Don José. If you could just see him soon. Today or tomorrow."

Again José Antonio nodded, more to be rid of him than in actual agreement. There had been this problem since last spring. Time for Archuleta to fill the old ditch and dig out the new channel. Time for a fence to be built. While Montoya did nothing. And now, please settle it in the next day or two.

"Next time," José Antonio said as the man rose to leave, "do not wait so long before you act. It makes it much more difficult."

"Sí, Don José. Thank you, Don José." And he was gone.

\* \* \*

So it went on the days that Don José Rafa was at home. Wives who came to complain that their drunken husbands had beaten them. Young lovers whose parents forbade them to see each other and who were determined, in spite of their parents, to love one another forever. Parents who despaired of what to do with a wayward son who was lazy and did not work or a daughter who was so promiscuous that they did not know the fathers of their grandchildren.

Over a period of months it seemed that all of Los Rafas passed through his sitting room, either physically or in gossiped words. He knew, through these visits, as much about Los Rafas as if he had made the rounds himself, from little adobe house to little adobe house, from verdant field to verdant field, from muddy irrigation ditch to muddy irrigation ditch. Only the priest rivaled him for intimate knowledge of the people of the area. And only God exceeded them both.

The light footsteps of his wife roused him. She placed a warm cup in his hand and sat on the chair beside him.

"It's been a long day," he said.

"How much did you give away this time?" Her voice was gentle, almost teasing, and his response was an arched eyebrow underlined by a slight smile.

He took a sip, savoring the warmth that made its way down to his stomach. "I'd give more if we were rich."

"We're rich enough."

They sat quietly, listening to the chair squeak as he slowly rocked. The bright light of day was softening and the warm air had cooled a little. From next door came Florinda's scream and the high-pitched responses from her daughters about why they could not come in and set the table for dinner. Then evening silence again.

This was José Antonio's favorite time of day, in the way that autumn was his favorite time of year. Work was over, one's energy spent, problems solved or put away for another day. The quarreling people had gone home. The smells of cooking in the kitchen perfumed the air and tantalized the stomach. The sun took its leave so that the bright, eye-blinking light became more benign; the air no longer assaulted the body with heat, but kissed it coolly to help soothe the fatigue of work. Then, with it all, the stillness. So one could ponder on what had happened that day. Try to understand what, in the whirl of a day's activities, one reacted to and acted upon without thought, sometimes without feeling, often without awareness, driven by instinct.

A slow, soft tread approached the open door. A shadow on the screen blocked the light from the dying sun. "Don José Rafa?"

Gregoria looked at him, then rose and returned to the kitchen. It was late for a visitor. Most would be home now, getting ready for dinner. He stood and crossed to the screen door instead of calling out for the man to enter.

"Don José Rafa?" The man peered through the screen, no doubt sensing the hesitation, the still-lingering suspicion of strangers that was a heritage from more dangerous times. "My name is Rudolfo Salazar. I live north of here, across the river near Alameda." José Antonio stood waiting. "I was told that you were the man to warn. It's about Los Hijos de Libertad."

The growl in José Antonio's throat could have been a greeting or an oath. He pushed the screen open and ushered the stranger to a chair.

"Thank you, Don José. My apologies for calling on you at this time of day. I was in Albuquerque on business and now I am on my way home. I do not come this way often. I only wish I could have come sooner to warn you before something happens."

"What about Los Hijos de Libertad?"

"I've only heard the name, the rumors, that it is a secret political organization that is trying to better things for the Spanish-speaking New Mexican. There has been talk about it all over Alameda. About

the ultimatum they issued to the local political leaders that will probably decide the election. Los Hijos have great power.

"Then last week a group of strangers appeared asking questions
about horses. Who owned them. About the numbers and kinds. About
their peculiarities. A hoof unshod or split. A peculiar gait. We thought
they were horse traders looking for bargains. But then why so many
together?

"Someone told them where they might find horses like those they
were asking about. When my neighbor who owned some was told about
his potential good fortune, he turned pale, and said he had to visit
a sick cousin in Santa Fe. He was gone the next day when the strangers
came by. I remember them as they passed. There were five. Led by
giant of a man, as wide as he was tall.

"The neighbor's wife rushed across the field to see me afterwards
with tears in her eyes. 'They threatened me,' she cried. 'They wanted
to know about the gray mustang with the split left-front hoof. Then
they wanted to know where my husband was. They asked what kind
of a husband would run away and let his wife stand up for him. Some
of them were talking to each other while the big man threatened me,'
she said. 'They mentioned Los Hijos de Libertad and how they would
fix those unmentionables. Then they rode off, promising to be back,
saying that if I valued my life and my husband valued his, he had
better be there when they came again.'"

"They mean great harm to Los Hijos, Don José. They said they
were certain that Los Hijos were from Los Rafas. When I asked in
town, someone told me that you were the man to see."

"Did any of these horse traders have a name?"

"Only the big man. One of the others called him Benito."

José Antonio closed his eyes for a moment. The midnight visit to
Plácido Durán had been stupid. If he had known the perpetrators,
he would have horsewhipped them himself. As it was, Benito Durán
would certainly take care of that.

But what should he tell this stranger who came to warn him? That
Los Hijos de Libertad was no mythic group of saviors but an unknown
gang of ruffians trying to intimidate a political candidate? No, he
thought. Why say anything. Even that Salazar's information was of
no use to him since he did not know who these men were and therefore
could not warn them even if he wanted to.

"Muchas gracias for the information, Señor Salazar."

"I only did what was right, Don José. I believe in what Los Hijos
are trying to do for us."

Salazar blinked a shy smile and took his leave. José Antonio stared out the screen door a moment, then joined his wife in the kitchen.

## 33

Francisco felt trapped. He was tempted by James Smith's offer of gain. The prospect of money was always alluring, even if he did not need it the way some of his neighbors did. He was his father's heir and there was no doubt about his inheritance. His sisters had received their shares as dowries. His brothers had renounced all but token shares when they had left New Mexico. So there was plenty of good land and a little money for him, even though Rafa fortunes were not what they had been during his grandfather's time.

On the other hand, the election of Plácido Durán was the key to Smith's financial opportunity. Francisco found it impossible to accept the bootlicker Durán, who toadied to the Anglos who ran New Town and had little concern for what he saw as the Hispanic needs. What would it profit him to gain Anglo money and lose his Hispanic soul?

Yet he could not completely dismiss the prospect. It tempted him. He would resist and the temptation would slink away . . . for awhile. Then it would sneak back, not yet acknowledging defeat.

He slammed the door of the house and trudged down the road toward the cantina, cursing under his breath. "Compadre!" a neighbor called. He waved back across the field and hurried to avoid a conversation.

The cantina was empty except for the bartender. "A drink," Francisco grumbled. The bartender made a sour face, matching Francisco's, and set a glass and bottle on the table.

The bell from the adjoining grocery store summoned the bartender. Francisco poured a shot and sipped it slowly. "Money isn't everything," he said to himself. "There are more important things than money."

He had poured a second drink before the bartender returned, followed by footsteps. "Rafa, how goes it?"

Francisco's face hardened and he answered without looking up. "Ignacio."

He wished that Armijo would go away. He could imagine the amused and superior look on the man's face. Knew what must be going through his mind: Well, I told you so, Rafa. If I had led that little expedition, Durán would have resigned right on the spot. Now it's too late. He's more determined than ever to be sheriff.

A heavy hand lit solidly on Francisco's shoulder. "Why so glum, amigo? Have you heard the news?"

He looked up in surprise. "You haven't heard?" Armijo whispered, dropping onto a bench beside him. "Benito Durán and his gang have been nosing around. Looking for horses." Francisco lifted his glass and downed the drink in one quick gulp. "That's no joke."

"What is it to me? Lots of people look for horses."

What did Armijo know? Francisco thought. All Armijo should know was that one of their group was the chief Hijo de Libertad. No one other than the chief knew the other men. And those men had not known the identities of their companions. The horses had been borrowed so they would not be recognized locally.

Ignacio leaned across the table, breathing into Francisco's face. "Listen. I hear the talk. Benito has been searching the countryside for a horse with a split left-front hoof. He's convinced that it was one of the horses ridden by what he calls 'Los Hijos del Diablo.' I hear he found such a horse across the river from Alameda. The owner is nowhere to be found, and if he knows what's good for him, he'll stay there."

"There are lots of horses with split hooves. And people reshoe their horses all the time."

"Maybe. But one thing for certain, Plácido is still our candidate."

The bright, shiny face beamed in silent accusation, feeding Francisco's anger and frustration. "Plácido was too stupid to heed the warning!"

"Because the threat was empty. 'Get out of the race or get killed!' was what he was told. Why haven't Los Hijos fired a shot at him, even if just to frighten him?"

Francisco wanted Plácido replaced in the worst way. Yet the thought of killing someone, in spite of the threats that night, disturbed him deeply. He was not his father's son for nothing. Never mind that his youngest brother had volunteered to be a soldier whose job it was to kill. It was something he knew he could not do and it angered him to be at such a disadvantage with Armijo.

"A threat is one thing," he said. "Doing it is something else."

"What good is a threat if it isn't carried out? Hell, man. This thing is a mess. I wish you had let me do it."

"Damn it, hombre!" Francisco said. "I came here to have a quiet drink. Who asked you to sit down and badmouth me?"

Armijo took a deep breath and held it, puffing up like a toad. His dark face turned a purplish red and he sputtered until he was able to speak. "Someone let us down, Rafa! The whole goddamned thing is —"

Francisco reached a hand into his pocket, slammed some change onto the table, and stomped out. "Stupid bastard!" he hissed. The son of a bitch playing God. You should have done this. You should have done that. Let him saddle his own horse and ride it.

The bartender yelled adiós. Francisco plodded grimly down the road, crossed the orchard, and headed toward the back field. Still cursing, he did not see his father standing beside the ditch, watching the flow of muddy water, until he was almost upon him. He stopped mid-curse as if he were a boy caught at something he shouldn't be doing.

José Antonio surveyed both sides of the ditch, then turned. "I was just seeing how straight and true it ran," he said. "Montoya and Archuleta are at it again."

Francisco closed his mouth tight to seal off the smell of whiskey. "I heard," José Antonio said, "that Los Hijos de Libertad are from Los Rafas." Francisco's mouth dropped open in surprise. "Where?"

"A little bird. The bird heard from Benito Durán himself. He was looking for a horse over near Alameda. He thinks he can trace it to the rider." Jesus! Francisco thought. Half the countryside knows. "It's no concern of mine."

José Antonio turned back to the ditch, once again studying its muddy flow.

"I'm going to the house," Francisco said.

He picked his way carefully through the orchard, feeling the effects of the drinks or was it the news of Benito's search? What did that bastard really know? he thought. One thing is certain. I'd better clean my gun.

## 34

The day's work was done. José Antonio and Leonardo sat under a tree in the late afternoon sun.

"Grandfather, did Don Pedro kill the lawyer?" Leonardo looked over his shoulder toward the shed.

"No. He had been drinking, you see. His hand was not steady and his eye not clear. What he had done was make a big commotion and frighten a lot of people. But worst of all, it had put him on the run."

\* \* \*

Suspicion is an insidious disease. A worm that grows inside you and feeds on itself as nothing else, until the worm becomes a snake and finally a dragon.

Thus it was with Don Pedro. When Jacob Schloss and partners were murdered, the sheriff suspected him or his friends. The attempt to shoot John Archer only confirmed the suspicion. When Don Pedro disappeared, the rumors began.

Few knew that he visited Rancho Los Palos in secret to bid farewell to his wife. Good Catholic that she was, she went to the little rancho chapel every morning, usually alone, although sometimes her maid accompanied her. Pedro waited early one morning to make sure she was by herself.

Rebecca knelt before a candle that dimly lit the wooden crucifix on the wall. She must have sensed his presence because she looked over her shoulder just after Pedro had followed her in. A look of shock came over her face as she saw him.

"Be quiet, my dear," Pedro whispered. She put a hand to her mouth and stared with wide eyes as he walked quietly toward her. "They are after me," he said. She nodded and her eyes filled with tears.

"They have been here. But the sheriff said you would never dare show your face where you might be caught."

She slid onto a bench and he sat beside her and embraced her. "I have to go into hiding." He took her by the shoulders and stared at her, fixing her features in his memory. "I don't know where yet. Someplace where the law will not find me. I will send you a message as soon as I find a place. I have cousins in Mexico. Perhaps there."

"Let me get the children and go with you."

He shook his head vigorously. "There is still the rancho. Some day it will be mine. That means it will also be yours and our children's. Not only must you look after our interests here, but it is safer than being on the run."

"I want to be with you, Pedro."

"And I with you, my dearest. But who will watch over my mother? Who will prevent her foolishness?"

She began to weep. "When will you send for me?"

"When I find a safe place. Soon. If for some reason you must leave the rancho, go to my cousin Macías in Monterey."

"Better I should return to Albuquerque."

"Monterey is closer and Macías will help you. It is a long, dangerous journey to New Mexico."

"Monterey then." Taking him by the hand, she knelt before the fluttering candle and prayed.

When he stood, she clung to him, and he felt almost too weak to leave as he kissed her tears.

"It won't be long, corazón," he said. He forced himself from her. The lighter it became, the more dangerous.

"Be careful, Pedro. I could not bear to live without you."

He did not look back as he rode away. One more glance from Rebecca and he would have stayed. Let them take him to jail. But then his better sense warned him that he had already been served with Yankee justice. He did not need another helping of that delicacy.

After he rode from Rancho Los Palos, it was rumored that he joined Joaquín Murieta. There were reports that he was in the goldfields, warring against Yankee prospectors who preyed on those with swarthy skins. Yankees were ambushed. Robbed. Hanged. Shot.

Like the elusive Murieta, Don Pedro was seen everywhere up and down California. Sometimes he was reported in a cantina in Monterey the same day that another report told of him riding hard through Santa Barbara. At other times he was rumored to be in San Diego or Los Angeles. Wherever he was seen, he was always on the run.

\*   \*   \*

"But Grandfather, if he did not shoot lawyer Archer, why did he run away? Men do not go to jail unless someone is hurt."

"Those were bad times, Leonardo. Don Pedro did not trust the courts or the sheriff. Men were hanged for less than what he did. The violence and lawlessness in the shanty towns in the gold country spread throughout Northern California. Especially among the former Mexican citizens. A law was passed, forcing foreigners to pay a tax before they could prospect for gold. Later, Yankee miners stopped them from seeking gold, even if they had paid their tax. The worst white scum from all over the world took the law into their own hands."

"But he did not even hit the lawyer with a bullet," Leonardo said. "Tell me. Did he kill Jacob Schloss and those other men?"

"No one knows. Pedro has never told me yes or no. He claimed that dozens at the rancho could have sworn that he was there the night Schloss was shot. But some will swear to anything. Especially relatives and servants."

"But do you think he killed Schloss?"

"I don't know, hijo. It really doesn't matter. That was a long time ago. Whether he did it or not, whether he deserved it or not, he has paid the price."

José Antonio watched his grandson's eyes widen and turn toward the shed. The boy spoke with a sense of wonder. "A killer who rode with Joaquín Murieta."

"No one is sure of that."

"What happened next? How did he get here? Where is his wife? She would be my great-aunt, wouldn't she?"

José Antonio leaned back against the tree and continued.

\*   \*   \*

Those were hard years throughout California, right after the discovery of gold. The man who started it all, Johann Sutter, an Anglo from Switzerland, was left destitute. The gold vultures ruined his land with their greed. Bandits owned the roads and honest people traveled armed and in fear. Among the Mexicans who rode the highways were those who called themselves patriots, resisting the avarice of the hordes

from the eastern United States. It was among these that Pedro Baca
claimed to ride, with no mention of Murieta or others whom the
authorities considered bandits.

As luck would have it, his career on the road was short. He was
surprised and arrested in Pacheco Pass while on his way to Monterey
from the central valley. He thanked the saints that he was not shot
or hanged on the spot. Even so, it took vigorous intervention by Pedro's
cousin in Monterey to keep him alive and in jail rather than kicking
his heels in a tree-top fandango.

The days turned into weeks. The mails were not dependable.
Highwaymen watched the stagecoaches for plunder. Although
Monterey was but a hundred miles from Rancho Los Palos, it might
as well have been a thousand. The jailers were not the most dependable of men. Letters that reached the jailers' hands from either side
of the bars often stopped there. Forgotten. Sometimes opened and read.
Or willfully thrown away. Pedro's correspondence from his wife was
a patchwork of messages and shifts in subject, each letter assuming
that he was aware of some previous message he had never received.
Those that he did get he read over and over, saving the fragile, folded
pieces as treasures.

"My dearest husband," one began. "The inevitable has happened.
Doña Beatriz has married the American lawyer in a ceremony that
would rival a royal wedding. How I wept, grieving that you could
not be here. Your mother was the happiest that I have seen her since
before your poor father died.

"As a wedding gift, he gave her that wretched mine that was your
undoing. Your mother claims that he bought it for the family to return
it to its rightful owners. If you had only known.

"The new Mr. and Mrs. Archer have gone on their honeymoon.
The rancho is almost as it was in days past except that you are not
here, my dearest. How I wish I could fly to you and hold you in my
arms again. Monterey is not so far and your cousin would be willing
to put me up when I visit. If only the roads were safer. If only I knew
for certain that they would let me see you. My life seems overwhelmed
by ifs.

"The children are well and send you their love. They are growing
and sassy and will soon be able to run the rancho by themselves. You
would be proud of them.

"May God keep you and speed you back to me. Your loving
Rebecca."

Not a word of what he really wanted to know. What was his mother's attitude toward him? She had married her gringo who was Pedro's enemy, yet Rebecca was still living on the rancho. During the solitary days in jail he would think about that. Would they drive her from what had been her home for so many years? He waited anxiously for the tear-stained letter that would tell him she had nowhere to go. That a vengeful mother-in-law and new husband had sent her packing. But nothing.

"My dearest Pedro. They would not let me see you when I went to Monterey. Macías did all he could to help me, but they refused. You were an enemy of the state, they said. A revolutionary. A dangerous man. They said things about you that I could not believe. 'No! No!' I told them. 'Not my Pedro. You are talking about the wrong man.'

"Macías had to carry me from the office. I felt such a fool. Then I gave Macías a message for you, but I never heard from you. Are you all right? Do they still keep you locked in that dismal hole or have they moved you to another place? Did you get my message? You must have. Even they couldn't be so inhuman as to prevent a husband and wife from exchanging letters."

He had never received the message from Macías. Never known that his beloved Rebecca had tried to see him. Then one day the whispered jail grapevine told him that Macías had been thrown from a horse and killed. Pedro felt more isolated than ever.

"Dearest husband. Your mother calls for you in her nightmares. As I told you in my last letter, she gets weaker and more ill. The doctor does not know what to do. John has even sent for a specialist from San Francisco. You should see the way he dotes on her. All of your doubts and suspicions of him would disappear."

A previous letter had never reached him so that this was the first he had heard of his mother's illness. And John. Rebecca referred to that lawyer as John. Outside jail things were changing, while inside his resentment stayed constant. "She says she wants to see you before she dies. That she wants her two men, you and John, to embrace like brothers. The two of you are all that she has in the world and you are more precious to her than the most priceless gem. More precious than life itself.

"The rancho is prospering, she told me to tell you that. And the children wait impatiently for their papá to come home. How we all wish you could be with us.

"Your loving wife, Rebecca."

The slow days of imprisonment became even more intolerable. What would he find outside when his time was up? A mother, his remaining parent, gone to heaven. A prospering rancho in the hands of that gringo lawyer. How much of it would be left to Pedro as his rightful inheritance? Perhaps nothing. He would find a wife grown old. Children grown and unrecognizable. The countryside Americanized. He would be a stranger in his own land.

It was this letter that firmed his resolve to escape. Where before he had ignored the jailhouse talk, he now listened warily, waiting for a plan to be proposed by those he thought capable of carrying it out.

When the opportunity came he did not at first recognize it. The prisoner was a gringo prospector. Scruffy. Unshaven. Blasphemous and suspicious to the point of paranoia. He had been brought in for murdering his partner, an Indian, in a quarrel over a mine.

"He tried to steal my map," the prospector hissed. His shifty eyes never focused on Pedro. His foul breath could have killed flies and Pedro turned away from him. "What's the matter? You think you're too good for me, greaser? Hah! I can buy and sell a dozen of you. My mine's worth millions, do you hear? And who the hell are you? Just another half-breed who probably cut up his sweetheart with a knife in some greaser cantina. Hah!"

On first meeting, Pedro thought seriously of strangling this foul creature. But the prospect of the gallows deterred him. "You stink!" he said. "I can't stand the smell of you and your money won't make it any better."

"Hah! Wouldn't you like some of my stinking gold? Don't try to fool me. You're all the same. Just pretending until you can find out my secret. But no one's going to find out."

"Your gold won't do you any good after they hang you. And that's what I hear they're going to do, prospector."

"Hah!" A shrewd gleam lit the prospector's eyes. He smiled his rotten-teeth smile and shook his head in a way that implied that he knew better.

A crazy man, Pedro thought. He kept an eye on this lunatic, as much to stay out of smelling range as from curiosity. He noticed interesting things. The guard did not seem to mind the prospector's stink as the two of them stood whispering through the bars like schoolgirls sharing a secret. At mealtimes, the toothy old stink seemed to get choice morsels, hiding his dish with one hand as he ate greedily with the other.

One day the prospector disappeared from the cell, then reappeared later washed and shaved with a change of clothing. He winked at Pedro. "I'm going to get out of this rathole," he said.

A prisoner in another cell laughed. "They're gonna hang you from a tall tree. They only had you clean up so they could stand to get near enough to drop the rope around your neck."

"Hah!"

Pedro watched the prospector without seeming to. He noticed the glances between the old man and one of the guards that seemed to signify something. He thought about the special treatment accorded this murderer. At first it added to his resentment and bitterness. These gringos all stick together, he thought. It does not matter how flagrant the crime. Better to befriend a murdering gringo than an upright Mexican. But then, realizing that something was brewing, he swallowed his anger and watched.

One night as he lay on the floor brooding, he heard tapping at the door. Footsteps shuffled across the cell.

"I've got it all set up," he heard the guard whisper.

"When?"

"Tomorrow night about this time. I'll unlock the cell and then disappear. The outside door will be unlocked. There'll be no one in the way. I'll see to that. There'll be a horse outside. But first you have to give me my half of the map." A tense silence, then, "No map, no unlocked door."

"And if I give it to you and you don't unlock it?"

"What good is one half of a map?"

"Bastard!"

"The map."

"I need a piece of paper and something to write with. I'll give it to you tomorrow. In my meal tin. Then I'll meet you where we agreed."

"There'll be a jacket and hat on the floor outside the door. Put them on and cover your face. If for some reason someone should be here, say you're looking for Jim Willets. He's one of the guards."

"What do you mean if someone is here? I thought you said everything would be all set? We was to be partners."

"You never know."

"Hah! You never know. Here I am taking this risk —"

"The only risk you're taking is hanging from the end of a rope. If it hadn't been an Indian, you'd be dead now. I'll give you just five minutes to get out, then I'm relocking the cell. I don't want anyone else to escape. It'll be hard enough explaining you."

"I got no choice, damn it!"

"Sure you have. A hanging."

Footsteps faded down the hall. Then the prospector quietly left the cell door.

The next night — early morning really — Pedro moved next to the prospector and feigned sleep. Every muscle, every nerve was alert as he waited. After the others had fallen asleep, he rolled over and placed an arm across the prospector's body.

"Goddamned greaser."

Pedro smiled in the dark. Some minutes later, certain that all but the two of them were asleep, he clapped his hand over the prospector's mouth, stifling the surprised groan. "Quiet," Pedro whispered, "or I'll kill you."

He gagged the prospector with his own dirty bandana and bound his hands behind his back with the man's own belt. Then he struck him a blow that rendered him unconscious.

When the cell door clicked open, Pedro waited for the footsteps to fade. Then he stood and cautiously left the cell. He scooped up the jacket and hat without breaking stride and donned them as he hurried down the corridor, scarcely daring to breathe. The outside door was unlocked. A saddled horse was tethered just beyond.

# 35

The American conquest and its aftermath had taken its toll on Don Pedro. John Archer's acquisition of the quicksilver mine had finally pushed him to the edge of madness, yet this was merely the culmination of all that had happened before. Each catastrophe had sapped his energy, assaulted his once serious and business-like mind, and filled him with the corrosive desire for revenge. Thwarted, this desire for vengeance turned inward. Even in jail, days of normality would, without warning, be interrupted by moody, withdrawn states where he did not recognize his jailers nor where he was. He would sit in a corner lost to the world around him, carrying out in fantasy all those acts that would right the injustices he suffered from the unbearable Anglo world.

Free from jail, all he could think of was to be reunited with his beloved family. Together they would escape from this gringo hell-hole. It no longer mattered that he was the last male Baca. With the Americanization of California he might not have anything to pass on to male heirs except a name besmirched by gringo laws.

Pedro remembered little of that desperate ride to Los Palos. Obsessed by the need to see his wife and his mother before her death, he rode oblivious to all but his own dark thoughts. Occasionally a landmark would remind him of some past happy time. But then, puzzled, as if it were from a life he did not remember, he spurred his horse on.

When he reached the foothills south of San José, he bore east to avoid travelers and isolated houses. Pausing to rest, he surveyed the beautiful valley that stretched north to San Francisco Bay. He wept as he saw the nearest boundary of Rancho Los Palos. He felt like a child returned to his mother after a long and painful separation. He could clearly see the Río Guadalupe crossing the valley toward San José. On the west the foothills stood in startled, green surprise at the flowering fruit trees below on the flatlands.

At dusk Pedro rode down from his vantage point toward the rancho. As he approached, he felt a flood of emotion at the familiar scenes softened by pleasant memories and the fading light. It had not changed in the time he had been away. If only he could return home in broad daylight and be welcomed with open arms.

As he drew near to the main casa, he searched the windows for light and saw the familiar glow in Rebecca's and his bedroom. "Well, my tired little mustang," he said, patting his mount on the neck, "we made it."

\* \* \*

A din of barking unsettled the quiet as Pedro slowly approached through the flowering orchard. He stopped to survey the house and barn and corral. One of the dogs stood facing the horse and rider, its front legs thrust stiffly at an angle, its head low and menacing, the vicious growl deep in its throat. The other dogs stood behind, yapping and howling.

"Gitano!" The lead dog looked up in surprise, then trotted forward wagging its tail. Pedro dismounted and extended a hand to the approaching Gitano. "Be quiet," he said softly, petting the beast on the head and shoulders. The other dogs followed in a wary rush, watching from a short distance.

After awhile the dogs left, one by one, as Pedro watched the house. He could see the lights in the windows. The one on the left was his wife's. Across from it on the other side of the balcony would be his mother's and Archer's bedroom. On the lower floor the kitchen was still lit and the servants were no doubt cleaning up after the evening meal. A short distance behind the corral was the bunkhouse where the workers were probably smoking and playing cards.

As first one, then another of the lights went out, Pedro grew restless and watched the window of his wife's room even more intently. Finally, unable to tolerate it any longer, he crossed the clearing.

The smells of dinner were still in the air and he realized how hungry he was. He had hardly eaten for two days, but it did not matter now. Quickly, quietly he climbed to the second floor and made his way to Rebecca's room. A light rap on the door. No answer. The whispered plea, "Rebecca!" Still no answer. He turned the knob and peered into the dimly lit room. It was empty and the furniture had been replaced with American pieces. What has happened? he thought. Has she changed rooms? But why?

Closing the door, he made his way around the balcony to his mother's room. It, too, was empty, though the furniture was as he remembered. A musty smell pervaded it, unrelieved by the scent of perfume or powder.

At the sound of footsteps he hid in the shadows against the wall. A servant he did not recognize entered Rebecca's room, rustled about for a few moments, then left after turning off the lamp. Who was she? She was not his wife's maid and surely Rebecca had not taken another. Old Carla had been with her for years.

A strange voice called out in the night air, a woman's voice, an Anglo voice. The servant answered, then a strange man's voice commented. For a fraction of a second Pedro thought in alarm that he had come to the wrong place. But then the solidity of the buildings, the familiarity of the landscape, reassured him that this was the place that was once his home. But who were these strangers? He would have recognized Archer's voice. There were no signs of Rebecca and Doña Beatriz.

Cautiously he descended the stairs and sneaked toward the kitchen to peer through the window. Most of the servants were strangers, although seated by the stove smoking a cigarette was the old cook who had served them for years. Two young girls bustled about her, cleaning up, and Pedro withdrew in confusion.

As he made his way back to the orchard, old Gitano followed him. He cast a glance toward the bunkhouse. He dared not enter. Who knows if anyone there would even remember him? He sat on the ground to wait out the night. Perhaps early in the morning while the family slept and the men started to work, he would see a familiar face.

It was not a familiar face but a familiar voice that greeted him at dawn. The words were spoken in the affectionate banter and tone of a child, an old ranchhand talking to the dogs as he approached the orchard.

Pedro stirred awake and drew back into the shadows. He looked, letting his eyes confirm what his ears had heard. Then he called toward the figure coming through the early morning mist. "Juan!"

The man stopped and looked around. The dogs barked their greetings, and Gitano approached, wagging his tail and body.

"Don Pedro." Juan's voice was full of wonder and surprise. He stood still, uncertain, as Pedro approached him. "I heard you had died, Don Pedro. May the saints be praised."

"Where is everyone, Juan?"

The old man's troubled look avoided Pedro's eager face. He touched forehead, breast, shoulders, and lips with thumb and forefinger of his right hand. "Doña Beatriz, your sainted mother, has gone to heaven," he said. "How we miss her. Had no one told you? But then, how could you have known? Everyone thought you were dead." Juan ran a hand across his eyes. "The señor, Don Juan, followed her shortly. They say he died of a broken heart, not like an Anglo but like one of us. He truly loved your mother though he was a lawyer and a man of business. It was a sorrowful day when the mistress and master were both gone."

Tears flooded Pedro's eyes. The enormity of it stunned him. Not just his mother's death; his wife's last letter had forewarned him. But the other loss, the loss of the rancho.

"Who are the master and mistress now?" The strangers whose voices he had already heard. With the strange maid.

"Don Juan's heir. His son. And his wife."

Pedro lashed out with a savage laugh. Juan recoiled. "It was the law, señor."

Pedro shook his head. This was the final legacy of his mother's lack of business sense. Rather than entering her marriage with an agreement, there was no doubt that it was the Yankee lawyer who had made arrangements. On her death the property became his. On his death it became his heirs'. "They thought you were dead, señor."

"And Doña Rebecca?"

Juan threw out his hands in helplessness. "Word came that they were
to move you to the prison at Point San Quentin. They said that you
had tried to escape but had been shot before you could get away. You
and two other men.

"Doña Rebecca was heartbroken. She had journeyed to Monterey
to see you, but they would not let her. Now this news just after Doña
Beatriz and Don Juan had died. It was as if there was nothing left
for her here. Even before the new master and mistress arrived, she
left for Mexico. To your family she said. It was a bitter day when
the last of the Bacas left and this became an American ranch."

Pedro stared past the orchard toward the main casa now visible in
the morning light. What more was there to lose? Only his life, and
that seemed worth little without his wife and children and home.

"My heart cries for you, Don Pedro."

Pedro stood numb with disappointment. There was nothing for him
here. Perhaps in Mexico he could find his wife and start life over again.
Many of the other once rich California Dons were now just simple
farmers. "Juan," he said. "Do not tell a soul that you have seen me.
They may be hunting for me here. As far as anyone is concerned,
you thought I died in an attempt to escape from Point San Quentin."

"Sí, señor. But what can I do? How can I help?"

"Wish me well. Then forget you saw me." Pedro mounted and rode
away. A man who had nothing and wanted everything.

*     *     *

"Well, Leonardo. That is Don Pedro's story."

"But what about Doña Rebecca?"

"He never found her. He looked for her in Chihuahua where he
had family, but they had not seen her. He searched the trails from
northern Mexico to California but to no avail. He became a wanderer,
making his living as he could, always searching. But he never found
a trace. Not a hint.

"Finally, Pedro gave up on California and searched the trails to
Arizona and New Mexico. There were rumors of Apache massacres.
He looked for survivors, hoping against hope that one might have in-
formation about a gentle Mexican lady with two young daughters.
But he found nothing.

"Eventually, as he grew old, he grew tired of wandering. His madness came upon him more frequently and he would find himself in places he did not recognize with people he had never seen before. He made his way here to his wife's only living relative, your grandmother. She added to those tattered letters that he carried other letters that Rebecca had written to her from California. Letters that told of the terrible happenings there. Letters that suddenly stopped."

"I never knew." There was awe in Leonardo's voice.

"It was more than the loss, though that is painful enough. What would you do if you lost family and home and wife and children? If the self-respect, the place you held in society had been destroyed? These are among the heaviest burdens a man carries in this life. But they are nothing compared to the poisonous acid of revenge that corrodes one's soul.

"It was hate, you see. Revenge that drove Don Pedro mad. If you can accept the will of God, you can make peace with whatever life sends you. You do not have to embrace it. You can weep and rage and hate it. But eventually you have to accept it or go mad. One always finds what one seeks. And if you seek only vengeance, you find mostly enemies. 'As you sow so shall you reap.' That's what the Bible says."

"But, Grandfather, these were enemies. It was the Americans that did all those terrible things to Don Pedro. If they tried to do that to me, I would fight back!"

"You're an American, Leonardo."

"I didn't mean that. You know what I mean."

"God has a way of evening things out. Perhaps it is only our turn to pay for what we did to the Indians. The Anglos' turn will come in time."

"We have to watch out, don't we? We have to be careful that the things that happened to Don Pedro do not happen to us."

"Of course. That is one of the reasons that I told you Don Pedro's story. Knowing it, you can watch out for your own life. But more than that, I think that one must forgive or he will carry his burden forever."

"But his family suffered those terrible things!"

"Yes."

"How can you forgive that? I would want to strike back!"

"That only prolongs the war. If there is to be an end to these wars, these hates, someone must take the first step. Someone must give up something and forgive. As the Lord says in His own prayer: 'Forgive us our trespasses as we forgive those who trespass against us.' It is much harder to accept being a loser than being a winner. Yet we must."

"In heaven, maybe, Grandfather. But here on earth people just cannot do that."

"*Will* not, Leonardo. Not *cannot.*"

"You really believe that, Grandfather?" José Antonio nodded. "I can see why you were once a priest."

"As you get older you will see more and more the futility of hate. At whatever level we war with others—our brothers and sisters, our wives or husbands, our children, our neighbors. Whatever weapons we use—not just guns or knives, but words or looks or thoughts—it only breeds more of its own kind. Jesus not only died for our sins, but also to show us the way even if it means our own personal loss.

"It is not easy. It never was. Hate is easier than forgiveness. But forgiveness is the only way."

Leonardo sat with an incredulous expression on his face. He has already lost his innocence, José Antonio thought. And when the best do not believe, where is the hope for the rest of us?

Finally Leonardo spoke; his face was tight, the words hesitant. "I heard, Grandfather, that your own brother was killed by the Anglos when they stole New Mexico."

"Yes." His answer was almost a sigh. "He was my twin. We were as much alike in some ways as two people can be. And yet so different in others.

"He was a soldier. He did not accept the American takeover and continued to fight after the surrender. He was killed in a battle at Taos."

"A hero!"

Again a sigh. "In a way. But his death did not change a thing. He could not embrace the inevitable so he died."

"Aren't you sorry?"

"Of course. I am always sorry when someone dies before his time. Especially my brother."

"Didn't you hate the Americans?"

"For awhile. But war is too impersonal. Your enemy one day is your neighbor the next. My brother's death was as much his own doing as it was that of the Americans."

Again silence. Leonardo appeared to puzzle over all he had heard. José Antonio felt distant from his grandson, as if there was now a wedge between them, the way it was when children grew up. When they became separate from their parents and grandparents, with ideas of their own. Leonardo was becoming a young man. In years past he would almost have been old enough for marriage.

A shadow fell across their silence. "It's late," Gregoria reminded them.

Leonardo looked up in surprise. "I'd better go. Good night."

José Antonio felt his wife's eyes on his back, but he did not turn around. "You think I shouldn't have told him."

"What good does it do? It's like the priests reminding us that the Jews killed Jesus. They forget that Jesus was a Jew and that the Jews living today had nothing to do with it. Why remember and point a finger of blame?"

"I really wanted him to know that Pedro's hate drove him mad."

"But you cannot tell one thing without telling the other."

José Antonio stared into the shadows of the darkening room. Maybe I was wrong, he thought. Maybe there are things best left unsaid. Stories best left untold.

# 36

Francisco stood resting his hand against the door. His irritation turned to anger as Florinda nagged at him from the kitchen.

"Where are you? You were here just a minute ago." Then her quick footsteps assaulted the floor the way her words buffeted the air, and she was staring at him from across the room.

"You're not listening to me." He closed his eyes and nodded. "Well, what are you going to do about it? Your father is filling that boy with nonsense and now he thinks that loco borracho is a hero of some kind. Joaquín Murieta's right-hand man. Leonardo imagines he's a brown-skinned Billy the Kid. He went off to the river to practice with the rifle."

"There's nothing wrong with a boy knowing how to shoot. It may come in handy some day — to hunt if nothing else."

"You're not listening to me. It's your father's stories that make me so angry. Making a hero of that lunatic. They should send him back to California where he would be right at home with the rest of those crazy people."

"Father is just telling him harmless stories. Leonardo is his favorite grandchild. Maybe he'll leave him the orchard in his will."

Florinda retorted with an explosion of air from her lips, a look of disbelief in her eyes. "We are his heirs. Why else would we live next door and put up with all this for so long?"

"I have to go to my meeting."

"Every time I want to talk to you, you have to go off to some meeting."

"Damn it! What do you want me to do?"

"Tell your father to stop telling him those stories. And stop going to so many meetings. I think you do it to get away from me."

If you only knew, he thought. "I have to be at the rally in Martínez Town. I'm on the committee. As for my father's stories, you tell him if it upsets you so much."

"He's your father!"

"I'm going. If we win the election there might even be a little money in it for us." For once she kept her mouth shut and looked at him with something akin to regard. "You never get anything if you don't earn it. The committee is my political work."

Francisco left before she could start up on him again. He could not understand what it was about Don José and Leonardo that angered her so. Jealousy perhaps. The boy listened to his grandfather more than he did to his mother. But a few harmless fairy tales never hurt a young person. Better that than some of the other things young people were up to nowadays.

Pablo Griego was waiting for him at the crossroads. They turned east, away from the river, ambling their horses toward Los Martínez on the outskirts of New Town, enjoying the afternoon sun and their conversation.

"So you heard, too?" Francisco asked. "What do you think he really knows?"

"¿Quién sabe? Benito is stupid, with a big mouth, so you never can be sure whether to listen to him or not. But I don't see how he could really know. Not unless someone told him."

"Who would tell him?"

Griego looked at Francisco with sorrow. "One of our little group?"

Francisco shook his head vehemently, even though he realized who Griego meant: Ignacio Armijo. "What would an informer have to gain?"

"Revenge. According to him we never listen to his advice or choose him for important jobs. Armijo is just crazy enough. But then maybe Benito Durán made a lucky guess. I would hate to think otherwise.

If someone told him, he would know for certain. If Benito knew, he would have acted by now."

Francisco agreed with the eminent sense of this. They rode in silence, past cornfields, in the direction of the Sandía Mountains. At the main road they turned south toward town.

"I'm sorry Don José is not coming," Griego said.

"He is not feeling well."

"They will miss him at the rally."

"We can handle it," Francisco answered testily.

Everyone missed his father at these functions. The implication was that they did not trust the son and Francisco chafed at this mistrust. He was a grown man. He did not need his father to tell him what to do.

Francisco felt for the pistol tucked in the waistband of his trousers. "I hear that we may get a few hecklers today," he said.

"So I've been told."

"It will be no place for an old man."

The fields of Los Martínez came into view. A few party workers had already gathered in the clearing alongside the little chapel to lead the cheering and applause and to watch for trouble. Francisco tensed when he saw the broad, thick back of Benito Durán directing the men who carried a barrel to a makeshift table.

"There he is," Griego said in an undertone. They exchanged wary glances, then dismounted and joined the group.

\*   \*   \*

The voters from Los Martínez turned out to hear Plácido Durán. Even the priest who only came once a month to say Mass in the little chapel made a special trip to give the invocation. Francisco listened half-heartedly as Durán gave The Speech again.

Throughout the afternoon he sensed Benito Durán watching him, but whenever he turned to challenge, the eyes turned aside. In the small group of workers the care with which Benito avoided him took on a special significance, while Plácido's initial hearty greeting seemed less real than usual, and he changed quickly to indifference, then avoidance.

"What do you think?" Francisco asked Griego after the crowd had broken up and drifted home.

"Same old faces. There's not a new vote in the bunch."

"I mean the Duráns."

"Plácido was trying too hard to be friendly . . . at first. Benito was too quiet. I had a feeling he was watching us."

"He knows something."

They joined the others in a corner of the clearing and stood beneath the gnarled apple tree at the edge of the dying orchard. Benito poured drinks from the still half-full barrel. They lifted their cups in a toast to their success.

Although it was still light as they rode home, Francisco kept looking back to see if they were being followed. When he saw nothing, he would shake his head, trying to clear it of the dulling effects of whiskey. Griego's eyes were mere slits as he leaned precariously astride his horse.

When they once again reached the crossroads, Griego was leaning dangerously to one side. "You should have stopped me from taking that last drink," he said.

Francisco rode alongside and pushed him back onto his horse. "I'll take you home."

Only afterwards, as he rode the lonely way back, was he suddenly aware of being alone. The early evening sky was turning gray. He stopped just before reaching the crossroads and listened. Nothing but the sounds of distant animals. The road ahead was clear. It was only a short distance home now.

He relaxed and smiled, remembering Griego's wife as she had opened the door and seen them leaning against each other. She had not said a word, just bustled them to the bedroom where he had helped Pablo to bed. Her thank you's politely and firmly pursued him back to the door. Only when he had mounted and headed down the road did he hear her first scream. It had startled him, then realizing what it was, he had laughed.

Now he clucked his horse toward the crossroads. As he drew near, the stillness became unnatural. Even the distant barking of dogs had faded.

Francisco slowed his horse and looked around. Over the barbed wire fences to the fields on his left and right. Across to the dark and empty building that was used as a chapel when the priest visited. Back toward the cluster of cottonwoods that guarded the edge of another cornfield.

As he entered the intersection of the two dirt roads, Francisco peered intently toward the chapel. What was that he heard? The scrape of a boot? The scampering of some night creature?

With pounding heart, he turned toward home, clucking his tongue to quietly urge his horse to hurry.

"Rafa!"

His blood froze and before it had melted, he heard the rustle, then the clomp of hooves behind him. He kicked at the flanks of his mount. Instead of bolting forward, it struggled against a tight grasp on the reins.

"Rafa!"

The voice approached from behind. Fear obscured his vision, though he could see six masked horsemen surrounding him. The man who spoke sat square and huge on his mount, the bandana covering the lower part of his face, but nothing could disguise that massive bulk.

There was a hint of triumph in the masked man's voice. "Welcome from Los Hijos de Libertad."

## 37

Gregoria's words gnawed at José Antonio when the opposite of what he had intended happened. Now Leonardo looked at Anglo neighbors with new eyes, with newly discovered animosity rather than just as other men who were his equals and with whom he must live in peace.

Outside, the clomp of hoofbeats announced Francisco on his way to Martínez Town. José Antonio wished that he were on his old horse joining him, but he felt unwell today. He felt his age. Aching joints. A stiff back. Legs like tree trunks. He was not certain if he had a fever; at times he felt flushed. But most of all he felt tired. And though he sat quietly, his mind would not let him rest. On and on. This and that. Back to his young manhood and the death of his brother. Over to California and the tragedy of the Bacas. Then to Leonardo and the unknown future.

Footsteps approached. Pedro Baca looked uncertainly at him, his madness having decreased at the price of his self-assurance. "Your son has gone away and left you alone," he said in a timid voice. "A person gets lonely." Pedro lowered himself onto a chair.

José Antonio wanted to be alone with his thoughts and his miseries.

Sometimes it was best to wallow in them until he became sick and tired of self-pity and shed it like a snake sheds its skin.

"You're feeling better," he said.

"I wish I had a son," Pedro said. "But only daughters. I have not seen them since they were little girls. They must be old ladies now, with children of their own."

Oh, Lord, José Antonio thought. If you must send me visitors, send me someone with a smile on his face. "There's a political rally in Los Martínez. I did not feel like going."

A look of alarm clouded Pedro's face. "Won't the Yankees try to break it up? In California they tried to take the vote from us, those who were part Indian. You have to watch out for them. You can't trust Yankees."

"Here we call them Anglos."

"They stole my rancho. You don't know how bad it can get. Just wait. Some day they will try to take yours too,"

Was this the beginning of another plunge into madness? José Antonio thought. How many years ago had all of this happened? Thirty-five? Forty? A lifetime. Three lifetimes for Leonardo. Memory was a sickness that never seemed to heal.

"You don't believe me." José Antonio tried to stem the rising hysteria in Pedro's voice by nodding that he did believe. "You think," Pedro went on, "that you are immune here? That you cannot be touched by Yankee — no — by Anglo madness? You think that your political rally will do you some good? That just because you elect a New Mexican that his Spanish surname and dark skin will make him other than an Anglo toady?"

"I have been called mad," Pedro said. "But when I see what is happening, I wonder who is really mad."

Pedro's face drained of animation. His eyes focused inward as if feeling old scars and how much they still pained him. "Death does not always come quickly. Sometimes it comes little by little, day by day, deceiving you into thinking you are truly living until that final day when it hits you like a shock. It's over. And you did nothing about it."

"I don't understand," José Antonio said. But deep down, cold fear surged through him, a sense of regret because, unlike his brother, he was letting death come to him slowly and unsuspectingly rather than in one outrageous burst of passion.

Pedro leaned forward and hissed. "The Devil speaks English. He is the brother of Death. What he does not take quickly, he takes slowly. It does not matter to him. He has plenty of time. Eternity."

You're crazy! José Antonio thought. He looked away; he knew Pedro's wild appearance might tempt him to harsh words. "I don't believe in the Devil," he said.

"But there is evil in the world. Evil ruined my life. Don't you believe in evil?"

He could not answer. Through his mind went the eternal unanswerable question: If God is good, why does He allow such wickedness?

"There is ignorance in the world," José Antonio finally said.

A crafty grin. "But why do the ignorant have bigger guns and more money? Why do the ignorant win while we lose?"

"God gave us free will, the freedom to choose, including the freedom to make the wrong choice."

"Ah!" Pedro snorted. "Fancy church talk. Nothing but words. *Be humble. Trust in God's grace.* But the boot on your neck when your face is in the dirt will not respond to prayer. I tell you, we have to get them before they get us."

There's no use arguing, José Antonio thought. The lunatic is right about one thing. Words. Nothing but words.

They sat in grim silence. From the kitchen came the sounds of Gregoria at work. The granddaughters ran past laughing. Chickens clucked and a goat bleated. There were hoofbeats of a passing horse and a rustle through the trees in the orchard. Reminders that without words life went on. That deep down one lived out his life in silent actions that spoke truer than the loudest harangue. That words could confuse, deceive, assault, persuade, and even impart the truth. But one could not always tell which. While with an action one knew what was happening, even though one might not know why.

"What will your rally get you?" Pedro asked.

"A new sheriff from our own political party who will interpret and enforce the law more equitably; favors for none or for everyone, not just for the privileged. He will appoint deputies, that is, give jobs to some who helped elect him. He will respond to abuses to our people and protect them. He will not arrest our people because of imagined abuses: 'suspicion,' 'intent,' 'looking or speaking different'—whatever some in power can use to bolster their positions and their prejudices. Most of all he will spread the power around so that we gain our share."

"But I hear that the present sheriff is a decent one, even though he is an Anglo."

"To whom does he owe his position?"

"You really think your man will be elected?"

José Antonio thought of Placido Durán and what a weak sheriff he would be. Intelligent enough. Ambitious enough. Crafty enough. But a pompous fool who needed his brute of a brother to protect him and carry out his dirty work. The first deputy appointed would be Benito Durán. A new regime conceived in nepotism leading to who knows what. But at least the men uptown would be watching Plácido. And the men uptown listened to their constituents — sometimes. To Smith and himself here in Los Rafas. To those in other placitas in the county.

"Do you really think you can win?" Pedro asked.

"I hope so."

"No matter who wins, the strings will be pulled by the Anglos in New Town. But I'm ready for them. They won't catch me by surprise again." He unbuttoned the flap of shirt just above his waist and leaned slightly forward. The handle of a knife glinted in the afternoon light.

José Antonio almost reached out and took it, but he was too surprised and then paralyzed by the thought of what this old fool might do.

Pedro smiled as if José Antonio's silence were an accolade. He pulled the knife from his waistband and held it across his two extended hands.

The oblong handle was made of wood, slightly rounded and roughly shaped. The crude blade had been filed sharp and ended in a blunt point. It was not one of those fancy store-bought knives made in a factory, but crude as it was it could still do damage.

"Where did you get that?"

A crafty grin. "I have my ways."

José Antonio took it as if accepting the offering. He turned it over, felt its weight and balance, then ran his thumb cautiously along the blade. "You could kill someone with this."

"Yes!"

José Antonio stuck the knife into the waistband of his own trousers. First shock, then anger crossed Pedro's face. He stretched a hand out, but José Antonio shook his head.

"It's mine! You have no right!" Again the shake of head. "I'm a Don. Dozens of servants obey me and the workers in the field tip their hats when I ride by."

"There are no Dons and precious few servants. We sons and grandsons of Dons are just farmers now. Americans even."

Pedro threw back his head and howled in frustration. There was a cry from the kitchen and Gregoria rushed in. "What are you doing?" José Antonio slid the knife from his belt and held it up safely out of Pedro's reach. She glanced first at one then the other. "So that's where it went." She riveted her eyes on Pedro.

"He took it to protect himself," José Antonio said.

"From what?" she spat at Pedro. "From the goats and chickens?" She snatched the blade and shook it threateningly at Pedro. "My grandson made this for me. Don't you dare take it again. Do you want me to lock you back in the shed?"

Pedro hung his head. "No señora."

"Then behave yourself."

# 38

The children had eaten and the time when Francisco should have returned had long passed. Florinda thrust her needle viciously, mending the tear in the heavy work pants. Behind her on the stove sat the lidded pot of frijoles and on the table the plate of cold, hard tortillas covered by a cloth.

Again and again she stabbed the work pants, pretending that it was Francisco she was punishing. "Miserable wretch!" she muttered. "Sitting with his drunken friends at some cantina not even thinking about me. ¡Política!" she spat. "Just another name for drunkenness. Another reason to stay away from home."

She ignored the sounds from the other room where the children went about their own business. The kitchen had been cleaned and put away except for the dishes left for her husband. The wood box had been refilled. All that remained was the endless mending.

"Mamá!" It was Rosa, the oldest of her daughters. "Carlos is hitting me!"

She stabbed her thumb with the needle and muttered a curse. "Shut up in there! If I have to get up you're really going to get hit! Leonardo, keep them quiet!"

A whispered exchange, then Leonardo's, "Yes, Mamá."

Time passed. She mended one garment, then the next, her anger flowing through her fingertips to the needle.

When she thought about Francisco again it was with anxiety rather than anger. It had passed from dusk to dark and he was long overdue even if he had stopped for a few drinks. She set her sewing on the table and stepped out the kitchen door to look past the orchard toward the road.

Only a light from the big house greeted her. There were three shadows in the window and she clenched her apron, twisting it in her fists. They had let the old loony loose again. She imagined him looming up out of the dark, his wild face peering through a window, his drunken eyes watching her with malice.

She shivered and looked toward the road. Only emptiness, silence. She turned and hurried in, slamming the door and bolting it.

"Leonardo!"

"Yes, Mamá."

She listened impatiently to the slow footsteps. Leonardo stopped at the edge of the kitchen, a worried look on his face. Good, she thought. Let him worry.

"Go tell your grandfather that your father has not come home and that I'm worried." The boy stood hesitantly. "Well, you heard me. Now go!"

"But what can Grandpa do?"

The blood rushed to her face. If he had been closer, she would have slapped him. "I don't want any back talk from you! Now you do what I say."

He spun abruptly and left.

*   *   *

What would he have done if he had married an ill-tempered woman like Florinda? José Antonio thought. How long could he have resisted beating her? Just a few minutes of her grating voice made him clench his fists. God knows, he tried to love his children's spouses, but sometimes God asked more than was possible.

For the third time she repeated her complaint. "The rally was supposed to be over by suppertime. He should have been home long ago. Now it's past dark. It's your fault. You never whipped him enough when he was a boy."

"Florinda! He's a grown man with a mind of his own. He's your husband and your marriage quarrels are your own. Now what is it that you want me to do?"

For a few seconds he thought that she was about to cry. "What is it that you want me to do?" he asked in a gentler voice.

"Go to the cantina and send him home. I'm ashamed to go there myself."

"If it will make you happy." José Antonio would have welcomed a thank-you from her, but he knew that was expecting too much. "How about it, Leonardo? Shall we go?"

"It's the least you can do," Florinda said.

José Antonio and Leonardo walked the moonlit path toward the junction of San Ysidro Road. "She could have sent me alone," Leonardo said. "She has done it before."

"Ah, yes."

Leonardo put a hand against José Antonio's arm. "Wait!" They stopped and listened, barely breathing. "Over there," Leonardo said, pointing.

José Antonio followed the dark shadow of the boy's arm toward the side of the road. "I don't see anything."

"Listen."

He heard the crunching. After his initial surprise, José Antonio recognized the familiar sound, an animal chewing on cornstalks. He strained his eyes, but saw nothing in the dim moonlight. It must be under the trees along the edge of the cornfield.

"Someone's cow," he said. "Let's get it before it eats its way to our field."

As they drew closer, Leonardo held onto his grandfather's arm. A low snort greeted them from the shadows.

"It's a horse," José Antonio said. He clucked his tongue, peering into the dark, hearing the snort as it approached.

"Negrito!" the boy said.

The old man strained his eyes at the dark shape clomping toward them. "He must have run away from the cantina."

"Come here, Negrito. Come here." Leonardo grabbed the reins. "I'll ride him to the cantina and get Papá."

They trotted off as José Antonio continued along the road. He felt uneasy about the loose horse. It was unlike Francisco to leave him untied, no matter how much he had to drink.

"Grandpa!" The shout startled him. Then the hoofbeats raced toward him, thundering in the dark. "A groan!" Leonardo shouted. "From the acequia!" Leonardo leaped from Negrito, helped his grandfather up, then leaped on behind him.

"¡Andale, Negrito!" the old man commanded.

"At first I thought it was a witch!" Leonardo shouted into José Antonio's ear. "But then I realized that Papá must have drunk too much and fallen off."

Since when could any amount of whiskey throw a New Mexican from

from his horse? If a rider could be placed onto his mount by whatever means, instinct alone would keep him on whether drunk or asleep. Even dead men were known to ride home without falling off.

"Over there!" The boy pointed across José Antonio's shoulder to the rise of earth where the dirt road crossed the ditch.

"Whoa, Negrito!"

The boy jumped down and bent low, peering into the shadows while José Antonio cursed his old body for not responding to the urgency that he felt. A low groan came from the rise of earth above the muddy waters of the ditch.

"I see him," Leonardo said.

Now José Antonio was on the ground, rushing toward the groan. The long, dark shape lay half-immersed in water, lying upslope as if trying to reach the top of the bank.

"Wait," José Antonio said. "I'll help you." They grasped the figure under the arms and carefully pulled it up. "Over here where we can see. Why isn't that damned moon brighter?"

The body was wet from flattened hair to soaked boots. Not a groan escaped, not a murmur. The old man and the boy squatted on the crest of the ditch catching their breath. José Antonio did not see signs of breathing and he leaned over touching the wet face with his nose.

"Is he dead?" Leonardo asked in a trembling voice.

Gently, José Antonio lifted the head, turning the face toward the dim moonlight. He gasped. He could barely recognize it for the cruel bruises that discolored and swelled it. From the torn mouth issued a faint trickle of blood. For an instant he thought it was a mistake. That it was not Francisco but someone else. A stranger.

Then his horrified eyes moved from the almost unrecognizable face to the familiar workshirt. To the worn, too-long leather belt looped through the silver Indian buckle studded with smoothed turquoise stones fastened tight around the thin muscular waist. Then the work pants with familiar patches, the left leg unnaturally bent.

This was no drunken man thrown from a horse. This was a man cruelly beaten beyond the point of punishment, beyond the loss of consciousness, with a viciousness that had intended to kill.

With tears in his eyes, trembling, José Antonio tried to hold back his nausea. He placed a hand against the torn and bleeding lips and hoped against hope. He cleared his throat before he turned.

"He's breathing," José Antonio said. "Barely. Go to the cantina. Bring some men and something to carry him in." The boy did not move. José Antonio growled in a sharp and urgent tone, "¡Andale!"

Leonardo jumped to his feet and disappeared into the dark. Gently, José Antonio placed the bruised head on the earthen slope. Then he crossed himself and began to pray.

## 39

José Antonio slumped on the earthen floor of the little house, his wife on a chair beside him. From the other room came the muffled sound of voices as the curandera went about her business, the doctor long since come and gone. The kitchen door opened and closed, the low murmur of voices faded, footsteps approached slow and heavy.

Florinda burst into tears as she entered, clutching her apron that she lifted to wipe her eyes. Gregoria went to her, encircling her long arms around the shorter, plump young woman.

"Oh, Mamá. He's going to die."

"What did the doctor say?" José Antonio asked.

Florinda wrenched herself from Gregoria's arms and thrust a wet, angry face at him. "Why do you think I called the curandera? That — that —" She could not find the right words.

"You know what I heard?" Florinda finally said. "That he isn't a doctor at all. That back in Missouri in some little gringo town people wouldn't even let him treat their dogs. The closest he ever got to blood was shaving customers when he was a barber. That's why he came west. So he could work on people too ignorant to know better. So when he killed someone, they would say it was God's will rather than that incompetent butcher."

José Antonio stirred uneasily, rubbing his tight shoulders against the adobe wall. The doctor was one of their major political contributors. A man of reserve and quiet generosity, educated in a medical college in Pennsylvania, who had probably only seen Missouri from the window of a passing train.

Florinda thrust her face at him challenging. "Well?"

"Nothing," he sighed. "What did he say?"

Outside, Florinda's sister-in-law, her brother Armando's wife, bullied the children into silence. "Your uncle's sick! Shut up that yelling or you'll make him worse!"

"It will be all right," Gregoria said to Florinda. "You'll see."

Florinda blew her nose into her apron. She spoke as if to the air, not looking at him. "His jaw is broken," she began, "and his teeth are loose.

"Though his eyes are swollen shut, he will see again. Only a few of his ribs are broken. He can lie on his back or lean on his left side without too much pain. His right hand is broken. The doctor is sure he will not have to amputate his right leg . . . if it does not get infected. When it heals he will not limp too badly."

She stopped and wiped her eyes with trembling hands. José Antonio's face drained of color as he listened to her litany of injuries. Florinda swallowed, then continued. "The doctor says that he will live, but he would not blame me if I called the priest to give him extreme unction." Then her thin shell of control cracked and her blubberings became incoherent. Gregoria led her to the chair and sat her down.

He wanted to ask her what the curandera had done. Later perhaps, but then perhaps not. He could guess what had happened. Herb-soaked compresses laid across cuts and bruises to soak up the poisons. A warm brew boiled from roots, leaves, stems, and pods, gathered and dried in the old Indian way, forced down the throat of the comatose Francisco. Bandages removed, then replaced after poultices made to ancient formulae were applied to the raw wounds. Was the doctor's science any better? Or José Antonio's prayers for that matter? One chose the magic of one's own prejudices, then left it in the hands of Fate or God or Science.

José Antonio stared at Florinda. When they had carried Francisco home cradled in a blanket, she had screamed her first outburst of hysteria: "What will happen to me now?" Me. Dependent me. Now who will plow the fields? And plant the corn? Who will bring in the harvest? Clear the ditches? Slaughter the goats? How can I do all that?

But women were widowed by other than death. By a husband's ill health, which when chronic was but a half-step from death. By drunkenness, which had forced Gregoria early to learn to do her widower father's work. By poverty, when one's husband did not have fields enough to provide for the family. Or sloth, the living death that like the others forced one to do alone what truly required two.

José Antonio did not begrudge her outcry. There were few he knew who had the strength to carry on alone. Florinda's branch of Chávezes was not known for fortitude any more than it was for calm.

Then, too, the fearful thought had crossed his own mind. For it was this eldest son of his who had stayed home and helped farm his father's fields with the unspoken agreement that they would be his some day. Now only Leonardo was left to work.

"Florinda!" Armando walked in with a quick nod to José Antonio. "We're going. Why don't we take the children for a few days? You have enough to worry about."

She nodded. "Tell Leonardo to stay," Gregoria said. "His mother will need him."

Armando sidled up to José Antonio, rolling his eyes toward the other room. "How is he, Don José?" His voice was low and somber, not his usual joker's playful chatter.

José Antonio held out a hand and Armando pulled him to his feet. The two tiptoed out the door with an exchange of concerned glances and a backward look at the women.

"It's touch and go," José Antonio said softly.

"Qué lástima."

"I'm glad you can take the children."

Armando took José Antonio by the arm and led him out of the house. "I'm worried about Florinda," he said. "She does not take these things too well. You know how she is. Christ! If she goes to pieces, this really will be a mess."

"Gregoria and I are here."

"It's not that I won't help," Armando said. "But there's only so much I can do. I have a family of my own to take care of."

"I know."

"You understand what I'm saying, don't you, Don José?" There was an urgency to his voice as if he wanted reassurance. "There's only so much that one man can do."

They stood in silence while Armando's wife rounded up the children. "Tell me," Armando finally asked, "has Francisco said anything about who did it?"

"No."

"I don't understand. They didn't steal his horse, if that's what they wanted. It happened near enough to the cantina that someone there might have heard something. How strange."

"Armando, what do you know about Los Hijos de Libertad?"

"Why would they attack Francisco?" Then, pondering a moment, he said, "I know no more than you. Probably less. Only rumors like those about that fool Plácido Durán. But," he said, shaking his head, "I don't see the connection between that and Francisco."

"Armando!"

He turned and waved at his wife, who had lined up the children beside the road. "There's a lot of mouths to feed," Armando said, "but then God will provide. Another cup of water in the pot of frijoles goes a long way. Adiós, Don José."

José Antonio watched them straggle homeward. When he turned, Leonardo was staring solemnly down the road after them.

# 40

Florinda, Gregoria, and José Antonio took turns sitting with Francisco, while Leonardo stood by to help. Now it was José Antonio's turn. He sat in the semi-dark and stared at the wall just above Francisco's head and just below the wooden crucifix. He listened for the slightest sound. A change in breathing. A shift in bed. A groan. Mumbled, almost decipherable words.

When Francisco slept calm and quiet, José Antonio rested. At such times he drifted, letting thoughts come of their own accord. Then suddenly, something would catch in the net of his mind and he would focus on it. Like now.

He could hear Sheriff Davis' words almost as if they were being spoken at this very moment. "If he dies," the sheriff had said, "we'll be looking for someone to charge with murder."

It had been matter of fact, as if discussing the price of corn. Another case for the sheriff, one of many, while it was a matter of despair, helplessness, and shock for the family.

"He didn't have any enemies, did he, Don José?"

"I . . . don't think so. Nothing serious. No feud or anything like that. Only . . ." He had hesitated, immediately sorry that he had spoken that one word. He would have let it drop, except that the sheriff had pounced on the hesitation as if it hid something important.

"Only what, Don José?"

"He's been very upset about the election."

The sheriff was silent for a long time. "How long have you known me, Don José?"

"Ten, fifteen years."

"And you think —?"

"No. It has nothing to do with you."

José Antonio looked at the square, serious man who had come about Francisco. The sheriff was an honest man, of this he had no doubt, and capable. If it had not been a matter of political party, he would have preferred him to Plácido Durán.

"What's been going on, Don José?"

What did the sheriff know already, if anything? Then the groan from the next room and the commotion from Florinda compelled him to tell what he knew. About Francisco's preference for a candidate other than Durán. Of rumors about Los Hijos de Libertad, whoever they were. About some suspected animosity between Benito Durán and Francisco.

"Do you think," Sheriff Davis asked, "that the men who threatened Plácido Durán are the same ones who attacked Francisco?"

"Who knows?"

They both knew what that implied. That the opposition party, the sheriff's party, or its supporters, felt threatened by Plácido's candidacy.

"Does that really make sense?" Davis asked.

"No, it doesn't."

"Why would my backers feel worried enough by Durán to threaten him? If Francisco prefers someone other than Plácido, he has more in common with them than not. Why would this same bunch nearly kill him?"

"I don't know."

"It doesn't make sense." The sheriff picked his Stetson up from the floor, preparing to leave. His voice lowered, taking on a more personal tone. "How is he?"

"It's in the hands of God."

Sheriff Davis was on his feet now, holding his hat in both hands. "If Francisco says anything, anything at all, that sheds light on this, let me know."

A groan interrupted José Antonio's reverie. He leaned in the chair, looking down at his son, ready for . . . he knew not what. Then a soft cry, a whimper, and some mumbled sounds that could have been words. José Antonio listened, alert like an animal sensing danger. He longed for a clue to those monsters who had done this frightful thing. But more important, he listened for coherent words as a sign of life, of a humanity emerging from under this mass of pain and bruises and broken bones.

He sat a long while, wishing that he did not have to breathe so he could listen more intently. He felt a presence behind him as silent as he and Francisco. Someone was in the doorway looking over his shoulder thinking much the same thoughts as himself and he turned and saw Leonardo in the dim light. They exchanged glances; words were not necessary. Then the boy disappeared as quickly as he had appeared.

José Antonio pondered over the strange, silent understanding he felt with his grandson. It reminded him of his long dead twin brother Carlos. Only with these two had he ever experienced this feeling. Although he was certain that his wife could read his mind, he could not always read hers.

How extraordinary that one could talk without words. As boys, he and Carlos had shared secret messages as if they were one body, one mind. They had but to look at each other and they knew what the other was thinking. In times of peril a warning might come from one to the other, even over great distances.

With Carlos this gift had faded as they had grown older. When Carlos had been mortally wounded in Taos, José Antonio had felt nothing. Whereas if it had happened when they were boys, he might have been struck dead in sympathy.

How mysterious to have experienced that closeness then lost it, then to have found it again with his grandson. It was almost as if he had lived two lives. Almost as if he had come upon his reincarnate self while his previous self still lived. Maybe, he thought, that is one form of immortality.

He felt the presence again, but this time he did not turn. "Yes?"

"I was just watching, Grandfather." There was a tremor in the boy's voice. "He was trying to talk to me this afternoon. 'Hijos,' he said. 'Hijos.' I thought he wanted Carlos and me, but when I leaned over to tell him that Carlos was at Uncle Armando's, he had fallen asleep."

"That's all he said?"

"Just 'hijos.'"

José Antonio stared at Francisco. When he looked back up, Leonardo had gone. He had not thought about it in a long time, but now he remembered old stories that his own grandfather had told him. About twins, including Carlos and himself. How in every other generation a pair of male twins was born to the Rafas. His own grandfather had been one of such a pair. José Antonio had been another. If the family were to continue as it had in the past, there should be a pair of twins among his own grandchildren.

But there were no such twins. What did that mean? That the family magic had run its course? It was not likely that Francisco would have more children. Not now. So it would have to be Carlos or Blas, although he could not believe that. The spell was broken. Things had changed. His hope for the future was in his grandson Leonardo. No more twins. No more magic. No more silly superstitions.

A sigh from the bed. A throat clearing. Then Francisco quietly continued sleeping.

"Hijos," José Antonio said aloud. Francisco could be calling for his sons or— Hijos de Libertad. But why them?

"José!"

"Shhh." He crossed his lips with a forefinger.

"It's Pedro," his wife whispered. "He has disappeared." Oh, Christ! he thought. "Along with my kitchen knife."

# 41

José Antonio and Leonardo took a lantern and went out into the night. First they searched the secret places where Pedro had hidden before. Behind the outhouse near the irrigation ditch. Under a favorite tree in the orchard. Then alongside the corral, after which they crossed the ditch to the north cornfield.

"Pedro!" José Antonio shouted. They stood listening along a row of growing corn, but there was no answer. Then they moved to another row where once again José Antonio shouted.

When they had finally searched their own farm, moving in a widening circle that brought them back to the main road, José Antonio stopped to catch his breath.

"Do you think he went to Esmerelda?" Leonardo asked.

"We'd better look. We can stop at the cantina on the way. Sometimes he goes there to beg for drinks."

He recalled one such visit when some of the loafers had had their fun with Pedro. The half-drunk old man had stood in the crowded room singing in a croaking voice while the crowd cheered. He finished a chorus and started to dance in the center of the cantina. As he turned unsteadily, Pedro had looked back and seen José Antonio at the entrance. The old drunk's face blanched. He lost his balance and toppled to the floor amidst the jeers of the crowd.

José Antonio had walked to the center of the cantina and immediately it became silent. "Just a little harmless fun," someone said.

"They owe me a drink," Pedro protested. "They promised me." Without a word, José Antonio had grabbed Pedro by the arm and led him out.

But the cantina was quiet tonight. Only the proprietor and his brother-in-law sat at a table talking in undertones. José Antonio waved at them, took a final look around, then left.

They continued along the road to the short cut across the Luceros' pasture which would bring them to the road near the Smith place. As they drew nearer, Leonardo slowed his pace. "Grandfather," he said, "is Señor Baca going crazy again?"

"I don't know, hijo. We'll see."

They stopped at the edge of the pasture to rest. The moon emerged from behind a cloud and soft light illumined the way. Up ahead about a half mile they could see the Smith house.

We'll have to lock him back in the shed, José Antonio thought. I should have heeded the warning when he showed me the knife. Crazy fool!

"We'd better move on, Leonardo. If we don't find him with the goats, we'll go back the other way on Rafas Road."

Their footsteps crunched along the moonlit path. As they approached the road, breathing heavily, a gunshot thundered in the distance. José Antonio put out a hand to stop the boy. The explosion lingered, reverberating in the night air. It was as if they were surrounded by sound, trapped in it, shocked motionless by the sudden, loud, angry rupture of the stillness.

At first José Antonio thought: Where did the fool get a gun? He felt Leonardo grasp him by the arm. In the distance he could see lanterns go on in the few houses set among the fields. Then a cloud obscured the moon and the path was dark, with only pinpoints of light showing from the houses.

"¡Andale!" José Antonio led the way, crossing the road to the other side, moving as quickly as his old legs could carry him. They could hear the shouting now.

"He headed toward the ditch!" someone yelled.

"Son of a bitch!"

José Antonio was overwhelmed by an ominous foreboding. "Wait!"

Leonardo whispered. José Antonio stared bewildered into the dark. Then he heard rustling in the cornfield.

The old man turned, feeling his grandson's grip tighten, trying to see through the dark. "There! Over to the left," Leonardo said, his voice rising and falling in fear.

At that moment the cloud cover passed. They stood transfixed, watching, as head and shoulders emerged from a row of corn, the hair wild and unkempt, the mouth flecked with saliva and gasping for air, the eyes like those of a wild animal.

"Pedro!"

Pedro answered with a wild groan. His frightened eyes widened. He came through the corn toward them, holding his left arm cradled against his body. Another shot exploded across the field and Pedro threw himself prostrate on the ground.

"¡Jesucristo!" José Antonio knelt and turned Pedro on his side. The cradled arm had fallen away from his body and he could see the blood on Pedro's shirt.

José Antonio motioned for the lantern. "My hand," Pedro groaned. He pulled his left arm to his side, unfolding his hand toward them. There was a gash across Pedro's palm, not a gunshot but a cut.

"There's somebody on the road!" The shout came from across the field.

Pedro tried to scramble to his feet, but he was too exhausted. "Don't let them get me," he pleaded. "They're trying to take my rancho."

"Stop over there!"

José Antonio stood and watched the light grow brighter as the lantern approached. He held his own lantern high so they could be seen.

"It's Don José Rafa," one of the men said.

"They said they'd get me," Pedro whined. "Last night when I was asleep they were coming through the walls into my room. I could hear the voices. 'We know,' they said. 'We've known all these years that you were the one.'

"They had been watching," Pedro said. "All during the trial in court. They had been in the mine, too. When I hired those men to kill those gringos, they had been hiding in the trees.

"No one else has ever known. I never told anyone, not even my wife. But they were there and they've been waiting ever since to get me. I heard them last night coming through the walls. My father was there, old Don Pedro, but they had tied his hands behind his back and gagged him so that all he could do was watch."

Pedro wheezed a crazed laugh. "Revenge is the sweetest fruit," he said. "The sweetest."

"Don José!" It was Wilhelm Kruger, whose place was just east of James Smith's over toward the river. He and Smith's foreman, Jesús Perea, approached cautiously.

José Antonio waited, a worried frown on his face, watching the rifles that the men carried.

"Don't let them — ," Pedro began. Then his eyes rolled so only the whites were visible.

"He's fainted," Leonardo whispered.

Jesús tightened the grip on his rifle and tilted it toward Pedro. "The bastard tried to knife me!"

Kruger looked at the fallen old man and then at José Antonio. "Well —" he sighed.

"I tell you he's crazy," Perea said. "Trying to screw the goats is one thing, but trying to kill me is something else."

"Get up!" Kruger commanded, prodding Pedro with the toe of his boot.

Perea glared at the fallen man. "I'll give the son of a bitch what he deserves!" As he raised his foot, José Antonio stepped in front of him.

"He's unconscious," José Antonio said. "Leonardo. You and Jesús pick him up and carry him to Smith's place. It's the closest."

Perea looked toward Kruger with an expression of confusion, as if wondering who was in charge. Kruger nodded his head toward the fallen man and Jesús handed him his rifle.

"Where's the knife?" Perea asked. Leonardo rummaged under the old man and handed the bloodstained blade to his grandfather. "Damn lunatic!" Perea said. "He ought to be locked up."

\*     \*     \*

The old man was so light that it seemed to Leonardo they were carrying a child. Smith ushered them into a bedroom and they laid Pedro on the finest bed he had lain on since his days in California. Perea sat near the door, his rifle across his lap, while Leonardo stood in the doorway to watch Perea and Pedro.

The boy could not think clearly. He was upset and confused by his father's condition. He had no idea of how it had come about or why. Yet he firmly believed that the old man who lay stretched on the luxurious bed was the victim of the same archvillains: the Anglos.

He glanced at Perea whose eyes were half-shut, watching the bed as if it held some wild beast. Leonardo's rage boiled and he trembled in frustration. If only I had my own rifle, he thought, I'd show them. Thinking mostly about his father and the men he imagined responsible for assaulting him.

He only half-heard the voices in the other room. "It was Jesse who saw him first, Don José. Out by the corral." Smith's voice was tense, pitched higher than normal.

"I was in here going over some work for the election. It's not that far off, you know. I was looking over the figures for Los Griegos when I heard the shouting and went to the back door.

"They were staring at each other in the half-light, poised like wrestlers gauging where and when to leap. Or like two tomcats eyeing each other before the screeching and clawing begin.

"'What do you mean, goddamned gringo?' I heard Jesse say. '¡Soy como tú, chingado!'

"'It's just a plot to divide us,' the old man said. 'They want to take my rancho and the easiest way is to divide us so we fight among ourselves instead of against the true enemy.'

"Jesse straightened up and laughed. He hadn't seen the knife yet. 'What rancho?' I thought. 'The crazy old loon doesn't even own a pot to boil frijoles in.' Jesse's laugh must have done it because it was then that the old man went for him with the knife.

"If he had been a younger man, he might have hurt Jesse. As it was, Jesse let out a yell you could have heard all the way down to the river.

"By the time I rushed through the door, Jesse had dodged and run for the rifle that he keeps in his room by the shed. The old man picked himself off the ground and wiped his hand on his shirt. Then he saw me and bolted into the cornfield.

"I went after Jesse. 'That crazy man tried to kill me!' he shouted."

"He's an old man," José Antonio said. "He gets confused."

"I've been very patient, Don José. For months he's wandered over here molesting my goats. Anyone could see that he was not all there, not quite right in the head. The goats were a lot of commotion, a lot of nuisance, but no real harm. It's not as if he actually raped a goat. But pulling a knife on Jesse is another matter. It might have been me or my wife."

"It was *my* wife!"

They turned toward Kruger, whose angry face stared accusingly at José Antonio. Kruger's long, hard fingers curled and uncurled around the stock of his rifle. His wrists protruded from the frayed cuffs of his faded workshirt; his overalls hung limp and dusty on his angular frame.

"He . . ." Kruger sputtered. "That crazy man. He bust into my house!" He looked at them, staring from face to face, trying to impress on them his fury at this violation.

"She . . . she was taking a bath. I was out back in the corral. That crazy man bust in. Just bust right in on her where she sat naked in the washtub.

"I come running when I heard her scream. She was standing there in the middle of the kitchen with the broom raised over her head, the water still dripping off her.

" 'In the cornfield!' she screamed. 'He ran into the cornfield!'

"I grabbed my rifle and chased after him. That's when I met Jesse coming up from the other direction."

"We just have to keep him locked up," José Antonio said.

"You're damned right," Kruger said. "And I mean to see it done."

"Pedro doesn't belong in jail," José Antonio said.

"The loony bin then!"

Old Pedro groaned and Jesús gripped his rifle tighter. Leonardo looked at the old man in alarm. The asylum?

"Let's just keep calm about this, Kruger," Smith said.

"The old man is crazy. A danger to himself and others. I'm going to report him. It's not just me. There's others around here who would do the same."

"I thought you were my neighbor, Mr. Kruger."

"Don José, this isn't a matter of neighborliness."

"Leonardo!" The boy met his grandfather at the bedroom door. The old man's face was ashen and his eyes were not so much angry as hurt. "I would like Jesús to drive Pedro home," José Antonio said. "With your permission, Mr. Smith."

"Jesse!" Smith called.

José Antonio took the rifle while Jesús and Leonardo carried the old man out to the buggy. Smith walked José Antonio outside as Jesús hitched up the horse; he put a hand on the old man's arm as he climbed aboard. "Kruger will cool off," Smith said. "I'll talk to him."

José Antonio turned his haggard eyes toward the screen door where Kruger stood watching. Smith gave him a final pat on the shoulder. "I'm sorry, Don José."

## 42

Gregoria had risen quietly, carrying her clothes to the kitchen where she started the fire. She would let José Antonio sleep in again today. He had stayed in bed all day yesterday, wrestling with his blankets in his half-sleep.

José Antonio had complained about Pedro, who once again was locked in the shed. Did he blame her becauses she took pity on the old loony and let him loose occasionally? Pedro was human too, no matter what crazy things he did. You cannot treat people like animals.

But she was worried about her husband. All of a sudden he looked his age. Especially the night when he and Leonardo had ridden back with Pedro in Señor Smith's buggy. She had heard the wheels creaking along the road, then up the path to the house. Heard the mumble of men's voices. Then, looking out the back door, she saw two of them carrying toward the shed a dark shadow like an elongated sack of meal.

After a bit the wheels creaked away. When José Antonio walked in, he sighed and merely said, "We found him. Here's your knife." And he handed her the bloodstained blade.

"Do you want some coffee?" He had nodded and sank onto the bench, his arms falling limp across the kitchen table. "You look all in, Tercero." He nodded again.

She had tended to him silently, knowing that he would tell her in time but that for now he needed to rest more than she needed to know. Leonardo had come quietly into the kitchen. "I'm going home, Grandmother."

Now the morning chill began to dissipate as the fire grew. Gregoria huddled close to the stove and dressed, taking care not to move too close to the hot metal sides. She sighed. How different it had been years ago when, like most of the poor paisanos around here, she had cooked and warmed herself by the heat of a fireplace. Not everyone could afford a stove and it made her extra warm to be among the privileged.

Fully dressed, she looked into the bedroom where José Antonio snored with a rumble. Gregoria then peered out the back door. A lamp shone in her son's house. Florinda must be up and about, ready to be spelled in her vigil. Gregoria would go and prepare breakfast before she took her turn watching at Francisco's bedside.

The shed was dark and silent. She remembered how she had washed the stain from the knife blade and hung it back on the wall with a shudder. For a few moments she thought that she would never be able to use it again, but she realized how silly that was. If someone had been killed with it she might feel that way. But it had only been a cut by a careless, crazed old man who had no more business playing with sharp toys than a small child.

José Antonio had been very upset about Kruger's threat to have Pedro committed. It was not like the old days when every little village could tolerate its idiot or its drunk. Now, somehow, in the bigger world where there should have been more tolerance for those who did not quite fit, there seemed to be less. "Hide him away! Get him out of sight! My God, what will the neighbors think?" Who cares? she thought. Next thing they will examine us before we go into town so that they can be sure we are clean enough.

She slammed the door in irritation. Startled, she looked back as if to apologize to the door, although she was really concerned about her sleeping husband.

Florinda stared mutely as she entered the little house. The fire was out and last night's dishes sat in disarray on the table. Florinda's hair was more unkempt than usual. The hollows of her eyes had sunk and the rings underneath had grown darker. Her skin was sallow, almost jaundiced, where it should have been a healthy tan.

Gregoria noticed that the wood box was empty, so she made two trips outside to the woodpile. She lit the stove, then went out once more, this time to the pump. She poured part of the water into a dishpan that she placed on the stove. Then she put on a coffeepot before she sat down.

Florinda was still in the same position as when Gregoria had first come in. It worried her that her daughter-in-law might not have the strength to cope. Like some, Florinda seemed best cast in the role of patient rather than nurse.

"How was he last night?" she asked softly. Florinda nodded, still staring. From the children's room came the stirring of someone up and dressing. "Are you all right?" Again Florinda nodded, but this time tears began to trickle down her cheeks.

"I don't know what will happen to our crop," she began. "We will all starve next year even if Francisco gets well."

"You have Leonardo. José Antonio. Your brothers. Neighbors. There will be people to help."

It was as if she hadn't heard. Or didn't want to hear. "What will happen to my poor little girls? No father. No food."

*No father?* Gregoria almost rushed to the bedroom to see for herself. "Has he taken a turn for the worse?"

No response. Not even a headshake. The tears flowed more rapidly. Finally a flicker broke Florinda's stare and she turned toward Gregoria. "No," she said. "I think he's getting better."

Gregoria's eyes narrowed as she studied her daughter-in-law. It was Florinda who had taken a turn for the worse.

"Why does everything have to happen to me?" Florinda wailed.

"Everything happens to everybody." Gregoria thought of that poor old crazy man locked in the shed across the yard. He had lost his home. His wife. His children. His mind. He too could whine that everything happened to him. Yet he had armed himself with a knife to take vengeance on the wrong man for some imagined offense. Now there was no doubt in Gregoria's mind that they would lock him up with other loonies.

"You've been working too hard," she said to Florinda. "Let me get you a cup of coffee."

They sat, holding their hands around the hot cups, listening to the sounds of morning. The rhythmic squeak of the pump. Then the splash of water on the ground. The front door opened and closed and the sound of bare feet approached. Sleepy-eyed, his wet hair slicked down, Leonardo smiled and helped himself to coffee. There were dewdrops of moisture on the thin dark hairs on his upper lip.

"Hijo," Gregoria said. "When you finish your coffee, go to the henhouse and see if there are any eggs. We'll have a treat for breakfast." He blinked his opaque eyes and smiled a sleepy smile.

Gregoria could see why this grandson was her husband's favorite. None of their own children had the same innocent intelligence. Nor any of their other grandchildren. José Antonio must have been such a boy, she thought. But she did not remember her husband as a boy. He had been a few years older than she, and in childhood that had been like a generation. How she did remember him was as a young priest. Serious, with a calm that gave people confidence that everything would be all right.

After breakfast Gregoria tried to comfort her daughter-in-law but finally gave up. The shell encrusted around Florinda had only one small opening, from which complaints issued forth. Gregoria had never understood why her son had married this woman, but now she realized that Francisco, being by nature quarrelsome, had chosen a mate with whom he could quarrel. From this unlikely pair had come Leonardo. Carlos, her other grandson, seemed more properly the child of Florinda and Francisco.

She washed the dishes, sent Leonardo to his work outside, and went to sit with Francisco. He lay in the unlighted room breathing so shallowly that she could hardly tell if he was alive.

Crossing herself, she whispered the words of her most powerful prayer, the Ave Maria, staring at him stretched out on the bed. Francisco was taller than his father, slimmer, like the men of her own family. His temperament, now subdued in illness, was unlike that of her father and uncles. They had been men of quiet resignation who evaded life with their liquor and their companionship with other men, while her son met life with an argument. Francisco was more like the Rafas who had passed away. Like José Antonio's brother Carlos, who had died fighting. Like José Antonio's father before old age had mellowed him.

In the middle of another Ave, the words automatic and unthought, she saw Francisco open his eyes slowly and calmly, fixing his gaze upon her. It was an alert stare, the energy shining forth even though the expression on his face did not change and he remained as still as ever.

So abrupt was the change that Gregoria stopped praying and returned his look in silence, watching for some sign: a word, a sigh, a blink.

Then, before she could decide what to say to him, he closed his eyes. It happened so quickly, so calmly, she almost doubted that it had happened at all. Yet she acknowledged it as a sign. He was getting better.

After a moment she resumed her prayer, lost herself in it, until sometime later — she didn't know when — a hand on her shoulder startled her. "Grandmother, Don Pedro is screaming from the shed."

She patted Leonardo's hand as she rose from the chair. "You sit with your papá. I'll be back soon."

\*     \*     \*

Mamá had stopped shuffling around the kitchen. Leonardo could hear her moving in the room where she slept instead of beside Papá.

It was quieter and more pleasant without his little brother and sisters. Even Mamá was quieter. Not screaming so much. Not after him to referee the little pedos, who seemed forever quarreling.

Only Pedro remained, with his hollering and screaming. Yet in the bedroom you could barely hear him through the adobe walls.

Shouting always upset Leonardo. What did all those angry people want? Why were they shouting at him? And now, Pedro's bellowing disturbed him in a different way. It was like the cry of a wounded animal. Like the frightened bleating of a goat before you slit its throat.

The shouting from the shed aroused a demon feeling that he had kept hidden deep inside. But his overwhelming anger at the state of the old man could no longer be restrained. That could have been *him* cheated like old Pedro had been cheated. That could have been *him* jailed. *Him* pursued. Shot at. Threatened. Cursed. Driven crazy. Because he too had a dark complexion and a name that went with it.

Just weeks ago Leonardo had been embarrassed by the old man. Had been angered at his crazy behavior. Had wanted to disown him. To deny that Pedro lived with Grandfather. That he was related by marriage to Grandmother. For so much of Pedro reminded the boy of himself—his brown face, his accented English, his Spanish name— that Leonardo wanted to obliterate everything that told the world they were two of a kind.

But his grandfather's story had been a revelation. A lightning rod for his sense of pride, his sense of honor, and his understanding that whoever attacked old Pedro attacked him. There was no way for him to be separate from this crazy old man.

A ghost-like groan startled him. Drew him back to that other crime perpetrated by those same unknown villains. His father assaulted by men whose hostile countenances Leonardo saw as pale, light-skinned. The politicians. It had to be them. Because if it were not, he could not imagine who it might be.

Again the groan. "No!" Francisco whispered with the little force his voice commanded. "Get away from me, you bastards."

"Papá?" Leonardo slid from the chair and leaned over the bed, not daring to touch his father for fear of causing him pain. Francisco did not seem to hear. Eyes closed, forehead beaded with sweat, his mouth twisted as he spoke through his nightmare.

"Hijos de Libertad!" he said. Then he started to laugh, until that quiet laugh turned into a cough.

"You can't fool me," he went on in his sleep. "I know. Yes, Benito, I know. So you'd better kill me, because if you don't—" Then a shudder passed through his body, trembling, wincing, drawing back as if he were reliving the attack. "No," he groaned. "Bastards. I'll get you for this, Durán. You'd better kill—"

Durán! Leonardo thought. Benito Durán! He was shocked that it had not been James Smith. Or Wilhelm Kruger. But then one did not have to be named Smith to be an Anglo. Being one was more than having a surname. It was a matter of loyalty. There were lackeys enough among their own people who would be loyal to the Devil himself for a price.

He did not hear the footsteps. "Francisco!" Florinda crossed the boy's line of vision, reaching over to shake her husband by the shoulder. "Are you all right, Francisco?"

Nightmare! Leonardo thought. The nightmare had passed from the dreaming father to the watching son. He knew that he must right the terrible wrong that had been done to his father. To old Pedro. To himself.

Without a word, he turned and left the room. He knew where his father kept it. It was still there. Clean. Oiled. Ready.

# 43

José Antonio had been sleeping lightly, resisting the drift to wakefulness, when he sensed Gregoria rise. In his state halfway between sleep and waking, he heard her move cautiously to the kitchen. Then the sounds faded and his awareness drifted away like smoke. Hours later it seemed, a shout startled him so that his body gave a little hop and he was wide awake, his heart pounding.

"¡Demonio!" he heard. "¡Me matan!"

My God! he thought, wondering what terrible thing was happening, until he recognized Pedro's voice. The lunatic was awake early this morning. José Antonio rolled to a sitting position on the edge of the bed, looked out the window at the bright morning, and groaned. It was later than he thought.

"¡Aquí vienen otra vez!"

He pulled on his overalls. Somehow Pedro must know that the doctor would come today to examine him at Señor Kruger's insistence, then report to the authorities. The thought was depressing. It did not take a medical expert to see that Pedro was loony. But a harmless loony. More a victim than a perpetrator of harm.

But José Antonio saw the inevitable. The examination. The questions. Just way stations on the road to the crazy house.

He took the key from a nail on the kitchen wall and ambled to the shed. As he fumbled at the lock, he heard breathing from the other side of the door and he knew Pedro was up against it listening.

"Good morning," José Antonio muttered.

"You're one of them. All night you've been coming through the walls, but now you're coming through the door to take me away. You want your revenge."

"It's José Antonio. I've come to let you out for awhile."

The disbelieving laugh ended in a cough. As José Antonio opened the door Pedro leaned back and blinked at the morning light. "You've been having bad dreams," José Antonio said. Then he heard light footsteps behind him.

"Have you been teasing him?" Gregoria scolded.

"We were just coming out for breakfast."

"All night they were coming through the walls," Pedro whined. "They're going to take me away. Even my darling Rebecca was there. With our little daughters who had grown old but with the same sweet faces and white hair and wrinkles. And Esmerelda," he added. "Esmerelda warned me that they wanted to take everything away from me. Everything. Rebecca, the little old girls, herself."

"Come along." José Antonio took him by the arm and led him toward the house.

"I'll make breakfast," Gregoria said.

José Antonio glanced across the yard to his son's house. "How is it over there?"

"He's better. Leonardo is with him now that Florinda has gone to bed."

José Antonio was tempted to go see for himself. It was a relief to hear good news for a change. But first things first.

*　*　*

Pedro was absorbed in the business of eating, focusing all his energy and attention to scooping the beans and chili onto pieces of folded tortilla that he popped into his mouth. José Antonio and Gregoria spoke as if he were not present, the way they might have spoken in the presence of a child.

"Pobrecito," Gregoria said. "With all that he's had to put up with. That damn Kruger. Pedro never did anything to him. When is the doctor coming?"

"Mid-morning. He's going to look at Francisco too."

"Then what?"

"I don't know.".

"Do you think Pedro knows?"

José Antonio looked across the table. Pedro raised his plate with both hands and held it out to Gregoria. "I don't know. At least he'll get plenty of free chili and beans there."

Gregoria brought the pan from the stove, spooning more onto Pedro's plate. "There, honey. Some nice frijoles for you. They make you strong." His face beamed in simple pleasure.

"I will miss him," Gregoria said. "When he's here it's as if my sister were still here."

José Antonio grunted and wiped his plate clean. "I'm going to sit with Francisco. You take care of him," nodding toward Pedro.


*   *   *


José Antonio sat beside Francisco, who lay quietly asleep. Only Florinda's rhythmic snoring from the other room rose above the silence.

For days he had taken his turn at the bedside and during the past few days he had seen the rapid blooming of strength in Francisco, like a flower unfolding. There was no longer any doubt that Francisco would live and recovery was just a matter of time.

"Well, hijo," he whispered, "You've been lucky. Men have died from less. Times like this remind me how cheap life is. When men sipping their whiskey in a cantina are shot dead for no reason, what can you expect? A sharp tongue just increases a man's chances of being assaulted. Maybe you'll learn from this."

José Antonio leaned back and took his rosary from his pocket. He ran thumb and forefinger over the first large bead and began to pray. Time passed, the silence broken only by the intermittent snoring of his daughter-in-law and an occasional quiet stirring by Francisco. He prayed the decades of Aves punctuated by a single Pater Noster. Round the cycle, not even thinking the words as his thumb and forefinger slid from bead to bead. He caught himself in this mindless rote and stopped. Might as well not pray at all, he thought. Or instead beat a drum like some savage Indian. Without thought, words were no longer prayers, only noises spiraling meaninglessly up toward the infinite. The sound of a falling tree or the quiet flow of the river were as much prayer as his thoughtless mumblings.

He looked up from his beads and saw Francisco, open-eyed, staring at him. They gazed silently at each other for awhile before José Antonio spoke. "Hijo."

"Papá."

"I'm glad you're better. God is watching out for you."

A weak smile. José Antonio felt embarrassed. He wanted to reach out and take his son's hand, but something stopped him. Just like a cold-fish Anglo, he thought. Annoyed at himself, he laid a hand on Francisco. He wished that he could give his son what he needed: health from old man to young.

This is the prayer I should be saying, José Antonio thought. Not words that I do not even think about. Lord, God. Thy will be done. If it is Thy will that my son should live, I would be most grateful.

He felt a feeble squeeze of his hand and when he looked, Francisco had closed his eyes. After a few moments he appeared to have fallen asleep again.

José Antonio dozed. The next thing he was aware of was the sound of Francisco's terrified voice. He listened, barely awake, trying to make out the words. Benito Durán? he thought. Los Hijos de Libertad? Then he shook Francisco, trying to rouse him from his nightmare.

"Benito Durán," José Antonio whispered, looking with dismay at his son. "But why?"

A voice from the other room called out. "My God! What's the matter now? Is he all right?" Then Florinda was beside him, running her fingers through her uncombed hair. "I can't even get a little rest without something happening," she complained. "Can't you keep him quiet? How can I do all that has to be done if I don't get my rest?"

"Has he been talking in his sleep?" José Antonio asked.

"How should I know? I don't listen. I have other things to worry about."

"Has Leonardo heard him?"

Florinda wiped at her eyes as she looked out the bedroom door.

"¡Desgraciado!" she muttered. "Where is that boy?" Then she rushed toward the kitchen. The back door slammed and he heard her scream, "Leonardo!"

\*    \*    \*

The day went slowly. The doctor, who was supposed to have come mid-morning, had not appeared yet, although it was now mid-afternoon. Leonardo had not shown himself either and José Antonio had tired of his daughter-in-law's complaints about it. He took his turn sitting with Francisco, then left the house to do those chores that his grandson had neglected.

It would have been helpful to have Pedro working with him. Pedro could at least do simple chores from instinct. But since José Antonio expected the doctor any moment, he left Pedro locked in the shed. He did not want to give the impression that he was lax in his custody of the old man. It was not just Kruger who had complained. There were others. Even Jesús Perea, in spite of Smith's attempts to keep him silent.

A door slammed and Gregoria crossed the orchard to Francisco's house, not seeing her husband as he sat in the shade. José Antonio rose and walked to the road. He gazed east and west. Nothing. Not even a distant cloud of dust. He stood a moment, then returned to the orchard.

"Well, where are you?" he said aloud in irritation.

Some moments later the bellowing began again. "My medicine!" came the shout. "¡Necesito mi medicina!"

With a sigh of irritation, José Antonio rose once again, walking past the shed to the pump. He filled a dipper and carried it to the shed, setting it down while he unlocked the door.

"Here."

Pedro smiled in anticipation. He took a deep swallow from the cup. His eyes mirrored immediate surprise. He spit out the mouthful and emptied the dipper onto the ground.

"This isn't my medicine."

José Antonio snatched the dipper from him and locked the door without a word. Damned drunken loony! He hung the dipper back on the tree beside the pump and walked irritably past the house to the road.

Off in the distance a small cloud followed the approaching horse and buggy like the dirty tail of a kite. When the buggy turned into the yard, José Antonio steadied the already steady horse more from impatience than from any real need. The doctor sat silent a moment and looked at him as if trying to decide what to say.

"I'm sorry I'm so late," he finally said. "There was an emergency."

The doctor looked up as the shout "¡Medicina!" came from the shed.

"That's him," José Antonio said.

The doctor alighted from the buggy and placed his hands on José Antonio's upper arms. "Let's go inside and talk a moment."

What was it that José Antonio sensed? Concern? Sympathy? Pity? A premonition of bad news? He had already mentally said his good-bye to Pedro.

The doctor kept a hand on his shoulder as they entered the house. "Sit down," the doctor said.

"What is it?"

"The sheriff's deputy should be here in a little while to explain."

"Explain what?"

"Oh, damn! I wish I didn't have to be the one to bring the news."

The doctor stared over José Antonio's right shoulder at a blank spot on the wall. "He's dead," the doctor said.

The old man felt his bones turn to jelly. As if some evil spirit breathed frigid air on him from a frozen mountaintop. He blinked in confusion. The shouting from the back of the yard grew louder. He knew that Francisco was next door being watched by Gregoria and that the doctor had not been there in several days.

José Antonio searched the doctor's face. Finally the man looked at him. "Your grandson," he said. "Young Leonardo."

I wish I could die, José Antonio thought.

# 44

The rude coffin lay across the two wooden sawhorses in the living room of the big house. The candles at both ends of the box had burned down to stumps of melted wax that flickered weakly.

José Antonio sat staring in the dark. The others had left long ago, having said the rosary, shared their impassioned tears of grief and consolation, and eaten what the black-garbed family women had prepared in the kitchen. Not even the smell of food lingered.

Francisco had insisted that he be carried to the big house for the rosary. He had sat mummy-like, wrapped in a blanket, among the crowd of relatives and friends and neighbors, barely alive himself, paying his last respects to his oldest son.

"It was my fault," Francisco had told him. "I talked in my sleep and he heard me."

"What does it matter who told him? He would have heard it somewhere sometime anyway."

"No!" Francisco's eyes had filled with tears. "I would never have told." His eyes flashed defiantly. "He would never have known."

"Until you had been strong enough to seek revenge yourself. Or Durán had come and killed you this time."

The skin had stretched tight across Francisco's skull, a living death's head. "I'll kill him anyway."

How could he argue with this ruin of a man? Hadn't he had the same thoughts himself? An eye for an eye. "Oh, Lord," José Antonio had said in prayer. "Help me to forgive . . . but not yet."

"My fault," Francisco insisted again.

And mine, José Antonio thought, filling the boy's imagination with stories of old pain inflicted by old enemies until he saw the world through old and unforgiving eyes instead of with the hope of youth. Leonardo's delusion was seeing himself as a young champion avenging old sins.

José Antonio turned to Francisco. "No. It was Benito Durán who pulled the trigger. His fault. And before that it was Benito Durán who nearly killed you. He and his Hijos de Libertad."

A look of pain had crossed Francisco's face. An anguish so deep that for a moment José Antonio thought that he would faint. Then Francisco's eyes were filled with tears, although he was frighteningly silent as they ran down his ravaged cheeks.

"He is with God and the angels now." José Antonio crossed himself.

"No!" He looked in surprise at his son's outburst. "What kind of God is it who takes the youngest and the best? I can't pray to such a God. Not anymore."

"You're just saying that because . . ."

"No! I won't pray to such a God."

"Then why did you insist on coming? You should be home in bed."

"I came for Leonardo. And to curse the God who would do this to him . . . and to me."

Then Florinda and Gregoria had come with the veloria who would lead the prayers. Afterwards came the others, whispering their condolences and glancing at each other when they saw Francisco. Throughout the rosary José Antonio saw Francisco's lips frozen shut, his stare fixed on the wooden coffin.

The sobbing of the women grew in an unbearable crescendo. The Aves of the whispering crowd were drowned in the moaning of a few. Finally, Florinda jumped to her feet in the midst of the crowd and screamed: "Oh, my baby! My boy!"

The whispered prayers continued, though eyes had turned. Gregoria and one of Florinda's sisters rose to comfort her, but before they reached her, Florinda toppled over in a faint.

The prayers rose in volume like the buzz of an excited beehive. They carried Florinda from the room. José Antonio noticed that Francisco had not even shifted his gaze. He continued to stare at the coffin though his lips moved in a sorrowful whisper. "All the crying and screaming in the world won't bring him back."

"Tercero." Startled, he looked up from the candle stumps. "Are you all right?"

Gregoria came behind him and put her hands on his shoulders. He leaned his head sideways to touch her hand, felt their moistness — she must have been wiping at her eyes — and looked up at her. "Sit down."

"He was your hope, wasn't he?" she said.

The dam broke. All the feeling built up during his conversation with Francisco, during the endless cycle of Aves and Pater Nosters, during the burning of the candles — all of the sorrow and anger and hurt burst forth and he cried like a hurt child, blinded by his tears.

He felt his wife's face against his, unable to distinguish her tears from his own. Her moans from his own. They cried together a long while, until there were no more tears and his dry, hollow eyes saw that the candles were out.

"It's hard not to hate," José Antonio said. "Damn it!"

"You always told me it did no good."

"I prayed to God to help me forgive . . . but not yet."

"Then when?"

"Never!"

She sprang back as if she had been struck. "Never belongs only to God. Never is like eternity. It's not something we decide, it's something we endure."

"Never!" he repeated, his voice hoarse with anguish.

"I've never seen you like this before," she said.

All he could do was shake his head because the tears began again.

\* \* \*

It is the story of our lives, José Antonio thought. The losers are told to forgive their trespassers, but they cannot. They carry their hurt and resentment with them, sometimes for generations.

The opening snap of the lock brought him out of his self-absorption. The shed door opened slowly and Pedro's wary eyes peered out at him.

"Come on," José Antonio said. "We have to go to the cemetery."

Pedro shuffled cautiously from the shed. "They're coming to take me away."

José Antonio shook his head as he led Pedro to the pump. "We have to go to the funeral. Wash up. I don't want you to disgrace us. You'll have to behave."

He pumped the handle as Pedro splashed his face and neck and arms, then shook himself like a dog before turning toward the morning sun to let it dry him.

"Gregoria has a clean shirt for you."

"They did it to another one of us, didn't they?"

Something about Pedro's expression, his tone of voice, broke through José Antonio's numbness. It was as if Pedro was in the eye of a hurricane, looking through his own madness from a core of sanity. *They,* José Antonio thought. It is always *they.*

"You know what happened," José Antonio said. "I told you."

"They did it again."

"What they?" José Antonio asked in irritation.

Pedro leaned toward him, looking around as if someone might be listening. "The Anglos," he whispered.

"Leonardo was killed by one of our own New Mexicans."

"No," he said. "They just want you to think that. He's really an Anglo. Can't you see that?"

"It was Benito Durán. And he's in jail."

Once again Pedro shook his head. José Antonio did not think of the literal meaning of the madman's words but of Benito Durán. How would he describe him? Ambitious. Grasping. A taker rather than a giver. Arrogant. Energetic. A seeker and user of power.

How would he describe so many Anglos? In much the same way. It was not just a matter of skin color or ancestry. It was also a matter of attitude and action. It knew no — or rather, it knew every — country, every race. Benito Durán was as much one in spirit as James Smith was in ancestry. That crazy Pedro was right.

A sly smile crossed Pedro's lips, a smile as if he knew something that José Antonio did not know. An indulgent smile that would have made an outsider wonder which one was mad. "They'll take it all," he said, "unless you fight back." Then his smile abruptly disappeared. "They're coming to take me and you're letting them."

A sigh. A doubt. Had Pedro been lucid when the doctor finally saw him? It was hard to know. He moved in and out of normality constantly. As if his madness were a secret creature imprisoned in his mind who made its presence known on whim, moving back and forth like a playful child maliciously irritating its parents.

"We're going to the cemetery. Go in and get your shirt. Then you can help me hitch the horse to the wagon."

"They're going to kill me at the cemetery. Once and for all. They've been after me most of my life. Now they're going to kill me and drop me into the ground."

"No. It's for Leonardo."

For a moment Pedro's eyes flickered as if he were trying to puzzle it out. "Leonardo?"

José Antonio took him by the arm and led him into the house.

*       *       *

They rode back along the dusty road in silence. Florinda lay stretched out in the bed of the wagon. Gregoria sat beside her holding her hand, while Pedro sat beside José Antonio. Francisco had been too weak to attend.

Behind, José Antonio could hear the squeak of Armando Chávez' wagon and the chatter of the children. They had cautiously progressed from the solemn quiet demanded of them at the funeral to a whispering exchange. When that had not been rebuffed, they had gradually escalated to more normal behavior.

During the funeral, Leonardo's brother and sisters had quietly joined their mother and grandparents as if they knew where they belonged. But once the rites were over, they had rejoined their cousins.

"Now I'm going to have a bed all to myself," he had heard Carlos confide proudly to a cousin. "I've never had my own bed before and neither have you." A childish fist in the ribs had cut short Carlos' bragging and he chased angrily after his cousin to repay him.

Carlos was no Leonardo, José Antonio thought. His surviving grandson's face was an angry mixture of the boy's father and mother. Then, of course, there were the granddaughters: Rosa, Gregoria, and Juanita. The eight-year-old Rosa was pretty, light-complexioned, dressed neatly as always, and bossy as befit the eldest sister. Gregoria, the middle girl, argued with her older sister, intense and feisty, plain and dark, with her unkempt neglected appearance a challenge thrown at the world by an intelligent child who knew too well that she wasn't pretty. And finally little Juanita, the baby, wearing what hand-me-downs Gregoria did not reduce to tatters, smiling from under the wave of reddish hair that was a throwback to distant generations. How could one not love these little granddaughters? But being female, they were but temporary custodians of the Rafa name. Not one of them would have children named Rafa. None of them budding flowers on the family bush. The rose had been cut down before the bud had unfolded.

His eyes misted with tears. Embarrassed, he glanced sideways. Pedro was watching him solemnly. "¡Andale!" he spat at the horses, snapping the ends of the reins to whip them along.

From the corner of his eye he could see Pedro still staring at him. It's over, he thought to himself. Dead and buried. The rose will never bloom.

From the wagon behind came the high-pitched shout of a child. "We're going to see Papá! He's going to be all right!"

He could still feel Pedro's eyes on him. It made him uncomfortable. Angered him. Just a few more days, he said to Pedro in his imagination. Then you'll be gone too. Somehow that thought soothed him, for seeing this survivor reminded him too much of the grandson who had not survived.

## 45

José Antonio knew that it was only a matter of time before they would be coming around. During the funeral he had acknowledged the silent nods and intense looks that spoke promises. Across the weed-covered cemetery, the open hole waiting to be filled, eyes sought him out. Sorrowful. Sympathetic. Yet business-like. Hard with intent on the world's work. Temporarily delayed by the chasm between them.

It did not take long before the first one came: the sheriff. The horseback figure came from the river, approaching slowly, almost casually. It was not the direction from which the sheriff would normally ride; town was south and east. It seemed almost accidental. A man about other business who just happened to be passing by.

"Don José!" The horse trotted into the yard and Sheriff Davis dismounted. "How lucky I am to see you."

"I was wondering when you were coming."

They silently entered the cool adobe. "I was down the road seeing about a little boundary dispute," the sheriff said. His voice was casual, as if this visit were nothing of much importance.

"Do you want to talk to Francisco?"

The sheriff frowned and glanced alertly at José Antonio. His speech quickened. "No. Not now, Don José. I want to talk to you first.

"I'm sorry about your grandson," he said. "I meant to speak to you at the funeral but somehow didn't." José Antonio nodded. "Durán is locked in jail under guard. There's a lot of strong feeling about this and I don't want anything to happen."

José Antonio's eyes burned like coals, and the sheriff looked away from him. "There are a few questions, Don José. I hope you don't mind."

"No."

"I don't know if you heard how it happened. There were witnesses."

José Antonio shook his head. What had he heard? Only the fact itself. From the doctor. And rumors.

"From what I can tell," the sheriff said, "Leonardo had come into town on his old horse carrying a rifle. No one thought much of that. Lots of men carry guns.

"He was seen riding out to Los Duranes. Benito's wife was home all day. She said no one came to the house. She saw no one around their place. Heard nothing unusual, except that their dogs barked and fussed worse than normal about mid-morning. She was in the kitchen and looked out, but didn't see anything.

"Later, about noon, Leonardo was seen riding into Old Town. He went into San Felipe Church, taking his rifle with him. He genuflected, made the sign of the cross, knelt with head bowed, and stayed awhile."

José Antonio looked up at the crucifix on the wall behind the sheriff. He began to tremble, feeling the tears starting to well up. Leonardo stopping to pray? For what? Revenge? The boy had prayed to the wrong God. For forgiveness? He had done nothing to forgive. Or perhaps from piety? A lifetime of habit may have turned his thoughts to where they should have been all along.

"After he left the church, he hung around the plaza for awhile, watching the passersby. A number of people saw him there. He seemed pleasant enough, although some wondered why he wasn't on the farm doing his work. Especially with his father laid up. But no matter.

"After loitering about the plaza for some time, he left abruptly. The conductor on the horse-drawn trolley saw him riding toward New Town with great urgency. He was seen in the saloons along Railroad Avenue, walking in, looking around, then striding out. Evidently he didn't find what he was looking for.

"He hung around one of the houses down at the end of the avenue, watching the entrance. All manner of men come and go. I have it on good authority that Benito Durán has a woman there that he visits."

"I did not think that my grandson was keeping company with whores," José Antonio said sharply.

"Whomever Leonardo was looking for did not turn up. Evidently he left about mid-afternoon. At any rate, he was next seen on the road to Old Town again. Passengers on a trolley saw him riding along. Then he must have seen someone because he shouted angrily at an approaching horseman.

"One of the passengers said that the two of them met in the middle of the road — Leonardo and Benito Durán. They must have had angry words. At least their faces looked red and angry. Leonardo reached to the side of the horse where his rifle was holstered. By then the trolley had gone past. The next thing they heard were two shots. When they looked back, Leonardo had toppled onto the ground and Benito sat looking down at him, his pistol in his hand."

José Antonio saw it all in his mind. The angry boy out to avenge his father. Looking for Durán in those places he was most likely to be found. Meeting him. And then —

"What did Durán say?"

"Self-defense."

"Do you believe that?"

"I'm here to find out what I can. It's for the court to decide. No one heard the words that they exchanged. They may have been threats, one way or the other. One witness saw Leonardo reach to the rifle holster on the side of his horse. The rifle was still in place after the shooting. No one saw the actual shooting; a dozen people heard it. What we have so far is Durán's word."

"Worth what?" José Antonio spat angrily. "Everyone knows what his word is worth."

"Was there any reason for the boy to quarrel with Benito?"

What did he know for certain? That Leonardo had overheard his father mumble a man's name in his sleep. That the boy had made an assumption. And José Antonio in turn had made another assumption: that Leonardo had gone out seeking revenge for his father.

"I don't know. He never said anything to me. He may have thought Durán had something to do with his father's beating."

"How did Leonardo behave? Did he give any indication?"

"We've all been concerned about Francisco. Taking turns caring for him. I never saw the boy that morning. If he had said anything before I would have remembered, but I don't."

The sheriff sat quiet for a moment, staring thoughtfully at his boots. Then he stood slowly, sighing. "I'd like to talk to Francisco if it's all right."

\* \* \*

They crossed the yard, scattering the flock of hens that cackled about, pecking the dirt. Gregoria looked out from the kitchen as they passed. Francisco, who was propped up in bed, slowly opened his eyes as they came in.

"Sheriff Davis wants to talk to you," José Antonio said.

"If you feel up to it," the sheriff said.

Francisco nodded. José Antonio offered the chair to their visitor and stood by the door.

"I hope the son of a bitch rots in hell," Francisco said.

"He's in jail. He'll get his day in court." A strange, luminous smile lit Francisco's face, a twisted smile with cruel intimations. "He's under guard," the sheriff said. "Nothing will happen to him before he goes on trial."

"The sheriff asked what I knew," José Antonio said. "I did not have much to tell him."

"Tell me, Francisco. Was there any reason for the boy to quarrel with Benito Durán?"

Francisco looked from one to the other, as if trying to fathom what they had already discussed. "Benito is a quarrelsome bastard. A bully. He has assaulted men before for no reason. The son of a bitch belongs at the end of a rope."

"I know all that. What I want to find out is if there was anything in particular between your son and Durán."

"No," he said. "Not that I know of."

"I heard," the sheriff said cautiously, "that he thought Durán had been responsible for your beating. That he sought him for revenge."

"Who would tell you a thing like that? Did you tell him, Papá?"

"Never mind," the sheriff said. "I heard from several sources."

"No!" Francisco answered.

"Is there any way Leonardo might have thought that Durán was responsible?"

"No!"

"Well, let me ask you about something else. I haven't seen you since your accident. Do you know who ambushed you or why?"

"No!"

"I heard something about Los Hijos de Libertad. Are they the ones who beat you?"

Francisco's face turned progressively more pale. José Antonio could see that he was tiring. What right did the sheriff have to keep after a sick man like that?

"It was night," Francisco said. "I couldn't see. I had been to the rally in Martínez Town and had a few drinks. Even if it had been light I might not have seen too well. All I remember is that there were five or six of them. One of them said something like, 'Welcome from Los Hijos de Libertad.' That's all I remember."

"Had you heard of Los Hijos before?"

"No!"

"Not even that visit to Plácido Durán?"

"Well, yes. That word spread all over the countryside."

"But other than that?"

"No."

The sheriff leaned back and looked at them both. "And you, Don José?"

"Everybody heard about the threat to Plácido. Especially those of us involved in the campaign. You know that as well as I do. As for who they are, I don't know. It seems to me that you should know more about that than us. It was our candidate who was threatened. And one of our campaign people who was attacked."

"You've known me for a long time, Don José. I don't work that way. In this case I don't have to. The election is as good as mine anyway. I couldn't have picked an easier opponent myself.

"But I didn't come here to argue politics. I'm here to do my job. Francisco, you're lucky to be alive. Now your son has been shot. That's more bad luck than any one family deserves.

"It just seems to me that if Leonardo thought Benito Durán was responsible for your attack, he would have cause to go looking for him. But if Benito belonged to Los Hijos, why would he threaten his brother? And why wouldn't his brother recognize him? No. It doesn't make sense."

"Listen, sheriff," José Antonio said. "Francisco is tired. He's still a sick man. He's had enough questions for now."

But Francisco's burning eyes stared at the sheriff. "Tell me. What does Benito say?"

"Self-defense. The boy went for his rifle after threatening him. He denies knowing anything about your beating or about Los Hijos de Libertad."

"Self-defense? Murder."

"What did the boy threaten him about?" José Antonio asked.

"Benito says that he accused him of ambushing his father. Of course he denied it. 'He's helping us win the election,' he said. 'Why would I do a stupid thing like that?' But Leonardo went for his rifle. Benito says he had no choice."

"Murderer!" Francisco cried. His voice was choked with tears, and the sheriff looked away, the business-like mask gone from his face.

"I think it's time to leave," José Antonio said.

The sheriff rose. "I'm glad you're getting well, Rafa. I'm sorry about your son."

José Antonio walked with the sheriff to his horse. "So Benito denies that he had anything to do with Francisco's attack?"

"He says he knows nothing about it." The sheriff lifted himself onto horseback. "What do you think, Don José?"

The dark brown eyes stared at him as if looking inside. José Antonio forced himself to hold the gaze, afraid that if he looked away it might be an admission of something. He shrugged and shook his head.

\*   \*   \*

"What did he want?" Gregoria asked.

"Just a few questions."

"You'd think he'd leave a sick man alone. Look at him. Out of here, Tercero. Leave him be."

"In a minute."

She frowned, took one last look at Francisco, who did not appear to have heard either of them, and left the room. José Antonio sat and waited. He followed his son's unfocused gaze to the brown adobe wall.

After a few mintues Francisco stirred and shifted his gaze toward his father. "Why are you holding back, Francisco?"

Francisco burst into tears. "It was my fault."

José Antonio waited, just as he used to when Francisco had been a boy. Of all his sons it had been this one who had wanted his approval the most, yet rebelled and fought the hardest. A difficult child to love. When José Antonio had gotten angry with him, it had made things worse. It was then that Francisco had fought and lied the most. So he had learned to wait the boy out.

A fly buzzed into the room and circled over the bed. Then its buzz grew louder, almost angry, and propelled it straight through the door toward the kitchen.

"I heard you cry out in your sleep," José Antonio said. " '¡Hijos! ¡Benito!' Leonardo must have heard too. Why didn't you tell the sheriff?"

"Durán was baiting me. I knew it was him, even with a mask. Somehow he had found out."

"You were one of Los Hijos."

"We wanted to scare Plácido out of the race. Instead, somehow, Benito found out who we were. At least he found me."

"The horses . . ." José Antonio said.

"Maybe I was to be the example. If the others saw what happened, they would be frightened. Benito's gang could have killed me. They could have shot me and dumped me in the ditch."

"Why didn't you tell the sheriff?"

"Then I would have to tell him about Los Hijos. How would it look? I couldn't prove that Benito was one of the men who ambushed me. He would have six witnesses who were with him in one of the whorehouses downtown."

"So you plan to do something about Benito yourself." It was a statement, not a question. "What good will that do? Although God knows I could kill him myself."

"I always remember the cemetery," Francisco said. "As a boy you would take me to visit Grandfather's grave. To help clear it of weeds. To straighten out the wooden marker. To paint over the legend. 'Francisco Juan Rafa. 1781–1857.' I felt a strange kinship because Francisco was my name, too. But since I was only a year old when he died, I had no memory or sense of the man.

"I . . . I learned my sense of family partly from those visits. I used to look at the other graves. At the dried flowers that someone remembered to bring. At the markers. I would read the legends. I can still remember some of them. 'Julián Martínez. Beloved son of Juan and Rosa. 1849–1851.' 'Eutemia Chávez. 1856–1857.' 'Baby Pérez. February–April 1863.' For every person who lived sixty or seventy years, there seemed to be two or three infants or young people.

"That was why my first child was so important. Why I rejoiced when Leonardo was born alive and survived. Why I feel the loss so much. My bitterness will poison me unless I do something about Durán."

José Antonio did not know what to say.

"I'm tired, Papá. I need to be alone." As José Antonio rose, the tired voice spoke to him again. "Papá." He turned and took Francisco's outstretched hand. "Will you keep my secret? I don't want anyone else to know. Not even Florinda."

He squeezed Francisco's hand and let it drop onto the coverlet, nodding at the wan smile as he left the room.

## 46

The next day Jesús Perea rode by. "He wants to see you," he said to José Antonio.

"Maybe tomorrow."

"He wants to see you now. It's important." José Antonio bristled at the insistent tone. An unspoken curse formed on his lips. "Do you hear me?"

"I'm busy, Perea."

The man twisted in his saddle. "I'll be in trouble if I don't bring you back."

"I don't work for Mr. James Smith. I don't give a damn if you do get in trouble. I have my own problems. I'll come when I'm ready."

"Damn it, Don José! There'll be hell to pay for this."

"¡Mierda!"

Viciously, Perea jerked the horse's head and spurred him down the road. "When I'm good and ready," José Antonio mumbled.

The following day Perea was back. "The patrón was not happy that you didn't come. He doesn't understand how you could say no."

"There are some things more important than an election."

"He wants to see you."

When José Antonio shook his head, Perea did not argue. He turned his horse with a parting shout, "I'd hate to be in your shoes, Don José!"

José Antonio watched him gallop off. There are things more important than a sheriff, he thought. Or a patrón.

The third day José Antonio was in the house resting when he heard the slow hooves, then the footsteps, followed by the knock on the door. The sound of voices came muffled through the house. His wife's and . . . He listened, the words indistinct but the sounds discernible enough. A foreigner? Smith.

"I came to express my sympathy, Don José. To see how Francisco was getting along."

"Please sit down, Señor Smith."

Smith's fingers played restlessly on the brim of his Stetson. José Antonio saw the quick, shallow breathing. Smith was used to men going to him, not the other way around. There was irritation in Smith's manner, yet he kept it under control.

"Jesse told me you were not well and could not come to see me. It's been a great strain, I'm sure."

Ah, truthful Jesús. "Yes."

"Our deepest sympathy for the loss of your grandson. Mrs. Smith especially wanted me to tell you how badly we feel."

"Thank you."

"I talked to the people downtown. There's a great deal of animosity toward Benito Durán here in Los Rafas. There have been rumors of a lynching."

"It's only talk. People are angry."

"It was a damned stupid thing for Benito to do. Especially with the election soon. The dumbest damn thing possible."

"It was more than that," José Antonio said. "My grandson was murdered." It was hard for him to hide the bitterness in his voice.

"Of course," Smith said. "That's the real tragedy of it all." He sat as if thinking about what to say next. José Antonio did not intend to help him and answered silence with silence.

Then, as if a decent enough time had passed, Smith spoke again. "There's an awful lot of money tied up in this election."

"Oh?"

"Didn't Francisco—" He caught himself. "No," he said. "You wouldn't have heard."

"Heard what?"

"About the money."

"Are you paying for votes?"

"You know that's against the law. No," Smith said. "But if the right man gets elected it could open up some possibilities that could make someone a lot of money."

"How could a sheriff do that? You'd need a judge."

"I've already said too much."

"But Plácido Durán is the right man?" Smith nodded. "He wouldn't have been elected before. Now . . . I'm sorry, Señor Smith. No one is going to make any money if it depends on Plácido being elected."

Smith rose and paced across the room. As he started to speak, Gregoria came in with a tray of chocolate and bizcochitos. The good cups, José Antonio noticed. A quick smile, then Smith's face closed like a door. When she left, he turned back to José Antonio.

"You don't think he can win?"

"Certainly not now. Look. Do you think I could vote for him after what his brother did? Could you? What about the rest of Los Rafas? You said yourself that there are rumors of lynching. The only election Plácido could win is at the end of a rope."

"You're sure?"

"I can only speak for Los Rafas. He'll be lucky to get a dozen votes here."

"There is such a thing as party loyalty."

José Antonio stared at Smith, trembling in anger. "I have always been a party man. Candidates come and go, but the party remains. I work for the party even when it picks a bad candidate. But my loyalty does not blind my good sense nor does it color my opinion. Plácido Durán is a disaster. He can do nothing but harm to us."

"You have a personal grudge against him."

"Yes. But that does not enter into my opinion. Damn it! If you don't believe me, talk to some people around here. Ask them if they'll vote for a man whose brother is a murderer."

The chair squeaked as Smith dropped heavily onto it. He crossed his legs and rocked the upper one back and forth. "It doesn't look good."

"No, señor."

"What do you think we ought to do, Don José?"

"I haven't had time to think about it."

"What do you think the voters want?"

"We're going to lose this election no matter what. We would have lost it anyway, but now we'll lose it worse. The voters around here have never liked Plácido Durán. They think the party was stupid to pick him. They think he toadies to some important Anglos downtown who like him because he does what he's told."

Smith's face reddened. "I think," José Antonio continued, "that if we ignore the shooting and run Plácido as if nothing happened, voters will think we're even more stupid. I think the best thing is for Plácido to withdraw and for us to run someone else. We'll still lose, but if we pick the right man we can lay the foundation for next time."

Through it all Smith sat red-faced, his lips clamped tight. His furious eyes glared at José Antonio. Sometimes, José Antonio thought, people did not want to hear the truth, but it had to be said to them anyway.

"You know," Smith said, "we depend on you for the political pulse of Los Rafas. And to deliver the vote."

There was such a forced emphasis in the words "Deliver the vote" that

José Antonio had to restrain a bitter smile. Yes, he thought. Wouldn't it be nice? Just say "Deliver the vote" and your political aides snap their fingers and all the sheep say "Baa-baa" and put their X in the right box. But life isn't like that. Oh, there are some you could bribe with a shot of whiskey or a silver dollar, but a lot more are going to do what they want to do and the hell with the bosses downtown.

"I do my best," José Antonio said. Thinking, the only votes anybody can truly deliver are those whose names are copied off the headstones in graveyards or those sheep who were given names and registered.

"You really think we should dump Plácido?"

"Yes!"

Smith sat mulling it over. The expression on his face shifted subtly until it finally set into a mask. "Who would you run in his place?"

"Enrique Martínez."

The only break in Smith's composure was a quick flickering of his eyelashes. "He may not be the favorite downtown," José Antonio said. "He has too much of a mind of his own. But that is exactly what makes him attractive. The dilemma, you see, is to run someone who can win but who the bosses don't have in their pockets. It's a matter of which risk you want to take."

"Goddamn it! I don't know if I could sell him."

José Antonio shrugged. What more could he say? It was up to Smith and his cronies in New Town. All he was supposed to do was deliver the vote.

"Why the hell did your grandson have to go looking for Benito? Why did the ape have to shoot the kid? Goddamn it!"

José Antonio looked at Smith coldly, the way he might have looked at a bug. A bug cannot help what it does. It can only act from its own nature. So why tell it that a boy's life was worth more than any number of elections? The bug wouldn't understand.

Smith rose and tapped his Stetson against his thigh. "I guess that's it, Don José." He glanced at the cup of cold chocolate and frowned. "Do you think I could pay my respects to Francisco?"

"He's still too weak for visitors," José Antonio lied. "I'll tell him that you asked about him."

"Tell him if there's anything he needs, anything at all, to let me know." Smith stepped to the door shaking his head. "These are difficult times, Don José. Difficult."

"Thank you for doing what you could for Pedro Baca."

Smith sighed. "It wasn't enough. Well, adiós, Don José."

"Adiós, Señor Smith."

## 47

Three months passed. How many times during those months had José Antonio thought about the terrible loss? Too many. But thinking did not resolve what he felt. It was not a problem of the mind. It was deeper, bigger, more important. The mind was a self-deceiver that tried to blindfold his heart, yet the heart somehow still saw the truth.

What have I done to deserve this? he thought during those months. Is it a sin to want so much for one's progeny? Even You have promised Your children eternal life in the hereafter. But what about eternal life here on earth, not for any one person, but for one's offspring? Is wanting that so much a sin?

Then he would open his Bible and turn to the passages that spoke to his pain:

"Naked came I out of my mother's womb, and naked shall I return thither: the Lord gave, and the Lord hath taken away; blessed be the name of the Lord."

"His remembrance shall perish from the earth, and he shall have no name in the street."

". . . I only am escaped alone to tell thee."

He would slam the book shut in anger. "No," he said. "I am not alone." It was then that he had gone to his son, who had suffered a relapse because of Leonardo's death. José Antonio sat by Francisco's bed every morning after that. In some ways it was more consoling than his rosary. Here was someone of his seed who reminded him that he had not escaped alone. Here was someone who would not let his remembrance perish, his name disappear. Here was someone who shared his guilt and on those days that Francisco was strong, they would talk.

"If only I hadn't . . ." Francisco would begin.

And I, José Antonio would think.

"But you, Papá. Why should He punish you?"

Even when humans do not see, He sees, José Antonio thought. Measured against God's perfection, no man can ever be completely innocent. Not even the purest of saints.

But finally he had to acknowledge to himself, even more than to Francisco, "I do not believe in God's wrath and vengeance. My God is a loving God. He does not punish us for our guilt, and therefore does not blindly punish us when we are innocent. There is no punishment in God. Punishment is the way of man's world. We justify our cruelty by blaming it on some higher power. It is our anger at failing to be perfect."

"If only I had not formed Los Hijos. Had not gone after Plácido. Had not . . ."

If only I had not left God's priesthood to serve a temporal master, my family, José Antonio thought. If only I had resisted the Yankee invasion with less forbearance. If only I had not told Leonardo Don Pedro's story. If . . . if . . . if.

Then, in an uncontrolled outburst, José Antonio said, "Sometimes I hate God!" Francisco looked at him with shock and fear. "His indifference throws us back onto ourselves. We must bear all . . . alone. We must carry on . . . alone. God the Father is not like human fathers who comfort us when we need it, who pick us up when we fall. It is His vast indifference that forces us to stand on our own, no matter how much we may not want to."

Then Francisco had reached for the old man's hand. They sat silently, basking in their mutual dependence, their mutual love. After a moment, Francisco let go of José Antonio's hand. "I mustn't dwell on Leonardo," he said. Just hearing the boy's name pained José Antonio. "I have another son. I have to take that worthless, angry lump of clay and make him man enough to carry on. Make him worthy of you, Father."

"Make him worthy of himself," José Antonio said.

From that day Francisco grew stronger. But for José Antonio it had not been so easy. He could say all the right words, but he could not always feel them in his heart. It was as if old flesh and old spirit did not heal as fast as they used to. As if the wounds cut deeper into the aged.

Now José Antonio could hear the children playing outside. Their shouts pierced the air joyously, the past months forgotten as if they had never happened.

The crops had been harvested with the help of relatives and friends and stored to last through the coming year. The frantic work days had eased into days of rest and calm. It was time to gather firewood for the cold months ahead. They would manage for another year.

He closed his Bible and set it on the floor beside his chair. "All right, Manuel!" he heard from outside. "You just wait!" Then the giggle of the girls as Carlos shouted angrily again. "You just wait!" The shouts of the children faded as they ran past the big house toward the ditch.

From across the yard men's voices grew louder. He heard the heavy thump of a cane on the wooden steps and then Francisco and Armando Chávez came into the room tentatively, as if they were not sure he would be there.

"Armando got the final count on the election," Francisco said. "Like we expected, the draft of the constitution for statehood was voted down. But for sheriff it didn't look bad. Maybe next time."

The younger men sat, nodding to each other and smiling. "I had the devil's own time getting the count for each area," Armando said. "Maybe they were afraid I was going to try to change the tally, but it's too late for that."

"Enrique Martínez is very pleased," Francisco said. "He carried Los Rafas. Not by much. But it's a miracle he carried it at all considering the mess the Duráns made of it." His face clouded for a moment; then it passed. "I think we can do it next time."

"He wants to come by and give you his personal thanks," Armando said. " 'As Don José goes, so goes Los Rafas,' he told me."

"He's always welcome."

Francisco leaned on his cane and looked intently at his father. "He still does not understand how he became our candidate."

"Smith suggested it," Armando said.

Francisco shook his head. "I don't believe it. Smith only helps those who are in debt to him. Enrique is too smart for that. What do you think, Papá?"

"I don't think Smith had any choice."

Armando lowered his voice conspiratorially. "It was a horse trade. They knew they couldn't win, but Plácido was too stubborn to drop out. So Smith offered to get Benito off with a light sentence if Plácido withdrew."

"They should have hung the bastard," Francisco said.

"Well, it didn't quite work out. Plácido withdrew all right. But even Smith couldn't fix the judge. Instead of self-defense they called it manslaughter and shipped him off to territorial prison."

"Where did you hear that?" Francisco asked.

"Oh, a little bird."

"Mierda."

The shouts of the children outside grew louder, their quarreling voices approaching the door. "¡Papá! ¡Papá! Manuel and Carlos are fighting again!"

Armando walked to the door, leaning his head and shoulders outside. "All right, damn it! I've had enough. Stop all the noise, or I'm going out there and whip every one of you." He returned to his chair, looking at José Antonio and Francisco in indignation.

Francisco's animation faded as he stared out the screen door. The sounds of the children touched José Antonio's heart. He could hear the voice that was missing. Hear the laughter that was no longer there. As he looked at Francisco, he could see in his son's face the hidden face of his dead grandson.

"Where's Mamá?" Francisco asked.

"At Consuela's. María is sick." María was one of their many grandchildren. "How's Florinda?"

Francisco nodded abruptly and shot a glance at Armando, who nodded in agreement. That bad? José Antonio thought.

The sounds of the children faded. The men sat silent, as if everything of importance had been said. We had a good crop this year, José Antonio almost said, but he realized that it was his nervous way of breaking the silence. The others already knew.

Francisco straightened up and looked around. "We'd better help Florinda with the children."

Then they were gone and José Antonio turned his chair so he could stare out the screen door. It had been three months now, yet it was as vivid as if it had been yesterday. He had not forgotten. He would never forget. The bitterness was almost gone, but the sorrow remained — an ache, a scar, a memory.

It is like being a farmer, he thought. All life is being a farmer. When he had been a young man, a priest, he had been a farmer of souls. Now, a grandfather, a patriarch, he was a farmer of future generations. Only this year's crop had not grown to fruition and there did not seem to be much hope for the future.

It was as if his heart needed weeding. A clearing of the debris that choked out the tiny green shoots of hope. Until the weeds were cleared, new seeds would not find their way down to soil and take root.

I feel barren, he thought. My heart is full of last season's refuse like the dry, yellow stalks in the cornfields outside. It's time to leave it alone, to let it lie fallow, until . . . But would there be another season for him? Another spring? Even the children at play brought him as much sadness as joy.

A door slammed, interrupting his reverie. Gregoria entered, a half-filled gunnysack in her arms. "Well, there you are moping again," she said irritably, "while I have to carry this ristra of chili all the way by myself."

He started to say something but then forgot what it was. She glared at him, then with a grumble turned and disappeared. He heard the sack drop onto— The table? A chair? The floor? He could hear her still grumbling in the kitchen.

Why hadn't she put the sack down when she came into the house instead of lugging it here? To show him, he realized. To flog at him in irritation.

"What the hell's the matter with you?" he shouted.

\*     \*     \*

That old bastard, Gregoria thought angrily. Moping as if we lost the only grandchild we'd ever have. Wallowing in the belief that this had never happened to anyone else in the world before. And would never happen again.

Then she heard his shout and she wheeled about, clutching her hands into fists and thrusting her angry face at him, shouting, "You know very well what's the matter!" as she stomped into the living room.

José Antonio looked at her in surprise. For a second she wanted to punch him one, but she just shook her head impatiently.

"It's been three months," she said. "I don't begrudge your grief. Lord knows there have been others of us grieving. The boy's parents for one. With Florinda still over there half out of her mind. And me. How could I not grieve for such a grandson? But there are other grandchildren. María is sick, and you didn't even go over there with me. I had to carry that ristra all the way across the fields by myself.

"What about Francisco? It was his son. After all he has been through he is hopping about with that cane like a three-legged burro, doing what he has to do.

"I'm getting tired of cooking your meals and washing your clothes while you sit like some martyred saint waiting to be lifted bodily to heaven because you've suffered so much.

"Damn it! I'm tired of your moping around. Nothing you can do will bring him back. Ever!"

He stared in surprise, his mouth half-open. His eyes moved uneasily, frightened, as she walked up to him and thrust her hands onto her hips and stared at him.

"Wha . . . what's the matter?" His soft voice cracked as he spoke. "Why are you so angry?"

She could see that he was on the verge of tears, but she did not let that soften her. "I want you up and about your business," she said. "No more sad sighs. No more hand-wringing. No more staring at the walls." She did not say what she was thinking: If you don't, you'll be dead in a matter of months.

"I . . . I . . ." He lifted his arms out helplessly.

As she watched his tormented face, her heart went out to him. She wanted to kneel beside him and take him in her arms, but she resisted the temptation.

"You loved him very much," she said in a gentler voice. His eyes were moist and shining.

"It's a terrible thing," he said. "But I loved him more than our own sons or our other grandchildren. Somehow he seemed closer to me than the others."

"It was because you were so much alike."

"There is vanity in that," he said. "But you are right. That's what I felt. Of all our children and grandchildren, Leonardo was the one I seemed to understand best and who understood me. We both felt it, the boy and I. I can't explain it. It just seemed natural."

"He was still a boy. He hadn't reached the age when he would go his own way, in spite of what you or anyone else thought. That's when the real test comes. When you can let them go their own way and still feel that closeness. The other is an illusion. It's easy to feel close to people who do exactly as you would."

She could tell that her words had hurt him. "You know that's true," she said. "Of all of them, each has been my favorite in turn. For different reasons and at different times. Yet I've been luckier than you. None of them have been enough like me for me to care for one more than the others."

"Vanity. God has a way of rubbing your nose in it to remind you that He is still God and you are only what you are. One of God's ants, of God's fleas, of God's mosquitos. And what you want is not of great importance in the ultimate scheme of things." He turned his face toward the ceiling and cried out in anguish. "Oh, God! It would be so easy to hate you!"

"And Benito Durán?"

"He is even easier to hate." He shook his head as if remembering something. "It would have been easy to organize a lynch mob. I watched Francisco and wondered what he was thinking. If he had been well enough, he would have led that mob himself. But now there is time. Durán will not be out of prison for a long while and perhaps by then Francisco will have lost his appetite for vengeance.

"As for me, I can hate; but I would not kill. At least I don't think so. No. My problem is not wanting to accept a death that happened too early."

But there was acceptance in his voice. The hopelessness seemed to be forgotten for the moment. Gregoria leaned against his chair and put a hand on his shoulder. "It will be all right."

"God willing."

\* \* \*

She had been gone for awhile, but it felt to José Antonio as if her hand had remained on his shoulder. The clucking of the hens grew louder and more rapid, then subsided. In his mind he could see them part before the rapidly striding Gregoria as she crossed the yard to Florinda's house.

How would he feel if she died before he did? The thought shocked him. He had never dared think that before in their almost forty years of married life. He had always taken for granted that they would go on together to the end. Yet he knew that it would not likely be so and he could not bear the thought.

He trembled with a cold chill. His teeth chattered like miniature castanets and his shoulders shuddered involuntarily.

I hope I go first, he thought in desperation. But then he realized that that would only be leaving the burden to her, and in frustration he began to weep.

The hot tears flowed down his cheeks, dispelling the cold and trembling. "Together, God," he whispered. But deep down he knew that although God had heard, since He heard everything, He might ignore the plea.

Whatever, José Antonio thought. If it comes I will have to accept it, no matter what.

Then the flow of tears began to slow and finally stopped. What if I were that other old man? he thought. Poor old Pedro. There is a man who has lost everything. A wife he has not seen for forty years, who might or might not be alive. Possibly in California or perhaps Mexico. Maybe even somewhere in New Mexico. Daughters he has not seen since they were small children. Middle-aged now, if alive. With children, perhaps even grandchildren, of their own. Descendants that Pedro Baca will never know.

A home stolen outright. Legally. With no recourse. Once a verdant rancho in Eden itself. Now God knows what kind of Anglo haven. A squalid farm town of loud and arrogant grabbers. A gabble of Anglo migrants who knew nothing of its history or of the people from whom they had stolen this paradise. Who cared even less. Like the livestock grazing the pastures with not a thought to the why and wherefore of it as long as their bellies were full.

Yes. A man who has lost everything. Except his life. To which he clings tenaciously even in madness. And as Pedro had once asked him: Who truly is mad? He or the ones who drove him to this state?

Compared to Pedro Baca, José Antonio thought, he had everything. Even now he could imagine that madman howling in the asylum for his medicine. For one more glassful to ease the pain. For one more hot tortilla to fill his stomach. For one more visit to Esmerelda. But never for it all to end.

I was wrong, José Antonio thought, in believing that Leonardo would learn from Don Pedro's story. I put too much on the boy. Too much maturity. Too much understanding. But not enough feeling, which was what drove him to something mad. Oh, Leonardo, he thought. Forgive me. If only I could do it over again.

A darkness came over him. He felt it lie heavy on his chest as if guilt itself, weighing three hundred pounds, squat obscenely there, grinning at him through bloody fangs.

"Go away," he said. But the thing just grinned more broadly.

"¡Mamá! ¡Mamá!" The high-pitched, childish scream came from the orchard.

Sluggishly, José Antonio shifted his gaze upward and out, staring at the wall in the direction of the scream. He recognized his granddaughter Juanita.

With a groan, he raised himself from the chair and walked slowly to the door. He pushed open the screen and slowly and carefully made his way down the wooden steps.

When he reached the corner of the house he could see them under the trees. Juanita was standing aghast, her hands at her mouth, while the other little girls watched briefly, then turned and headed toward the ditch.

The dust was flying. Mumbled groans and curses punctuated the thrashing and pummeling. Then Juanita looked up, her eyes wide. "Grandpa! Grandpa! Carlos and Manuel are killing each other!" The other little girls turned around in the midst of their stroll, giggled, then ran off while Juanita started to cry.

José Antonio hurried toward the boys who were pounding each other. "All right, you ruffians. Stop it!" But they did not hear and they only looked up when José Antonio reached over and pulled Manuel off the smaller Carlos.

As Carlos jumped to his feet, he aimed his hate-filled eyes at his cousin and charged, fists swinging. "I'll kill you!" he screamed. "I'll kill you!"

José Antonio held him off with a palm on the boy's chest. "Now stop it! That's enough!" Then to Manuel. "You're bigger than . . ."

But before he could finish, Manuel angrily screamed, "He started it! It was his fault!"

Meanwhile, Juanita watched through teary eyes, staring in fascination at the blood flowing from Carlos' nose. When the boys had calmed somewhat, she spoke directly to Carlos. "I'm going to tell Mamá. You just wait." She turned and rushed toward the house.

"Now you boys behave," José Antonio warned. He took a handkerchief from his pocket and gave it to Carlos.

"He called me a name," Manuel said. But his words had already lost their anger. "He hit me first. He got what he deserved."

José Antonio turned Manuel around, pointing him toward the house, and gave him a push. "You go to your father. I'll talk to him later."

Then he turned to his grandson and took back his handkerchief. The boy's face was a furious red, streaked with a mixture of dust and sweat. The blood from his nose had started to congeal, giving him a crusted red-brown mustache that almost blended into his red face. Carlos leaned against José Antonio's extended palm and thrashed his upper body about, as if rejecting the restraint, although his fisted hands were stiff against his sides. José Antonio's eyes flared and for an instant his other hand almost leaped out to slap Carlos.

"Stop that!" The boy stopped and looked up at his grandfather. "Now over to the pump!"

José Antonio worked the handle while Carlos splashed his face with water. "Once again," he said. "Your upper lip." Then he wiped at his grandson's face with the handkerchief.

It had grown still outside. Juanita had flounced into the house and Manuel had disappeared behind the corral. The other little girls had long since gone over the ditch toward the farthest fields.

José Antonio looked down at this grandson of his. Little devil, he thought.

"Teach me to fight," Carlos demanded.

"What was that?"

"Teach me, Grandpa. I want to beat that Manuel good." The sound of his own voice seemed to feed the boy's anger. "I'll kill him!" he shouted. "I'll just beat him to pieces."

"All right. That's enough."

A sullen look. A quivering lower lip. Then Carlos looked away. His voice was softer. Pleading. "Teach me, Grandpa."

"Why?"

Carlos looked up in surprise. "So I can beat him up." Any fool can see that, his expression seemed to say.

"Why?"

The boy's face reddened even deeper, and his eyes narrowed angrily. "Grandpa, I just told you."

"Manuel said you started it. You hit him first."

"He called me a baby."

"Why?"

Carlos seemed to swell up with frustration and he blinked his eyes to hold back the tears. "Nobody can call me a baby!" he shouted. "I'm not!" José Antonio turned the boy's angry face toward him and stared down into his eyes. "I asked him to come spend the night at our house. I have a bed all to myself now, but it isn't the same without Leonardo. I . . . It felt strange sleeping alone.

"He . . . he called me a baby. Said that I was just afraid and that if he stayed over I'd wet the bed and him too. So I hit him."

Not enough sense to refrain from hitting someone bigger, José Antonio thought. But deep down he felt a heaviness because he was really thinking about Leonardo.

"Was it worth it? Was it worth getting beat up?"

"Leonardo would have," Carlos said. "Leonardo wasn't afraid. That's why . . ."

José Antonio put a hand over the boy's mouth. He couldn't bear to hear what his mind had already heard: ". . . he was killed."

Carlos shook his head free and looked up at his grandfather as if a thought had struck him. He whispered in awe. "I want to be just like him."

"The first thing to learn," the old man said, "is that not everything is worth fighting over. Some things are, but they are rare and precious."

"What, Grandpa?"

He put him arm around the boy's shoulders and led him to the shade of an apple tree. "First I have to tell you a story. About how the Rafas came to be in this place."

"Our ancestors were explorers," Carlos said. "Conquerors."

"And conquered. But there is more to it than that. To live in the future, you must know what happened in the past." His fight with Manuel forgotten, Carlos leaned against his grandfather, sweaty and warm, sensing that something important had changed in his life. "You see, Carlitos, some day you will be your father's heir. The way your father will be my heir. You will be the man of this farm. And it is time to start learning."

"Tell me, Grandfather."

José Antonio patted him on the shoulder and cleared his throat. "Once upon a time," he began, "there was a land called New Mexico . . ."